HWARHATH STORIES:
Transgressive Tales by Aliens

Hwarhath Stories:

Transgressive Tales by Aliens

by

Eleanor Arnason

SEATTLE

Aqueduct Press, PO Box 95787
Seattle, WA 98145-2787
www.aqueductpress.com

Copyright © 2016 by Eleanor Arnason
First edition, first printing, June 2016

ISBN: 978-1-61976-095-0
Library of Congress Control Number: 2015960967
10 9 8 7 6 5 4 3 2 1

Cover: Planetary Nebula NGC 6302
NASA, ESA, and the Hubble SM4 ERO Team, September 9, 2009

Book Design by Kathryn Wilham

Printed in the USA by Thomson Shore, Inc.

Acknowledgments

The Semen Thief, originally published in *Amazing Stories*, Winter 1994

Lovers, originally published in *Asimov's Science Fiction*, July 1994

The Small Black Box of Morality, originally published in *Tales of the Unanticipated*, Spring/Summer/Fall 1996

The Gauze Banner, originally published in *More Amazing Stories*, 1998

Dapple, originally published in *Asimov's Science Fiction*, September 1999

The Actors, originally published in *The Magazine of Fantasy & Science Fiction*, December 1999

Origin Story, originally published in *Tales of the Unanticipated* #21, April 2000

The Potter of Bones, originally published in *Asimov's Science Fiction*, September 2002

The Hound of Merin, originally published in *Xanadu*, 1993

The Garden, originally published in *Synergy SF: New Science Fiction*, 2004

The Woman Who Fooled Death Five Times, originally published in *The Magazine of Fantasy & Science Fiction*, July-August 2012

Holmes Sherlock, originally published in *Eclipse Online*, November 12, 2012

To Patrick Arden Wood

CONTENTS

INTRODUCTION

Humanity has encountered only one other species able to travel among the stars. This species, who call themselves the *hwarhath*, or "people," are also the only intelligent species so far encountered. Of course, we interest and puzzle and disturb each other.

Why have neither of us encountered an intelligent species without FTL travel? Surely they ought to be more common than species with FTL. Why are the two known intelligent species so alike? The physical resemblances are striking; and the cultural differences, while large, do not make us utterly unintelligible to one another.

Many human and *hwarhath* scientists explain this as an example of convergent evolution. Other scientists, mostly human, argue that the two species are related, although distantly. We know organic molecules appeared early in the universe's history, not on planets, which did not yet exist, but in the space around stars. As planets cooled and became solid, the molecules rained down on them, becoming the basis for life.

We know that life can travel from planet to planet, embedded in ice or as free-floating spores. Life on Earth traces its descent from Martian life forms, blown off their home planet by meteor impacts more than three billion years ago. There are still organisms on Earth, deeply buried anaerobic and thermophilic microbes that are virtually identical to what remains of Martian life.

Can microorganisms or their spores travel from star to star? It seems likely. Microscopic travelers have been found in the

Oort clouds that ring many planetary systems and in interstellar space. We don't know for certain if such travelers have actually carried life from one system to another. But a number of scientists, mostly human, believe they have, and argue further that the microbes' genetic material was—and is—predisposed to evolve in certain ways. If the star-faring travelers ended on similar planets, these scientists say, they would evolve into similar organisms.

Opposing thinkers say it's ridiculous to suppose that the genetic material in a bacterium is preprogrammed to become (to give one example) a five-fingered animal. The fact remains that both humans and the *hwarhath* have four fingers and an opposing thumb.

Perhaps it's simple accident that the first species that humanity met is so similar to us. Other, stranger creatures may await us in more distant stellar systems. Maybe we have already met intelligent aliens and not recognized them.[1]

There are *hwarhath*, most of them not trained in science, who argue that the similarity is due to their Goddess's sense of humor. Humanity, they argue, is a distorted reflection of the People, designed to call into question many assumptions about the nature of evolution and moral behavior. The Goddess loves to trip up, surprise, and astound. She is the great magician, pulling birds out of her sleeves, turning fish into *tli*.

Other *hwarhath* say there is more here than mere surprise and the Great Mother's love of jokes. "Surely we can learn something from a people so similar, yet different. The Goddess is full of tricks, but not (to our knowledge) malicious."

As far as can be determined, the stories in this collection were all written after the *hwarhath* learned enough about humanity to realize how similar (and different) we are. Our existence has

---

1   I am indebted here and elsewhere to Dr. Anna Perez, who has graciously shared her knowledge of human and *hwarhath* xenobiology with me.

called into question many ideas about life and morality that most *hwarhath* would have called certain a century ago. With two exceptions, the stories don't deal with humanity directly. Instead, the authors are looking at their own culture through lenses created by their knowledge of us. Reading this fiction, we can begin to learn about our neighbors in known space. We may even learn something about ourselves.

The most dramatic differences between *hwarhath* and human culture, the ones that bother both species, lie in the area of morality; especially as morality pertains to sex, reproduction, and violence. Early in their history, the *hwarhath* made a rigid division between sex for procreation, which had to be heterosexual, and sex for pleasure, which is homosexual. Humans find this division almost impossible to believe. However, the *hwarhath* point out, they have always found it perfectly reasonable and natural; and it eliminates accidental children. Every child is the product of an agreement between two families. Since *hwarhath* families vary in size between 1,000 and 100,000 members, this means a lot of people are involved in the creation and raising of each child. A child's death by neglect or abuse is a crime with several thousand perpetrators, and any family that tolerates harm to children risks its own existence. Who, ask the *hwarhath*, would interbreed with a family that does not care for its own?

A second benefit of *hwarhath* morality is that it keeps men and women apart. Traditionally, male culture is violent. The *hwarhath* believe this is a result of male natures and not to be condemned. One of the five traditional male virtues is violence.[2]

Through most of their history, *hwarhath* men and women have had separate spheres of action. The women control the home, breeding, child-rearing, and their own lives. The men do dangerous work at the perimeter. Prior to modern times, the majority of *hwarhath* societies had strict rules about proper work

2 The other four are loyalty, piety, discipline, and directness.

3

for women and men. This has changed since the development of space travel. Most men live in space now, and the two sexes are so separate that both have to do most kinds of work, though child rearing remains female. The traditional work rules varied from one society to another, but two rules were universal: only men fought wars, and it was never permissible for a man to harm either women or children. These last two rules have not changed in modern times.

When the *hwarhath* began to understand humanity, they were shocked to discover that an intelligent species could produce accidental children and permit men to bring male violence into the home. They tried to deal with this disturbing information through theory and art. Most of the stories in this collection deal, in one way or another, with the morality of sex and violence.

Knowledge of humanity has led some writers to question other aspects of traditional society. Is it right to condemn heterosexuality so absolutely? Is it a good idea to place society and the family "in front" of individuals, as the *hwarhath* have usually done, or should individuals have some freedom? At what point does individuality become chaos? How important is love? Or loyalty? How dangerous is conservatism, a strong trait among the *hwarhath*, to the future of the species? Conversely, are the new ideas that come from humanity likely to destroy *hwarhath* culture?

All the stories in this collection were written in *Eh Ahara*, the traditional language of diplomacy and trade. It is no more difficult to learn than many human languages.[3] Although highly inflected, it is surprisingly regular and logical, due to generations of work by grammarians, logicians, and ordinary people. Nonetheless, the usual problems of translation remain. No two

---

3   This is the greatest problem currently facing human and *hwarhath* students of linguistics. If grammar is innate and genetic, as we believe it is, how can a species that belongs to a different evolutionary line create a grammar humans can understand? It is absurd to think that microbes are preprogrammed for language.

languages have exactly comparable ideas. To give one example, the *hwarhath* word for piety—used by many of the home world's languages—is *chulmar*. This word also means having a good sense of humor. If a story says a certain person has *chulmar*, it may mean she is pious, or that she tells good jokes, or that she can take a joke, or all the preceding. How can this be conveyed in English? How can the translator distinguish between Gesh Hala, the hero of "The Hound of Merin," who is clearly good humored, and Eh Manhata, famous for his extreme piety, but never described as humorous or good humored?

In addition, an ordinary human reader is not going to understand many of the cultural references. Because of this, the stories cannot be translated exactly as they are written. Extra information must be added. In some cases, the information has been incorporated into the stories, a violation of the integrity of the text, perhaps; but footnotes on a story that was not originally footnoted is also a violation. In other cases, the information has been provided through a foreword or footnotes. Readers can decide for themselves which technique works best.[4]

The collection is deliberately popular and accessible, intended for as wide a range of readers as possible. Because of this, some of the ordinary rules of scholarly translation have been ignored or modified. If we are to share the universe with other beings, we should make an effort—all of us—to understand them; and if over-careful fidelity and precision stand in the way of understanding, then they must go, at least in this book. More scholarly works will doubtless be produced.

Rosa Haj.
Independent Scholars Union
North American Central Region

---

4   Scholars writing other scholars for would prefer footnotes or hyperlinks, of course, as well as a literal translation. But as the old saying tells us, you cannot please everyone, so you ought to please yourself.

Historical Romances

Official *hwarhath* literature, the work taken seriously by scholars, is poetry and drama. These are the works taught in schools and studied at institutions of far-in-front learning. Prose fiction is a popular art form, regarded with suspicion by cultural moralists and the *hwarhath* academy. It is the tales of romance and adventure loved by men, and the family sagas read by women; it is usually published anonymously, with no information that will enable readers or the government to discover those responsible.

In general the state ignores popular fiction. It is an irritation, not a social danger. If fiction writers do not usually end in prison, they also do not get the *hwarhath* equivalent of grants or tenure, and their work is not published or performed on the information nets. Prose fiction remains an ink-on-paper art form, read widely but with some embarrassment. The *hwarhath* know they ought to be reading something edifying: a heroic tragedy or a linked-stanza poem about the people who created their civilization.

Most of the stories are what one would expect of popular fiction: escapist fantasies, which enable the *hwarhath* to endure the demands put on them by society. In the romances, young men triumph over monsters, enemies, and fate. In the family sagas, canny women rescue their families from destruction and bring them forward to prosperity and power.

Most prose fiction readers have little interest in mimetic (realist) stories. They know their own lives already. If they want to

learn about other parts of *hwarhath* society, they turn to travel-
ogues, biographies, memoirs, and cultural studies. All of these
are respectable and easily available. There is no need to go to a
sub rosa bookstore and worry about being seen.

As is true on Earth, *hwarhath* modern society is highly struc-
tured, with few areas of freedom. With nine billion people in our
home system, we have long since lost the unknown and empty
regions where freedom and adventure might lie. FTL explora-
tion is capital intensive, requiring an elaborate technology and
the cooperation of many people: hardly the final frontier, if by
frontier we mean the territory for which Huck Finn lit out.

The *hwarhath* home system has a far smaller population; the
best estimates are under a billion. However, good communication and a gift for organization have left no areas on the home
planet or in the home system beyond the knowledge and control
of senior relatives and the state.

Like humans, the *hwarhath* turn to the past or future when
they fantasize. The most popular type of fiction is the historical
romance, followed by the scientific romance, which can also be
called science fiction, though the first term is closer to the *hwarhath* original.

While historical romances are an accepted (though covert)
genre, the stories here are all—in one way or another—trans-
gressive, both of the rules of the genre and of the moral values of
hwarhath society. They treat heterosexual love and heterosexual
prostitution, cross dressing, the breaking of breeding contracts:
all profoundly disturbing behaviors, which would not appear in
a typical romance. The stories challenge *hwarhath* ideas of their
own history. Who are they, really? Where do they come from?
Are they as moral as they have always believed?

The *hwarhath* prefer their literature short or, if not short,
modular. The usual length of their plays is a human hour. Their
poetry is made of stanzas that are complete in themselves,

though, in longer works, they are connected through a complex system of repetition and anticipated change. Most of their prose fiction is under 40,000 words when translated into English.

However it's common for stories to have sequels, not always written by the same author. In many ways, this is like a time-honored human art form: fan fiction. Nowadays, of course, most fan art is electronic, the most common forms being metamorphic animation technology (MAT) dramas and games. *Hwarhath* fiction writers, denied access to electronic media, are forced to use paper and ink—not an entirely bad thing, according to readers. A book made of paper does not interfere with the operation of electronic equipment, nor will electronic equipment interfere with the operation of the book; it requires no power source other than the reader; it is difficult to damage a book so badly that it can't still be used; a book is easy to carry and hide; and one can read it in a soaking pool.

Included in this collection are three linked stories ("The Actors," "Dapple," and "The Potter of Bones"). Most likely they were written in a southern hemisphere language, then translated into *Eh Ahara*. Because of this, a stylistic analysis is difficult, perhaps impossible. There is no way to tell if the stories were written by one person or three.

The Hound of Merin

There was a lineage named Gesh, which held land in the hill country at the western edge of the Great Central Plain. The land was good, with plenty of water and timber. The valley bottoms were flat and arable. But the Gesh were not lucky, especially when it came to war. They became involved in a struggle with one of their neighbors, a large and powerful lineage named Merin. The struggle went on for years. At times there was peace, but it never lasted. In the end there was a decisive battle, and the men of Gesh lost.

Imagine a fortress town overlooking a valley deep in the hills of Gesh. There are high walls made of stone covered with pale blue plaster, narrow streets, and houses built around courtyards. Sunlight enters, filling the courtyards, slanting into shadowy rooms. The women of the lineage go about their business more quietly than is usual and with only a few jokes. Their children are with them. (Where else would they be?) One of the children is a boy named Hala, thirteen or fourteen, not quite old enough to go to war.

Days pass. It's autumn. The fields have been harvested, and the trees on the hilltops are changing color. Finally a message comes, brought by a single man. His *tsin* is stumbling with exhaustion as it comes through the gate. The man can barely stand once he has dismounted.

He tells the women, his aunts and senior cousins, that everything is over. The men of Gesh are dead, killed by the enemy or by their own weapons. The Merin are a day behind him at the most. What mourning they want to do will have to be done now, along with preparations to greet their new relations.

After he delivered the message the last man of Gesh went into an inner courtyard.

There he knelt in the dust and sunlight, taking out his knife. The women and children were safe from harm, and there was nothing more he could do for them. No man willingly falls alive into the hands of the enemy.

The boy Hala followed the man to the courtyard. A balcony went around it on the second story, roofed over but open toward the courtyard. The boy stood there, in the shadow, looking down at the man as he cut his throat.

A body empties itself as it dies, releasing whatever is in the bladder and bowels. Most likely this happened, but the story does not tell that part. It speaks of red blood rushing from the wound in the throat, and how the man's body collapsed onto the dusty white pavement. Gesh Hala decided then that he would never belong to Merin.

He left the body for the women to care for and went down to find the man's riding animal. That afternoon he cared for the *tsin*. In the evening, he led the animal out of the fortress. It could not be ridden. He walked through the fields, over the dry stubble, leading the *tsin*, then up into the hills. He spent the night there, hidden by the forest. In the morning, he went on, still leading the animal. It was still too weak to ride.

He did not see the soldiers of Merin arrive or the greeting they received from his female relatives. The mourning was over by then. The body of his cousin was cremated. Surely there had been time for that. The children had been dressed in their best clothing and told how they must speak to their new uncles and cousins.

Most likely Hala went east toward the Great Plain. He would have kept to the high ground, where the forest would protect him. There were trails made by animals. The men who had known the trails and could have followed him were dead, and the animals were shy: no danger, unless he did something really stupid.

Imagine him, moving through the shadows below the trees. Around him the foliage is green and blue-green, copper-red, the rich brown of weathered bronze. The ground is dry. The air smells of autumn, whatever that aroma may be on this planet and in this country. The *tsin* follows him, a large quadruped that looks something like an antelope. Its horns have been cut off close to its head and capped with metal. (This was always done to the animals used in war.) Most likely, the *tsin* is striped. The animals with solid coloration are rare and expensive.

We don't have a description of Hala as a boy. I see him as tall and thin, maybe a little gawky. At a distance, he'd pass for human, except for the fur that covers him. It is short and thick and grey. When he moves through a patch of sunlight, the fur shines like silver. He wears the usual costume for a male of that era: a kilt and sandals. There is a knife in a sheath at his side. This is how I imagine him, as he leaves everything he knows behind: the land of Gesh, his family, his name, and his childhood. It's unlikely that he understood what he was doing. He acted in response to grief and rage and maybe to some odd trait in his personality. How could he possibly know, at the age of fourteen, what he was getting himself into?

There are many versions of the story of Hala. Some are brief and stick to known facts. Others elaborate, filling all the empty spaces. These long tales, which are known as *tsugalin* or "lies," tell us what happened next in detail. But it's all made up. All we know for certain is that the boy was on his own.

This was the age called the Unraveling, when there was almost continual war. Old families were destroyed. Old alliances were torn to pieces. The world was full of people who no longer had a lineage. They were outlaws—thieves, beggars, prostitutes, and mercenary soldiers, living as best they could. Living badly, for the most part. Life has never been easy for people without a family. Hala became one of these people. He lived among the shadows for more than fifteen years.

When he comes back into the light, he is a man of thirty, a soldier employed by Eh Manhata, war leader for the new alliance that by now has begun to dominate the Great Central Plain. By this time Hala has his nickname. He is called *sul*, after an animal that the People use for hunting. The animal is large, fierce, relentless, and loyal. The closest equivalent animal on Earth would be a hunting dog. So Hala's name can be translated as Hound-Hala. According to the histories, he was a respected captain in the army of Eh Manhata.

His old enemies, the Merin, were allied with Eh, as they had been for several generations, and they had troops in the army. The man leading the troops was a son of Merin named Ie. So now the two main characters in the story have been brought together. At this point most of the stories describe Hala for the first time.

He was tall for a man of the People, which probably means his height was somewhere in the area of 175 centimeters. His body was broad and powerful-looking. According to many of the stories, "it was evident that his life had not been easy." This probably means that he was scarred. His fur was pale grey. His eyes were ordinary blue. (Remember that these "ordinary" eyes would have been entirely blue, with no white showing, and the pupils would have been rectangular and horizontal like the eyes of a sheep or squid.)

The stories tell us that he was a good comrade and an excellent soldier. Men liked him, though "he was one of those people who always keep their ideas in back." He kept secrets, this means. He was not forthcoming.

When he spoke, he was to the point. When he moved, his motions were rapid and decisive. But he knew how to wait, and it was no problem for him to be silent.

Merin Ie was a few years younger, about the same height as Gesh Hala but more slender. His fur was dark grey. His eyes were blue-green. He was the favorite son of a powerful lineage: well nourished, confident, happy with a quality that the People call *kahtiad*. It means upright, in-front, clearly visible, sincere: a person who says what he thinks and goes in a straight line toward his goal. According to the stories, he was a good soldier, though not as good as Gesh Hala, and a good leader. His directness made it easy for him to deal with other people, and he was intelligent and observant. An ardent young man, but not a fool. He had several nicknames. One was "Malachite" and referred to his eyes. Another was "The Beautiful." A third was "The Well Adorned." This last probably refers to the way he dressed, but there is a possible *double entendre*.

Both men held ranks that put them on the army council. It was not possible for Hala to avoid the son of Merin, though he must have wanted to, and Merin Ie had no idea that Hala was (or had been) Gesh.

The old quarrel lay between them like a sword covered with blood. But Merin Ie did not know this, and he fell in love with Hala Sul. No one knows exactly why. What could have been so attractive about this tough soldier-for-hire, this man out of the shadows?

Most likely, Merin Ie was not especially serious at first. It would be a camp romance, lasting a few days or maybe a tenth of year. How could it be anything else? Hala was nameless. Not the kind of man one would choose for a long-time love affair. But when he approached Hala, the man said no.

This is the part of the story that the People find really hilarious. It is their version of a rolling-around-on-the-floor joke. Hala Sul was nameless to other men, but he knew that he belonged to one of two lineages. If he was Gesh, then Ie was an enemy. If he was Merin, then they were relatives. In either case, they could not be lovers.

He could not explain to Ie what was going on. If the Merin decided he was Gesh, they were almost certain to kill him. If they decided he was a cousin—well, he still had no desire to be one of them, though his anger had almost vanished over the long and difficult years. Now, more than anything else, he wanted to make a decent living and stay out of trouble.

The other aspect of his problem was this: Hala was in love with Ie. This also strikes the People as very funny.

The situation was impossible. Hala did his best to avoid Ie. When they had to be together, Hala was polite and unfriendly. It did no good. Ie's affection, which had not been much at first, at least according to the stories, grew strong now. He became crazy in love. Whenever Hala turned around, there was the son of Merin.

The stories about Hala treat this period in one of two ways. Either they emphasize the romance, describing how the proud and beautiful son of Merin is pushed back (i.e., brought down) by love. Or they emphasize the humor. Isn't it funny to see Merin Ie make a spectacle of himself, languishing in a conspicuous fashion around the camp? Isn't it funny to watch Hound-Hala push away the only man he has ever loved?

This went on until Eh Manhata called Hala to his quarters. "Why don't you go to bed with this man? Then maybe he will be able to think about something except your body, and we can all get back to the important business of war."

Hala can do nothing except tell him the truth.

This may be the moment to speak about Eh Manhata. He led the alliance that became the Ten Wound Together and then the Weaving. In the end, this turned into the government of the planet. In so far as the People have a Founding Father, he is it. They respect him for his religious piety, which no one has ever questioned, and for his devotion to his family. He was a loving son and brother who never went against the women of his lineage. No one can argue with his skill as a soldier. No one can fault his drive to power. But he is a disturbing man.

There is no evidence that he cared for anyone except his mother and sisters. He had many male relatives, who fought alongside him for years and died in his campaigns. No stories tell of his affection for these people. He had allies outside his lineage, but no close friends. The first descriptions of his sexual behavior date from a hundred years after his death and may not be reliable. They say, when he decided he needed sex, he would point to one of his officers—someone who was not a relative—and tell him to spend the night. His officers accepted this as one of their duties. It was not an especially difficult one. His sex drive was not strong, and there was nothing perverse about his sexual habits.

This is the man who listened to Hala's story: a man who understood nothing about love.

He had never been interested in Hala's past. Why should he have been? The world at that time was full of people without families. Some were like Hala, refugees from lineages that had been destroyed. Others had been driven out of their families. The age bred many criminals. Manhata didn't ask the men he hired where they had come from or what crimes they might have committed.

But now he became furious. Hala had kept secrets from him. He had injured his plans. This was a betrayal, and—in any case— he could not leave Hala in the camp, in front of Merin Ie, driving the man even further into craziness.

He told Gesh Hala that he no longer had a job in the army of Eh. "If I ever see you again, I will have you killed."

Then he told his soldiers to beat Hala and throw him out of camp. This was done. In a day or two, Merin Ie noticed that Hala was gone and asked about him.

"He is a man of the shadows with no loyalty to anything. He has left us. He will not return."

According to many versions of the story, Merin Ie tried to find Hala, questioning people in the camp. He found out nothing. The soldiers who knew what had happened kept quiet out of fear. Later on, the stories say, whenever Ie sent messengers anywhere, he told them to ask about Hala. It was years before he got any news.

At first, he moped, having trouble paying attention to anything except his own unhappiness. But his relatives told him this was unmanly and disloyal. He had to pull himself together, they told him, and get back to thinking about the war.

"The man left without saying a word. He has no interest in you, cousin. Let the wind take him and blow him away! Don't think about him any longer."

In the end, the son of Merin listened to his cousins, though he did not forget Hala. He merely put that memory off to the side.

What happened to Hala? The most reliable stories give no information. He goes back into the shadows and is not seen again for almost five years. The lying stories describe many adventures.

According to the most famous tale, he was found, almost dead, by a camp follower.

This person was a woman who made her living by divination and prostitution. The divination was, of course, a legitimate activity. The prostitution was the worst possible kind of crime, since her customers were men who felt a need to have sex with a woman.

This story is unlikely. Eh Manhata is famous for his absolute hatred of heterosexuality except for the purposes of procreation. He would certainly not have allowed a heterosexual prostitute to follow his army, though how he would have gotten rid of her is a bit of question. Manhata was very traditional; he would have found it difficult to coerce a woman and impossible to harm one.

But there would have been no problem with any man who visited a female prostitute.

Manhata would have had the man killed in the most unpleasant way available.

But if the story is unlikely, it is also entertaining. It says that the prostitute nursed Hala back to health. He would have died without her. The soldiers had done a good job of beating him.

When he had recovered, he asked what he could do for her. She said her work was dangerous. A man who was willing to have sex with a woman was capable of anything. She never knew when one of her customers would turn on her, driven by guilt and horror at what he was doing or had just done. She needed a bodyguard.

The story says Hala took the job and remained for some time in the shadow camp that followed after Eh Manhata's army. The people there were diviners, gamblers, prostitutes, dealers in drugs and *halin*, criminals of every variety. They had little loyalty to anything, and little honor. How could they? Loyalty and honor are like trees that grow from a great root system. The root system is kinship. When it is no longer healthy, the trees that grow out of it must die.

Hala liked the woman, though not in a way that was sexual, and he felt grateful to her. In any case, where did he have to go? Though it was dangerous for him to stay so close to Eh Manhata.

He told the woman about this problem. She boiled up a dye and combed it into his fur, turning him from grey to black. Hah! It was strange to have a woman who was not a relative touch him, but it had to be done. Now the soldiers coming into the shadow camp would not recognize him. He was no longer Hala of the shining silver-grey pelt. Instead, his fur was drab, and his eyes in contrast seemed brighter and paler: no longer ordinary. He kept out of sight as much as possible, especially during the day. At night, the woman's customers arrived, some to learn their fortunes, others to have sex. Hala stayed close to the woman's tent, listening for any sign of trouble. It was not work that he found pleasant. The People have a proverb, which is very close to "beggars can't be choosers":

"There are few choices beyond the firelight."

In the end, the story tells us, the woman became pregnant. There was always the risk of this, though the woman knew as much as anyone about ways to prevent conception, and most of the men who visited her did not ask for "the act that causes procreation." For one thing, it was a lot more expensive than the other things she did. For another, there are degrees of perversity. Most of her customers were willing to be satisfied with less extreme versions of the crime. (Some, no doubt, were repelled by the idea of doing for pleasure what should be done only to create people. Others may have lacked imagination: they wanted to do with a woman what they had done with men.)

In any case, the woman got pregnant. Think of what this meant in this society. Remember that these people drew—and draw—a line between sex for pleasure and sex for procreation. Sex for pleasure is between people of the same gender. Sex for procreation is (of course) between members of different genders. It is not something done casually. Children do not come out of nowhere, by accident. Children come from families. They are the product of negotiations between lineages and of matings that have been formally arranged. If a woman without a family becomes pregnant, it is almost certainly evidence that she has done something immoral.

She tried every way she knew to end the pregnancy, but nothing worked, though several of the methods made her sick. The fetus remained inside her. She decided she had to tell Gesh Hala what was going on.

It's hard to explain how disturbing this situation was to him. For one thing, the People keep their men firmly away from the concerns of women. Men belong on the perimeter, guarding the lineage and its land. What happens at the hearth is not their business. If the women decide now and then that an abortion is necessary, most likely because something has gone badly wrong with the pregnancy, the men are not told about it. If certain children die as soon as they born, the men are not given details.

Now Hala was faced with the worst possible kind of problem: a problem that belonged to women. What he knew—what he'd been told his entire life—was that his first duty was to keep women and children from harm. Even in the shadows, this lesson had not been forgotten.

He was horrified that the woman had tried to kill the child inside, since she was healthy, and there was no evidence that there was anything wrong with the child. But that, in the end, was not his decision. He had no right to an opinion about the making or raising of children.

Everything he had ever learned told him that he could not let the woman deal with her problem alone. So they discussed the problem, Hala feeling more uncomfortable than he had ever been in his life. The woman knew a midwife, who'd be willing to help her, but this person was not close. They would have to leave at once, while she was still able to travel.

They bought two *tsina*: lazy bad-tempered animals that cost far too much. The good animals had all been bought by the army of Eh Manhata.

They rode south and west. Once again it was autumn, but this time the season was rainy and cold. The roads were muddy tracks. There were few other travelers. The war had produced too many criminals. It was dangerous to leave home.

Often, when they reached a caravanserai, they found it half in ruins and empty except for themselves. The local families had forgotten their old duties: there was no wood or food in the storerooms. Even the supply of water was uncertain. Wells had fallen in. The ceramic pots designed to hold rain had broken. Once they found the body of an animal floating in a water storage pond, huge and bloated. Hala could not tell if it had gotten there on its own or been put there.

A long hard journey. They made it finally to the village where the midwife lived. Her house was gone. Nothing remained except burnt pieces of wood. Hala left the woman in a thicket and went to ask questions.

"That witch and pervert! We drove her out and made sure there was nothing for her to come back to."

"You did that to a woman?" asked Hala.

"You could scarcely call her a proper woman. She belonged to that horrible new religion that says that the Goddess has two forms. We couldn't have that in our village."

The world was becoming a truly bad place, thought Hala. He went back to the woman and gave his news.

It was true, the woman told him. Her friend had been a follower of the religion that says the Goddess has a mate, equal to
her. Together they had created the universe. In this religion, sex
between men and women was tolerable and maybe even holy,
since it was a replica of the act between the Goddess and her
Other Self.

Hala felt as if he was sinking deeper and deeper into excrement. He was not the passionate and romantic boy who had
left Gesh more than fifteen years before. He had done things
he did not like to remember and lost some—maybe most—of
his faith in the honor and decency of people. Even his faith in
the Goddess was not what it had been. But he had not become
entirely cynical. He still could tell the difference between right
and wrong, and there were certain kinds of behavior that would
never be acceptable to him.

"Why did you know this person?" he asked the woman.

The woman said she was a follower of the same religion.

"Why?" asked Hala.

"Because if I don't have that, I have nothing. The old ways
don't work beyond the perimeter. You know that, Hala Sul. The
old Goddess, who spoke to me when I had a family, has not said
a word since I moved out of the firelight. I must believe in something. I will not believe that my life is entirely empty and wrong."

No question about it. He had gotten mixed up with a whore,
a pervert, and a heretic. When he died, he would certainly turn
into one of those unhappy ghosts who roam the world, complaining about their past and trying, without success, to undo
or remake their lives. He might even become the worst possible
kind of ghost: one that was deliberately evil. Hala shivered and
noticed how cold the thicket was. Ground and air were damp,
and the woman was coughing. She had begun to develop an ug-
ly-sounding cough several days before.

That brought Hala back to the situation at hand. He was
going to have to find a dry place and some firewood. Maybe the
villagers would give him some food—or sell it. He had a silver

bracelet that he'd managed to hold onto this far. He rose and went to get a blanket for the woman.

They went north from the village, looking for some sign of the midwife or other people who believed in the heretical religion. Several times, Hala asked the woman if they could stop. They had lied before, using the name of a lineage far to the west and saying they were brother and sister, caught in the war and trying to get home. Let them do it again, said Hala, and stay in a village till she had recovered her health.

"I want to be with people I trust when I have the child," said the woman.

By this time she was probably a little crazy from illness, but Hala didn't know this. All his training told him that women's problems had to be left to women. He had no right to interfere. His job, only and always, was to guard.

One morning he could not rouse the woman. He felt her skin where it was bare, on the palms of her hands and the soles of her feet. It burned. Her lips were dry and cracked.

He looked at her, her belly swollen till she looked like the animal floating in the pond, and he listened to her breathing. The sound was harsh. He could tell she was struggling. The sickness in her lungs had gotten suddenly much worse.

Well, this was the end to their argument. The woman would have her child wherever he could find people. Hala cut branches and made a litter to sling between the *tsina*. They didn't like this innovation, and he had to beat them. They were not the kind of animals that listened to reason. Finally, they quieted down, and he lifted the woman into place. He led the animals down out of the hills.

As he'd hoped, there was a village at the edge of plain: twenty tumble-down houses belonging to a lineage he'd never heard of. The people looked gaunt, even though it was harvest time, and they were not happy to see strangers, but they took the woman in. What else could they do? She had her baby and died. This took several days. In the meantime, the baby was nursed by a woman in the village. Gesh Hala waited and tended his animals. Finally, the woman he knew—the diviner—was gone. The villagers said they could not care for the baby. Times were hard. The winter coming on looked bad.

Where could he take the child? Gesh Hala asked.

The next village to the north was more prosperous, and the people were odd. Who could say what they would do?

He went north, carrying the child. The weather had cleared by this time. The sky over him was blue, and the wide plain began to dry, though there were still pools of water in low places. He came finally to the village of odd people. They seemed ordinary enough to him.

Their houses were kept up, and their gardens looked orderly. He told his story, as much of it as was decent.

They listened and said they would keep the child. Did he want to give the little girl a name? He thought for a moment, then said, "Geshani."

Fine, they said. The name would be given. He lay down to sleep, not worried for the first time since he learned that the woman—his friend—was pregnant.

In the morning, an old woman came to him, thin and bent over, her fur as white as snow.

"You said that you were searching for a midwife."

"Yes," said Hala.

"I am that person. Tell me who the woman was."

He gave his friend's name.

"Hah!" said the old woman. "Now, tell the real story, the entire story."

What did he have to lose? He told the story. The old woman listened, looking interested and grave.

Finally, he was done. The old woman said, "Everyone in this village follows the new religion. We believe that this division between men and women is contrary to the will of the Goddess and her Mate."

Hala made some kind of noncommittal answer.

"And we believe that the world is coming to pieces because people have ignored the true wishes of the Makers of Everything. Surely, this is the last age. Surely, something new and different has to happen."

"Maybe," said Hala. "But that isn't my concern. I have done the best I could for the diviner and her child. Now, I think I ought to go and find a new job elsewhere."

He waited until the child had been named in a ceremony that made him uneasy. There were two people officiating, one a woman and the other a man. They were called "mother" and "father." This seemed perverse to him, but the child got a name that meant "woman of Gesh," and that gave Hala a kind of satisfaction. He rode north, skirting the plain, and came finally to the town that was not held by Eh Manhata or his allies. There he found work as a guard.

Time passed. The war continued, but Hala was out of it. Sometimes he heard news of Eh Manhata or Merin Ie. That world, of the army and the war, seemed almost as remote as the world of his childhood. Now he lived in a world of petty merchants and little caravans. He made enough to live on, and, after a while, he stopped fearing the son of Eh. Who would ever find him in this dusty, unimportant town? Or in any of the towns he visited when he guarded traveling merchants?

Now the story moves to the meeting that young men love. Hala is traveling with a caravan. It stops for the night in a caravanserai. Great stone walls shut out the windy plain and, for once, there is wood in the storerooms. They build a fire. The merchants start drinking. Hala watches his soldiers to make certain they remain sober.

Another group of travelers arrives, coming in through the iron gates: a war band, their clothes glittering with gold. Is there a problem here? Gesh Hala walks toward them. When he gets close, he realizes that the leader is Merin Ie. He stops, hoping that the darkness will hide him.

Ie moves forward. "I think I know you."

"Is that so?" asks Gesh Hala.

The son of Merin moves closer to Hala and grabs his shoulders, turning him so the firelight shines in his face. "Hound-Hala!"

There was nothing for Hala to do, except admit that he was himself. The war band dismounted and made camp within the walls of the caravanserai, and the son of Merin invited Hala Sul to join him for a jug of *halin*.

What could Hala do? It would have been discourteous to say no. And hah! The son of Merin was lovely! His fur shone like steel. His eyes were like malachite. His clothing was richly ornamented with gold.

They settled at a distance from the fires. (There were two now; one for each company.) For a while they drank and spoke about neutral topics. Finally, when he was a little drunk, Merin Ie said, "Why did you leave? I tried to find you, Hala, year after year. I just heard about a soldier in the west, a man named Hala who might be you. I thought I would go and see." He reached out and touched Hala gently on the shoulder.

It was time to explain, Hala thought, and told his story, though he did not talk about his interview with Eh Manhata, and he said nothing about the diviner. Only that he was Gesh or maybe Merin.

"Let's get up and walk," said Merin Ie.

They went through the gate. The sky was full of stars. The flat, dark plain stretched to the horizon.

"Do you want to kill me?" the son of Merin asked.

"No," said Gesh Hala. As far as he was concerned, the old quarrel was over. He could get up no enthusiasm for it.

"I have not forgotten you, Hala," said Merin Ie. "And I haven't met a man I liked more."

Gesh Hala tried to explain about his lineage a second time. If he was Gesh, they were enemies. If he was Merin, they were cousins, and a love between them would be incestuous.

Merin Ie listened patiently, then said, "If you had been adult when the Gesh came to an end, we would have been enemies.

My family would have killed you. If you had stayed one day longer with your female relatives, you would have become Merin, and we'd be cousins. But neither of those things happened, and we cannot make them happen now. No one can change the past, not even the Goddess.

"You aren't Gesh. That lineage no longer exists, except in the minds of people and barely even there these days. You can't be part of something that has no real existence. That is like—what? Sailing on a ship that burned and sank a generation ago. Or living in a house out of a dream. It can't be done.

"Life is life, Hala Sul, and ideas are ideas. You have been mixing them up.

"As for Merin, I think the time when you could join is over, but maybe not. I'd sooner have you as a lover than as a cousin, Hala, but if you want to belong to Merin, I am willing to speak to my female relatives. It's possible that they will make an exception. Families have been known to adopt adult men in the past."

"No," Gesh Hala said. He did not want to be Merin.

"So," said Merin Ie. "What's the problem? You are a person without a family, which is sad. But in this age, many people have no family."

They stopped and faced each other. Merin Ie took hold of his shoulders again and pulled him close and kissed him. It was not the superficial kiss of friendship, but, rather, the deep kiss of love.

After a while, they went back in through the gate and gathered blankets and went up into one of the towers. There they made love. Hala wasn't certain it was morally right. But something had broken inside him, some wall or locked door. Instead of moral questions, he thought of Merin Ie's body and his own loneliness and desire.

In the morning they parted. Hala escorted his merchants to their destination, then quit his job and rode to join the son of Merin. The two of them were together through a summer of military campaigns. In the autumn, the war slowed down for a while and Hala went to Merin with his lover.

Hah! This was difficult! He was afraid that one of his old relatives would recognize him.

But over twenty years had passed, and the middle-aged soldier looked nothing like the boy of Gesh. Fortunately for him, Hala was a common name, and the world was full—as Merin Ie had told him—of people without families. No one was suspicious.

It's possible that the son of Merin consulted with his female relatives, and they told him he was right: Hala belonged to no family. Or maybe he kept the whole thing a secret. This isn't known.

The two men stayed together for close to thirty years, and Hala fought with the Merin in the endless war. Eh Manhata never did anything to either man, in spite of his threat to Hala. Maybe he decided the original problem had been solved, and if he killed Hala, he would have another quarrel on his hands. He had plenty to occupy him. In time, Hala's nickname changed. He became Merin Sul, the Hound of Merin, and that is the way he is known to history.

He never had a family name, though other lineages offered to adopt him, as years passed and he became famous and the Merin increasingly powerful. He refused them all with courtesy.

Merin Ie died at the age of sixty of a minor wound that became infected. He made it home to Merin, though he was no longer rational by the time they reached the big main gate. Hala got him off his *tsin* and carried him up to a bed, helped by other men. Then the women took over, though Hala was always there, sitting next to Ie, holding his hand, talking to him. Ie never answered or said anything that made sense.

After he died, Hala got up and stretched, rubbing his cramped arms and hands. People spoke to him. He ignored them and went down to the stable. His favorite *tsin* was there, a big male with red and white stripes. He got the animal ready to be ridden and led it into the main courtyard. More people spoke. He brushed past them and mounted the *tsin*, turning it toward the main gate. One of Ie's sisters stood in his way.

"Will you move?" said Hala.

"Where are you going?" the sister asked.

Hala shook his head, trying to clear it. Grief filled him like a great heavy stone. His tongue seemed incapable of motion. There were no ideas in his mind.

"If you want to ride out and be alone for a while, that is fine. I'll let you. But if you are trying to leave us, Merin Sul—No! You'll have to ride over me."

"It is over," he said finally. "I am done with you."

"What did you love?" asked the sister. "Not the son of Merin! You know if he'd been able to, he would have asked you to stay. Do you think we want the dishonor of sending you out into the world? Do you think we want the pain of losing you as well as Merin Ie?

"And how can we replace both of you? What kind of situation will you leave us in?"

"You don't know," said Hala. "You can't understand."

"You have lived among us for thirty years, and fought in our war band, and stood—always!—next to my brother. This is what I understand. I will not let you go."

Hala sighed finally and dismounted, leading the animal back into its stable. Men came to care for it. He walked back to the room where Ie's body lay. He sat down in a corner and wrapped his arms over his head, remaining there motionless and silent. The women of the house moved past him, getting his lover's body ready for cremation.

The next day Ie was burned. His ashes were buried on the hill above the Merin fortress. Hala watched all this without expression. When it was over, he walked off by himself and was gone until evening.

When he came back, he went to Merin Ie's sister, who was the leading woman of the lineage.

"I'll stay," he said. "I'll do what Merin asks of me. I want one thing only in return. When I die, bury me in the graveyard by the old fortress of Gesh."

The sister looked at him for a moment. "This tells me something I didn't know before."

Hala waited.

"It will be done," the sister told him.

"Good," said Hala, and left.

He stayed with the Merin until he died at the age of a hundred. He was in good health until his last days, and he kept traveling until he was past ninety. He had gotten into the habit of going places when he was young.

When he was almost eighty, he made a trip onto the Great Central Plain. By this time, peace had been established in most areas, and Hala didn't need more than a small retinue. They stopped one evening in a caravanserai. It was in good repair, he noticed. The storerooms held wood and food. They built a fire and settled down for the night. Then a second group arrived: soldiers wearing the insignia of Eh.

Hah! They were curt and efficient. They searched the building, then said, "You can't stay here tonight, old man."

One of the soldiers of Merin started up and opened his mouth. Hala raised a hand and asked, "Why not?"

"Someone important is coming. We can't let him share this building with the likes of you."

"Very well," said Hala and stood up, his joints making noises. The soldiers of Merin gathered around him, looking angry.

"Be patient, children," Hala said. "And think of who must be coming."

They led their animals out onto the plain and made a second camp. After a while, more soldiers arrived, coming out of the twilight. They entered the caravanserai. Hala watched them. He saw no one special among them. Night fell. He drank a little *halin*. His body was aching more than usual, and the *halin* helped. The soldiers of his retinue talked quietly. They had been with him long enough to know when he needed to be left in peace.

Finally, a shape came out of the darkness. A harsh voice said, "Hala Sul."

Hala lifted his head and then his hand in greeting.

"My men said they had pushed an old man out into the night. What old man? I asked.

They didn't know, they told me, but the men who traveled with him wore the sign of Merin. Fools, Hala! I am surrounded with people who cannot think. Come in."

He got up and followed Eh Manhata through the gate.

The soldiers had built a fire in one of the inside rooms. There were chairs, old but in good repair, and a table with a big crack going through it, still usable. The walls had been painted with a scene: a battle. Hala could make out that much, but no more. The paint was badly faded and great patches had flaked off.

Manhata waved him into a chair.

Hala settled and groaned.

"Right enough," said Manhata. "You are almost as old as I am. How could they possibly not recognize the Hound of Merin?"

"One old man looks like another," said Hala. "Except you, of course, Manhata."

Manhata made a noise that indicated disbelief. He was still impressive, his fur as grey as iron. There was no white at all in it. (Hala by this time was the color of snow.) His body had lost muscle and fat, so the big heavy bones were clearly visible. His face still wore an expression of command, made—if anything—more evident by the years.

He settled opposite Hala and filled two cups with *halin*. They began to talk, two old men in the firelight. By this time, Eh Manhata was beyond a question the most powerful man in the world. He was also alone. His last sister had died. He had no one to turn to for advice. In a year or two, he would make a stupid mistake and find himself in a trap, and then he would be dead, killed by enemies who got nothing out of his death.

Hala had twenty years to go. He would die in bed in the fortress at Merin. His lover's nieces would keep the promise their mother made. Half the promise, anyway. His ashes were divided. Part was buried in the graveyard at Merin, and part went to Gesh to the hill above the ruins of the town where he was born.

But none of this was known to the men, as they talked in the caravanserai. The meeting seems actually to have taken place, but there are only lies and speculations about the conversation.

One story has Eh Manhata asking if the two of them—he and Gesh Hala—had ever been sexually involved.

"Once or twice," Hala Sul answers.

"I can't remember," says Eh Manhata.

Hala smiles. He has kept most of his teeth. "It wasn't worth remembering, son of Eh."

Manhata asks Hala what happened, after he was beaten and thrown out of camp.

"A long story," Hala says. "I found out that life is even more complicated and difficult to understand that I had already suspected. And I re-found Merin Ie."

"You could have saved me trouble, if you had decided to have sex with him earlier. What difference would it have made? The problem you had with him—I can't remember what it was—something to do with your families. Isn't that right?"

"Yes," said Gesh Hala.

"It stopped being a problem, and you ended in his bed. For how long?"

"Thirty years, and fifteen years in Merin since he died."

"Such a long time!" Manhata turned his cup, looking at the fire. He said nothing for a while, then began to speak of the past: the battles and campaigns that had made him the foremost man alive.

Hala listened and commented from time to time. Finally, Manhata grew tired and a little drunk. He dozed off in his chair. Hala went to find the soldiers of Eh.

"This happens," one of them said. "He is no longer the man he used to be. We apologize for the way we treated you, Hala Merin Sul. We didn't recognize you."

Hala said it wasn't important and went out to where his men were camped and settled by their fire.

When he got back to Merin, he told the senior women about his meeting with the son of Eh.

"His own men say that Eh Manhata is failing. I don't know if he'll go quickly or slowly, but Merin needs to be ready."

The women agreed with him. Plans were made and instructions given to the men who led the Merin war bands. (There were three by this time.)

When Eh Manhata was trapped and killed, the soldiers of Merin knew how to act. They did not become involved in the struggle that broke out as soon as Manhata was dead. Instead, they pulled back to guard the boundaries of their own country, consulted with other lineages they were especially close to, and waited to see how events would go forward.

In time, it became evident that Eh was not going to produce an adequate leader. So the Merin threw in with Ahara, and this turned out to be a wise decision. All this happened because of Hala Sul.

As mentioned before, he died in Merin when he was almost a hundred years old. His mind remained clear until the end, and there wasn't a lot of pain. The women of the lineage took care of him. The men came in to pay their final visits, full of respect and grief. When he looked out the window, he saw the hills of Merin, their foliage autumn brown and green.

It was a good death, the stories tell us, and a really fine joke. Although he was a quiet man, he had a good sense of humor, and he must have enjoyed the situation. What an ending for the boy of Gesh!

After he was gone, the Merin began to name their sons after him. "Hala" became their favorite name for a male child, and other lineages began to make jokes about the number of Halas in Merin.

This habit has continued into modern times. Even today there are so many men named Merin Hala that nicknames have to be used. But no one is ever called Hala Sul.

THE LOVERS

There was a woman of the Ahara. She came of a good line within the lineage[1] and grew up to be tall and broad with thick, glossy fur. Her eyes were pale gray, an unusual color in that part of the world. From childhood on, her nickname was Eyes-of-crystal. If she had a fault, it lay in her personality. She was a bit too fierce and solitary.

Her home was in the town of Ahara Tsal, which stood on top of the Tsal River bluffs. To the west and south lay the farms and pastures of her lineage: a flat, rich land. To the north and east was the river valley, wide and marshy and full of animals. Eyes-of-crystal liked to go down there into the wilderness and ride and hunt. Her mother warned her this was dangerous.

"You'll get strange ideas and possibly meet things and people you don't want to meet."

But Eyes-of-crystal refused to listen.

Don't think this is a story about how she met ghosts or bandits or some horrible great animal like an *ulkuwa* and learned that her mother was right and she ought to have stayed at home. That's another story entirely, and maybe a good one. But the pain that Eyes-of-crystal encountered did not come from disobedience, and it did not come to her when she was away from home.

As mentioned before, she grew up to be large and strong. When she was twenty-five, her relatives decided to breed her.

1 Literally, "of a good thread within the woven cord."

At this time, the Ahara were the second most powerful lineage in the world, and this young woman came from a line that produced really fine children. The Ahara wanted to breed her with someone important. They looked around, and who did they see? Eh Manhata, who was the greatest warrior of the age. His lineage, the Eh, stood in front of everyone else. They had no equals. Only the Ahara came close.

So the young woman's relatives entered into negotiations with the senior women of Eh.

Eyes-of-crystal knew about this, but paid as little attention as possible. She had never wanted to be a mother, but she had always known that she had no choice. At times, she wished that she had come from a less excellent line. If only there had been something wrong or unhealthy about her immediate family! Maybe then she would have been left alone.

But her brothers and male first cousins were sturdy fighters. Her sisters and female first cousins were producing babies like furry butterballs. Every relative was co-operative, moral, intelligent, and well-put-together.

What a curse, thought Eyes-of-crystal, and went back down to the river to hunt. There, in the dark forest of the flood plain, she found a kind of peace. Often she found animals as well and brought them home, dead and bloody, across the back of her well-trained *tsin*. Imagine her as a kind of Diana, a gray-furred virgin huntress, about to lose everything she valued.

After a while, her mother called her in for a conference. One of her uncles was there as well, her mother's full brother, a soldier of middle age with a great scar across his face and one eye missing.

"You know that we have been speaking with the Eh," her mother said. "We wanted Eh Manhata as the father of your child."

"Yes," said Eyes-of-crystal. "I know this."

"He is not available," her mother said. "According to the Eh, they can't afford to take him out of the current war and send him here."

"There may be more going on than we can see," her uncle added. "I have never heard of Eh Manhata fathering any children, even in those periods when the war has slowed down."

Her mother's head tilted in the gesture that can mean either agreement or consideration. "There are men, even great men, who are not able to father children for one reason or another."

Eyes-of-crystal knew the reasons, of course. The People do not enjoy thinking about the unpleasant aspects of life, any more than humans do. But if a thing is unavoidable, then it must be looked at, and they have never misled their children about what was involved in producing the next generation.

Some men were infertile, and others were impotent. These were physical problems and comparatively rare. The most common problem was one that humans would call psychological, and the People would say was moral or spiritual. There were men who simply could not overcome their natural aversion to sex with women. They were fine with other men, but put them in breeding situation and nothing happened.[2]

"They have offered us Manhata's full brother," her mother said. "He has fathered a number of children, and most of them look good. Your uncle has met him, which is why I asked him to be present in this conference."

"They are twins," her uncle said. "When they came out into the world, Manhata was already bigger and stronger. He has always been quicker and more forceful than his brother. There are people who say he took something from his brother in the womb. I wouldn't be surprised."

"This doesn't sound promising," Eyes-of-crystal said.

"There's nothing wrong with Eh Shawin. He looks very much like Eh Manhata, though he isn't as tall or broad, and something is missing, as I said before. Manhata is like a man in sunlight: no one can overlook him. Shawin is a man at the edge of a forest, in shadow and not entirely visible. But he's a good soldier, and no

---

2   Literally, "nothing came forward." The *double entendre* is in the original.

one has ever questioned his courage or intelligence. And he is Eh Manhata's only full brother."

"No mating can tie us closer to Eh than this one," her mother said. "And no lineage is more important to us. If we're lucky, some of Manhata's qualities will show up in your child or children."

"You want me to do this," Eyes-of-crystal said.

Her mother said, "Yes."

She agreed. A message was sent to Eh. Eyes-of-crystal took her bow and went down along the river to shoot birds.

This happened in the late spring. Eh Shawin did not arrive until mid-summer. He came alone, which was not surprising. The road from Eh to Ahara was usually safe, and his brother was leading a campaign in the north against the Alliance of Five Less One. All his male relatives would be there. In peaceful times, of course, they would have ridden with him and made rude jokes about heterosexuality. It is always the job of one's male relatives to demoralize, while the men of the other lineage are required to be friendly and encouraging.

In any case, Shawin appeared alone at the gate of Ahara Tsal. The guards asked him to wait and sent a messenger ahead. There was time for her family to gather in the courtyard of their great house: her mother, her aunts, the older female cousins, and the two old men who were not at war.

Eyes-of-crystal was on a balcony. There were rules and courtesies in a proper mating. One does not meet the man right off, but there was nothing wrong in watching, as she did.

He rode in. His animal was dusty and tired, but had a good shape with powerful haunches and shoulders and a wide head that might indicate intelligence. It was solid brown, a rare and expensive color.

The man was as dusty as the *tsin* and dressed like an ordinary soldier. But he swung down gracefully, and, once he was on the ground, she could see he was tall, standing eye to eye with her mother and looming over the two old men, as they came forward to welcome him.

37

All the rituals of greeting were performed. It seemed to her that Shawin moved through them with unusual precision, like the traveling actors she had seen now and then. They came to Ahara Tsal and set up their stage in the main square. There they danced and told the stories of heroes. It occurred to her as a child that she wanted to be two things: a soldier or an actor. Both were impossible.

One of her sisters was on the balcony with Eyes-of-crystal. She looked down at the man in the courtyard and said, "He isn't much to look at, is he?"

Eyes-of-crystal held her tongue, though there was plenty she could have said. The sister had mated for the first time with a son of Merin, a beautiful man who liked fine clothing and jewelry. His eyes had been blue-green, the color of malachite. His manners had been good enough, especially at first. But it had taken her sister a long time to get pregnant, and the man became obviously restless. He was anxious to get back to the war and to his lover, the men of Ahara said.

When he learned that the sister was finally pregnant, he let out a shout of joy, and he left as soon as he decently could.

Eyes-of-crystal mentioned none of this. For one thing, the sister was still pregnant and with twins, if her size was any indication. Discomfort had ruined the woman's usually good disposition, and it was never a good idea to criticize the father of an unborn child.

Eyes-of-crystal kept her lips firmly closed over the *hwarhath* proverb that means, "Handsome is as handsome does."

The next day she was introduced to the man. He'd taken a bath and put on a new kilt covered with embroidery. The grip of his sword was white bone bound with rings of gold. His fur was brushed and glossy.

That was as much as she learned about him. Their meeting was formal and brief; the words they spoke to each other were set by tradition. When they had finished, her great-uncles led

Eh Shawin off to meet with other men. She went off with her female relatives.

For the most part, the *hwarhath* would prefer not to think about what their ancestors had to go through before the development of artificial insemination. But the information is there if you want to look for it, and the author of this story clearly did her research.

Remember that heterosexuality was—and is—frightening to the People. In it lies the power of generation and destruction. They know—and have always known—that the survival of their society depends on keeping men and women apart. But, through most of their history, the survival of their society depended on mating.

They did what humans also do, when faced with something frightening and unavoidable: death, for example, birth, or marriage. They used ritual to protect the act and limit it and direct its power. They used humor and drugs to diminish their fear.

Eh Shawin spent the day with the men of Ahara, talking and getting a little drunk. Eyes-of-crystal spent the day getting ready for the night, and the author of the story describes every detail: the ritual bath, the ceremonies of protection, the comic skits performed by female cousins, the elaborate mating robe.

Most likely, there is an element of malice in all this description. "Look, look," the author is saying to her readers. "This is what you are trying to forget. This is where we come from. It's as inescapable as shit."

Finally, at nightfall, Eyes-of-crystal was led up to the mating chamber: a large circular room high in a tower. Most of the space was filled by a bed, its wooden frame elaborately carved. Two chairs stood by a window. A lamp burned on the table between them. Eyes-of-crystal sat down. Her robe was stiff with embroidery. There was no way to relax. She had been given a potion, so the bed did not frighten her. Her relatives fussed around, straightening the cover on the bed, trimming the wick on the lamp, offering good advice.

At last, there was the sound of male voices, mostly drunk, at the bottom of the tower. The women grew silent. Eyes-of-crystal heard footsteps on the stairs: one person only, climbing steadily. The others had stayed behind, as was proper. One fellow kept shouting, "Good luck!"

A couple of the women whispered angrily. This was a serious—a sacred—business, and it ought to be carried forward with gravity. A little bit of something to drink did no harm. But men never knew when to stop. Any excuse for a drinking party!

The door opened, and there Eh Shawin was. A torch shone in back of him, so he was edged with red and yellow light. A moment later, he was in the room and standing in the shadows along the curving wall.

The women left. Several of them touched Eyes-of-crystal as they passed her, but no one spoke. There was only the rustle of clothing, the slap of sandals on the bare stone floor, and the breathing of an especially large and solid aunt as she went down the winding stairs. Last to go was Eyes-of-crystal's mother.

Eh Shawin closed the door, came over and sat down in the chair across from Eyes-of-crystal. Now she was frightened, in spite of the potion. He leaned forward and looked at her, frowning. "They have drugged you."

"Yes."

He sighed. "The first night is always like this. I'm going to tell you something, Ahara Pai, though I don't know if you'll be able to understand it at the moment. Still, I believe in acting directly[3] and in saying what's in my mind.

"There are many families who want to interbreed with Eh, and all of them are interested in having my brother as a father. But, as you probably know, our lineage cannot let him leave the field of battle.

3   Literally "with *kahtiad.*" This is the most important male virtue. If a man has it, he is steadfast, forthright, honest, and sincere. He travels like an arrow that is well made and well shot, straight to the target.

"Because I'm Eh Manhata's twin, I've been sent on trips like this—" He paused. "More times that I can remember. I know far more about this situation than is usual for a man, and I have formed my own opinions about how to go about producing children."

Eyes-of-crystal would have been shocked, if she had been sober. Thanks to the potion, she remained calm.

"These drugs and rituals do nothing good! The woman is frightened, and the man would be, if he wasn't drunk, as he usually is. It's surprising he remembers what it is he has to do. In my opinion, everything goes best if the two people are sober and comfortable with one another. The woman seems to get pregnant more quickly, and it's my impression that the child turns out better. And so I have developed my own way of doing this. I try to make it as ordinary as possible."

"Do your female relatives let you have these opinions?" asked Eyes-of-crystal. "It seems odd."

He glanced up and smiled briefly. "Remember that they've known me from childhood. Eh Manhata is fierce. I am stubborn."

He changed the topic then and asked her about hunting. The man of Ahara had told him she liked to hunt. It was an unusual trait in a woman, but not wrong or shameful. His home was on the plain. What was the great river like for hunting?

She tried to answer him, but she was frightened, and the drug made it hard for her to think and speak. Her mind kept coming back to the present situation, though with decreasing fear. For one thing, his questions were so ordinary. For another, the drug was making her sleepy. Her thoughts moved more and more slowly, like people wading through a heavy fall of snow.

"Maybe we should have this conversation another time," Eh Shawin said finally. He paused, then continued, his voice quiet and gentle. "There is one thing I have never been able to change. Your relatives and mine have expectations about what will happen tonight. We must meet those expectations.

"I can do the thing slowly and try to find some way to make it pleasant for you, or I can do it quickly and get it over."

"Quickly," said Eyes-of-crystal.

Eh Shawin inclined his head in the motion of agreement, then asked if she wanted light or darkness.

"Darkness," said Eyes-of-crystal.

He licked his fingers and put out the lamp.

The home world of the People has no moon, but the stars are brilliant, and the People have better night vision than humans. Most likely, the man and woman could see each other as they undressed. Maybe their eyes gleamed occasionally, reflecting starlight. Their dark, solid bodies must certainly have been visible as they moved past the star-filled windows and settled on the bed, which was covered with a mating blanket of bleached fabric as white as snow or bone.

The author of the story does not tell us any of this, though she describes their mating with clinical detail. Most likely, she was working from the old mating manuals, which are still available in libraries, though not (of course) in sections that children can access. There is no reason to believe that she is writing from personal experience.

After they finished, the man went to sleep. Eyes-of-crystal lay next to him, looking out a window at the sky. She could see the Banner of the Goddess, the Milky Way.

What had the Goddess been thinking of, when she devised this method for making people? It was like a great, ugly knot in the net of kinship and cooperation and love that held all of them—women and men, adults and children—together. Impossible to understand!

She woke in the morning and found Eh Shawin gone, though she could see the place where he'd lain. Her body hurt. She got up groaning and went down to the women's bathroom. There was hot water ready and a cousin to help her.

Hah! It was good to wash and then soak in a tub of clean water scented with herbs. The cousin was middle aged, but had never been bred. One of her feet was twisted. It had been that way from birth, and this was not a trait the Ahara wanted continued. She barely spoke to Eyes-of-crystal, either out of envy or embarrassment.

At last, Eyes-of-crystal got out of the tub and rubbed herself dry. The cousin brought a fresh new tunic. She put it on. Her female relatives would be waiting for her in the eating room and the kitchen. She had no wish to see them. Eyes-of-crystal thanked her cousin and went out to the stables.

Light slanted in the little, high windows. The air smelled of hay and *tsina*. Most of the stalls were empty, the animals gone to war. But a few remained: the mares and geldings that children rode and her own hunters. She went to look at her favorite, a blue-gray stallion. His legs and hindquarters had white stripes, and his horns were as black as obsidian.

Eh Shawin stood at the end of the stall. "A fine animal," he said. What do you call him?"

"Direct Action."

"A good name. I talked to your mother this morning and explained that I don't want to inconvenience your male relatives. There are so few home at present, and most are so old! They don't have the energy to be entertaining a guest. And I do best in these situations, if I keep regular hours and maintain my ordinary habits. So—" He glanced up briefly and smiled. "Your mother has agreed that it makes better sense for me to go out riding with you. I get the exercise I need, and the old men of Ahara get their rest."

It wasn't like her mother to agree to anything unusual, but Shawin was clever and plausible. There are men who know how to charm women, just as there are men who know how to charm men. These two qualities don't usually come together in one person. Eyes-of-crystal had the impression that Eh Shawin was no exception to this rule. Her male relatives did not dislike the man, but it wasn't likely they'd go out of the way for him.

"My *tsin* hasn't recovered from our journey yet, but one of your cousins has offered me this animal." He led her to another stall.

She knew the animal there: a large gelding. Its color was solid purple-brown.

"He told me its name is Consistent Behavior, which sounds promising, though I'm curious why an animal this color was gelded."

She knew and told him. The animal had a sullen disposition. This wasn't a problem for riding. "Unless you want to go quickly." But Consistent Behavior was no good for hunting, and the animal would have been dangerous in a war.

Eh Shawin laughed.

"My cousin meant no discourtesy. You see how little we have available." She gestured around at the empty stalls.

"I don't take offense easily. That's my brother."

They saddled and rode out. The author of this story is anonymous, but she almost certainly came from one of the lineages along the river, maybe from Ahara. Her description of the country is detailed, and it reads like real experience, not something she got out of a book.

They went east along a narrow trail that led past fields of *hwal* and *antim.* The sky was clear except for a handful of high clouds, and the air smelled of dust and dry vegetation. Small bugs filled the weeds along the trail. The names of the bugs are given: sunfly, hopper, *pirig, heln,* and scarlet warrior.

Eh Shawin asked about hunting a second time.

Eyes-of-crystal told him about the many fine animals and birds to be found in the marshes along the River Tsal and in the flood plain forest.

It was obvious that he knew about hunting. The questions he asked were intelligent. But he had never spent much time around water. She told him about the giant fish that lived in the river. They were longer than a man and had teeth like knives. Their dispositions were nasty. Her people hunted them with nets and spears.

"That must be something," Eh Shawin said, and then exhaled loudly. They had come to the top of the bluffs. In front of them was the river valley, wide and deep, full of many channels that wound through the forest and marshland, so the entire valley was like a belt made of strips of colored leather woven together: green, blue-green, brown, and pale red.

The two of them dismounted and let their animals graze. They spoke more about hunting. He reached over and stroked her shoulder the way a female lover might. Eyes-of-crystal frowned. After a moment he took his hand away and leaned back till he was lying full-length on the stony ground, his hands forming a resting place for his head.

Now she was made uneasy by his silence. "What is your brother like?" she asked.

He glanced at her. In the bright sunlight, his pupils had contracted into lines she could not see. His eyes were like windows onto an empty, blue sky.

"That's a question I've heard before. 'Tell us about Eh Manhata, Eh Shawin.'"

"Does it make your angry to be asked?"

"No. It's always been obvious that he was something special, even when we were children. Everyone knew if he lived to be a man, he would be either a hero or a monster.

"He is fierce and without fear, commanding, strong, clever about war. No one can match him as a leader in battle. So long as he's alive, our lineage will always win.

"He loves our mother and our female relatives, and he never acts without consulting them—except on the battlefield, of course. He is loyal to Eh. He respects the Goddess."

He stopped talking. There was no noise except bugs singing in the vegetation.

"I know all this," said Eyes-of-crystal.

"Then you know Eh Manhata." The man sat up. "Let's ride more."

That day they stayed on the plain above the river. In the afternoon, they returned to Ahara Tsal. At night, they mated again in the tower room. It was as unpleasant as the first time, but she didn't lie awake for as long afterward.

The weather remained hot and dry: good late summer weather. They got in the habit of going out almost every day. Eyes-of-crystal showed the man of Eh her country: the cultivated fields, the marshes and forest. They hunted the animals available in that season, before the fall migrations began. The man was a good companion: patient, observant, respectful of her skill and knowledge, unmoved by violence and death.

She liked him, though she had never expected to like a man who was not a close relative and thought he did things that made her uneasy.

One afternoon Eyes-of-crystal shot a *ral*[4] in the marshes along the river. The animal went down, but it wasn't dead. It struggled to rise, making a bleating noise. Eh Shawin was the one who dismounted and cut its throat. As he stuck the knife in, the ral jerked and twisted its neck. Blood spurted onto his clothing, and he made the hissing sound that indicates anger or disgust. He finished killing the *ral*, then pulled off his tunic and sank it in a pool of water. Naked, he eviscerated the animal. She had never seen an adult man without clothing. It made her uncomfortable.

She kept herself busy with the *tsina*. Her Direct Action was not troubled by the scent of blood, but the animal Shawin was riding—a young stallion that she had not finished training—was fidgety. He might try to run.

When Shawin had finished, he waded into the water and washed himself, then the tunic.

"Put that on," she said when he came back to shore.

"Wet? No."

4   This is a marsh-dwelling quadruped herbivore. Its body is like a small antelope or deer, except for the broad three-toed feet. Its head is surprisingly large and looks as if it might belong to a refined wart hog. The males have tusks. Both sexes have little piggy eyes and large mobile ears, which are striped lavender and pale yellow inside. Their backs are dull red, almost the same color as the dominant vegetation of the marshes. Their rumps are yellow, except around the anus, where there is a circular area that is entirely hairless. The bare skin is bright pink.

"I don't like this."

For a moment he said nothing, but concentrated on wringing out the tunic. Then he glanced up briefly. "There's no one here except the two of us, and we have been spending every night in the same bed, neither of us wearing anything. Do you really think we need to be formal?"

"Yes."

"Maybe you ought to go on ahead," Eh Shawin said. "You'll have to take the *ral*. My *tsin* isn't going to be willing to carry it."

She did as he suggested and rode home alone, troubled by the memory of him, his fur slicked down by water and his body evident. He was rangy with large bones and long muscles, narrow everywhere except through the shoulders. Made for speed rather than endurance, Eyes-of-crystal thought. In a way beautiful, though not with the sleek beauty of a woman.[5]

He ought to be more modest. He had not seemed especially bothered by the fact that he was naked. Maybe he had spent too much time fulfilling mating contracts. It had become ordinary for him to be around women who were not relatives and to do things with them that most men did only once or twice in their lives.

That evening, in the tower room, she asked about his behavior.

"If I hadn't washed the tunic right away, the stain would have sunk in, and I like that tunic. It's almost new, and I don't know if you noticed, but the embroidery over the shoulders is really fine. I shouldn't have worn it for hunting. I wasn't expecting to make quite so big a mess."

"Are you this way in battle?" she asked. "Fastidious?"

"No. Of course not. Though I never like it when something good is ruined: a piece of clothing, a weapon. But I don't think about that till later. In battle, there are only two things on my mind: staying alive and following my brother's orders."

5   The build described here is not typical of male *hwarhath*, who tend to be solid with torsos that go straight up and down. The author is giving us a male protagonist who is a bit odd and humanish in appearance.

There was something in his voice when he spoke about his brother that troubled her. "Do you like him?"

Eh Shawin glanced up. The room was dark except for a single lantern, flickering on the table between them, and his pupils had expanded to wide, black bars. "Manhata? What a question to ask." He licked his fingers and put out the light.

One of her cousins was home from the war while an injury to his leg healed. By this time, he was starting to hobble around, and he asked Eh Shawin to practice fighting with him. This was something women were not supposed to watch, but Eyes-of-crystal climbed onto a roof that overlooked the fighting ground. The two men used swords, the long heavy kind that had only one purpose. No man ever carried a weapon like that, unless he was going to war. Eh Shawin handled his sword with ease. He was obviously a better fighter than her cousin, and this was not due simply to her cousin's injury. He was as quick as she had expected and strong as well. Lovely to watch, the woman thought as she crouched on the roof tiles. If she had a son, this quickness and strength would be useful. If she had a daughter, maybe the child would get Eh Shawin's discipline. With luck, his oddness would not be transmitted.

Her time for bleeding came. So did the blood: she wasn't pregnant. She stayed away from him for several nights, as was customary.

"That tells me I have another 40 days here," Eh Shawin said. "I'm not sorry, though I have to say your male relatives are boring. But I like you, and my lineage does not have another breeding contract that requires me. Once you are pregnant, I will have to rejoin the army."

"You don't like the war."

"It's been going on a long time. After a while, everything seems as if it's happened before. There are only so many ways to kill and die. Even my brother has not managed to find much that is new in those areas."

"You are very peculiar," said Eyes-of-crystal. "I hope it doesn't come out in your children."

He laughed. "No one has complained to my female relatives."

This conversation took place atop a river bluff. They ended in this place often. He shared her love of the wide river valley. The foliage was getting its autumn colors. The river was dark brown like weathered bronze, except where it reflected the forest or the sky. Everything seemed to be shifting and changing. She looked out and thought of traveling like a tree floating in the water or a bird rising on the wind.

Maybe when this was over and she was pregnant, she would go to visit another town. There were several lineages nearby that were closely tied to Ahara. She had relatives, women who had been fathered by men of her lineage. She even had a former lover, a woman of Shulnowa. They had met at a festival and visited back and forth, and then the war grew dangerous for a time, and they exchanged tokens and messages. That ended finally. But maybe she could go to Shulnowa and visit one of her minor cousins. Maybe she would meet the lover. How could she avoid it in a town that size?

Eh Shawin ran a hand down her arm, stroking the fur. "I think I'd like to have sex right now."

"Here? In the sunlight?"

"We aren't getting anywhere by having sex in the dark."

Her bleeding had stopped the day before, so it was possible, though it seemed wrong. She tried to remember some rule that forbade sex outdoors while the sun was up. Nothing came to mind, and she had done such things with her lover. But that had been at festivals and with a woman. Surely sex for procreation ought to be done in a less carefree manner.

He leaned over and kissed the rim of her ear, then touched his tongue to the bare skin inside.

They had sex on the river bluff in a meadow of dry plants. A group of hunting birds soared overhead. At one point, early on, she looked up and saw them rising in a wide circle. Later, she found she had become preoccupied. The bright open world seemed to darken and turn in upon itself, and she was not aware of much except her body and Eh Shawin's body.

When they had finished, they lay a while together, listening to bugs sing around them. The birds had gone. Finally, Eh Shawin yawned and sat up. "That's something I haven't done before." He grinned at her. "There's more variety in sex than in war, in my opinion, anyway."

They got up and brushed each other off, then put on their clothing and went to find their *tsina*.

After that, they got in the habit of having sex beyond the town walls. It was the right time of year. The ground was dry, and the biting and burrowing bugs had mostly vanished. Now and then, there was some kind of distraction: a *tsin* would come close while grazing. Once, a fat little *tli* came up to see what they were doing. It stopped just outside reach and reared up on its hind legs, folding its paws against the white fur of its chest.

"Fill your eyes, little trickster," said Eh Shawin.

The animal seemed to listen. It tilted its head and watched them until they were done. Then, as they moved apart, it moved away.

They still slept in the tower room. By now, she had gotten used to sharing a bed with him. His scent was familiar, and it was comforting to lie against his broad back. Every few days her mother would ask how everything was going.

"Fine," she would answer. Finally she said, "I think I'm like my sister."

Her mother frowned. "In that case, we'll have the man with us all winter. I suppose I shouldn't complain. It gives your cousin someone to practice fighting with."

One morning she woke early and heard the cries of birds as they flew over Ahara Tsal. The fall migrations were beginning. There would be good hunting in the marshes along the river. She prodded Eh Shawin. Half awake, he agreed to go into the valley with her. After breakfast, they saddled their *tsina*.

The morning air was cool, and thin banners of mist floated over the surface of the river. The mist would be gone in less than an *ikun*,[6] and the day would be hot by noon. But at the moment she could feel the sharp edge of autumn. She carried her strung bow. Her quiver hung from her saddle. Eh Shawin had brought a pair of throwing spears. He wasn't really in the mood to kill anything, he told her. "But a ride is fine. I can watch you shoot down birds. And if we encounter anything large, I'll be ready."

There were plenty of animals in the valley, but she didn't see the birds she wanted: the ones she had heard as they flew over. She and Eh Shawin kept going, following a road that wasn't much used. Midway through the morning, two men appeared ahead of them, riding *tsina*. They came out of the underbrush and reined their animals, blocking the road. One had a shield on his arm.

Eh Shawin had been riding in back of her; now he came up alongside. There was a spear in his hand. "Let me take care of this." She reined Direct Action, and he moved past her. He was riding her young stallion, Hope-for-the-Future.

The two men turned their animals so they were facing Shawin, and one drew a sword, a long weapon of war.

Something made a noise behind her. She glanced around: two more men came riding toward her. They looked like soldiers who had gone to hell, ragged and dirty. One man wore a metal helmet. The other wore a leather cap. Both held battle-swords.

She glanced back at Shawin. He'd thrown his spear, and one of the men in front was falling, shouting as he slid onto the ground. The spear was in his chest.

Shawin pulled the second spear from its holder.

The two ragged soldiers came up on either side of her. One glanced over. "We're sorry that this has to happen in front of you, but, as you can see, we're desperate. It will be over quickly." Then they rode on. Direct Action shook his head. She tightened the reins. There was nothing she could do.

6   A *hwarhath* measure of time: one tenth of a standard *hwarhath* day, 2.31 human hours.

Among the *hwarhath*, warfare is entirely a male activity. The *hwarhath* men direct their violence exclusively toward each other. They do no physical harm to women and children, strange as this may sound to humans. But there is a *quid pro quo*. The *hwarhath* teach their women that they must never fight. Eyes-of-crystal knew that she was almost certainly safe. Unless these men were crazy, they would not touch her. But Eh Shawin was going to die, and all the rules of right behavior told her that she had to look on. This was the way it had always been done.

The man of Eh glanced back. He must have seen the two new soldiers. A moment later, he was charging at the man in front of him, spear in hand. Their *tsina* met. Her young stallion screamed, and a man shouted, she didn't know which one. They were tangled together, their animals turning in a circle. The other bandits reined, as if they were trying to see a good way to attack.

There was no way for Eh Shawin to win. His animal was untried. He didn't have the right kind of weapons. A hunting spear and a sword that was little more than a dagger! As ignorant as she was, she knew this was a bad situation. Finally, he was outnumbered. Her male relatives did not speak much about war, but she had heard them say, "As a general rule, big wins over little, and many over few."

Eyes-of-crystal pulled an arrow from her quiver. She fit it into her bow and pulled back the string. Hah! This was easy! They were much larger than a bird and hardly moving. She let the arrow go. It went into the neck of the man in the leather cap. He screamed, a noise almost like the one made by her young stallion.

The man in the helmet twisted around, a look of horror on his face. "No!" he shouted.

Her second arrow went into his chest. Her third went into his throat, and he fell. One foot stayed in its stirrup. He ended on the ground with one leg up. His *tsin* was thin and needed a grooming, but evidently it had been well trained. The moment its rider fell, it stopped moving, except to shake its head. Not that it made any difference. The rider was dead. His *tsin* could have dragged him across the valley and done no further harm.

The man she had shot first, the one in the leather cap, was still on his animal, bent over and holding onto the animal's neck. Blood poured down his back.

Beyond these two, Shawin still struggled with the third man. They were on the ground now, though she hadn't seen how this had happened. Their *tsina* danced around them. The men were entangled. Eyes-of-crystal could not risk a shot.

She waited, bow in hand. The struggle ended, and Eh Shawin stood up. His tunic was torn and dirty. He held his little sword. The blade was covered with blood.

"That seems to be it," Eh Shawin said.

Eyes-of-crystal leaned to one side and vomited.

After she finished, Eh Shawin helped her dismount. He was unharmed, except for a few small cuts. "Though I've been beaten like iron on the anvil, and I'll feel it tomorrow. If your relatives think I am going to be good for much of anything in the next few days—"

"I killed them," she said.

"Two of the four."

She went on, speaking disjointedly. How could she tell her relatives? What would they do? No woman of the Ahara had ever gotten involved in a battle.

"None that you have been told about," Eh Shawin said. He turned and watched the one man still alive. His *tsin* had become nervous finally and begun to step sideways like a harvest dancer. Then it shook its body, and the man slid off and lay motionless on the dusty road.

"I'll pull out the arrow and drive in my second spear. It's broken, but no one will know when that happened, and you will have killed only one man then."

That was more than enough, said Eyes-of-crystal.

He tilted his head in agreement, then walked over to the man he had killed with his short sword. "I killed this fellow, then captured his sword." He bent and picked it up. "And used it to kill the last man with two blows, one to the neck and one to the chest. If I make cuts that are big enough, no one will notice the arrow wounds. So two men died from my spears, one from my short sword and one from this." He lifted the battle sword. "What a hero I am! They'll make up poetry about me in Ahara." He looked at her, meeting her gaze. "And you behaved like a decent woman and watched the fight, never moving a hand."

She spoke again. The story was unlikely. She wasn't a good liar. It would be better to tell the truth.

"If you admit to behavior this unusual, your relatives may decide it wasn't a good idea to breed you," Eh Shawin said in answer. "And if you are pregnant already, they might decide to kill the child. Then all my hard work will have been wasted. I'd prefer that my children live, unless they are damaged in some way.

"And I'd prefer that your life be happy. It isn't likely to be, if you admit to violence. Lie to the best of your ability. That ought to be sufficient. Remember what you have just seen. If you're upset and don't make a lot of sense, your family will understand.

"And while it's unlikely that I could kill four men, my brother has done as much and more. Maybe I had for once his determination and power."

She agreed finally, and he did as he had planned, like a manager setting up the opening of a play. Bloodflies had begun to gather, their bodies shining like sparks of fire in the hazy sunlight. He ignored them, cutting the arrow from the one man with his hunting knife. He worked deftly, making the wound only a little larger, then drove in the broken spear, grunting with the effort. Then he moved to his second victim and used the borrowed battle sword to slash new wounds. The bloodflies hummed around him and crawled on the dead men.

A play would begin with the corpses lying on the stage, looking far more splendid than these fellows. One by one, the corpses would rise, turning into handsome warriors, who would explain to the audience how they came to their present situation, acting out the quarrels and moral dilemmas that led to death.

Let nothing like that happen here, said Eyes-of-crystal to the Goddess.

At last, Eh Shawin was done preparing the stage, He gathered the men's weapons and loaded them on their *tsina*, then tied the animals to a lead and gave the lead to her. They mounted and rode back toward Ahara Tsal.

They stopped once by a stream. Eh Shawin washed her arrows, which he had kept, then handed them to her.

"I don't want these."

"I don't want them found anywhere close to the place where these fellows died. Someone might wonder. And I can't think of a better place to hide arrows than in a quiver. Get rid of them later."

She put them in her quiver, and they went on.

Hah! It was an event when they arrived at the town, leading four animals, Eh Shawin covered with blood. He did most of the talking, while her relatives comforted her.

Male relatives saddled their *tsina* and rode to find the bodies, led by Shawin. He was fine, he said. A little tired and sore. But he would have no trouble riding back into the valley. The men of Ahara gave him sideways glances that indicated respect.

Her female relatives gave her a bath and put her to bed. After a while, she went to sleep, waking in the middle of the night.

Shawin was settling into bed next to her. She spoke his name.

He said, "We followed their trail back for a distance. There were only four of them. Bandits, your kinfolk say. Men without a lineage. The world is full of people like that these days. They must have wanted to rob me. The Goddess knows their animals are in bad condition, and they had nothing of value except their battle swords. Hah! To end like that!" Then he went to sleep.

She stayed awake. He had bathed, and he smelled of clean fur and aromatic soap. She found the odor comforting. All at once, she was unwilling to have him leave.

What lay in front of her, after he was gone? Being pregnant and then nursing a child. Then, maybe, if she could convince her relatives that she had no interest in children, she would be free for a while. That happened sometimes. There were women who could not manage to get interested in motherhood. Other women raised the children they bore.

But if the child turned out well, they would breed her again, maybe to someone like the son of Merin who had fathered her sister's just-born child.

And all the while, she would have the secret of her violence in her mind. What if her child was a girl? The trait might be transmitted. She might begin a line of female monsters.

As might be expected, she did not sleep any more that night. In the morning she was queasy and threw up. Not a good sign, the woman thought.

But the next day she was fine, and the day after she and Eh Shawin went riding, though not down into the river valley. Instead, they wandered among the fields, now mostly harvested, and went up onto the bluff to their favorite place. They dismounted and sat a while, watching the hunting birds that soared over the valley, circling and chasing one another, not out of anger or from a need to mate, but only (the old women said) for pleasure, from joy in their skill.

Finally Eyes-of-crystal began to speak. She had not been able to shake off her feeling of horror at what she had done, and she did not like to think of living her life with a secret like this one.

"You are not the only person with a secret," Eh Shawin told her gently.

"Not like this," she answered. "And it isn't my secret alone. You know it also."

"I'm not going to tell, dear one."

She glanced at him, surprised. He had used a term that belonged to a lover.

He was lying comfortably full-length on the ground, his eyes half closed, his hands folded over his belly. "You are young enough to think that people are the way they appear from the front and that they ought to be so. What am I? A loyal son of Eh, who carries out an embarrassing obligation as I am told to by the senior women of my lineage?"

"I don't know what to think of you," said Eyes-of-crystal.

"I have never been much interested in sex with men. That is one thing I have in common with my brother, though we differ in our attitude toward sex with women. The idea repels him so much that he has always refused to carry out any breeding contract. I like what I do, though my attitude toward the individual women varies. Still, none of them has ever been stupid, and all of them are in good physical condition."

He smiled at her. "Our lineage has been lucky. They have one son who wants to spend his entire life fighting and killing, which has been very useful, and another son who is willing to put the same kind of effort into mating.

"And I have been lucky. If my brother had been ordinary, I would have spent my life having no sex or sex with men, or I would have become a pervert, sneaking after women. Such men exist, though they are not common, even in this age where everything seems to be unraveling.

"Instead, I am here with you, for which I thank the Goddess and Manhata."

She couldn't think of what to say. They were both monsters, though in different ways. She had acted in a way that no woman ever should, though she had been unwilling and was now remorseful. His actions were proper. He had done as his female relatives told him. But his thoughts and feelings were perverse.

"What kind of child is going to come from this mating?" she asked finally.

"I don't know," said Eh Shawin. "But the passing of traits is not a simple process, as we know from breeding animals as well as people, and we both have many good traits. I think it's likely that the child will be fine."

She looked out at the river valley, then up at the birds, still soaring over the bluffs. A crazy idea came into her mind, and she told it to Eh Shawin.

Why couldn't they go off together? The world was full of people who wandered, having lost their homes in the long war. She could disguise herself like a man. Such things were possible. The actors who came to Ahara Tsal played women convincingly. Or else they could claim to be relatives, a brother and sister. She would not have to hide the person she was from the rest of her family. If the child turned out badly, at least it would not be one of the Ahara. He would not have to go back to the war.

He listened to her patiently. When she finished, he said, "How would we earn a living? I have only two skills, fighting and making women pregnant. The second one would be useless, if I didn't belong to a powerful lineage. As for the first skill, I don't want to become a bandit like those men in the valley."

They could hunt, said Eyes-of-crystal.

"And live like animals in the wilderness?"

They could sell whatever they didn't need, meat and fur.

"Most land is held by some lineage or other. Do you think they'll give us permission to hunt? Do you think people will refrain from asking questions, if we bring the hides of animals into a town? I'd be executed as a thief, and you would be sent off to survive as best you could. Most likely, someone would take you in. Even in this age of unraveling, there are people who will not let a woman come to harm. But you would not be the daughter of a famous lineage, and you would not be loved as you are here.

"And if there were more children, what would happen to them? I don't want my children to be beggars."

"Is there nothing we can do?" asked Eyes-of-crystal.

"What we are doing," said Eh Shawin.

After that she was silent, watching the birds.

It was midwinter before her relatives were certain that she was pregnant. The snow was deep by then and the winter unusually cold. Eh Shawin stayed on till spring, though she no longer spent time with him. She saw him, now and then, at a distance.

When the thaw was over and the roads comparatively dry, he rode off with a group of her male relatives who were returning to the war. She was sick that day and did not see him go.

The children were born at harvest time: two boys, large and sturdy. The older became Tsu, which was an old name among the Ahara. The younger became Ehrit, which means "deriving from Eh."

She nursed them for a year, as was customary in those days, then turned them over to one of her sisters and went back to her old habits. But hunting interested her less than it had. She missed having company, and she felt less safe than before. What if other bandits came into the river valley? Would she become violent again? Would they become violent?

Gradually, she became more like other women, though she never became entirely ordinary. She remained more solitary than was usual, and she did not lose her fondness for riding. Now she followed the trails that went through cultivated land, and she kept her eye on the fields and pastures. When she took out a weapon, it was usually to deal with some wild animal that was doing harm to her family's herds and crops.

Although she wasn't especially maternal, she wasn't able to leave her twins entirely in the hands of her female relatives. Maybe if they had been ordinary, she would have been able to ignore them. But they were clever and active and clearly in front of most other children.

When they were two years old, her family bred her again. This time the man came from one of the small lineages that existed at the edges of Ahara.[7] He was solid and handsome with

7   The old term for families like this was "side-clingers," though the word can also be translated as "shelf fungus" or even "barnacle." They were too small to survive on their own, so became allies of some large and powerful lineage, which chose not to absorb them for various reasons. Most powerful was the need to have a nearby source for breeding and sexual partners. In the area where this story takes place, the incest taboo forbade—and still forbids—sex

a fine glossy coat, and he did what he was asked to do with determination and competence. But he was obviously embarrassed, and it was clear that he preferred to spend his time with her male relatives. Eyes-of-crystal felt disappointed, though this didn't make any sense. The man behaved exactly as he was expected to, and he was never discourteous. She got pregnant almost at once. The child was a girl who inherited her father's solidity and lovely fur. What about this mating could cause dissatisfaction?

In time, another gift came from this mating: the man's sister, who was as solid and handsome as her brother and who (unlike him) was comfortable around women. Eyes-of-crystal met her at a festival, and they fell in love. This was (the author tells us) no ordinary casual bed-friendship.

It's important, at this point, to realize that the *hwarhath* tend to see women as less romantic and more promiscuous than men. Living on the perimeter, men have time and opportunity for love. But the women live at the center of the family, surrounded by relatives, and their strongest ties are usually with kin. For women, sexual love tends to be a matter of brief couplings at festivals or long-term, long-distance romances where the two lovers visit back and forth, but are more often apart than together.

Occasionally, female lovers will move in together, and this has happened more often in modern times. Conservatives see it as yet another example of how society is going to hell in a hand basket. What is going to become of the People, if women languish and hold onto one another like men? Who is going to look out for the family and children?

In the age of Eh Manhata, this kind of female affection-beyond-the-family was unusual, but it did occasionally happen, and the author of this story, who apparently is determined to break all the ordinary rules of romantic fiction, gives her heroine a lover who is willing to move away from home. The woman was

of any kind within a lineage. As the lineages grew larger and larger, this began to be a problem, which was solved—at least in part—by the accumulation of clingers.

maternal and had no children of her own, the author tells us, and she found Ahara Pai's children more interesting than her nephews and nieces.

It's possible that the lover was added to the story to give it a happy ending. The *hwarhath* insist on happy endings in their romances, though their idea of a happy ending is not always the same as ours. Or maybe the author put the lover in to shock and perturb.

Eyes-of-crystal was bred three more times. Each time the man was different and came from a different lineage. The author gives the names of lineages, but they would mean nothing to a human reader. Two were important. One was another clinger. The children—two more girls and a boy—were healthy enough to keep, and all of them grew up to be promising, though none equaled the twins. They really were exceptional boys: quick, well-coordinated, intelligent, forceful, good-humored, and charming.

"This is the spirit of Eh Manhata showing," said her family relatives.

No, she thought. The intelligence and good humor came from Eh Shawin. So did the charm, though the boys were able to get what they wanted from both women and men.

Occasionally she heard news about Shawin. Her kinfolk took an interest in him now. His life continued the way he had described it. He was often away from the army, fulfilling contracts his relatives had made. It seemed as if he almost never failed. The children he fathered were strong and healthy. They made it through the dangerous years of childhood with little trouble. His kinsmen began to call him The Progenitor, and this became the nickname that everyone used.

He was less impressive in the war. Not a bad soldier, her male relatives said, but not what they would have expected from Eh Manhata's twin. "Or from the man who killed those four bandits in our valley. Hah! That was an achievement! We still tell people about it! But he has never done anything comparable."

When the twins were fourteen, there was a festival at Tai-hanin. Eyes-of-crystal went, along with other women and enough men to provide protection, though the war had moved to the east by now, and all of Ahara and Eh lay between them and the nearest enemy. Her younger children stayed at home, as did her lover, but the twins were old enough for traveling, and they joined the party.

One evening they came to a caravanserai. There were people there already: a small group of soldiers from Eh. One of her male cousins went to speak with the soldiers. When he returned, he said, "Eh Shawin is there. I asked him over. He's never met his sons."

Soon the man himself appeared, walking out of the shadows into the light of Ahara's fire. No question that he had gotten older. He was still tall and rangy, but he moved stiffly now. The fur on his shoulders and upper arms had turned pale silver-gray. But when he saw her, he smiled, and his smile was unchanged: brief, but affectionate in a way that was not common among men of the People.

She was right, thought Eyes-of-crystal. The boys got their charm from him.

Her cousin stepped forward and introduced the boys. Eh Shawin looked at them. They had shot up in the last year, and it seemed likely that they would be as tall as he was. At the moment, they were thin and as leggy as *tsina* colts. Like colts, they were nervous and shy. They hung back and ducked their heads, unwilling to meet Eh Shawin's gaze, though they gave him many sideways glances. But there is nothing wrong with shyness in young men and boys, and their manners were good. They answered his questions promptly and clearly, Ehrit doing most of the talking, as he always did.

Finally, Shawin ran out of questions. The boys were given leave to go, and he came over to Eyes-of-crystal. It wasn't required that the two of them talk, but it was permissible.

"You've done a good job," he said.

"My sisters more than I," she said. "And my lover, though I taught the boys to hunt, and that was enjoyable."

He asked if she had other children. She named them and their fathers.

"Your relatives have been keeping you busy," he said.

"Not as busy as the Eh have been keeping you, from what I hear."

He laughed and inclined his head.

They spoke some more about the twins. She praised their qualities, while he looked across the fire. The boys were sprawled on the far side. They had gathered stones and drawn lines in the dirt, and were playing a game of strategy. Now and then one or the other would glance up and see Shawin watching, then glance back down.

"So everything has turned out well," Shawin said finally. "You have a lover and six fine children, and I have my life, which has turned out better than I expected. Hah! I was frightened when I first realized where my sexual interests were likely to lead me.

"I thought our relatives had been wrong. They worried about Manhata becoming a monster. He was always so relentless, and he cared for so few people and none of them male. But I was the one who was the monster. I thought, they will find out and kill me, or I will kill myself. But none of that has happened."

"Have you never wanted a lover?" asked Eyes-of-crystal.

He glanced at her sideways and smiled. "How could I have one?—I'll do what I can for your boys when they join the war, though they aren't going to need much help, being Ahara and having the qualities you describe. But I find it pleasant to do what I can."

They said goodbye, and he walked back to his campfire, pausing on the way to speak again with his sons.

Eh Shawin lived to be almost eighty, and Eyes-of-crystal reached a hundred, but they never met again, at least so far as the author tells us.

The last part of her story is devoted to the twins, who grew up to be fine soldiers and famous men. When Eh Manhata died at the age of eighty-five, betrayed and murdered by men he trusted, it seemed as if the alliance he had created would be destroyed. It was Ahara Ehrit who held everything together, not through violence, but through negotiation. He was helped (he said) by the fact that the world was full of the children of Eh Shawin. Often, when he met with other lineages, he found that he was talking to a half-brother. And there were certain traits that appeared over and over in Shawin's children. They were reasonable, flexible, good-humored, and willing to make the best of the situation. If they had to, they could fight, but it wasn't their preferred way to solve problems.

Ehrit is known to history as The Negotiator or The Weaver. Eh Manhata began the alliance that finally became the world government, but Ahara Ehrit saved it.

His brother Tsu was better at warfare, and this also was useful to the alliance. He was among the best generals of his generation, though no one in it could equal Eh Manhata. Still, Ahara Tsu won most of the battles he fought. His nickname was The Sword of Ahara. In the opinion of Ehrit, his qualities came from their mother. He was more courageous than was typical of the children of Eh Shawin, more relentless, more disciplined, more bloody-minded, and more bent on going his own way, though he always listened to Ehrit, and discipline and loyalty kept him from doing anything seriously off to the side.

Neither of them inherited Eh Manhata's great force of character. But the new age did not need this quality. They both had lovers, men who stayed with them for years, and though both of them fathered children, so far as is known they did so without pleasure.

∞ ∞ ∞

Two Notes on the Translation

In its upper course, the River Tsal is confined by high bluffs of sandstone and limestone, but farther to the south it runs between low banks across a level plain. In modern times, engineers have built dams and levees to control it, but, in the old days, the river changed course often. Its name comes from these changes in course. Tsal means loose, unfastened, unconnected, wandering, and homeless. Another meaning has been added in the last few years, since the People encountered humanity and the human concept of freedom, which does not (apparently) exist in any *hwarhath* society. Tsal is the word they use to translate the English word "free." This story, which may be (in part) about freedom, is set by the Loose or Homeless or Untethered or Free River.

In the main *hwarhath* language, there is no way to speak of people without mentioning their gender. The language has singular female, singular male, singular of undetermined gender, female plural, male plural, mixed plural and undetermined plural. There is no mixed plural form of the word "lover." Lovers are always both female or both male. The author of this story could have made up a mixed (heterosexual) form of the word. It would have been recognizable, and her readers would have been shocked. But for once she played it safe, or maybe she wanted her readers to come to the center of the story—its hearth or meaning—slowly. The title she gave the story, assuming that it was given by her and not by a nervous publisher, is best translated into English as "The Breeders." But this title doesn't sound right to humans and distorts the meaning of the story, which is, after all, about love.

THE ACTORS

There were two women who fell in love. At first this was no problem. Their families were allies and trading partners whose ships plied the narrow ocean between the coast of Sorg and the Great Southern Continent.

The northern family was Sorg itself. Numerous, prosperous, clever, and arrogant, these folk gave their name to an entire region.

In recent centuries the coast of Sorg has been improved in many ways: land drained and turned to agriculture, canals dug to carry away excess water and for transportation. The coastal people still prefer boats to the railroad, which they claim is noisy, dirty, and unnatural. "If the Goddess had meant us to ride on iron rails, she would not have given us so much water."

Most of the year a steady wind blows off the ocean. Modern silent windmills stand everywhere, their metal blades flashing "like a flock of little suns" in the words of a famous poem. These power the country's many drainage pumps and the even more numerous air cooling machines, which make the climate of Sorg tolerable to foreigners as long as they remain indoors.

In ancient times, the coast was a place of brackish marshes, slow rivers, shallow bays, and heat. The inhabitants would have been grey if they'd kept all their fur, as they do now, being influenced by air conditioning and the opinions of other cultures. In those days, however, both men and women cropped their outer layers of hair, leaving only the soft white undercoat; and many decorated themselves by shaving certain areas down to the bare dark skin.

Imagine a folk with snowy fur so short that it hides no detail of the bodies underneath. Dark lines zig-zag or coil over their angular shoulders and long narrow backs. (The Sorg have always been a tall and bony people.) Often their faces are partially shaved as well, becoming patterned masks from which stare eyes as blue as the ocean. Savages, we'd call them now. In their time they were matriarchs, warriors, explorers, and merchants.

Their country was rich, providing them with fish, shellfish, birds of many kinds, and *luatin*, which came into the coastal bays to breed. Though it is never easy to kill these massive animals, lust makes them less wary than usual, and many of the bays could be turned into traps. In the coastal marshes the *wis* plant bloomed, red as blood or fire. Its sap made (and makes) a famous scarlet dye.

The southern family was Helwar. Their home was an island that lies off the north-east corner of the Great Southern Continent. A polar current runs up the continent's eastern coast and coils around the island, bringing cold water, cool air, rain, and fog. The rain nourished the Helwar forests; the icy current gave them fish; the cool air made their flocks grow long thick wool. The family wealth, such as it was, came from these four sources: fish, wool, lumber, and ships. At the time of this story the Helwar made the best ships in the world.

It was the Helwar ships, seen in their own harbors and other places, which drew the Sorg south, traveling in wide wallowing barges better fit for rivers than the ocean. As rich as they were, they lacked the Helwar skill. To gain it, or at least the use of it, they offered an alliance.

How could the Helwar refuse these towering, white and black people? An agreement was made and confirmed with gifts, though the Sorg did not offer the one gift that makes an alliance unbreakable: their men as fathers for Helwar children. No bond is stronger than kinship. The offspring of such a mating would connect the two families as long as they and their descendants lived.

The Helwar made hints, which the Sorg pretended not to understand. Growing desperate, for they really wanted this alliance, the Helwar matriarchs made an offer of their own. They would send the five best and most promising young men in their lineage north to father children among the Sorg. The Helwar's new allies hesitated and consulted among each other, while the Helwar waited anxiously; and some of the islanders began to mutter that this might not be such a good deal. Maybe they ought to find more willing trading partners. Finally the Sorg agreed, though in a way that seemed grudging and reluctant.

"This is a beginning," said the Helwar matriarchs to each other. "Once they have our ships, they will understand the appeal of a stronger alliance."

When the Sorg left, five Helwar men—sturdy warriors— traveled with them. The motion of the Sorg barges was terrible, they reported later. "No wonder these folk want our ships. And the heat of their homeland! We're surprised that we didn't shrivel up like fish in a smoke house. But the job is done. All five women are pregnant."

Reassured, the Helwar built ships for their new allies: deep-hulled ocean flyers. When the ships were finished, sailors had to be trained; and this is how this story's heroine came to Helwar. She arrived in the southern autumn, along with other young folk, female and male. All had short hair. Many shaved. What a sight they must have been among the furry, fog-grey southerners!

The Helwar divided them, assigning each gender to the proper kind of ship. Like most of the peoples of the narrow ocean, they had both male and female vessels. The former explored new regions and traded in areas known to be dangerous. The latter kept to established routes, doing business with allies.

Sorg Ahl ended on the *Foam Bird*. The captain—Helwar Ki—was short, sturdy, and as grey as the winter ocean or the cloud-wrapped peaks of her island home.

Now we have brought together the story's first pair of lovers, as gangling Ahl walks up the gangway of the *Bird*, carrying her journey bag over one shoulder. Ki looks down at her, admiring the foreign woman's grace and evident confidence, but despising the unfamiliar haircut.

There are dark triangles below Ahl's eyes, both pointing down. A third triangle, this one pointing up, occupies most of her forehead. Rows of dark squares go down her arms. A final downward-pointing triangle rests between her upper pair of breasts, in no way concealed by her vest, which seems scanty to Ki.

The ship had two private cabins. One was for the captain. Ki put the foreigner in the other one, safely away from the rest of the crew. She was the only daughter of Sorg on board.

At first, as might be expected, Ahl kept herself aloof, though she was a hard worker and eager to learn. Then one day Ki noticed Ahl had stopped shaving. She asked about this.

"It's not easy to shave on board a ship," the northerner answered. "Especially in the weather we've been having, and I don't enjoy the feeling that ice-cold rain and spray produce when they beat against my bare skin. Finally—" She gave Ki a sideways glance. "I'm tired of looking like a foreigner."

After that Ahl became more friendly. By midwinter she'd stopped cutting her fur. "You people look so comfortable," she told Ki, and ran a hand along the other woman's arm, ruffling, then smoothing the winter-thick hair. Ki noticed she was falling in love, but kept quiet, having no idea how to court a person who came from so far away.

In early spring they carried a cargo of pickled fish to a harbor on the eastern coast of the Great Southern Continent. The trip was stormy. By the time they reached land and tied up in protected water, all of them were exhausted. Nonetheless, most of the crew went on shore. The lineage that held this part of the coast was connected to the Helwar by generations of interbreeding. They all had relatives in the houses that lined the harbor town's narrow, winding streets.

Ki and Ahl stayed on board; Ahl because she was not kin to anyone in the town, Ki out of courtesy and affection. The storm had blown out to sea, and the sky in the east was black; but where their ship rested, the sun shone, and the clouds were mostly white. Farther west, above low hills covered by a semitropical forest, the sky was clear. Hah! It was pleasant to lie on the *Foam Bird*'s deck, sharing sunlight and a jug of *halin*. Ahl had unfastened her vest. Her four breasts were visible: rather flat, especially the lower pair, but with prominent nipples and large oval areolae so dark that they seemed black. Ki felt desire, stronger than before. Something about the day—the stillness, the brightness, their fatigue, the jug of *halin*—made it possible for her to speak. Voice halting, she confessed her love.

Ahl listened courteously, head tilted, blue eyes half closed. When Ki finished, she said, "If that's so, why don't we have sex?"

Ki could think of no reason not to.

An awning had been raised in the middle of the ship, and thick rugs laid under it, so crew members could sleep in open air. They went there and, in the dim light coming through the canvas, gave each other pleasure and release. When they were done, Ahl rolled onto her back and sighed. "It's been a long time."

"Do you have a lover at home?" asked Ki.

"I did, a woman whose family is closely tied to mine. Most likely, she has found someone else by now."

Ki repeated that she was in love.

Ahl raised herself on one elbow and looked at the little southerner. "More likely you find me interesting because I'm foreign."

No, said Ki. It was the true emotion. To prove this she listed the qualities she loved: Ahl's hardworkingness, her courage, her even temper, her sense of justice. "There ought to be a fifth quality, but it doesn't come into my mind."

"This sounds like respect to me," said Ahl.

"Well, then, I love your thin body, your small breasts, your silver fur, your laugh, and the place between your legs, which has a taste faintly reminiscent of fish."

Ki loved fish, especially when just pulled from the ocean and lightly cooked in the grill on deck, so this was not an insult.

Ahl laughed. "Maybe you're in love. Let's continue and see what happens next."

At first they tried to be secret. But it's difficult to keep anything hidden on a ship full of women. Soon Ki's cousins took her aside. "Stop this acting and sneaking back and forth between cabins. Everyone knows what's going on. Be open and honest!"

The two women became acknowledged lovers, holding hands in public, kissing and using the personal form of "you" and "she." This continued until Ahl's training ended and she was ready to go home.

"I'm going to ask my mother to send me back here as soon as possible," she told Ki. "I don't know if I'm in love; it's not a word that comes easily to me; but I know I'll miss you and the *Foam Bird*."

Ki could say nothing. All her words had become stuck together in a lump at the back of her mouth. Sorrow lay in her mind like a heavy stone.

They parted, Ahl going up a gangway onto one of the ocean-flyers that Helwar had built for Sorg. The flyer spread its sails like great, white wings and carried her away across the ocean. Little Ki went back to her own ship to grieve.

The trip north was easy, except for the jokes that everyone made about Ahl's long fur. She ignored her relatives, remaining quiet and aloof.

"Is anything wrong?" they asked finally.

"I'm thinking,"

"Don't make yourself ill with ideas."

At home it was the dry season. The marshes of Sorg baked under a cloudless sky, their vegetation turning yellow. The great house where Ahl's mother lived was surrounded by gardens, kept watered except in times of severe drought. Ahl carried her journey bag past brightly colored ornamental plants. She dropped the bag in the entrance room and went looking for her mother.

The matron's favorite place was a porch at one end of the house. The walls were carved wood screens, pierced by many holes. White gauze curtains hung inside the screens, keeping out most bugs, but admitting whatever light and air came though the holes.

This is how you should imagine the room: mostly shadow, but flecked with sunlight, which has been slightly dimmed by its passage through gauze. In the middle is a large square table, where Ahl's mother does her accounts, arranging colored stones in rows. Now and then a gust of wind stirs the curtains. When this happens, the room's pattern of light and shadow flickers and shifts.

"Well," the matron said, looking at her daughter. "You need a haircut."

"It's cold in Helwar; I'm planning to return there."

Her mother frowned, then moved a stone from one row to another. "I'm not certain the alliance will hold."

"Why not?"

"They are a small lineage and far away. Aside from their ships, they aren't important. Allies should be neighbors or lineages so powerful they can't be avoided. That's the rule. Everyone knows it." Ahl's mother lifted her head, giving her daughter another look. "None of the children fathered by Helwar is alive."

"What happened?" Ahl asked sharply.

"One woman was not pregnant, though she seemed to be; or possibly she miscarried almost at once. Another woman miscarried at midterm. Two women remained pregnant, but their children died at birth." Her mother's tone permitted no questions. Maybe the children had been deformed or too weak to survive.

72

If so, the midwives would have killed them, rather than let them die slowly or live in pain.

"There's one you haven't accounted for," Ahl said.

"Your cousin Leweli." Her mother looked down again, pondering an arrangement of red and reddish-purple stones. "She went hunting in the marshes. Her boat was found later, floating upsidedown. She was not found. She and the child she carried have gone to the same place."

The land of death, Ahl thought. Leweli was dead. "You think this is a sign. The agreement with Helwar is unlucky."

"Maybe. They are a long way off." Her mother paused, white-furred hand hovering over a red stone. "And not important."

Ahl went to her room and unpacked, feeling grief for Leweli, who had been a distant cousin but a close friend, also for the other women who'd lost their children. Lastly, she grieved for herself and Ki.

In time—not her first day at home, nor the second—it occurred to Ahl that Leweli's death was strange. Her cousin had been a fine hunter, not in the least bit careless. Yet she had gone into the marshes alone while pregnant and done something so stupid that it killed her and her child.

Was this likely?

No.

She would go into the marshes and speak with a cousin who lived there. This woman, closer to Leweli than anyone, might know what had happened.

The next morning Ahl saddled a *tsin*, riding past fields and orchards. The sky, as usual, was cloudless and brilliant. The road was dusty, even when it reached the marshes and wound among waterspears. The plants were in blossom, their tall stalks topped with bladelike flowers as blue as the sky.

The woman Ahl went to visit was named Merhit. A witch, she lived by herself in a thatched hut by one of the marsh's many slow-moving channels. This kind of behavior would not have been tolerated in any other kind of woman. But holy people make their own rules. If they want to live alone, they can.

Ahl reached the hut at noon, dismounted and tied her animal in the shadow of a tree. The witch was sitting in an arbor made of driftwood branches overgrown with vines. For the most part the wood was hidden, but here and there a small piece showed, white as a bone among glossy leaves.

"Well," said Merhit. "You are back."

Ahl squatted, pushing her wide-brimmed hat off her head.

"And you need a haircut," said the witch.

"It was easier to get along with the Helwar if I looked like them. I've fallen in love with one of their daughters, though I don't imagine we have much of a future, if the alliance turns out badly."

"It has turned out as planned," the witch said. "We have the ships we desired and no permanent entanglement in the south."

Ahl considered this remark while looking at the channel's dark water dotted with red-orange flowers. These were not *wis*, as you might think, but a closely related plant, which had no commercial value, though it was lovely. "What happened to Leweli?"

"You know that five women mated with the men of Helwar. One had a mother who might be called weak. She didn't want her daughter to carry a child for most of a year, then lose it."

"What do you mean?" asked Ahl.

"It had been decided that none of the children would live beyond birth."

"Why?"

"The matriarchs of Sorg do not want this alliance. We are a proud family, also careful. The Helwar live far off and have nothing to recommend them except their skill in building ships. We have the ships now."

"They won't last forever. What if we need more?"

"That problem will be dealt with when it comes forward and can be seen. Our family is proud and careful, but does not always look into the distance."

Ahl considered this information, squatting in dust and heat. No question about what the witch was saying: their relatives had decided to kill whatever children came from the Helwar interbreeding. A contemporary woman would be sick with horror or at least uncomfortable. What did Ahl, a woman of the middle distance in time, feel?

Remember how many children died in the days before modern medicine. Those who were deformed or sickly died at once, of course, as they still do. It is a kindness we owe our kin. But many strong and healthy children died as well, due to illnesses that can now be prevented or cured. As a result, in many cultures, babies were called "guests" or "visitors" until they reached the end of their first or second year. Often they were not given a permanent name until it seemed likely they'd remain; and women tried to keep from loving these nameless children too much. If they had thought all the little ones they buried were true people, instead of beings who would turn into people in time and with luck, the women might have died of sorrow.

Because of this, Ahl saw the situation differently than we do. The two children who were killed at birth might have died later. How did she know for certain they'd been healthy? The idea was disturbing, but it did not make her sick.

"What happened to Leweli?" Ahl asked again.

"The mother I mentioned told her daughter to pretend pregnancy. The daughter told Leweli what was going on. By this time Leweli was pregnant; and it turns out she is one of those women who can't bear to lose a child. She knew if she stayed in her mother's house and had the child delivered by midwives, it would die. She came to me."

"She is alive," Ahl said.

"As is her daughter," said the witch. "A fine healthy child, though she has a definite southern look, which I don't find attractive."

"Where?" asked Ahl.

"In the marshes," said the witch after a pause. "I'm not happy about this. The air here breeds too many diseases. As you know, I can foretell the future. The child is important. I knew it the moment I saw Leweli's distended belly. I want the two of them in a place that's safe."

"What can I do?" asked Ahl after a moment.

"Take them to Helwar."

"How?"

"My vision does not see."

Ahl left, taking a different route, since she wanted time to think. The day grew hotter. She started panting and remembered an inn at the marsh's edge. With luck it was still in business. She made a detour and found the building, standing in the shade of a good-sized *atchul* tree.

Secondary roots hung from the tree's branches, forming a greenish-white curtain. A few had reached the ground and burrowed down, becoming runners that would in time, at a safe distance from the parent tree, send up shoots. This is the *atchul*'s preferred way to grow, though it also flowers and can produce seeds. In youth—and this *atchul* was comparatively young, though larger than usual—it is surrounded by a veil of roots, none thick, most ending in midair.

In middle age the roots increase in size; many dig into the earth. Instead of a veil of white filaments, they become a sturdy net. Outside the net, beyond the shadow of their mother, daughter trees rise, stretching out their branches and producing their own curtains or veils..

As the tree reaches old age the roots thicken even further, weighing the branches, pulling them toward the ground. Now the tree stands within a cage made of itself. In this cage, in time, it dies.

The tree is fairly common in the southern marshes, though rare elsewhere. Because of its behavior it has several nicknames: the Veil Tree, for obvious reasons, and the Sewing Tree, because of the way it grows, roots descending, then rising as another tree, then re-descending, as if it were stitching its family into the soil, generation after generation.

Finally it is called the Mother Tree because it reminds people of their mothers: large formidable women who sew or figure their accounts in rooms where gauzy curtains hang and billow.

Ahl pushed through the veil of roots and saw the inn clearly. It was more run-down than she remembered, but a cart stood at the entrance. Brightly painted in a foreign style, it must belong to travelers. Ahl dismounted and led her animal into the courtyard.

Two *tsina* stood there, old and bony. One was apparently lame as well. A man stood next to it, examining a forefoot. Something there, in the horny pads or the fissures between the three broad toes, disturbed him. He groaned softly, released the foot—the *tsin* put it down gingerly—looked up and greeted Ahl in a courteous, despondent tone.

Not her concern. She returned the greeting, tied her animal and went inside.

A man sat there. Like the man outside, he was a foreigner with uncut fur. But the man in the courtyard had been middle-aged, while this fellow was barely more than a boy, slender and graceful, though not—it was obvious to Ahl—entirely sober at the moment. He lounged on a bench, his back against the rough trunk of the *atchul*, which formed one wall of the room. The other walls were plastered and white rather than grey, though almost as rough as the *atchul*.

The innkeeper was female and a true daughter of Sorg: tall, thin, white and black. Ahl got beer from her. "Is there another place to be?"

"There is only the patio," the innkeeper said, her tone apologetic.

Anything would be better than sharing a room with an unrelated man. Ahl went out, finding an area paved with stone, shaded by the *atchul*'s leaves and curtained by its roots.

Hah! Better! There was even a breeze that stirred the hot air, bringing the aroma of summer vegetation to her nostrils.

She sat down, tasted the beer—it was cool in her mouth and pleasant on her tongue—then thought about her current situation.

Merhit was asking her to oppose her own mother, as well as all the other senior women of her lineage. No woman did this lightly. Many women—most women—would never do it.

But it was wrong to make a contract with the intention of breaking it, and even more wrong to break a contract made solid by children; and to break it in such a way!

No one would question the right of senior women to examine newborn children and decide, "This one should be kept. This one should not."

The job had to be done. A decent self-respecting family, one such as Sorg had always been, could not allow any of its members to die slowly. Nor could a decent family let children who had come out badly continue to live. What future did they have? How could they be happy or useful? The children who were killed held no grudge, as was known by the behavior of their ghosts.

The ghosts of adults are almost always resentful and dangerous. Hungry and angry, they haunt the living, looking for revenge or restitution. But the ghosts of newborn children cause no trouble. They appear in the houses where they were born and died, as if they don't know where else to go, causing no trouble, merely lingering. In time they grow dim and transparent. Finally they vanish. No one is the worse for them. This proves no wrong has been done. The children have lingered out of ignorance and confusion, not because they were angry or felt they had been dealt with unjustly.

The job of judging fitness to live was necessary, but it was the kind of decision that could not be left to the mothers who had borne the children. Young women as a group were unsuited to this kind of work, and men were obviously utterly unfit. Beyond question the job was best done by matriarchs full of experience. They judged, then made sure the children—the ones not kept— died without pain.

The children were not always sickly. In times of famine Sorg women had killed healthy children. A great loss, but unavoidable. In addition, Ahl had heard of families who used infanticide to control the number of males and females in each generation. If times were difficult and violent, it made sense to have sons. In good times, one wanted daughters. As far as Ahl knew, the Sorg had never done this. Always confident and proud, they trusted in the Goddess and their own ability to turn any healthy child to a good use, providing the rains fell and crops rose from the soil.

Maybe she would be justified in opposing the matriarchs of Sorg in this case, though the idea made her queasy. But how could she get Leweli and the child away? By ship, of course. But a ship that belonged to Sorg would not take them, and what story could she tell to foreign sailors? Two women alone were certain to look odd. Why weren't they traveling with kin?

The innkeeper came out. "Those men are quarreling."

"Hah?"

"Quietly, and in a language I don't understand. None the less, it's a quarrel. I didn't want to stay."

Ahl tilted her head in agreement. It was the worst kind of discourtesy for men to argue in front of unrelated women.

"They're actors. Something happened to split their company. These two are all that's left. For some reason they don't want to go home, though it's difficult to see what else they can do."

"Actors are often men of irregular behavior" Ahl said. This was a way of saying the men might be in trouble with their families. A terrible idea, but such things happen, and happened more often in the period of this story. It was the age called the Unravelling. An apparently endless war raged to the north of Sorg, on the continent's Great Central Plain. For a while it had seemed that the great warleader Eh Manhata would bring peace by defeating all rival armies. But Manhata had died a year before, and the war continued with increased savagery.

The innkeeper sat down and drank from the cup she carried. "I've thought they might be criminals or outcasts, though they're both very civil, and the older man has been through here before, causing no trouble.

"I saw him act the last time. He had a company of five, and they did the death of some hero. I forget which one, but he had a red robe and died impressively, after a lot of talk—about honor, mostly, as I remember. When the talk stopped, he gave a yell, and crash! Down he went! The men of Sorg are usually quieter when they die. What is there to talk about, anyway, in these situations?"

Ahl could think of no comment, though she'd enjoyed the few plays she had seen. She finished her beer and went to get her *tsin*, going around the outside of the inn, so as to avoid the quarreling men. When she looked closely, she saw the cart was shabby, its carving worn, its paint chipped and faded.

She got home at dusk. Great tall clouds were blowing in from the south-west. Lightning flickered around their tops.

The storm broke after dark. Thunder woke Ahl. She lay in bed, listening to wind and rain. This was the way summer ended in her country. The season for safe ocean travel was almost gone. The task she had been given would become more difficult with every day that passed.

She went to Sorg Harbor the next morning. This was not a harbor town like the ones she had visited in the south: rows of houses climbing over hills; steep streets paved with stone; marketplaces, also paved; and gardens, mostly private; but the people of the far south were not clutching, nor did they live in fear of thieves. It was a habit for them to share their gardens with passersby. Not everything, but something. Vines grew on the tops of walls. Pots of flowers stood by doors. Trees were left untrimmed, so their branches stretched over the street, dropping seeds in spring and leaves in autumn. In one town Ahl had walked through clouds of floating gauze. In another the streets had been carpeted with leaves as orange as fire. In a third there had been flowers, tiny and purple, dotting pale grey paving stones. Looking up, she had seen a flowering tree.

The Sorg preferred living on the farms established by their ancestors, and they saw no reason to make the stays of foreign visitors comfortable. Their harbor town consisted of storage barns. Here and there it was possible to find an inn, though most foreign sailors and merchants stayed on their ships, which were more pleasant and less expensive. The streets were unpaved and badly rutted. Unused ground was either bare or full of weeds.

The harbor itself was a wide bay. Five docks extended into it. Two were for local fishing boats, empty at present: the boats were at work far out on the ocean.

It was the other docks that interested Ahl. Five deep-bellied freighters were tied along them. Shading her eyes, she surveyed each deck. All the sailors were black and white: members of her lineage or of closely allied families.

This was bad news, but it might not be the only news. Ahl reined her *tsin* at one of the taverns along the waterfront. These were the only structures in town that looked welcoming and pleasant. They were a kind of building that used to be common along the south coast. A wooden framework is anchored in large ceramic pots. Vines grow out of the pots and over the frame, creating an arbor open on one side. The taverns all looked toward the harbor. What else would interest sailors?

Inside were benches and more pots, these with narrow mouths. Beerflies whirred around them or crawled on their lips.

Ahl dipped beer into a cup, paid for it, and sat down.

"Where are you from?" asked a black and white sailor.

"Sorg."

"You need a haircut, then."

"I've been traveling. I'll find a barber now that I'm home."

The sailors went back to their conversation, which was about ships, as are all conversations in a harbor town. A Batanin women's ship had left the day before, early enough so the storm wouldn't have caught it close to shore; and there was a Taig ship outside the harbor, waiting for high water.

"It will be men," a male sailor added. Obviously he was Sorg, or he wouldn't have been sitting with Sorg women, even in an arbor with an open front. "The Taig women don't travel. The ocean is dangerous, they say, and uncomfortable."

The other sailors—all women—grinned, tilting their heads in mocking agreement. The Taig women were right, of course, but there was more to the ocean than danger and discomfort. Let the Taig be timid, if they wished. The women of Sorg would sail, having confidence in their new ships and their family's traditional courage and strength.

No other foreign ships were expected.

Ahl drank her beer and left, riding home thoughtfully.

"Where have you been?" her mother asked.

"At Sorg Harbor."

"You are turning into a restless woman, and you still need to get a haircut."

"You're right that I've become restless," Ahl said. "I think I'll pay another visit to the marshes."

"Better that than the ocean," her mother said. "But I expect you to settle down soon."

The next day Ahl took her questions to the marsh witch and found Leweli visiting. Her cousin's fur—like her own—had not been cut recently, though for a different reason. The marsh was full of bugs, Leweli said. She wanted as much protection as she could get. "And Merhit, in spite of all her skills, is not a barber."

The fur had grown to its full length and was as grey as fog. The baby nursing at Leweli's upper left breast was the same color, though dappled.

"I've never seen anything like this before," Leweli said, sounding worried.

"It's common among the island folk," said Ahl. "Baby spots they call the condition. The spots usually fade, though now and then a person remains dappled. I have seen old grandmothers with spots and venerable men as well."

Her cousin frowned, looking at the child, who had finished eating and gone to sleep. "I hope they fade. Though I don't suppose it will matter, if she spends her life in a marsh."

"She won't," Merhit said firmly.

At this point Ahl explained her problem. How could she take Leweli and the baby south, if there were no ships in port except those belonging to relatives? "I could make up a story, explaining why we need to go south. But I have never been a good liar."

"This is true," said Leweli.

"And you know that any Sorg captain would check the story with my mother."

"You will have to go in disguise," said the witch. "How fortunate that both of you have uncut fur. You can pass as foreigners."

"Until we open our mouths and Sorg voices come out," Ahl said. "In any case, it's too late in the season. I don't think any of our family's ships will be going out again."

The witch frowned and was silent for a while. Finally she said, "The Taig ship will be leaving. Go with them."

"Two women and a child, traveling alone? How likely are they to take us?"

"This plan is doomed," said Leweli. "I'll have to stay here with you, Merhit."

"First of all, the marsh is unhealthy," the witch replied. "Secondly, I have visitors. Sooner or later you will be discovered. Imagine the trouble we'll be in then. Finally, I know the child belongs with her father's kin. I have seen that."

No way to argue with a witch who's had a vision. Ahl was silent. Leweli placed the baby in a basket lined with vegetation. The tiny hands were closed. Ahl couldn't see the bare skin of the palms. But the soles of the feet were visible and dark grey. So were the four nipples, emerging from the fog-grey fur like buds.

Even the dappling seemed lovely to Ahl, since it reminded her of the Helwar and Ki.

"Tell me everything that has happened to you since you left my house two days ago," Merhit said finally. "Maybe there's something that will help me find a path out."

Ahl complied. After she finished, Leweli said, "Would the actors take us north with them? It sounds as if they're in trouble already; they might not mind a bit more trouble, especially if we paid them."

Ahl realized she hadn't thought about money. "Do we have any?"

"I do," Merhit said. "So does your mother."

"Are you suggesting that I rob my mother?" Ahl asked, horrified.

"One thing at a time," said Merhit. "I want to answer Leweli first. You shouldn't go north. There's a war on, as you ought to remember, and it has gotten so bad that even women aren't entirely safe. I've heard stories of bandits—" She paused, apparently unwilling to continue. "The child belongs in the south."

The child opened her eyes, revealing sea-grey irises. It was a southern color. Leweli had blue eyes, as did Ahl and Merhit and almost all the Sorg.

"Have you named her?" Ahl asked, remembering Ki's grey eyes.

"Not yet. When I need to call her something, it's Darling or Dapple. A real name will come later, if she lives."

"I'm going to meet with the actors," Merhit said. Moving quickly, as witches do when they have made up their minds, she saddled her *tsin* and rode off. This was not the animal we know in modern times, descended from chargers used by warriors on the Great Central Plain. Instead, this was a swamp *tsin*: short, stocky, thick-legged and broad-footed. Its coat was greenish-tan with pale, thin, vertical stripes, which enabled it to blend with the marsh reeds. No breed of *tsina* is better over dubious ground. No breed is harder to find if it doesn't want finding.

Ahl knew all of this, of course, and paid no attention to the *tsin*. Instead she settled down to admire the baby and talk with her cousin.

Admiring a baby takes time, if it's done properly; and talking about one's family takes even longer. The afternoon passed without notice. All at once the light was slanting, and the witch rode back in view.

"Well?" asked Ahl.

Merhit dismounted, groaned and rubbed her behind. "It's just as I thought. I know the actor. He's been here often, though his former tours were luckier. What the innkeeper told you is true. His company has split apart, and he is left with one companion. They don't want to go back north. 'War is bad for every kind of art,' Perig said to me, 'except the art of war.' There may be other reasons, unpaid bills or the kinds of trouble actors get into.

"I offered him money to go south across the ocean and take the two of you, disguised as actors. Obviously it's a dubious enterprise, but he's desperate; and he knows I'm a good and reliable witch. I cured him of a throat inflammation that wouldn't go away. That was several years ago, but an actor remembers!

"He'll meet the two of you tomorrow at sunrise on the marsh road. Keep going till you meet him."

"Are we leaving already?" Leweli asked in a worried tone.

"Of course not. He has to train you. I'll mind the baby."

That was that. Ahl rode home on her animal, which was a crossbreed, larger and swifter than a true marsh *tsin* and less careful about where it put its feet: a good animal for ordinary use and warfare on solid ground.

That evening she sat with her mother and two aunts in a porch with gauze curtains. Hanging lanterns filled the room with light. Ahl's senior relatives sewed, while Ahl sharpened a favorite knife. Long and narrow, it was the best tool she had for cleaning fish.

"We're getting tired of waiting for you to settle down," an aunt said.

"We don't usually produce flighty women in this house," the second aunt added.

Ahl's mother kept at her cross-stitch, saying nothing, though she glanced at her daughter.

"Give me a few more days," Ahl said. "It's disturbing to live in a foreign place."

"We'll remember this in the future," her mother said.

The aunts tilted their heads in agreement.

"If we send any of our family off a second time, it will be men."

"Or women who are not promising."

"Though your kin haven't come back restless, as you have," Ahl's mother added.

Ahl ran her whetstone along the knife's blade. "What can I say?"

"There is nothing to say," her mother replied. "Remember who you are. And do!"

Ahl excused herself soon after that and went to her bed, not through the house's winding corridors, but outside though the garden. The air was cool and full of the scent of herbs. The sky was clear and starry. A meteor blazed in the north. Watching it, she swore two things. By the Goddess, she would find her way back to the Helwar and Ki. By the Goddess, she would not turn out like her mother!

She made the morning rendezvous on time. The men stood on the road, sun rising behind them. They'd brought their one healthy *tsin*, which grazed nearby. As Ahl dismounted, Leweli arrived on the witch's *tsin*.

"We went to the harbor yesterday," the older man said. "The Taig ship was planning to leave tomorrow, but will wait one extra day. Everything must be ready by tomorrow night. A challenge, let me tell you! But actors are used to rapid changes of plan and fortune."

"This is true," said the younger man with a glinting smile.

The men pulled clothing out of their animal's bags: male tunics, belts, swords and strips of fabric. "Put these on," the older man said. "Use the strips of fabric to bind your breasts till they're as flat as you can make them. We'll take a walk down the road while you dress. Be rapid! We have one day to teach you how to behave like men."

They worked till noon, the women walking and turning, bending, hefting tools and weapons, speaking. The men watched and made comments or demonstrated the right way to stride and pull a sword. At midday they rested in the shade of an *atchul*, a sapling with no secondary roots, which had apparently popped up out of nowhere. The mother tree was nowhere in view.

The older man, whose name was Perig, said, "I think you'd best pretend to be actors who specialize in female parts. They are usually tall; and they often have feminine mannerisms." He paused and gave the women a quick sideways glance. "I really can't imagine you as the kind of actors who play warriors or romantic leads."

"Well enough," said Ahl. "I've never wanted to be a soldier, even in pretense."

"They have the best roles," said the older man in a comfortable tone.

"I prefer lovers," said the younger man, whose name was Cholkwa.

"Well that you should," said Perig. "You have the beauty and grace required of such roles."

"But not the passion and darkness required of heroes," added the younger man. This sounded like an old argument, possibly a teasing one, though Ahl couldn't tell for sure.

"That will come. Youth is not a time for passion."

"It isn't?" asked Ahl, surprised.

"The young experience lust, which is a fine and useful feeling. How else can a young man move away from his mother? How else can he form friendships? And the best friendships are those formed when young. But real passion, the kind that can be acted, comes later. You'll see this, when you see me act."

When noon was past they got up and practiced more. At last, when the sun was low in the west, the actors called a halt.

"I've done what I can," Perig said. "Meet us here tomorrow at mid afternoon, and bring the money for our passage. The Taig will want to be paid the moment we're on board."

Leweli tilted her head. The two kinswomen rode off together. When they were safely away from the men, Leweli said, "Merhit has a message for you. Bring what money you can find."

"She wants me to rob my mother," Ahl said.

"Yes." Leweli reined the witch's *tsin*, though it wasn't easy, since the animal knew it was going home. At last it came to a halt. Ahl stopped her more-obliging animal.

"We both know your mother has a cache under the floor in her counting porch. Most likely you know the exact stone and how to raise it."

"This is horrible," Ahl said.

"It was horrible for me when I realized they were going to kill my child, not because it was sick or deformed, but to escape an agreement they never intended to keep. Obviously it is shameful to rob one's mother. But haven't we been shamed already? What have our relatives left us in the way of honesty and honor?"

Ahl groaned and tilted her head in agreement.

That night she went to her mother's counting porch and pried up the right stone. Gold shone in the light of the tiny lamp she carried: coins, bracelets, chains, ingots and works of art that were too badly damaged to be shown: a mounted warrior with a missing head, a *luat* with two missing flippers, a statue of the Goddess in her guise of creator. The statue was hollow and had gotten crushed. Ahl could still recognize the Great One, her tools in her hands, the hammer that beat out the heavens, the axe that chopped out the earth; but it wasn't easy.

Coins would be the safest. They were least likely to be missed. She gathered two handfuls, then replaced the stone and hurried away, feeling self-disgust.

It was impossible to sleep now. Instead she went to the stable and saddled her animal. In the first light of dawn she rode to the marsh. The day was hot already; Ahl felt queasy; it wasn't a real sickness, she decided, but rather fear and shame. When she reached the witch's cabin, she found Merhit outside, crouched next to a fire, brewing a potion. "It will keep the child sleepy and quiet. I have a wicker chest to put her in. She'll be able to breathe. Did you bring the money?"

Ahl pulled it out. Merhit examined the coins, putting several off to the side. "These are distinctive. Better to take only coins in common use. The ship will be in harbor tonight. Board after dark. By sunrise you'll be on the open ocean. I'll hide your animal. When you are missed, your relatives will think you've run away or died in the marsh like Leweli. No one will connect you with a band of actors going south by sea."

"The innkeeper knows there are only two men in the acting company."

"Maybe two of their companions came back. Maybe they found new companions." The witch stirred her potion, looking thoughtful. "Maybe I should talk to the innkeeper. She knows I met with the actors; and your mother knows that you have been visiting me. I'm a closer neighbor than your mother or any of the matriarchs. She won't talk, if I tell her not to. But I have to say this business of weaving plots isn't easy. I'm going back to ordinary magic as soon as you and Leweli are gone."

When the potion was cooked through and cooled, she fed a spoonful to the baby.

"Why are you doing this now?" asked Leweli.

"To make sure the dose is right. People vary in how they respond to magic, and it's always hard to judge how much to give a baby."

Soon Dapple was asleep, lying in the green shade of the witch's arbor. She looked, Ahl thought, like a *sul* cub: new-born, soft and round, still covered with down. All too soon the down is lost, giving way to rough fur and scales. But for a while such cubs have an unequaled charm.

Merhit poured the rest of the potion into jars and sealed them, pausing now and then to examine the baby. "The dose is right," she said at last. "This is a healthy sleep, neither light nor heavy. She held out a spoon made of horn, yellow and translucent. "Take this. Always use it. Give the child a spoonful when you want her to be quiet, but never more than five times a day."

"Is the potion dangerous?" Leweli asked.

"All magic is dangerous," Merhit said.

A little after noon, the women set off. Leweli and Ahl rode double. Merhit, on her marsh *tsin*, carried Dapple in the wicker chest.

When they reached the rendezvous, the men were there with their one healthy animal, loaded with baggage now. "Take your costumes and go down the road," Perig said. "We'll load your bags while you change."

"Not the baby," Leweli said. "It's hot already and will get hotter. I don't want her in that box."

"What are you going to do with her?" Cholkwa asked.

"Carry her till the sun goes down."

The two men looked at each other. "Very well," said Perig. "But if anyone comes, you'll have to hide in the marsh."

Leweli agreed. The two women changed clothing, Ahl binding all four of her breasts. Leweli, however, left her upper pair free and used the binding strip to make a sling for Dapple. "If she wakes, I can feed her."

They rejoined the men, and Perig said, "Another thing has occurred to me. By the time we reach Sorg Harbor, you are going to smell of milk and the baby."

"This is true," said Merhit, who was still on her *tsin*, watching everything.

"I also have a solution to this problem," Perig said. "Or rather, Cholkwa does."

The young man looked puzzled.

The older man smiled. "He likes perfume and always has a jar. We'll pour it over Leweli—"

"What?" cried Cholkwa.

"When we reach the south, dear one, I'll buy you more."

Cholkwa opened his mouth.

"You can argue on the way," said Merhit. "Be careful! And be lucky!" She turned her *tsin* and rode off, leading Ahl's animal.

The journey to Sorg Harbor was uneventful. They met no one.

Only a fool would travel through weather like this, Perig remarked. Late in the afternoon they took shelter against the heat, resting in the shadow of a half-grown *atchul* tree. Sister trees stood in the distance, but Ahl couldn't find the mother. Had it fallen? Was this an omen? Would she ever see her mother again? Imagining the matriarch's fury, Ahl decided she might not want to.

At sunset the four continued on their way, trudging through the long summer dusk into a starry night. By the time they reached Sorg Harbor the buildings were dark.

They stopped. Leweli put her baby in the wicker chest and, with Ah's help, strapped her upper breasts. The two men went off to relieve themselves. When they returned, Perig got out the perfume and dowsed Leweli.

"Too much," said Cholkwa. "You know what she smells like now."

"Like a man who sells the use of his body to other men," said Perig cheerfully. "Better that than a mother. In the future, please remember to use the male pronoun when speaking of Leweli or Ahl. They are men now."

"With a baby in a box," said Cholkwa.

"As you say," Perig agreed in the same cheerful tone. He looked toward the women. Ahl could see starlight shining on his eyes. "You need new names. How does Lewekh sound? And Ahlin?"

"Good enough," said Ahl.

Perig led them through dark streets. A few dim lanterns shone in the harbor, aboard docked ships. One was the Taig *Far Traveler*. A sleepy male voice asked, "Who?"

"The actors," said Perig.

"Come on board."

Tired and half-asleep, Ahl helped unfasten the chest. She and Leweli carried it into a cabin. A lamp hung from the ceiling; the still air stank of burning fish oil. Ahl forced open the cabin window. "It'll be better once we're under way."

"Good," said Leweli.

The men followed with bags, then left again. The *tsin* had to be delivered to its new owner. Ahl searched the cabin. A row of cabinets went along one wall. Inside were five hammocks, neatly rolled, and five pots of fired clay, good-sized and glazed inside. The lids fit tightly. One was clearly for urination. She could tell by the shape and the emblem drawn on the outside. She didn't know the purpose of the others.

Leweli spread her bedroll on the floor, but Ahl—a sailor— hung up one of the hammocks, fastening it to iron hooks in the cabin walls. Along with the lamp and the cabinets, these were the cabin's only furniture. A spare folk, the Taig.

Lying in her hammock, she regarded the lamp, which was iron and shaped like a fish with bulbous glass eyes. Light shone out of the eyes and through a hole in the fish's back: Taig art. The Sorg would never make anything so grotesque. Thinking this, Ahl went to sleep.

Waking, she felt the ship in motion. The fish was dark. Daylight came through the window. She could make out Leweli, sleeping next to the wicker chest, one hand on it. The men were not present. Had they slipped off in the night? Were she and Leweli alone among male strangers? A disturbing idea! She rose and used the pot-for-urination, then went on deck. Perig and Cholkwa were there, leaning on the ship's side, watching blue waves go past.

"Good morning, Ahlin," Perig said. "Cholkwa is a little queasy. I thought he'd be better up here."

"And you?" asked Ahl.

"No kind of travel bothers me."

She stayed a while with the men. For better or worse the journey had begun. There was a kind of relief in simply beginning. As to the end, who could say? With luck, she'd find Ki.

The first two days of the voyage were bright, with a strong wind blowing out of the north. Nothing could be better! They sped toward Helwar over foaming water. Leweli stayed in their cabin, afraid that the Taig sailors would see through her disguise, afraid as well to leave the baby alone.

"A good actor and a bad traveler," Perig said in explanation. "Poor Lewekh is often queasy, but if you could see him play a matron mourning the death of her male relations! A stone would groan and grieve!"

"I would like to see this," said the Taig captain politely.

Ahl preferred to be on deck, listening to Perig tell stories about his acting career, though he never mentioned the trouble that had left him with one companion.

At night they had to share the same cabin. The two men slept on the floor, keeping as far from the women as was possible. They were not perverts, Perig said in a reassuring tone. "Neither one of us has ever touched a woman, except for close relatives when we were children. Nor will we. Men like us are never used to fulfill breeding contracts. What lineage would want the kind of traits we have?"

This was true, Ahl realized. The most important male virtue is directness. How could an actor have this quality? Surely—to do his work—he had to be devious. Nor did it seem likely that an actor's life would encourage loyalty, the second male virtue. Always traveling, living a series of lies, how could men like Perig and Cholkwa be loyal, except possibly to one another?

In thinking this, Ahl showed the prejudice of her time. Now we understand that honesty can manifest itself in more than one way, and that people can travel long distances from home without becoming disloyal.

But it wasn't simply prejudice that made her think of actors as men of doubtful virtue. In those days acting was a trade halfway in shadow. Many actors were runaways, and not a few were criminals: thieves and prostitutes, usually, though there had been one famous acting troop, which supplemented its income with banditry.

"Understandable, given the quality of their acting," Perig said when he told Ahl about this group. "Eh Manhata caught them finally and told them to put on a play. Maybe they thought he'd leave them alive, if they could please him. They did their best, and he had them all beheaded. It wasn't a judgment on their acting, but it could have been."

Were her two companions thieves? Ahl wondered uneasily, then remembered that she was a thief and beyond question disloyal to her family. In addition she was pretending to be a man. Hah! She was most of the way into darkness! Maybe she ought to finish the job and become an actor, though women never did.

On the third day the wind shifted, blowing out of the west. Black clouds loomed there, lighting flashing around them: the first autumn storm. The Taig men reefed their sails. In spite of this the ship's speed increased. The waves grew taller and changed color, becoming dark green with thick white streaks of foam. The air filled with flying spray. "Get below," the Taig captain said to them.

They obeyed. Lewli was in the cabin already, throwing up in a pot, which had not been used till now.

"This is turning into a difficult situation," Perig said.

"Yes," said Cholkwa in a strange voice and found a pot of his own.

The cabin window was already shut. Ahl checked to make sure it was secure, then sat down. The ship was well-made, though not of Helwar quality; and the crew were good sailors, the captain especially. Nonetheless they might go down. Such things happened. It was terrible to sit here quietly! She mentioned to Perig that she was trained as a sailor.

"The captain sent us below for a reason," he replied. "Respect his knowledge; and remember how wet it is on deck. If you go

up, you ⎫ ⎫⎫ked at once. It will cling to your
body. The ⎫ ⎫⎫ know you're a woman."

This wa⎫ ⎫⎫. Ahl tilted her head in agreement. Above her
the fish lamp swung back and forth, casting shadows that danced
over the walls. Leweli and Cholkwa were still throwing up. Perig
sat on the floor, arms clasped around his knees, in a pose of patient endurance. Seeking distraction, Ahl opened the wicker
chest. The child Dapple slept quietly, as if in the witch's arbor.
She laid a thick cloth over her legs for protection, then lifted
the child out. How delicate the body between her hands! How
soft the fur! How light the weight when she laid Dapple in her
lap! Ahl watched the baby sleep, the tiny chest rising and falling
gently. The eyes were not perfectly shut. Now and then, when the
lantern's light shifted, a gleam shone between the grey lids. Hah!
It made Ahl feel tender! As did the loosely curled hands, their
nails uncut and curving over the fingertips like claws.

It occurred to her that the potion's magic might work on
full-grown people. At the moment Leweli and Cholkwa were
both lying down. If they were making any noise, Ahl was not
able to hear it over the sound of water rushing, the creak and
groan of wood. But neither looked comfortable.

So Ahl laid Dapple in the chest, then filled the horn spoon
with potion, bringing it to her cousin. Leweli glanced up, her
expression despairing.

"Try this," said Ahl, kneeling.

Leweli hesitated. The ship made a sudden loud noise and
shuddered around them. That was enough. Leweli took the potion.

If that was the right dose for a child, then the mother needed
more. Ahl went back to the jar.

When she finished with Leweli, she took the jar to Perig and
explained her idea, speaking loudly through the ship's noise. The
actor smiled and carried the jar to his companion.

Leweli and Cholkwa dozed, looking more comfortable now.
Perig sat as before. After a while Ahl began to feel queasy. The
jar of potion was still mostly full. She ate a spoonful. The flavor

was medicinal, sharp and herby. Soon she noticed her body was relaxing. Instead of fear and nausea, she felt a pleasant drowsiness. She lay down, one hand on the chest where Dapple slept, dreamt of Ki and woke to a banging noise.

Was the ship breaking apart? No, it was the Taig captain, beating on their door. The storm was as bad as ever, he told them. All the sails were gone, pulled down or blown away. Still the ship drove east, far off course already. "Pray for us, if you think the Goddess will listen; and if you have charms or know any spells, use them now!"

Then he was gone. The fish lamp swung back and forth. Looking across the cabin, Ahl saw Perig's mouth moving.

"Are you reciting magic spells?"

"Speeches out of the plays. Everything I can remember in praise of the Goddess, courage and luck."

This didn't seem useful, but could hardly do harm. Ahl gave more potion to the invalids, the child and herself. Time passed. Now and then, among her dreams, she thought she heard Perig's voice, speaking of honor and fate.

Finally—was it on the third day or the fourth?—the motion and noise decreased. Perig left the cabin, coming back to say, "The captain thinks we'll survive, though we're far east of the route he planned for us; and I have never seen an ocean like this one."

Ahl couldn't stay put. Pulling a vest over her tunic, she went on deck. The smooth planks shone with water. The air tasted of moisture and salt. Looking up, she saw the main mast still intact, though loose ropes flapped around it, holding pieces of broken spar like fish in a net.

On every side waves rose like mountains capped with snow. What a sight it was! But the ship was moving like a ship, climbing the dark blue slopes, sliding down into deep blue valleys. Before this, when the storm was at its worst, the ship's motion had reminded her of an animal fighting as the butcher's helpers dragged it into the butcher's killing yard.

They were going to live.

The next day was cloudless. Ahl and Perig opened the cabin window and emptied the various pots. None the less the cabin's air remained less than pleasant. The two of them spent most of the day on deck. The waves had decreased in size; and the Taig sailors put up a sail.

"We can steer now," the Taig captain said. "Though not well. We have to put in for repairs. I'm at the eastern edge of my knowledge, beyond all certain ports; and we can't turn back and sail across this wind until the repairs are made."

"Is that so?" said Perig in his usual tone of friendly interest.

"What then?" asked Ahl.

"There are islands out here," the captain answered. "I've heard other captains describe them, and they're marked on my maps, though this far out the maps are unreliable. Some are uninhab-ited, which would be fine. Others are inhabited by honest fishing people, which would be even better. What I'm worried about is pirates. Also monsters, though I'm not sure the monsters are real. There's no question about the pirates."

The day after they spotted land. A sailor climbed the main mast. Coming down, he reported no signs of habitation. But there were plenty of trees and a broken coastline that might pro-vide a harbor.

"We'll try it," said the captain.

At sunset they anchored in a little bay edged by sand. Be-yond the sand were ledges of rough-looking, dark-brown rock. Trees grew atop the ledges, their foliage the color of weathered bronze. The place made Ahl uneasy, though the harbor water was still and clear, the sky bright and almost cloudless.

They would spend the night on board, the Taig captain said. Was he simply being cautious, or did he feel—as Ahl did—that the island brooded and held secrets? Being the captain, he did not have to explain himself.

In the morning, men went ashore. They returned midway through the afternoon, having gone around the island. It was empty of people, though there were plenty of birds. The sailors brought back firewood and fresh water from a spring. Hah! It was sweet to drink!

"I don't imagine you'll be any help in repairing the ship," the Taig captain said to Perig and Ahl. "But you can work on shore. We'll need more wood, more water, and if any of you know how to hunt or fish—"

"Lew—," Ahl said and paused, then continued. "Lewekh is a fine hunter, though what he knows best is marshes."

"Cholkwa and I have lived off the land," said Perig.

"Do what you can," said the captain.

Cholkwa had no problem with this idea. But Leweli refused. "I can't leave the child alone. What if she wakes and begins to cry? What if she becomes ill? Men can't take care of children."

"The child is healthy as a *tsin* and sleeps like a rock," said Ahl.

"Usually," said Leweli. "But I will not leave her."

In the morning the three of them set off. It was another bright day. Small clouds dotted the sky. A mild wind blew, stirring the bronze-brown forest, making spots of sunlight dance over the ground. There were no trails. Obviously, no large animals lived on the island, though—as the sailors had said—birds were plentiful. So were edible plants, and Perig turned out to be excellent at finding these. Soon he had a basket full. Ahl knew most, though he was especially happy with something she hadn't seen before. "*Tsin* ears," he called the plant. It was fleshy and looked like its name, except for its color, which was a reddish-purple. The plant grew on tree trunks, so it looked as if the trees had ears and were listening: an eerie sight. Perig cut them off, using a knife. The cut ends did not bleed, a relief to Ahl.

On the far side of the island was a moor, covered with low vegetation. The birds there were large and heavy, like the *halpa* that the People raise on many parts of our home planet. Like *halpa*, they flew when startled, but only for a short distance. Then they dropped down and tried to run.

"This can't be called a sport," said Cholkwa and shot one. Seen close, it was covered with glossy brown feathers, except for its legs and feet, which were naked and bright blue. There were areas of bare skin on the head, circling the animal's round yellow eyes, so it seemed to wear spectacles, though this image would not have occurred to Ahl. In her age spectacles were rare, and it's likely that she never saw a pair.

"What do you think?" asked Cholkwa.

"It looks like a *halpa*," said Perig. "Except for the blue skin. Maybe it's a relative. If so, it ought to be tasty, especially in a stew with my ears."

They spent the midday killing birds. All had the same areas of blue skin, so it wasn't a disease, a thought that had occurred to Ahl. When they had enough, Perig found a long straight branch. They fastened the birds to it by their bright blue feet and carried them back this way, Cholkwa at one end of the stick, Ahl at the other. The wind had died. Ahead of them a trail of smoke rose into the cloudless sky.

"They must be heating pitch," said Perig. "The ship was taking on water, the captain said."

"How could it not?" asked Cholkwa. "If I had known what kind of trip this was going to be—"

"We couldn't stay in Sorg," said Perig. "Nor return to the north; and we have survived the journey."

"Wait till we've reached our destination before you say that," replied Cholkwa.

They reached the inlet in late afternoon. The ship's cook, a burly man with grey-brown fur, descended on them and seized their birds. Perig followed with his tsin *ears*.

Dinner was roast bird. The cook would use the ears tomorrow, Perig said. "The men are hungry. A stew takes time; and *tsin* ears require special preparation. I have to say the birds taste fine roasted. I'm almost certain they're related to *halpa*."

"How did they get here?" asked Cholkwa. "They could hardly fly."

"Maybe they've been here all along," Perig said. "Placed by the Goddess when she made the world."

"Or maybe people left them," said Ahl, licking her fingers.

"That's possible," Perig admitted.

Most of the sailors stayed on shore that night, as did Perig and Cholkwa. Ahl suspected the two men were interested in sex, now that they were safe and could get away from their female companions. Nothing could be done in the cabin. No self-respecting male would do anything so intimate in a room containing women. But on a dark beach, surrounded by other men— She envied them and went back to the ship.

The next day the Taig captain said, "I'm tired of your comrade's laziness. What is his excuse today? Sickness? An unlucky omen?"

"He still hasn't recovered from the storm," said Ahl.

"Nonsense," said the captain. "He will go on shore. You said he's a good hunter. We need food, and he clearly needs exercise and fresh air."

Argument was impossible. Leweli went with Ahl and the actors, though she looked unhappy and began complaining as soon as they were in the forest.

"Merhit is a good witch," said Ahl. "I'm confident her magic will keep the child safe. We have no choice, cousin. A captain must be obeyed."

This time the birds were harder to find, but at noon they came on a flock, all grouped together in an open space on the moor, scratching with large blue feet and pecking. It was easy to kill as many they were able to carry. Laden with their prey, they returned to the beach.

The pitch pot was turned over, and a black pool of pitch lay next to it. Bodies, the Taig sailors almost certainly, lay scattered on the sand.

"Bad luck!" said Perig.

Could they flee? Ahl glanced around. The forest was close, but not close enough. Ragged strangers moved toward them, holding bloody swords.

Perig stretched his arms out to the side. His hands was open and empty. "Obviously we can't fight you. But I ought to mention if you kill us, you will be killing a pair of women."

"What do you mean?" asked one of the men. His accent was thick, but Ahl could understand him.

Perig gestured. "Those two are women."

The man frowned. "They don't look it."

"Ahl, pull off your tunic," Perig said.

She did as he asked, dropping the tunic and unfastening the band that held her upper breasts. The moment she was bare, the men looked down. This was encouraging. In spite of being pirates, they had not lost all sense of right behavior.

"Put on your tunic," said one of the men in a stifled voice.

She picked up the tunic and pulled it on.

"There is a baby on the ship," Perig continued in his usual pleasant voice. "The other woman, the one holding the stick with birds, is the mother. I assume you're planning to kill us or maroon us. But you can hardly kill women or maroon them with unrelated men."

"How do you know what we can do?" asked the man who had spoken first. Most likely he was the leader.

The men around him looked uneasy. One said, "Jehan," in a nervous tone.

"And why are these women traveling in disguise with men who aren't relatives?" added the man named Jehan. "I know foreigners lack self-respect, but this seems worse than usual."

"Why don't you disarm us, which is the obvious next step, and then we can talk," said Perig. "If you've left the Taig cook alive, you might give the birds to him."

Jehan swung his sword. Perig fell.

"Goddess!" cried Cholkwa, falling to his knees beside his lover. Ahl was certain now. She heard love in the young man's anguished voice.

Perig sat up, feeling his head.

"I used the flat," said Jehan. "But if he keeps talking, I'll use the edge."

"He'll be quiet," said Cholkwa and stood, helping Perig up. His hands, on the older man, seemed as careful as if he were holding a fragile treasure: something made of glass and gold.

"Now," said Jehan. "Give us your weapons."

They went down the beach, still carrying their birds, surrounded by pirates. Now Ahl could see beyond the Taig ship. There was another ship, somewhat smaller, outside the harbor entrance, blocking escape. Obviously it belonged to the pirates. Squinting against the glare of sunset, she tried to make out details, but couldn't tell if there were pirates on the Taig ship.

Clearly they held the beach and the remaining sailors on shore: a group of seven, two injured, one badly. The Taig cook was wrapping an already-bloody bandage around his chest. Guards stood around the prisoners, holding weapons that had belonged— Ahl was almost certain—to the Taig.

"Are the rest dead?" asked Ahl.

"Some," said the cook in an angry voice. "Most were on the ship, repairing the rigging. They are still there, guarding it against capture."

One of the guards said, "My cousin Jehan thought it would be a good idea to attack from the land. That's where you seemed to be, if your smoke was any indication. If we came sailing in from the west, you'd see us and make preparations. Better to circle to the south—the island would hide us—and land a party in the little southern harbor, then come through the forest and take you by surprise."

"It worked," said Jehan stubbornly.

"We don't have their ship," said the guard.

"We'll get it," Jehan said. "In the meantime, we have dinner."

"And two women," said one of the other pirates.

"What?" asked the guard. He was a stocky man with dark fur going silver over his shoulders. In Ahl's opinion, he looked sensible, not a trait she associated with piracy.

"I'm a woman," said Ahl. "And so is she."

"This is turning into a perplexing mess," the guard said. "What are two women doing on a Taig ship, disguised as men? Taig women don't travel, and why would any woman disguise herself as a man? Surely you know how dangerous it is! We could have killed you by mistake."

"Can I speak?" asked Perig.

"If you want to," said the guard. "And have something useful to say."

"He's one for chattering," said Jehan in a warning tone.

"Let him chatter," said the guard. "I want information."

"These two women needed to get south in a hurry and went in disguise because they couldn't find a women's ship."

"Are you related to them? You don't look similar."

Perig hesitated briefly, then tilted his head in assent. "The women in our lineage are tall and have an authority we men lack."

"Which lineage?" the guard asked.

"Tesati," said Perig.

"Not one I know."

"It's to the north," said Perig. "At the edge of the Great Central Plain. Or rather it was there. The Unraveling has destroyed much. Another family overwhelmed ours. The men are dead, except for us."

"Why are you alive?" asked Jehan.

"We weren't home when the end came. Cholkwa and I are actors and often travel."

"Actors!" said the guard, looking interested.

"When we did come home, we found—" Perig smiled briefly. "No home. Our male kin were dead. The family that killed them, the Chaitin, had gathered in our female relatives and the children. We should have killed ourselves. It would have been the decent thing to do. But we found these two hiding out, along with Leweli's baby. They didn't want to be Chaitin. There are women who hold this kind of grudge."

Everyone was listening intently, of course. It was a good story, told excellently. But now Ahl saw a look of confusion on the Taig cook's face, followed by a look of horror. The cook was remembering the night before, she thought. Perig and Cholkwa had made love on the beach. The Taig sailors had noticed and been undisturbed. Traveling companions often give each other this kind of comfort, provided they are the same sex and not related. But if the two actors belonged to the same family, the act was incest. The cook opened his mouth, then closed it and glanced down, going back to work on his injured comrade.

A near thing! And not over. The cook might still decide to denounce the actors.

"Maybe we should have given our kinswomen to the Chaitin," Perig said. "They would have been safer; and there is always something offensive about the idea of women without a family. Such things happen to men. We know it! But women should live inside a double wall of matriarchs and soldiers.

"These ethical problems are never easy to untangle. In the end we decided to rely on the old rule, which says that men should not make decisions for women. That power lies in the hands of their mothers and their female relatives; and they were not available, nor were they kin, since they had become Chaitin, while these two remained Tesati. They asked us to escort them south; and we agreed out of loyalty, which is not the foremost male virtue. That, of course, is directness or honesty. But loyalty is one of the five."

"I told you he talked a lot," said Jehan.

"Are you really actors?" asked the guard.

"Why would I lie?" asked Perig.

"I've never seen a play," the guard said. Ahl heard longing in his voice.

"Well, then," Perig said. "Let the Taig cook fix our birds. You can feast tonight and see *The Death of Eh Manhata*."

"He's dead?" cried the guard. The other pirates made noises indicating surprise.

"What happened?" asked Jehan.

"He was betrayed by men he trusted, captured and—" Perig stopped. "The play will show you. Wait till tonight."

"It's all very well for you to talk about waiting," Leweli said. "But I have a child on board the Taig ship. I need to get back to her."

"We can't let you go," said Jehan.

"Why not?" asked the silver-backed guard.

"For one thing, the Taig might be willing to surrender their ship in order to get these two women back, especially if they have a baby on their hands."

"You are willing to hold women hostage?" asked Perig in a shocked tone.

Jehan frowned and raised his sword.

"Don't kill him," said the guard. "I want to see the play."

"For another," continued Jehan, "we can't let the women tell the Taig whatever they may have found out about us. What if they've realized how few of us there are? And how difficult it will be for us to take the ship?"

A look of pain crossed the guard's face. "Very well," he said. "Keep the women here."

The pirates untied the cook's feet, so he could work, helped by pirates. Soon a new fire was burning, and the cook was eviscerating birds. As for Ahl and her comrades, they settled in the sand close to the Taig prisoners. The guard settled with them, obviously anxious to talk. His name was Jehan, he said, the same as his cousin. Though he was Jehan Silverback, and his cousin was Long Jehan.

"Long?" said Perig. "He's no taller than you are."

"That isn't the way he's long," said Jehan Silverback, then looked embarrassed. "It's hard for me to remember these two are women."

"This isn't a situation where it's easy to remember anything having to do with manners," said Perig. "Though I'm glad to know you're a self-respecting man. How did you end in this line of work?"

He came from an island, said Jehan Silverback. "Where exactly I won't tell you, in case we decide to let you live." It was one of two islands that lay remote from all other land. The guard's family lived on one island. Another lineage— "our breeding partners"—lived on the other. Both islands were steep and stony, surrounded by rocks and shoals. Not much to look at, according to the guard, though his voice sounded affectionate to Ahl. "But the cliffs are full of nesting birds; and the waters next to shore are so full of shellfish that they are like stones on a beach; and there are plenty of fish."

The problem was the islands were treeless. The islanders lived in houses made of stone and sod. Their fuel was driftwood and the oil of marine animals.

Lacking timber, they could not build boats. Without boats, they would not be able to fish or reach their neighbors. "We might not starve, since we could still net birds and gather shellfish. But how could we breed without boats to carry men from one family to the other? We'd die out, unless we were reduced to in-breeding." There was horror in the guard's voice as he said this. "We are pirates because we can't buy the ships we need. Nothing we have to sell is of sufficient value."

"Couldn't you cut timber on an island like this one?" asked Ahl.

"We gather wood for ordinary uses on this island," the guard said. "And we could make some kind of wretched little dinghy from the timber here. But a good ship requires large trees, metal tools and fittings, fabric for the sails, rope and—most of all—skill."

"You want the Taig ship," said Perig.

"Yes. We thought we were in luck when we saw your smoke. Since the island is uninhabited, we knew that meant a ship, most likely one that had put in for water and repairs. The sailors would be tired from fighting the storm, which blew them here; they would be preoccupied by work; and they would not expect any trouble. Why should they, in a place this remote? Things didn't turn out exactly as we expected. But we have prisoners, eleven of you now. If we can't take the ship by force, maybe we can strike a bargain."

"It really doesn't seem wrong to you, holding women and a baby hostage?" asked Perig.

Jehan Silverback scratched his forehead. "It's a difficult situation and not one we expected. No one lives in this part of the ocean except us and our neighbors. When ships come here, it's usually to fish or hunt. The crews are male. What family would risk its women on work that is hard and dangerous and unpleasant, and which does not require any of the usual female skills? One does not negotiate with a storm or a fish."

There were, of course, many families whose women fished. But Ahl was not going to argue with this pirate, who seemed to have strong opinions about women's work. Nor did she wish to bring up the worst danger of this region, the one that would almost certainly keep women away: murderous pirates.

"You have never encountered a women's ship?" asked Perig.

"To the west of here we have," the guard said. "Not often, since we rarely go far into the narrow ocean. When we realize that a ship is crewed by women, we let it go with an exchange of greetings. We are not monsters! My cousin is right. You talk too much."

Perig said, "Let me go and help the cook. Then you'll be free of my foolish questions."

Jehan Silverback gave permission. The rest of them stayed where they were. By this time the sun was down and the sky darkening. Lamps began to glimmer on the two ships. This was a frightening situation, though not as frightening to Ahl as it would be to a modern woman. Having met the humans, we know that it is possible for a species to flourish in spite of behavior that our ancestors would find unthinkable; and we wonder if our own behavior is fixed. Could our men turn into monsters like human men? Could they turn on women and children? Is it possible that violence has no natural limits?

None of these questions occurred to Ahl, sitting on the darkening beach in another age. Instead she worried about the baby on the Taig ship. Surely it would wake soon, be hungry and cry. She worried about the possibility that her shipmates and the two actors would die, if not tonight, then tomorrow; and she worried about the rest of this unlucky trip. Would they ever get to Helwar? Would she ever see Ki again? But she did not fear harm to herself or Leweli. Was she right to be fearless? At this distance in time we cannot say.

As dark closed around them, the cooking fire burned more brightly. Working in a red glare, the Taig cook roasted birds, while Perig prepared his *tsin* ears. Dismembered, the birds went into an iron pot with water, the ears and herbs.

"This is something," said Jehan Silverback. "A proper feast and then a play. We never have events like this on our island."

Soon there was food, *halin* and fresh clean water, drawn from one of the island's springs. None drank water, except the prisoners.

"Eat moderately," Perig whispered as he settled next to Ahl.

"Why?" she hissed.

"The ears have to be prepared in just the right way. If not, they are toxic. Not fatal, but I hope—"

A pirate glanced at them. Perig stopped talking.

He had poisoned the stew. She whispered a warning to Leweli.

"This is likely to be a long night," her cousin whispered in answer.

While the pirates ate, Perig and Cholkwa consulted. Their costumes and props were on the Taig ship, so they borrowed from the pirates and prisoners: a long red ragged cloak, a stained yellow tunic, a staff with impromptu ribbons. They set torches on long poles in the sand and drew lines to mark a stage.

Then—the pirates full of food, but still drinking—they began.

This was *The Death of Eh Manhata*, Cholkwa announced. A true story, acted by men whose native home was on the Great

Central Plain. "We have not lied. This story is the way things actually happened."

The first scene was between Perig in the red cape and Cholkwa. Perig was Manhata: arrogant and confident, the greatest man in the world. Cholkwa was a younger relative, worried about his kinsman. He was too trusting, Cholkwa said. The men who sought a meeting with him were liars. They would betray him.

Strutting back and forth, the red cape swirling, Perig said, "Nonsense."

It really was remarkable. Perig, who had always been mild and reasonable, in no way formidable, now held everyone's attention. It seemed to Ahl that he had grown in size. His stride was forceful. His voice commanded. Even the cloak had changed, becoming—how could Ahl describe it?—richer and heavier, fit for a great leader, a warrior without equal.

In vain Cholkwa argued. Perig would not listen. Off he went to the foredoomed meeting.

Cholkwa left the circle of torchlight, returning shortly in the stained yellow tunic. Now he was one of the false allies, a wheedling plausible man, who had been—one sensed—handsome in his youth and was still in the habit of behaving seductively.

How did Cholkwa manage this? His own good looks were mostly gone; and he seemed older. The stained tunic helped, making him look seedy, but it was something more. The way he held himself? His voice? He didn't command attention like Perig; and Ahl could still see him inside the character he played, the way one saw people inside festival dolls, when firelight shone through the stick and cloth bodies. None the less, he impressed her.

Ahl leaned forward, intent. Around her the pirates and prisoners were silent.

At first Manhata was oblivious. The other man, the ally, praised, made promises, even flirted, though carefully. Manhata ignored the flirtation and accepted the praise, expecting nothing less. Gradually Cholkwa's manner changed. Sharpness crept in.

He began to mock the old warrior at the same time that he became more openly seductive.

A disturbing scene. Around her the pirates shifted and muttered. One stood up, stumbled into the bushes and threw up.

Understandable, though maybe it was the stew.

It took a long time for Manhata to understand what he was hearing. Finally he turned on the ally, shouting, "How dare you?"

The ally explained. The trap had closed. Manhata's men, the guards he'd brought with him, were dead by now. Manhata would join them soon. "You have lived too long and become a fool, deserving of a shameful death. I promise you, old man, that is the kind of death you'll get."

What happened next was impossible to understand. Perig barely moved, yet she could see every idea and feeling in his mind. Disbelief came first, then anger—a brief hot flash, then fear. How was this possible? Manhata was fearless. As she watched, Perig grew smaller, collapsing in on himself like a festival doll at festival end, when the sticks that hold it up are folded. Now she saw Manhata's age. He was more than eighty at the time of his death. His life had been one of constant violence. Who knew how many injuries he had endured? Surely his body must have reached its limit. And he was alone. His sisters, who had guided him through his long career, were dead. What was left for him, except his terrifying reputation?

Courage was left. She could see that now, as the old man straightened, meeting the gaze of his former ally.

"Do what you will," Manhata said. The pirates sighed. As they did, Perig stepped out of the torchlight. Cholkwa joined him. A moment later the young man returned wearing his own tunic. Now he was a messenger, bringing news of Eh Manhata's death. He stood quietly, looking out at the audience, and described what happened next. It had been a bad death, long and deliberately painful; and Manhata handled it less than well. The Man Who Broke Lineages was himself finally broken. Ahl had heard most of this before. It was no more pleasant a second time.

Of all the brutal things done during the Unravelling, this was the worst. Around her the pirates gasped and groaned. "Why?" cried more than one.

"His former allies wanted us to remember him this way," said Cholkwa. "If he had died in battle or by some ordinary form of execution, his reputation would not have been diminished. But this—"

"You should have lied," said Jehan Silverback. "You should have given him the death he had earned. How can you cooperate in something so contemptible?"

Perig stepped back into the torchlight. The red cloak was gone. He was Manhata no longer. "Anyone can be broken," he said in his ordinary, quiet, even tone. "No one escapes shame except through luck. This is something that Manhata may have forgotten, for a while at least. But he learned it at the end.

"That's one thing to remember. The other is, his enemies are fools."

"Why do you say that?" asked Jehan Silverback.

"In old age, when he no longer had his sisters to advise him, Manhata acted in ways that must be called foolish. This can't be denied. It's true as well that his courage failed him at the end.

"But think of the rest of his life! I'm from the plain, as my cousin told you. For more than fifty years, Manhata rose above the rest of us like a thundercloud that would not dissipate. Every time we looked up, there he was—his head in sunlight and lightning around his shoulders. Can a year or two of folly, a day or two of pain unmake a life like his?"

"Yes," said Long Jehan.

"No," said Jehan Silverback.

"Time will determine," Perig said in his usual reasonable tone.

That ended the play. The pirates continued drinking. By now they were obviously intoxicated. Several more threw up, lurching past the prisoners into the forest shadows. Long Jehan grabbed Cholkwa's arm, pulling him down on the sand beside him. Perig settled by the other pirate cousin. Ahl couldn't tell if

Jehen Silverback had ordered him to do so or asked him. Maybe Perig was acting on his own, trying—like Manhata—to beg a better ending.

"I think it's time for us to leave," said Leweli quietly.

"Mother told me men were disgusting after they'd been drinking for a while," Ahl said in agreement.

Maybe they could say they needed to urinate, Ahl thought. That would get them to the forest. But no ruse was necessary. The pirate closest to them slumped over suddenly, his cup spilling from his hand. The next fellow over had already risen and was stumbling toward the Taig prisoners. Why, Ahl didn't know or want to know. She and Leweli rose together, stepping backward into the black forest shadow. No one called out.

Instead of entering the forest, they went along its edge, keeping in the shadow. Hah! It was dark! But there were stars above them and lamps on the two anchored ships. When the beach ended, they clambered over rocks, going out on the promontory that formed one side of the harbor. Someone by the pirate's fire was screaming. Ahl didn't think it was from pain or fear.

Finally, when they were a good distance from the beach, Leweli said, "This will do."

The two women dove into the water and swam toward the Taig ship.

Remember that Sorg is marsh. No one grows up there without learning to swim. Ahl was excellent and Leweli even better. Side by side, they stroked through the cold still water, making no sound. On shore the pirates were shouting at one another. Had they discovered the missing women? Or were they quarreling, as drunks will do?

When they reached the ship, Ahl grabbed the anchor chain. It made a noise. A moment later she saw a shape above her, leaning over the ship's side. Metal gleamed in starlight.

"It's Ahlin," she said quietly. "With Lewekh. We escaped."

Ropes came down. They climbed up.

"I hope you'll be able to do something about that baby," said the Taig captain.

"You found it," said Ahl.

"Hard to miss it, once it began to cry."

"I'll take care of Dapple," said Leweli and went toward their cabin.

Ahl stayed with the captain, telling him about the situation on shore.

"The actor tried to poison them," he said, leaning on the railing and looking at the figures that moved around the pirate's fire. "They don't look dead to me."

"He said it wasn't fatal. They are certainly intoxicated, though that might be due to *halin*."

"They don't seem to be looking for you, which suggests an unusual degree of intoxication. Either they haven't noticed that you're gone or they no longer care." The Taig captain paused, evidently thinking. "I could wait and hope they lose consciousness. But I think it'd be better to move before the other pirates—the ones on board the pirate ship—notice something is wrong. Do you want to join the attack, or are you a woman like your friend?"

"I'm a woman," said Ahl.

"How about the other two?"

"Perig and Cholkwa? They're men. When I left, it seemed to me they were trying to seduce the two chief pirates."

"With luck, that will prove distracting. I'll leave some men here, in case the pirates on the ship decide to move." The captain made a noise that indicated irritation. "This would be much easier if I didn't have to worry about enemies on two sides. Not to mention a ship with damaged rigging. As the proverb says, when luck turns bad, it turns bad."

"True enough," said Ahl. She went down to the cabin and found a knife. Leweli was nursing the baby, who was quiet now.

"The Taig men are going to attack," Ahl said.

"In which direction?" Leweli asked.

"Shore."

Leweli tilted her head, regarding the child. "A hard decision. I'm glad it's not one I have to make. But the party looked as if it might become ugly. Maybe it should be broken up."

Ahl went back on deck, carrying the knife. The Taig sailors were clustered on the landward side of their ship. After a moment Ahl realized they were lowering a boat. "Quietly," said the captain to them. "Act with care."

There was a soft splash as the boat hit water. The sailors climbed down and rowed away, their oars making almost no sound.

The remaining sailors posted themselves along the rail, some watching the shore, while others kept an eye on the pirate vessel. A man said, "They'd be crazy to bring the ship in at night with the tide low, but they could send a boat. The captain says you're a woman. Why are you traveling in disguise?"

Ahl said, "I can't tell the story now. Later, if we survive."

After that, they waited. The fire on the beach was burning low, and only a few figures remained around it. Most had wandered into darkness, though she could still hear them howling like *sulin*.

Finally, when she began to wonder if the Taig boat had sunk, a shout came over the water: sharp and commanding. Not a drunken howl. A battle call.

Men ran into the firelight, carrying weapons. The sailors around Ahl exhaled. "Hah! Taig!"

Behind her Leweli said, "The baby's asleep at last. What's going on?"

"The battle has begun," said Ahl.

They were too far away to see anything clearly. Ahl longed for a looking-into-the-distance tube. Such things existed at this point in history, and she had seen them in the south. But the Taig ship didn't have one. The battle was small dark figures, meeting in dim light. There was more shouting, then a high shrill scream that did not end.

One of the Taig sailors said, "Don't you think you ought to go below deck? It can't be good for a mother to see this kind of violence. Or any woman, for that matter."

"Is that what's worrying you?" asked Ahl.

"Of course not," said another man. "We're worried about our kinsmen on shore. But there's nothing we can do about their situation. So my cousin here is taking the only action he is able to take. I have to say he's right. It's the reason our women don't travel. No mother—or future mother—should watch while men kill each other. It's bound to do something to the milk."

"If not to the milk, to the mind," said a third man. "What kind of mothers are you two going to be after a trip like this one?"

Enough, thought Ahl. She and Leweli went down to the cabin. The porthole was open. She found she could see the beach. The fire had been scattered and was mostly out. She thought she could see motion, and there was still noise. Apparently the battle continued.

"How could I be a worse mother by traveling than by staying home?" asked Leweli. "If I had stayed in Sorg, Dapple would have died."

"Nothing men say about child-rearing is worth attention," Ahl said. "I wish I could see more clearly."

Finally—it must have been an *ikun* later—she heard noises on deck. The Taig sailors returning? Or a pirate boarding party? Leweli lay asleep. Ahl stood and pulled her knife.

The noises continued, none of them loud. Surely this meant it was the Taig sailors. Ahl relaxed, then grew tense again as the cabin door opened. She'd forgotten to bar it. Too late!

The actors entered, both unsteady. Perig's tunic was torn, and Cholkwa had a bandage wrapped around one arm.

"That," said Perig as he settled on the floor, "was the worst evening of my life."

"You, at least, didn't have Long Jehan in your hands," said Cholkwa. "Goddess!" He leaned against the open doorway. "Don't get comfortable. We're sleeping on deck."

"Are you all right?" Perig asked the women.

"Yes," said Leweli. "It was a fine performance."

"Which part?" asked Cholkwa. "The lies Perig told about our history or the play itself or the way the two of us behaved with Jehan and Jehan?"

"We didn't see the last," said Ahl.

"Good," said Perig.

"The play," said Leweli.

"Wasted on louts," said Cholkwa. "Get up, old man."

Perig groaned, stood and searched in his baggage until he found a tunic, faded but clean and untorn.

"That will do," said Cholkwa. "You needn't look pretty. There's no one left to charm."

"It's over?" asked Ahl.

"There's still the pirate ship," said Cholkwa. "But the pirates on shore are prisoners or dead. Perig needs sleep. So do I."

Then they were gone. She'd heard about the kind of mania that overcomes some men after battle. That must be what she'd just seen, unless it was the effect of *halin* and the *tsin* ears.

Cholkwa, who had always seemed a bit sullen, had shone with happiness, so beautiful—in spite of his rumpled fur—that even a woman could see his beauty. Perig had seemed tired, nothing more. Maybe it was too soon for him to feel happiness. Maybe he'd done too much.

That night she dozed rather than slept. Often she was awake, or in a strange state between sleep and waking. At dawn she went on deck. The Taig sailors were up, watching the pirate ship.

"Leaving, I think," said the Taig captain.

Sails billowed out, filling with wind. The anchor went up, water dripping and flashing in the first rays of the rising sun.

"They've decided to abandon their kin," said one of the Taig sailors.

"What do you expect of pirates?" said another sailor.

The ship headed north and west, vanishing at last among the waves. When it was gone, the Taig captain said, "We need to spend another day here. I want the two of you—the women—to stay on board."

"Why?" asked Ahl.

"What we have to do on shore is not pleasant."

Cremate their dead, Ahl thought, and kill the remaining pirates. Cremation did not bother her, though it took a primitive form in her era; but the cremation of Taig men belonged to Taig men. The other activity was male as well.

"We'll stay on board," said Ahl.

Perig and Cholkwa went with the Taig men. Ahl and Leweli went to the cabin. The day had a mild wind, enough to carry the pirate ship away, but not enough to bring fresh air through the porthole. The room seemed stifling to Ahl. The baby fretted. "She misses her potion," Leweli said. "But I'm not giving her any more, unless she becomes impossible."

The baby became impossible and got more potion. "Just a little, to make her quiet."

Ahl went through her baggage and repacked everything, made sure her knives were sharp, then went on deck.

"Something has occurred to me," she said to a sailor. "If you build a fire for cremation, it may attract more pirates."

"We thought of that," the sailor said. "We won't cremate our men until we're ready to leave. What the captain is doing now is questioning the pirates. When he's done, they'll be killed and buried. No reason to burn them. We don't intend to take their ashes home."

"I haven't heard anything," Ahl said.

"Our men went inland with the pirates. The captain didn't want to bother you. Sound carries well over water, especially on a day like this."

There were dark shapes on the beach, laid in a line. The Taig dead, almost certainly. One man stood by them, leaning on a spear. No one else was visible. A bright hot day. The air barely moved. Bugs would be gathering around the Taig bodies. Not a pleasant job the watcher had.

Would it be pleasanter to be inland, torturing the captive pirates?

Ahl shook her head, thinking life was full of difficult choices.

In late afternoon the sailors came back, Perig and Cholkwa with them. Ahl waited on the deck. Cholkwa looked sullen again, while Perig looked grim.

"That's done," the older man said. "The Taig know how to reach the pirates' homes, though the pirates certainly did not want to give out the information."

"Goddess," said Cholkwa.

"They said they weren't going to harm you," Perig told Ahl. "They let you go, they said, though my impression at the time was they hadn't noticed your disappearance. Jehan and Jehan certainly seemed busy with other things. I don't remember anyone coming to tell them that you were gone, though I was occupied at the time."

"You shouldn't talk about such things to women," said Cholkwa.

"You did last night."

"I was drunk."

The sailors set to work on their repairs. Most looked grim, though a few seemed satisfied. The next day the ship was ready to go. They took it out of the harbor, anchoring where the pirate ship had been, then rowed back to burn their kinsmen.

This was done at night. Looking through the porthole, Ahl saw the great red glare of the funeral fire. The air smelled of wood smoke and burning flesh. By morning the fire was out. No smoke rose into the cloudless sky. The Taig let out their sails, going west and south over an ocean dotted with foam.

Once the island was gone from sight, the Taig captain called them all on deck. "I want to know the truth about you people. I've heard one story about you that is obviously untrue; and our cook says there's another story, which you told the pirates. Is there a third story? A fourth? A fifth?"

Perig glanced at Ahl. "Tell him what you know," she said.

Perig did, describing how he and Cholkwa and been stranded in the country of the Sorg. "Like a *luat* trapped in a too-shallow lagoon." Just when they reached desperation, the witch appeared and made her offer: money to go south, if they would escort two women in disguise. "It was wrong to do it, of course," Perig said. "But we had no alternative."

The Taig captain glanced at Ahl. "Why did you need to flee your home, escorted by unrelated men? Surely this is shameful behavior."

Ahl told her story: how the Sorg matrons had decided to kill five children in order to get out of a business contract. One child was left alive, the baby in the cabin. She and Leweli had decided to save it, advised by the witch who hired Perig and Cholkwa. "She said it was the right thing to do."

"You've put us in a bad place," the captain said. "It's too late in the season to turn back and risk more storms. In addition, if I returned you to Sorg, the Helwar would be angry; and no one makes better ships than they. But if I take you to Helwar, as I intend to do, I'll make bad enemies among your kin. Why couldn't you let the child die? The crime—if it is a crime—would not be yours, but would belong to your mother and the other matriarchs. It's wrong to take on too much responsibility."

"That may be," said Ahl. "But it's done."

The cook, who had been listening, said, "It's my belief that those of us who were taken prisoner would have died, except for the actors' cleverness. Now that I know they are not perverts and committers of incest, I can be grateful. Granted, it's odd for men to travel with unrelated women, but every man is supposed to help women in need of help; and healthy babies should not be killed, especially to escape from a business contract. Where will we be, if people don't keep the agreements they make? I don't intend to tie my mind into knots by trying to make sense of this situation. Go with the simple solution, kinsman! Thank these folk for their help, and deliver them to Helwar."

"A good cook is always worth listening to," the captain said. "I will take your advice."

The ship continued west and south, carried by a mild and steady wind. Leweli spent most of her time in the cabin, caring for the baby, who was often awake, now that she no longer got the potion. Without the witch's magic, the child proved as irritable as any ordinary baby.

"And maybe more so," said Ahl to Perig, while explaining why she spent most of her time on deck. "I'm willing to save the child from death and maybe ruin my own life by doing so; but I will not listen to her cry."

Several days later, Ahl asked, "Did the *tsin* ears work the way you expected?"

"Not entirely," Perig said. "If you peel them before cooking and cut off the base, they are an ordinary food, except for being unusually tasty. But if this isn't done, they cause visions, followed by stupor. In my home country diviners use them to look into the future. They wear headdresses in the shape of *tsin* ears." Perig glanced sideways and smiled. "Foreigners think the headdresses are funny; and maybe they are; but the visions are often useful, though only if the person involved has been trained."

"Wasn't it dangerous to give something like that to pirates?"

"The situation was dangerous already. The pirates were going to kill all of us, except possibly you and Leweli. It seemed like a good idea to try everything: the *tsin* ears, drama, sex—if the pirates wanted sex, as they obviously did. Anything to distract them and delay the moment of killing. I thought if they began to see visions or fell into a stupor, maybe we could escape. Or maybe the Taig sailors would attack, or the Goddess reach down her hand and lift us all to safety. Who can say?" For a moment he was silent, looking out at the ocean. "If I'd had the witch's potion, I would have used it. But it was on the ship. I used what was at hand."

Ten days later a sailor vanished. The ship was searched. He wasn't found.

Perig told Ahl about it. "They think he went overboard last night. He was one of the men held prisoner by the pirates, a young man, good-looking."

Odd, thought Ahl. She didn't remember a good-looking man among the prisoners.

"After they were drunk, several of the pirates approached him. He wanted nothing to do with them. It's not a good idea to say 'no' to a drunken pirate. For one thing, they won't listen."

"He killed himself out of shame," Ahl said.

"The Taig believe so, though it doesn't seem to me especially shameful to endure what can't be prevented. Maybe he thought he could have behaved in a more disciplined and undemonstrative fashion. Or maybe he wanted the memories of what had happened to stop. He should have waited. Most memories grow less sharp in time."

It seemed wrong for a man to die on his way home, in good weather, after danger was past. Was what he had experienced so terrible? Hadn't the two actors gone through something similar and made jokes about it? She asked Perig about this, speaking carefully, since most men don't enjoy discussing sex or violence with women.

Obviously Perig was under no obligation to answer her; no matter how indirectly she asked her question, it was rude. But he did reply, his tone courteous and more serious than usual.

"Remember how Cholkwa and I make our living. Actors spend most of their time traveling. Any business that is carried on away from home is risky.

"Remember also that no man can expect help in a foreign country. Especially, no man can expect help given freely. That is done for women and children, but a man is expected to pay in one way or another. Actors learn to do what is necessary, and we make jokes about these necessary actions. Why not?"

She thought she understood what he was saying, and it fit with everything she'd heard about traveling players. They lived at the edge of morality. How could they feel shame in the same way as other men? After all, they sold strangers the right to stare at them and said the most intimate things, which ordinary men would reveal only to their closest relatives or friends, in loud voices in public.

"Was the Taig youth right to die?" she asked. "Is that what a man of ordinary honor would do?"

Perig glanced at her sideways. "One who isn't an actor? I think not, though it isn't my business to judge any of the Taig. He should have waited and spoken with his relatives. It's not a good idea to kill yourself without permission. Now his mother has lost a son, and the men on this ship have lost a cousin. Did he have the right to deprive them of so much just because the world is not as safe and pleasant as he imagined?"

A troubling conversation. Ahl was no longer sure she could disentangle right from wrong. The threads seemed knotted together. When she pulled on a bright one, she found something dark, while the dark threads often led to something as bright as gold or silver.

Ahl pondered morality while the ship continued south. Looking around, she began to see evidence that land was near. Clouds like towers stood at the horizon; and there was an increase in the number of birds. Next came an island: a bald rock that rose straight out of the ocean, useless to anyone except the birds. Another island followed, equally bare and sheer. Finally they passed a fishing boat, wallowing home with as many fish as it could carry. The Taig sailors shouted and waved message banners. The fishers replied with their own shouts and flags.

"We'll be in harbor before dark," the Taig captain said.

Soon after that Helwar came in view. Its forested peaks rose into a wreath of clouds; and mist lay in the upland valleys like handfuls of unspun wool. Off the north coast rain fell like a curtain made of gauze. Ahl's mind filled with happiness.

One troubling idea remained. "I have a final question," she said to Perig, as they watched Helwar approach.

"Surely you can stop asking questions now."

"What broke apart your acting company?"

He was silent for a moment. "That's my business."

"It's obvious that you and Cholkwa have a secret," Ahl said. "I think I know what it is."

"Do you?" he asked.

"You've have been lovers for a long time; everything about you suggests as much; and he's still young. It would surprise me if he's twenty-five."

"You think I'm a child molester," said Perig.

"Well," said Ahl. "I've met every other kind of criminal on this journey."

"It hasn't been a lucky trip," Perig admitted.

"How old was he when you met?"

Perig turned, leaning his elbows on the rail and looking around to see who might be near. "What are you going to do with this idea?"

"Nothing. You got us out of Sorg and saved us from the pirates. Except for you, they might have killed Leweli and me, or adopted us and taken us home to their miserable island. I will not repay you with harm."

"Hah," said Perig, the long slow exhalation that can mean anything. For a while he was silent. Ahl waited, her eyes on the cloud-capped island.

At last Perig said, "He was fourteen when he left home. His family had been destroyed in the war, and he refused to join the lineage that had killed all his male kin."

"Was that family the Chaitin?" asked Ahl. "Is he Tesati?"

"Yes. I didn't know his family name at first, nor did he know mine. Actors use their personal names, so as not to embarrass their families. He was a beggar I found on the road, fed and cleaned and found to be lovely.

"I said he could stay with the company if he was old enough, but I wouldn't have an unrelated child traveling with me. Of course he told me he was adult. He wasn't lying by much. He'd been on his own for almost a year by then.

"We were lovers before he reached his fifteenth birthday, and before he learned my family name. When he learned it, he tried to kill me, though it wasn't a serious effort. I took the knife away from him, and he explained."

"You are Chaitin," Ahl said, not certain what she felt. Confusion? Horror? A need to laugh? This is the kind of joke the Goddess loves to play: two-sided like a sword, with sharp edges that can cut to the bone. When the joke is especially fine, when the Great One brings it down like a blade on her victim, piety requires that everyone—even the victim—laugh. But Ahl had never been religious.

"Yes," said Perig. "He's angry at me for telling his story to the pirates; but I had to think quickly; and it's always a good idea to stay close to the truth when lying. So I turned one fierce and stubborn boy into a pair of women, and I turned myself into a hero. Art is full of such transformations."

"The cook was right. You are a committer of incest."

"No," he said firmly. "Cholkwa was never adopted by my family. Therefore what we did was not incest. But it would have been, if I'd dragged him home and said, 'Here's a cousin I found at the side of the road.' The actors in my company knew what we'd been doing. The story would have come into daylight; and my hair goes up when I think of how my mother would have responded.

"In any case, Cholkwa didn't want to join the Chaitin, and I didn't want to give him up."

"He stayed with you, after finding out who you were?"

"I'm Chaitin Perig when I'm at home, which isn't often. The rest of the time I'm Perig the actor. The answer to your question is 'no.' He ran away. I followed and dragged him back, partly because I knew how dangerous the plain was for someone like him—alone, without a family. But mostly because love had made me crazy.

"The second time he came back on his own. What else could he do? Starve on the plain? Live among criminals and learn to be like them? I offered him safety and the chance to learn a skill more honest than robbing travelers."

"And this is what broke apart your company?"

"After so many years," Perig said in admission. "I really thought we could hide the secret forever. But we don't always get along. We had a quarrel that was overheard. When Cholkwa has been drinking, he drags the past forward. The actor who overheard us is Chaitin. As far as he was concerned, it was incest. In addition, I had robbed our family of a child who had grown up to a perfectly acceptable young man. Even worse, my cousin had been interested in Cholkwa, though nothing had happened. Imagine how he felt! He had been on the edge of perversion without knowing it!

"Of course he made a lot of noise, and the other men decided the company was unlucky. That was true enough. I can't blame them for going.

"I don't think my cousin has a future as an actor. He's stiff as a plank and far too moral. It was a mistake to take him into the company. But when a relative asks a favor, it's difficult to refuse."

Ahl looked at her hands, almost seeing the tangle of darkness that filled them. Perig was wrong about his lover. A man could be kinless. So could a woman, though it wasn't common. But every child must have a family. Cholkwa could not be Tesati, since that lineage was gone; and no other lineage had adopted him. Therefore he was Chaitin, or had been until his fifteenth birthday. When the two of them first had sex, it was incest and the molesting of a child, but only by a few days, twenty or thirty. How could wrong behavior be a matter of timing? She asked Perig this question.

"Everything is a matter of timing," Perig said. "When the witch came with her offer, I thought, 'What fine timing! What excellent luck!'" He gave Ahl a sideways glance. "If you keep quiet about our story, this may still be true. Cholkwa and I can still recover."

"I have already promised to cause you no harm," Ahl said. "I want this journey to end. Too many bad things have happened since I left Helwar. I've learned too many things I didn't want to know."

"You would ask questions," Perig said.

"I'll stop. All I want now is Ki and a safe place to stay."

Perig turned, looking at the cloudy island. "You have almost reached safety. With luck, Helwar Ki will be waiting."

As the fishers had promised, they were in harbor by sundown. The two women hurried onshore, Dapple in Leweli's arms. By nightfall they were in a great house, surrounded by matriarchs, telling the story of Sorg's betrayal. Ki was there, leaning over the back of her mother's chair, looking both grim and happy. Even in the midst of her dark narration, Ahl felt happy as well.

When the story was done, a matriarch spoke. Large and solid, well into middle age, she still had her baby spots. Her son had fathered Dapple, though the women from Sorg didn't know this. "If Sorg wants to escape our alliance so badly, let them go! It's no loss, since they have shown themselves to be cheats of the worst variety. What kind of people enter into a contract, intending to break it? What kind of people breed children, knowing the children have no future?

"We need to tell everyone in the narrow ocean about this behavior. No one should trust the Sorg, and no one will, once this story has traveled. As for the child, it's my advice that we adopt her and her mother."

Grey eyes met blue-grey eyes. One by one, the women of Helwar tilted their heads. A quick decision, you may say. Remember how angry the Helwar must have been, and remember that every child must have a family.

Leweli was invited to stay in the great house, along with Dapple, but Ahl went back to the *Foam Bird* with Ki. A fine rain was falling, dimming the lights of Helwar Town. The ships in harbor seemed ghost-like, though the *Bird's* deck was solid enough, once they set foot on it.

Ki's cabin was exactly as Ahl remembered. Hard to imagine anyone moving Ki's large bed. Made of carved wood, it was fastened to the wall and floor for safety in turbulent weather. The hanging lantern was too fine to change. Five *luatin* curled around a bronze bowl. Their eyes and teeth were gilded. One held a silver fish in its mouth. Another held a bronze harpoon no longer than Ahl's smallest finger. The weapon was broken; a torn rope—made of twisted gold wire—flew out from it. Who could say what had happened to the *luat* hunter?

In the lantern's bowl a seed oil burned, aromatic and bright.

"Nothing is missing, except your belongings," said Ki to Ahl. "You can bring them tomorrow."

They drank *halin*. Ahl spoke of her journey: the storm, the pirates, the actors' cleverness.

"And courage, I should think," said Ki. "It must have been frightening to act in front of criminals. As for deliberately seducing men like that— Surely every instinct and every idea of morality would push one back."

"Maybe," said Ahl in a tone that lacked conviction. According to Perig, his motivation had been fear of death, rather than courage; and she doubted that ideas about morality had much effect on either man.

"You owe them a lot," said Ki firmly. "As do I and all the Helwar."

This was true. Ahl tilted her head in agreement.

They moved on to other topics, then into Ki's large bed. Tangled with her lover, smelling and tasting Ki, Ahl forgot—for a while—her uncertainty; though the person she had been, the always confident daughter of Sorg, was gone; and never, in a long life, did she regain her family's absolute, unquestioning self-assurance.

The rest of the story can be told quickly. Ahl refused adoption, since it would end her romance with Ki. Instead she remained Sorg until her kin disowned her. Then the Hasu, who were neighbors of the Helwar, adopted her as a courtesy. For the rest of her life, she was Hasu Ahl, though she visited her new family only rarely, preferring to stay with her lover and Leweli.

Perig and Cholkwa formed a new company and brought northern theatre to the Great Southern Continent. Previous to this, the southerners had told stories through a combination of narration and dance. The new style was recognized everywhere as an improvement. To actually see heroes, as they struggled! To hear their voices! To have their anguish made so vivid that it could be felt! This was something!

The two men remained lovers, though their relationship was difficult. At times they quarreled so badly that one or the other left the company. During one such period, Perig came to Helwar. Cholkwa was on the continent, in a far southern area where the people were barely civilized, but great lovers of drama, especially the comedies for which (it turned out) Cholkwa had a gift.

"A surprise to me," said Perig to Ahl. "I never thought Cholkwa would do so well dressed up as an animal with an erect penis. As we age, we learn who we really are. But," he added, while turning a cup of *halin* between his hands, "the plays are really clever. Cholkwa can write comedy. Who can say, maybe it's more difficult than the kind of writing I do."

After he drank some more, he said, "The problem is the secret we share. One should never base love on something that must be hidden. It's like building a tower in a bog. Nothing is solid. Cracks run everywhere."

"You could live apart," said Ahl.

"And you could leave Helwar Ki."

In the end, the actors formed two companies, but remained acknowledged lovers. They organized their tours so they met often. Towns vied to be their meeting place. Even in later years, when there were many companies in the south, no one could equal Perig as a tragic hero or Cholkwa for humor.

As for Dapple, she was given the name of Helwar Ahl and used it while growing up. But after she was an adult, she became interested in acting and formed the first women's company anywhere. Even now, women in theatre, actors and playwrights, call her "mother" or "the originator."

Because acting was a dubious activity in those days, especially for women, she went back to her baby name. In this way, the Helwar were not embarrassed. Nor was her aunt Ki's lover.

Nothing remains of the plays written by Perig and Cholkwa, but we have fragments of Dapple's work. No one has ever written more beautifully in her native language, and much of the beauty remains in the various translations. There are many of these. As the witch predicted, Dapple became famous. Even now, after centuries, her words are like diamonds: pure, hard, angular, transparent, full of light.

DAPPLE

There was a girl named Helwar Ahl. Her family lived on an island north and east of the Second Continent, which was known in those days as the Great Southern Continent. (Now, of course, we know that an even larger expanse of land lies farther south, touching the pole. In Ahl's time, however, no one knew about this land except its inhabitants.)

A polar current ran up the continent's east coast and curled around Helwar Island, so its climate was cool and rainy. Thick forests covered the mountains. The Helwar built ships from the wood. They were famous shipwrights, prosperous enough to have a good-sized harbor town.

Ahl grew up in this town. Her home was the kind of great house typical of the region: a series of two-story buildings linked together. The outer walls were mostly blank. Inside were court-yards, balconies, and large windows provided with the modern wonder: glass. Granted: the panes were small and flawed. But some ingenious artificer had found a way to fit many panes to-gether, using strips of lead. Now the women of the house had light, even in the coldest weather.

As a child, Ahl played with her cousins in the courtyards and common rooms, all of them naked except for their fog-grey fur. Later, in a kilt, she ran in the town streets and visited the harbor. Her favorite uncle was a fisherman who went out in morning darkness, before most people woke. In the late afternoon, he returned. If he'd been lucky, he tied up and cleaned his catch, while Ahl sat watching on the dock.

"I want to be a fisherman," she said one day.

"You can't, darling. Fishing is men's work."

"Why?"

He was busy gutting fish. He stopped for a moment, frowning, a bloody knife still in his hand. "Look at this situation! Do you want to stand like me, knee deep in dead fish? It's hard, nasty work and can be dangerous. The things that women do well—negotiation, for example, and the forming of alliances—are no use at all, when dealing with fish. What's needed here," he waved the knife, "is violence. Also, it helps if you can piss off the side of a boat."

For a while after that Ahl worked at aiming her urine. She could do it, if she spread her legs and tilted her pelvis in just the right fashion. But would she be able to manage on a pitching boat? Or in a wind? In addition, there was the problem of violence. Did she really want to be a killer of many small animals?

One of the courtyards in her house had a basin that held ornamental fish. Ahl caught one and cut off its head. A senior female cousin caught her before she was finished, though the fish was past help.

"What are you doing?" the matron asked.

Ahl explained.

"These are fish to feed, not fish to eat," her cousin said and demonstrated this by throwing a graincake into the basin.

Fish surged to the surface in a swirl of red fins, green backs, and blue-green tails. A moment later, the cake was gone. The fish returned to their usual behavior: a slow swimming back and forth.

"It's hardly fair to kill something this tame—in your own house, too. Guests should be treated with respect. In addition, these fish have an uninteresting flavor and are full of tiny bones. If you ate one, it would be like eating a cloth full of needles."

Ahl lost interest in fishing after that. Her uncle was right about killing. It was a nasty activity. All that quickness and grace, gone in a moment. The bright colors faded. She was left with nothing except a feeling of disgust.

Maybe she'd be a weaver, like her mother Leweli. Or the captain of a far-traveling ocean-trader, like her aunt Ki. Then she could bring treasures home: transparent glass, soft and durable lead.

When she was ten, she saw her first play. She knew the actors, of course. They were old friends of her family and came to Helwar often, usually staying in Ahl's house. The older one— Perig—was quiet and friendly, always courteous to the household children, but not a favorite with them. The favorite was Cholkwa, who juggled and pulled candy out of ears. He knew lots of funny stories, mostly about animals such as the *tli*, a famous trouble-maker and trickster. According to the house's adults, he was a comedian who performed in plays too rude for children to see. Perig acted in hero plays, though it was hard to imagine him as a hero. The two men were lovers, but didn't usually work together. This was due to the difference in their styles and to their habit of quarreling. They had, the women of Ahl's house said, a difficult relationship.

This time they came together, and Perig brought his company. They put on a play in the main square, both of them acting, though Cholkwa almost never did dark work.

The play was about two lovers—both of them warriors— whose families quarreled. How could they turn against one another? How could they refuse their relatives' pleas for help? Each was the best warrior in his family.

Though she hadn't seen a play before, Ahl knew how this was going to end. The two men met in battle. It was more like a dance than anything else, both of them splendidly costumed and moving with slow reluctant grace. Finally, after several speeches, Perig tricked Cholkwa into striking. The blow was fatal. Perig went down in a gold and scarlet heap. Casting his sword away, Cholkwa knelt beside him. A minor player in drab armor crept up and killed Cholkwa as he mourned.

Ahl was transfixed, though also puzzled. "Wasn't there any way out?" she asked the actors later, when they were back in her house, drinking *halin* and listening to her family's compliments.

"In a comedy, yes," said Cholkwa. "Which is why I do bright plays. But Perig likes plays that end with everyone dead, and always over some ethical problem that's hardly ever encountered in real life."

The older man was lying on a bench, holding his *halin* cup on his chest. He glanced at Cholkwa briefly, then looked back at the ceiling. "Is what you do more true to reality? Rude plays about animals? I'd rather be a hero in red and gold armor than a man in a *tli* costume."

"I'd rather be a clever *tli* than someone who kills his lover."

"What else could they do?" asked Perig, referring to the characters in the play.

"Run off," said Cholkwa. "Become actors. Leave their stupid relatives to fight their stupid war unaided."

It was one of those adult conversations where everything really important was left unspoken. Ahl could tell that. Bored, she said, "I'd like to be an actor."

They both looked at her.

"You can't," said Perig.

This sounded familiar. "Why not?"

"In part, it's custom," Cholkwa said. "But there's at least one good reason. Actors travel and live among unkin; and often the places we visit are not safe. I go south a lot. The people there love comedy, but in every other way they're louts and savages. At times I've wondered if I'd make it back alive, or if someone would have to bring my ashes in an urn to Perig."

"Better to stay here," said Perig. "Or travel the way your aunt Ki does, in a ship full of relatives."

No point in arguing. When adults started to give advice, they were never reasonable. But the play stayed with her. She imagined stories about people in fine clothing, faced with impossible choices; and she acted them out, going so far as to make a wooden sword, which she kept hidden in a hayloft. Her female relatives had an entire kitchen full of knives and cleavers and axes, all sharp and dangerous. But the noise they would have made, if they'd seen her weapon!

Sometimes she was male and a warrior. At other times she was a sailor like Ki, fighting the kinds of monsters found at the edges of maps. Surely, Ahl thought, it was permissible for women to use swords when attacked by monsters, rising out of the water with fangs that dripped poison and long curving claws?

Below her in the barn, her family's *tsina* ate and excreted. Their animal aroma rose to her, combining with the scent of hay. Later she said this was the scent of drama: dry, aging hay and new-dropped excrement.

The next year Cholkwa came alone and brought his company. They did a decent comedy, suitable for children, about a noble *sul* who was tricked and humiliated by a *tli*. The trickster was exposed at the play's end. The *sul*'s honor was restored. The good animals did a dance of triumph, while the *tli* cowered and begged.

Cholkwa was the *tli*. Strange that a man so handsome and friendly could portray a sly coward.

Ahl asked about this. Cholkwa said, "I can't talk about other men, but I have that kind of person inside me: a cheat and liar who would like to run away from everything. I don't run, of course. Perig would disapprove, and I'd rather be admired than despised."

"But you played a hero last year."

"That was more difficult. Perig understands nobility, and I studied with him a long time. I do as he tells me. Most people are tricked and think I know what I'm doing. But that person—the hero—doesn't speak in my mind."

Ahl moved forward to the play's other problem. "The *sul* was noble, but a fool. The *tli* was clever and funny, but immoral. There was no one in the play I could really like."

Cholkwa gave her a considering gaze, which was permissible, since she was still a child. Would she like it, when men like Cholkwa—unkin, but old friends—had to glance away? "Most people, even adults, wouldn't have seen that. It has two causes. I wrote the *sul*'s lines and, as I've told you, I don't understand nobility. The other problem is my second actor. He isn't good enough. If Perig had been here, he would have made the *sul* likeable—in part by rewriting the lines, but mostly because he could play a stone and make it seem likeable."

Ahl thought about this idea. An image came to her: Perig in a grey robe, sitting quietly on a stage, his face unmasked and grey, looking calm and friendly. A likeable rock. It could be done. Why bother? In spite of her question, the image remained, somehow comforting.

Several days later Cholkwa did a play for adults. This event took place at night in the town hall, which was used for meetings and ceremonies, and also to store trade goods in transit. This time the back half was full of cloth, big bales that smelled of fresh dye: southern blue and the famous Sorg red.

Ahl snuck out of her house after dark and went in a back door, which she'd unlocked earlier. Climbing atop the bales, she settled to watch the play.

Most of it was past her understanding, though the audience gasped, groaned, clapped and made hissing noises. Clearly, they knew what was going on.

The costumes were ugly, in her opinion; the animals had huge sexual parts and grimacing faces. They hit each other with padded swords and clubs, tumbled and tossed each other, spoke lines that were—as far as she could tell—full of insults, some sly and others so obvious that even she made sense of them. This time the *sul* was an arrogant braggart with a long narrow head and a penis of almost equal size and shape. The *tli*, much less well endowed, was clever and funny, a coward because he had to be. Most of his companions were large, dangerous, and unjust.

It was the *tli*'s play. Mocking and tricking, he won over all the rest, ending with the *sul*'s precious ancestral sword, which he carried off in triumph to his mother, a venerable female *tli*, while the *sul* howled in grief.

The Sword Recovered or The Revenge of the Tli. That was the name of the play. There was something in back of it, which Ahl could not figure out. Somehow the *sul* had harmed the *tli*'s family in the past. Maybe the harm had been sexual, though this didn't seem likely. *Sulin* and *tli* did not interbreed. Puzzled, she climbed down from the bales and went home. The night was foggy, and she almost lost her way in streets she'd known her entire life.

She couldn't ask Cholkwa to explain. He would have told her relatives that she'd seen the play.

After this, she added comedy to her repertoire, mixing it with the stories about heroes and women like her aunt, far-travelers who did *not* have to die over some kind of unusual ethical dilemma.

The result was a long, acted-out epic tale about a hero, a woman sailor, a clever *tli* and a magical stone that accompanied the other three on their journey. The hero was noble, the sailor resourceful and the *tli* funny, while the stone remained calm and friendly, no matter what was going on. There wasn't any sex. Ahl was too young and the adult comedy had disgusted her. It's often a bad idea to see things that are forbidden, especially if one is young.

In the end, one of her cousins—a sneak worse than Cholkwa in the children's play—found out what she was doing and told her senior female relatives. "Clearly you have too much free time," they said, and assigned her work in the house's big weaving room. The sword was destroyed, along with the bits of armor she'd made. But her relatives decided the *tli* mask, constructed of bark paper over a frame of twigs, was good enough to keep. It was hung on the weaving room wall, where it stared down at her. Gradually, the straw whiskers disappeared and the large eyes, drawn in ink, faded.

Don't think that Ahl was too unhappy, or that her relatives had been unjust. Every child has to learn duty; and she'd gotten bored with her solitary play, as well as increasingly uncomfortable with hiding her props. Better to work at a loom and have ideas in her mind. No sneaking cousin could discover these, and everything she imagined was large and bright and well-made, the swords of real steel, sharp and polished, as bright as the best glass.

Two years passed. She became an adequate plain weaver, but nothing more. "We thought you might have a gift for beauty," said her mother. "The mask suggested this. But it's obvious that you lack the ability to concentrate, which is absolutely necessary in any kind of art. Anything worth doing is likely to be slow, difficult, and boring. This is not an invariable rule, but it works in most situations."

"Give her to me," said Ki. "Maybe she'd be happier in a more active life."

Ahl went to sea. At first, it was not an enjoyable experience, though she had little problem with motion sickness. Her difficulty lay in the same region as always: she spent too much time thinking about her stories. As a result, she was forgetful and careless. These are not good traits in an apprentice sailor; and Ki, who had always seemed pleasant and friendly at home in Helwar, turned out to be a harsh captain.

At first, the punishment she gave to Ahl was work. Every ship is full of nasty jobs. Ahl did most of them and did them more than once. This didn't bother her. She wasn't lazy, and the jobs—though nasty—required little thought. She could make up stories while she did them.

Her habit of inattention continued. Growing angry, Ki turned to violence. On several occasions, she struck Ahl: hard slaps across the face. This also had no effect. The girl simply did not want to give up her stories. Finally, Ki beat her, using a knotted rope.

Most likely this shocks you. Nowadays we like to believe that our female ancestors never did harm to one another. It's men who are violent. Women have always used reason.

Remember this was a sailing ship in the days before radio and engines. Weather satellites did not warn sailors of approaching storms. Computers did not monitor the ship's condition and send automatic signals to the Navigation Service. Sailors had to rely on their own skill and discipline.

It was one thing to be forgetful in a weaving room. If you fail to tie off a piece of yarn, what can happen? At most, a length of cloth will be damaged. Now, imagine what happens if the same person fails to tie a rope on board a ship. Or forgets to fasten a hatch in stormy weather.

So, after several warnings and a final mistake, Ahl received her beating. By this time she was fourteen or fifteen, with a coat of fur made thick by cold weather. The fur protected her, though not entirely; and later, when she remembered the experience, it seemed that shame was the worst part: to stand naked on the ship's deck, trying to remain impassive, while Ki used the rope she had failed to tie across her back.

Around her, the other sailors did their work. They didn't watch directly, of course, but there were sideways glances, some embarrassed and others approving. Overhead the sky was cloudless. The ship moved smoothly through a bright blue ocean.

The next day she felt every bruise. Ki gave her another unpleasant cleaning job. All day she scraped, keeping her lips pressed together. In the evening she went on deck, less stiff than she'd been earlier, but tired and still sore. Ahl leaned on the rail and looked out the ocean. In the distance rays of sunlight slanted between grey clouds. Life was not entirely easy, she thought.

After a while, Ki's lover Hasu Ahl came next to her. Ahl had been named after the woman, for reasons that don't come into this story; and they were alike in several ways, being both tall and thin, with small breasts and large, strong, capable hands. The main difference between them was their fur. Hasu Ahl's was dark grey, like the clouds that filled the sky, and her coloring was solid. Our Ahl was pale as fog. In addition, she had kept her baby spots. Dim and blurry, they dotted her shoulders and upper arms. Because of these, her childhood name had been Dapple.

Hasu Ahl asked how she felt.

"I've been better."

They became silent, both leaning on the rail. Finally Hasu Ahl said, "There's a story about your childhood that no one has told you. When you were a baby, a witch predicted that you would be important when you grew up. She didn't know in what way. I know this story, as do your mother and Ki and a few other people. But we didn't want your entire family peering at you and wondering, and we didn't want you to become vain or worried; so we kept quiet.

"It's possible that Ki's anger is due in part to this. She looks at you and thinks, 'Where is the gift that was promised to us?' All we can see—aside from intelligence, which you obviously have—is carelessness and lack of attention."

What could she say? She was inattentive because her mind was full of stories, though the character who'd been like Ki had vanished. Now there was an orphan girl with no close relatives, ignored by everyone, except her three companions: the hero, the *tli* and the stone. They cared for her in their different ways: the hero with nobility, the *tli* with jokes and the stone with solid friendliness. But she'd never told anyone about her ideas. "I'm not yet fifteen," Ahl said.

"There's time for you to change," Hasu Ahl admitted. "But not if you keep doing things that endanger the ship and yourself. Ki has promised if you're careless again, she'll beat you a second time; and the beating will be worse."

After that, Hasu Ahl left. Well, thought our heroine, that was certainly a confusing conversation. Ki's lover had threatened her with something like fame and with another beating. Adults were beyond comprehension.

Her concentration improved and she became an adequate sailor, though Ki said she would never be a captain. "Or a second-in-command, like your namesake, my Ahl. Whatever your gift may be, it isn't sailing."

Her time on board was mostly happy. She made friends with the younger members of the crew; and she learned to love the ocean as a sailor does, knowing how dangerous it can be. The coast of the Great Southern Continent was dotted with harbor towns. Ahl visited many of these, exploring the steep narrow streets and multi-leveled market places. One night at a festival, she made love for the first time. Her lover was a girl with black fur and pale yellow eyes. In the torchlight, the girl's pupils expanded, till they lay across her irises like bars of iron or narrow windows that opened into a starless night.

What a fine image! But what could Ahl do with it?

Later, in that same port, she came to an unwalled tavern. Vines grew over the roof. Underneath were benches. Perig sat on one, a cup in his hand. She shouted his name. He glanced up and smiled, then his gaze slid away. Was she that old? Had she become a woman? Maybe, remembering the black-furred girl.

Where was Cholkwa?

In the south, Perig said.

Because the place was unwalled and public, she was able to sit down. The hostess brought *halin*. She tasted it, savoring the sharp bitterness. It was the taste of adulthood.

"Watch out," said Perig. "That stuff can make you sick."

Was his company here? Were they acting? Ahl asked.

Yes. The next night, in the town square.

"I'll come," said Ahl with decision.

Perig glanced at her, obviously pleased.

The play was about a hero, of course: a man who suspected that the senior women in his family, his mother and her sisters, had committed a crime. If his suspicion was true, their behavior threatened the family's survival. But no man can threaten any woman with violence, and no man should turn against his mother. And what if he was wrong? Maybe they were innocent. Taking one look at the women, Ahl knew they were villains. But the hero didn't have her sharpness of vision. So he blundered through the play, trying to discover the truth. Men died, mostly at his hands, and most of them his kin. Finally he was hacked down, while the women looked on. A messenger arrived, denouncing them. Their family was declared untouchable. No one would deal with them in the future. Unable to interbreed, the family would vanish. The monstrous women listened like blocks of stone. Nothing could effect their stubborn arrogance.

A terrible story, but also beautiful. Perig was the hero and shone like a diamond. The three men playing the women were grimly convincing. Ahl felt as if a sword had gone through her chest. Her stories were nothing next to this.

Afterward, Ahl found Perig in the open tavern. Torches flared in a cool ocean wind, and his fur—touched with white over the shoulders—moved a little, ruffled. Ahl tried to explain how lovely and painful the play had been.

He listened, giving her an occasional quick glance. "This is the way it's supposed to be," he said finally. "Like a blade going to a vital spot."

"Is it impossible to have a happy ending?" she asked, after she finished praising.

"In this kind of play, yes."

"I liked the hero so much. There should have been another solution."

"Well," said Perig. "He could have killed his mother and aunts, then killed himself. It would have saved his family, but he wasn't sure they were criminals."

"Of course they were."

"You were in the audience," said Perig. "Where I was standing, in the middle of the situation, the truth was less evident; and no man should find it easy to kill his mother."

"I was right years ago," Ahl said suddenly. "This is what I want to do. Act in plays."

Perig looked unhappy.

She told him about her attempts to weave and be a sailor, then about the plays she had acted in the hayloft and the stories in her mind. For the first time, she realized the stories had scenes. She knew how the hero moved, like Perig acting a hero. The *tli* had Cholkwa's brisk step and mocking voice. The stone was a stone. Only the girl was blurry. She didn't tell Perig about the scenes. It would have been embarrassing to admit that this quiet aging man lived in her mind, along with his lover and a stone. But she did tell him that she told stories.

He listened, then said, "If you were a boy, I'd go to your family and ask for you as an apprentice—if not this year, then next year. But I can't, Ahl. They'd refuse me and be so angry I might lose their friendship."

"What am I to do?" asked Ahl.

"That's a question I can't answer," said Perig.

A day later, her ship left the harbor. On the long trip home, Ahl considered her future. She'd seen other companies of actors. Perig and Cholkwa were clearly the best, but neither one of them would be willing to train her. Nor would any company that knew she was female. But most women in this part of the world were broad and full-breasted, and she was an entirely different type. People before, strangers, had mistaken her for a boy. Think of all the years she had acted in her loft, striding like Perig or mimicking Cholkwa's gait. Surely she had learned something!

She was seventeen and good at nothing. In spite of the witch's prediction, it wasn't likely she'd ever be important. It seemed to her now that nothing had ever interested her except the making of stories—not the linked verse epics that people recited on winter evenings, nor the tales that women told to children, but proper stories, like the ones that Perig and Cholkwa acted.

Before they reached Helwar, Ahl had decided to disguise herself as a boy and run away.

First, of course, she had to spend the winter at home. Much of her time was taken by her family. When she could, she watched her uncles and male cousins. How did they stand and move? What were their gestures? How did they speak?

The family warehouse was only half-full, she discovered. This became her theatre, lit by high windows or (sometimes) by a lamp. She'd bought a square metal mirror in the south. Ahl leaned it against a wall. If she stood at a distance, she could see herself, dressed in a tunic stolen from a cousin and embroidered in the male style. Whenever possible, she practiced being a man, striding across the wood floor, turning and gesturing, speaking lines she remembered out of plays. Behind her were stacks of new-cut lumber. The fresh, sweet aroma of sawdust filled the air. In later life, she said this was the smell of need and possibility.

In spring, her ship went south again.

In a town in the far south, she found an acting company, doing one of Perig's plays in ragged costumes. It was one she'd seen. They'd cut out parts. Her bag, carefully packed, held boy's clothing, a knife, and all her money.

So, thought Ahl. That evening she took her bag and crept off the ship. The night was foggy, and the damp air smelled of unfamiliar vegetation. In an alley, she changed clothing, binding her four breasts flat with strips of cloth. She already knew where the actors were staying: a run-down inn by the harbor, not the kind of place that decent female sailors would visit. Walking through the dark streets, bag over her shoulder, she was excited and afraid.

Here, in this town, she was at the southern edge of civilization. Who could tell what the inland folk were like? Though she had never heard of any lineage that harmed women. If things got dangerous, she could pull off her tunic, revealing her real self.

On the other hand, there might be monsters; and they did harm women. Pulling off her tunic would do no good if something with fangs and scales came out of the forest. At most the thing might thank her for removing the wrapping on its dinner.

If she wanted to turn back, now was the time. She could be a less-than-good sailor. She could go home and look for another trade. There were plenty in Helwar, and women could do most of them. She hadn't really wanted to fish in the ocean, not after she killed the fish in the basin. As for the other male activities, let them have fighting and hunting dangerous animals. Let them log and handle heavy timbers. Why should women risk their lives?

She stopped outside the inn, almost ready to turn around. Then she remembered Perig in the most recent play she'd seen, at the moment when the play's balance changed. A kinsman lay dead at his feet. It was no longer possible to go back. He'd stood quietly, then lifted his head, opening his mouth in a great cry that was silent. No one in the audience made a noise. Somehow, through his silence and their silence, Ahl heard the cry.

She would not give that up. Let men have every other kind of danger. This was something they had to share.

She went in and found the actors, a shabby group. As she had thought, they were short-handed.

The senior man was pudgy with a scar on one side of his face. "Have you any experience?" he asked.

"I've practiced on my own," said Ahl.

The man tilted his head, considering. "You're almost certainly a runaway, which is bad enough. Even worse: you've decided you can act. If I was only one man short, I'd send you off. But two of my men are gone, and, if I don't find someone, we won't be able to continue."

In this manner she was hired, though the man had two more questions. "How old are you? I won't take on a child."

"Eighteen," said Ahl.

"Are you certain?"

"Yes," she answered with indignation. Though she was lying about almost everything else, eighteen was her age.

Maybe her tone convinced the man. "Very well," he said, then asked, "What's your name?"

"Dapple," she said.

"Of no family?"

She hesitated.

The man said, "I'll stop asking questions."

She had timed this well. They left the next morning, through fog and drizzling rain. Her comrades on the ship would think she was sleeping. Instead, she trudged beside the actors' cart, which was pulled by a pair of *tsina*. Her tunic, made of thick wool, kept out the rain. A broad straw hat covered her head. Oiled boots protected her feet against mud and pools of water.

From this point on, the story will call her Dapple. It's the name she picked for herself and the one by which she was known for the rest of her life. Think of her not as Helwar Ahl, the runaway girl, but Dapple the actor, whose lineage did not especially matter, since actors live on the road, in the uncertain regions that lie between family holdings and the obligations of kinship.

All day they traveled inland, through steep hills covered with forest. Many of the trees were new to her. Riding in the cart, the pudgy man—his name was Manif—told her about the company. They did mostly comedies, though Manif preferred hero plays. "These people in the south are the rudest collection of louts you can imagine. They like nothing, unless it's full of erect penises and imitations of intercourse; and men and women watch these things together! Shocking!

"They even like plays about breeding, though I prefer—of course—to give them decent comedies about men having sex with men or women having sex with women. But if they insist on heterosexuality, well, we have to eat."

This sounded bad to Dapple, but she was determined to learn. Maybe there was more to comedy than she had realized.

They made camp by the side of the road. Manif slept in the cart, along with another actor: a man of twenty-five or so, not bad looking. The rest of them pitched a tent. Dapple got an outside place, better for privacy, but also wetter. The rain keep falling. In the cart, Manif and his companion made noise.

"Into the *halin*, I notice," said one of Dapple's companions.

"And one another," a second man added.

The third man said, "D'you think he'll go after Dapple here?"

It was possible, thought Dapple, that she'd done something stupid. Cholkwa had warned her about the south.

"He won't if Dapple finds himself a lover quickly," said the first man.

This might have been a joke, rather than an offer. Dapple couldn't tell. She curled up, her back to the others, hoping that no one would touch her. In time, she went to sleep.

The next day was clear, though the ground remained wet. They ate breakfast, then struck the tent and continued inland. The change in weather made Dapple more cheerful. Maybe the men would make no advances. If they did, she'd find a way to fend them off. They might be shabby and half as good as Perig and Cholkwa, but they didn't seem to be monsters or savages; and this wasn't the far north, where a war had gone on for generations, unraveling everything. People on this continent understood right behavior.

As she thought this, one of the *tsina* screamed and reared. An arrow was stuck in its throat.

"Bandits!" cried Manif and shook the reins, shouting, "Go, go," to the animals.

But the shot animal stumbled, unable to continue; and the second *tsin* began to lunge, trying to break free of the harness and its comrade. The actors pulled swords. Dapple dove into the edge-of-forest brush. Behind her was shouting. She scrambled up a hill, her heart beating like a hammer striking an anvil, though more quickly. Up and up she ran, hoping the bandits would not follow. At last she stopped. Her heart felt as if it might break her chest; her lungs hurt; all her breath was gone. Below her on the road was screaming. Not the *tsin* any longer, she thought. This sound was men.

When she was able to breathe, she went on, climbing more slowly now. The screaming stopped. Had the bandits noticed her? Had they counted the company? Four of them had been walking, while Manif and his lover rode. But the lover had been lying in back, under the awning, apparently exhausted by his efforts of the night before. If the bandits had been watching, they might have seen only five people.

No way to tell. She continued up the hill, finally reaching a limestone bluff. There was a crack. She squeezed her way in, finding a narrow cave. There she stopped a second time, leaning against the wet rock, trying to control her breath. Somehow she'd managed to keep her bag. She dropped it at her feet and pulled her knife.

For the rest of the day she waited, then through the night, dozing from time to time, waking suddenly. No one came. In the morning she went down the hill, stopping often to listen. There was nothing to hear except wind in the foliage and small animals making their usual noises.

The road was empty, though there were ruts to show that a cart has passed by. Dapple saw no evidence that a fight had ever taken place. For a moment she stood with her mouth open, wondering. Had it been a dream, the attack and her flight from it? Or had the actors managed to drive off the bandits, then gone on, condemning her as coward? Across the road a bird took flight. Large and heavy, it was mottled black and white and green. Not a breed native to Helwar, but she knew it from her travels in the south. It ate everything, plant and animal, but had a special liking for carrion.

Dapple crossed the road. On the far side, beyond the bushes, was a hollow. Something lay there, covered by branches and handfuls of leaves. She moved one of the branches. Underneath was the shot *tsin*, dead as a stone; and underneath the *tsin* were the actors. She couldn't see them entirely, but parts protruded: a hand, a leg to the knee. One face—Manif's—stared up at her, fur matted with dark blood, one eye already gone.

Shaking, she replaced the branch and sat down before she fell. For a while, she did nothing except rock, her arms around her knees, silent because she feared to mourn out loud.

Finally, she got up and uncovered the grave. There was no way for her to move the *tsin*'s huge body, but she climbed down next to it, touching the actors, making sure they were all dead.

Everything she touched was lifeless. There was nothing in the grave except the corpses. The bandits had taken everything else: the cart, the surviving *tsin* and the company's belongings.

There was no way to bury the actors properly. If she tried, she would be leaving evidence of her existence.

She climbed back out of the grave. Where should she go? Back to the harbor town? But the bandits had obviously been waiting along the road, and they might have gone back to waiting. If so, they were likely to be where they'd been before: somewhere to the east.

If they intended to set an ambush farther west, surely they would have done a better job of covering the bodies. Birds had found them already. By tomorrow this spot would be full of noisy, filthy eaters-of-carrion.

It's possible she wasn't thinking clearly in reasoning this out. Nonetheless, she decided to go west. According to Massif, there was a town less than a day's journey away: solid, fortified and fond of acting. Slinging her bag over her shoulder, Dapple went on.

The road wound through a series of narrow valleys. After she had gone a short distance, she saw the cart ahead of her, motionless in the middle of the road. She glanced back, planning to run. Two men stood there, both holding swords. Goddess! Ahl glanced at the forest next to her. As she did so, man stepped out of the blue-green shadow. He also held a sword.

"I should have gone east," said Dapple.

"Some of our cousins went in that direction. Most likely, you would have met them."

Was this the moment to reveal she was a woman? "Are you going to kill me?"

"That depends on what you do," the man said. "But I'd prefer not to."

The other bandits came close. There were four of them, all dressed in worn stained clothing.

"He's handsome," said the youngest fellow, who had a bandage wrapped around one arm. "Worth keeping."

"For what purpose?" asked Dapple, feeling uneasy.

"We'll tell you later," said the man from the forest.

After that, they took her bag and knife, then tied her hands in front of her. The man with the injured arm took the rope's other end. "Come along, dear one. We have a long way to go before nightfall."

He led her off the road, onto a narrow path. Animals had made it, most likely. A second man followed. The others stayed behind.

The rest of the day they traveled through steep forest. Now and then the path crossed a stream or went along a limestone outcropping. Dapple grew tired and increasingly afraid. She tried to reassure herself by thinking that men rarely killed women, and rape—of women by men, at least—was an almost unknown perversion.

But women rarely traveled alone. Obviously they came to little harm, if they stayed at home or traveled in large companies; and this was the south, the region where civilization ended; and these men were killers, as she had seen. Who could say what they might do?

For example, they might kill her before learning she was a woman. Was this the moment to tell them? She continued to hesitate, feeling ashamed by the idea of abandoning her disguise. She had wanted to be different. She had planned to fool other people by using her intelligence and skill. Now, at the first setback, she was ready to give up.

What a finish to her ambitions! She might die in this miserable forest—like a hero in a play, though with less dignity.

Worst of all, she needed to urinate. She knew from Perig and Cholkwa that all actors drank moderately before they went on stage. But she hadn't thought that she'd be acting this afternoon. Her bladder was full and beginning to hurt.

Finally she confessed her need.

"Go right ahead," one of her captors said, stopping by a tree.

"I'm modest and can't empty my bladder in front of other men."

"We won't watch," said the second bandit in a lying tone.

"Let me go behind those bushes and do it. You'll be able to see my head and shoulders. I won't be able to escape."

The bandits agreed, clearly thinking that she was some kind of fool. But who can explain the behavior of foreigners?

Dapple went behind the bushes. Now her childhood practice came in useful: unlike most women, she could urinate while standing up and not make a mess. From situations like these we learn to value every skill, unless it's clearly pernicious. Who can predict the future and say, this-and-such ability will never be of use? She rejoined the bandits, feeling an irrational satisfaction.

At nightfall, they came to a little stony valley far back in the hills. A stream ran out of it. They waded in through cold water. At the valley's end was a tall narrow cave. Firelight shone out. "Home at last," said the bandit who held Dapple's rope.

They entered. The cave widened at once. Looking around, Dapple saw a large stone room. A fire burned in the middle. Around it sat women in ragged tunics. A few children chased each other, making shrill noises like the cries of birds. At the back of the cave were more openings, two or maybe three, leading farther in.

"What have you brought?" asked one of the women, lifting her head. The fur on the woman's face was white with age; and the lenses of her eyes were cloudy.

"A fine young man to impregnate your daughters," said the man holding the rope.

The old woman rose and came forward. Her body was solid, and she moved firmly, though with a cane. Bending close, she peered at Dapple, then felt an arm. "Good muscle. How old is he?"

"Tell her," the man said.

"Eighteen."

"Men are active at that age, no question, but I prefer someone older. Who knows anything about a lad of eighteen? He hasn't shown his nature to the world. His traits may be good or bad."

"This is true, mother," said the man with the rope. "But we have to take what we get. This one is alive and healthy. Most likely, he can do what we need done."

Dapple thought of mentioning that she could not impregnate a female, but decided to wait.

"Come over to the fire," the old woman said. "Sit down and talk with me. I like to know who's fathering the children in our family."

Dapple obeyed. The man went with them. Soon she was on the stone floor, a bowl of beer next to her. In her hand was a piece of greasy meat, a gift from the old woman. Around her sat the rest of the family: thin women with badly combed fur. Most likely they had bugs. One held a baby. The rest of the children were older, ranging from a girl of four or five to a boy at the edge of adulthood. The boy was remarkably clean for a member of this family, and he had a slim gracefulness that seemed completely out of place. The other children continued to run and scream, but he sat quietly among his female relatives, watching Dapple with eyes as yellow as resin.

The man, Dapple's captor, sat in back of her, out of sight, though when she moved her bound hands she could feel him holding the rope.

There had been five families in these hills, the old woman said. None of them large or rich, but they survived, doing one thing or another.

Five lineages of robbers, thought Dapple.

"We all interbred till we were close kin, but we remained separate families, so we could continue to interbreed and find lovers. The rest of the families in this region never liked us and would have nothing to do with us. We had no one except each other."

Definitely robbers.

In the end, the large and powerful families in the region combined against the five. One by one, they were destroyed. It was done in the usual way: the men were killed, the women and children adopted.

"But our neighbors, the powerful ones, never allowed any of the people they adopted to breed. They would not let women and children starve, but neither would they let traits like ours continue. We were poisoned and poisonous, they said.

"Imagine what it was like for those women and children! It's one thing for a woman to lose her family name and all her male relatives. That can be endured. But to know that nothing will continue, that her children will die without children! Some of the women fled into the hills and died alone. Some were found by us. We took them in, of course, and bred them when we could. But where could we find fathers? The men who should have impregnated our daughters—and the women we adopted—were dead.

"We are the last of the five families: more women than men, all of us poor and thin, with no one to father the next generation, except travelers like you.

"But we refuse to give up! We won't let rich and arrogant folk make us vanish from the world."

Dapple thought while drinking her beer. "Why did your men kill the rest of our acting company? There were five more—all male, of course, and older than I am."

The bandit matriarch peered past Dapple. "Six men? And you brought only one?"

"They fought," said the man behind Dapple, his voice reluctant. "We became angry."

The matriarch hissed, a noise full of rage.

"One other is still alive," the man added. "My brothers will bring him along later."

"You wanted to rape him," said the matriarch. "What good do you think he'll be, after you finish? Selfish, selfish boys! Your greed will destroy us!"

Obviously she had miscounted, when she climbed into the actors' grave. Who was still alive? Not Manif. She'd seen him clearly. Maybe his lover, who was young and handsome.

"Don't blame me," said the man sullenly. "I'm not raping anyone. I'm here with this lad, and I haven't touched him. As for the other man, he'll still be usable. No one wants to make you angry."

The matriarch scratched her nose. "I'll deal with that problem when your brothers and male cousins return. In the meantime, tie up this man. I need to decide who should mate with him."

"Why should I do this?" asked Dapple. "There is no breeding contract between your family and mine. No decent man has sex with a woman, unless it's been arranged by his relatives and hers."

"We will kill you, if you don't," said the man behind Dapple.

"What will you do if I agree to do this very improper thing?" The people around the fire looked uneasy.

"One thing at a time," said the matriarch. "First, you have to make one of our women pregnant. Later, we'll decide what to do with you."

Dapple was led into another cave, this one small and empty except for a pallet on the floor and an iron ring set in the wall. Her captor tied her rope to the ring and left her.

She sat down. Firelight came from the main cave, enough to light her prison. She tried to loosen the knots that held her. No luck. A cold draft blew down on her. At first she thought it was fear. Glancing up, she saw a hole that led to starlight. Too far for her to reach, even if she could manage to free herself, and most likely too small to climb through. Only a few stars were visible. One was yellow and very bright: the Eye of Uson. It made her think of Manif's one eye. How was she going to escape this situation? The hole seemed unreachable, and the only other route was past the main cavern, full of bandits; and she was tired, far too tired to think. Dapple lay down and went to sleep.

She woke to feel a hand shaking her. Another hand was over her mouth.

"Don't make any noise," a voice whispered.

She moved her head in a gesture of agreement. The hand over her mouth lifted. Cautiously, she sat up.

The fire in the main cave still burned, though more dimly. Blinking, she made out a slim figure. She touched an arm. The fur felt smooth and clean. "You are the boy."

"A man now. Fifteen this spring. Are you really an actor?"

"Yes."

"My father was one. They told me about him: a handsome man, who told jokes and juggled anything: fruit, stones, knives, though they never let him have sharp knives. After he made my mother pregnant, they kept him to impregnate another woman and because they enjoyed his company. But instead of doing as they planned, he escaped. They say they'll never trust another foreigner—or keep a man alive so long that he knows his way through the caves. His name was Cholkwa. Have you ever heard of him?"

Dapple laughed quietly.

"What does that mean?" asked the boy.

"I've known him all my life. He stays at my family's house when he's on Helwar Island. Though he has never mentioned meeting your kin, at least when I was around."

"Maybe we weren't important to him," the boy said in a sad tone.

Most likely, Cholkwa kept silent out of shame. His own family was far to the north, across the narrow ocean, and she'd never heard him speak about any of them. Maybe he had no relatives left. There'd been war in the north for generations now. Sometimes it flared up; at other times it died to embers, but it never entirely ended, and many lineages had been destroyed.

He was a decent man, in spite of his lack of kin. How could he admit to breeding without a contract arranged by the senior women in his family? How could he admit to leaving a child who was related to him—granted: not closely, but a relative none the less—in a place like this?

"Will your relatives kill me?" Dapple asked.

"Once you have made one of my cousins pregnant, yes."

"Why are you here with me?"

"I wanted to know about my father." The boy paused. "I wanted to know what lies beyond these hills.

"What good will it do for you to know?"

There was silence for a while. "When I was growing up, my mother told me about Cholkwa, his stories and jokes and tricks. There are cities beyond the hills, he told her, and boats as big as our cave that sail on the ocean. The boats go from city to city, and there are places—halls and open spaces—where people go to see acting. In those places, Cholkwa is famous. Crowds of people come to see him perform the way he did for my family in this cave. Are these stories true?"

"Yes," said Dapple. "Everywhere he goes, people are charmed by him and take pleasure in his skill. No actor is more famous." She paused, trying to think of what to say next. The Goddess had given this boy to her; she must find a way to turn him into an ally. "He has no kin on this side of the ocean. Most likely, he would enjoy meeting you."

"Fathers don't care about their children, and we shouldn't care about them. Dead or alive, they do nothing for us."

"This isn't true," said Dapple with quiet anger. "Obviously, it makes sense for a child to stay with her mother and be raised by maternal kin. A man can't nurse a baby, after all; and few mothers could bear to be separated from a small child. But the connection is still there. Most men pay some attention to their children, especially their sons. If something happens to the maternal lineage or to the relationship between a woman and her family, the paternal lineage will often step in. My mother is from Sorg, but she quarreled with her kin and fled to my father's family, the Helwar. They adopted her and me. Such things occur."

"Nothing has happened to my family," the boy said. "And my mother never quarreled with them, though she wasn't happy living here. I know that."

"Your family is not fit to raise children," said Dapple. "You seem to have turned out surprisingly well, but if you stay with them, they'll make you a criminal; and then you'll be trapped here. Do you really want to spend your life among thieves and people who breed without a contract? If you leave now and seek out Cholkwa, it may be possible for you to have a decent life."

The boy was silent for a moment, then exhaled and stood. "I have to go. They might wake."

A moment later, she was alone. She lay for a while, wondering if the boy would help her or if there was another way to escape. When she went back to sleep, she dreamt of Cholkwa. He was on a stage, dressed in bright red armor. His eyes were yellow and shone like stars. Instead of acting, he stood in a relaxed pose, holding a wooden sword loosely. "All of this is illusion and lies," he told her, gesturing at the stage. "But there's truth behind the illusion. If you are going to act, you need to know what's true and what's a lie. You need to know which lies have truth in back of them."

Waking, she saw a beam of sunlight shining through the hole in her ceiling. For a moment, the dream's message seemed clear and important. As she sat up, it began to fade and blur, though she kept the image of Cholkwa in his crimson armor.

One of the bandit males came and untied her. Together they went out, and she relieved herself behind the bushes.

"I've never known anyone so modest," the bandit said. "How are you going to get a woman pregnant, if you can't bare yourself in front of a man?"

A good question, Dapple thought. Her disguise couldn't last much longer. Maybe she ought to end it. It didn't seem likely the boy would help her—people didn't turn against their kin, even kin like these—and, as long as the bandits thought she was a man, they might do anything. No rules protect a man who falls into the hands of enemies. She might be dead or badly injured, before they realized she wasn't male. But something, a sense of foreboding, made her reluctant to reveal her true nature.

"We have sex in the dark," she told the bandit.

"That can be managed," he replied. "Though it seems ridiculous."

Dapple spent the rest of the day inside, alone at first, in a corner of the cave. The other bandits did not return, and the matriarch looked increasingly grim. Her kin sent their children outside to play. The men were gone as well. Those who remained—a handful of shabby women—worked quietly, giving the matriarch anxious glances. Clearly this was someone who could control her family! A pity that the family consisted of criminals.

At last the old woman gestured. "Come here, man. I want to know you better."

Dapple settled by the fire, which still burned, even in the middle of a bright day. This wasn't surprising. The cave was full of shadows, and the air around them was cool and damp.

Instead of asking questions, the woman grumbled. It was hard work holding together a lineage, especially when all the neighboring families were hostile, and she got little help. Her female relatives were slovenly. "My eyes may be failing, but I can still smell. This place stinks like a midden heap!" Her male kin were selfish and stupid. "Five men! And they have brought me one, with another promised, though I'll believe in him when he appears."

All alone, she labored to continue her line of descent, though only one descendant seemed really promising, the boy who'd been fathered by an actor. "A fine lad. Maybe there's something potent about the semen of actors. I hope so."

Evening came. The missing bandits did not appear. Finally the old woman looked at Dapple. "It seems our hopes rest in your hands—or if not in your hands, then in another part of your body. Is there a woman you prefer?"

Dapple glanced around. Figures lurked in the shadows, trying to avoid the matriarch's glance. Hard to see, but she knew what was there. "No."

"I'll pick one, then."

"There is something you ought to know," Dapple said.

The old woman frowned at her.

"I can't impregnate a woman."

"Many men find the idea of sex with women distasteful," the matriarch said. "But they manage the task. Surely your life is worth some effort. I promise you, you'll die if you don't try."

"I'm a woman," said Dapple. "This costume is a disguise."

"Ridiculous," the matriarch said. "Decent women don't wear men's clothing or travel with actors."

"I didn't say I was a decent woman. I said I was female and unable to father children. Don't you think—since I can't help you—you ought to let me go?"

"No matter what you are, we can't let you go," said the matriarch. "You might lead people to this cave." Then she ordered her kin to examine Dapple.

Three shabby women moved in. Standing, Dapple pulled off her tunic and underpants.

"No question about it," one of the women said. "She is female."

"What wretched luck!" cried the matriarch. "What have I done to deserve this kind of aggravation? And what's wrong with you, young woman, running around in a tunic and tricking people? Have you no sense of right behavior?"

There were more insults and recriminations, mostly from the old woman, though the others muttered agreement. What inhospitable and unmannerly folk! Dapple could hardly have fallen into a worse situation, though they weren't likely to kill her, now that they knew she was a woman.

At last, the matriarch waved a hand. "Tie her up for the night. I need to think."

Once again Dapple found herself in the little side cave, tied to an iron ring. As on the previous night, stars shone through the hole in the ceiling, and firelight came down the corridor from the main cave, along with angry voices. Her captors were arguing. At this distance she couldn't make out words, but there was no mistaking the tone.

This time she made a serious effort to untie the rope that held her. But her hands had been fastened together, and her fingers couldn't reach the knot. Gnawing proved useless. The rope was too thick and strong. Exhausted, she began to doze. She woke to a touch, as on the night before.

"Is it you again?" she asked in a whisper.

Dapple

"My grandmother has chosen me to impregnate you," said the boy, sounding miserable.

"What do you mean?"

"If you can't father children on our women, then we'll father children on you and adopt the children, as you were adopted by your father's family. That plan will do as well as the first one, Grandmother says. The others say she's favoring me, but I don't want to do this."

"Breed without a contract? What man would? What are you going to do?"

"Have sex with you, though I've never had sex with anyone. But Grandmother has explained how it's done."

"You have reached a moment of decision," said Dapple. "If you make the wrong choice now, your life will lead to ruin, like the life of a protagonist in a hero play."

"What does that mean?"

"If you have sex with me against my will, and without a contract arranged by my female relatives, you will be a criminal forever. But if you set me free, I will lead you to your father."

"I have a knife," said the boy uncertainly. "I could cut you free, but there's no way out except through the main cave."

Dapple lifted her head, indicating the hole in the ceiling.

The boy gazed up at the stars. "Do you think you could get through?"

"I'd be willing to try, if there's no other way. But how do we reach it?"

"Standing on my shoulders won't do. It's too far up. But I could go outside and lower a rope. Can you climb one?"

"I've worked as a sailor," said Dapple. "Of course I can."

"I could tell them I need to urinate. I know where there's a rope. It could be done. But if they catch us—"

"If you stay here and do this thing, you will be a thief. Your children will be thieves. You'll never see the cities beyond these hills or the ships as big as caves."

159

The boy hesitated, then pulled his knife and cut Dapple free. "Wait here," he said fiercely, and left.

She rubbed her hands and wrists, then stood and stretched. Hah! Hah! How stiff she was!

Voices rose in the main cave, mocking the boy, then dropped back to a murmur. She began to watch the hole.

After a while, a dark shape hid the stars. A rope dropped toward her. Dapple grasped it and tugged. It held. She took off her tunic and tied it to the bottom of the rope, then began her climb, going hand over hand up the rope. Cold air blew past her, ruffling the fur on her arms and shoulders. It smelled of damp soil and forest. Freedom, thought Dapple. A moment or two later, she reached the hole. Hah! It was narrow! As bad as she had feared!

"Can you make it?" the boy whispered.

"I have to," Dapple said and continued to climb.

Her head was no problem, but her shoulders were too wide. Rough stone scraped against them. She kept on, trying to force her body through the opening. All at once she realized that she was stuck, like a piece of wax used to seal the narrow neck of a jar. Dapple groaned with frustration.

"Be quiet," whispered the boy and began to pull, leaning far back, all his weight on the rope. For a moment she remained wedged in the hole. Then her shoulders were through, though some of her fur remained behind. Her elbows dug into dirt. She pushed up. The boy continued to pull, and Dapple popped into freedom. She stretched out on the damp ground, face down, smelling dirt, the forest and the night wind.

"You have no clothing on!" the boy exclaimed.

"I took my tunic off," said Dapple. "I knew the fit would be tight."

"You can't travel like this!"

She pulled the rope out of the hole, retrieving her tunic and putting it on.

"Better," said the boy, though he still sounded embarrassed.

He had wrapped his end of the rope to a tree. She undid the knots and coiled the rope. "A knife, a rope, and four sound feet. I'd like more, but this will have to do. Let's go."

They set off through the forest, the boy leading, since he had good night vision, and this was his country.

"When will they discover that we are missing?" Dapple asked after a while.

"In the morning. Tonight they'll drink and tell each other rude stories about sex. Grandmother gave permission. It's lucky to do this, when people breed."

It was never lucky to breed without a contract, Dapple thought, but said nothing. How was this boy going to survive in the outside world, knowing so little about how to behave? She'd worry about that problem when both of them were safe.

They traveled all night. In spite of the boy's keen eyes, the two travelers stumbled often and hit themselves against branches, sometimes thorny. No one living in a town can imagine the darkness of a forest, even when the sky above the trees is full of stars. Certainly Dapple had not known, living in a harbor town. How she longed for an ocean vista, open and empty, with starlight glinting off the waves!

At dawn, they stopped and hid in a ravine. Water trickled at the bottom. Birds cried in the leaves, growing gradually quiet as the day grew warmer. Exhausted, the two young people dozed. Midway through the morning, voices woke them: men, talking loudly and confidently as they followed a nearby trail. The boy peered out. "It's my relatives," he said.

"Is anyone with them?" asked Dapple fearfully. What would they do, if one of the actors had survived and was a prisoner? It would be unbearable to leave the man with savages, but if she and the boy tried to free the man, they would be killed or taken prisoner like him.

"No," said the boy after a while. "They must have killed him after they finished raping him. My grandmother will be so angry!"

These people were both monsters and fools. Was there anything she could learn from the situation? Maybe the nature of monsters, if she ever had to portray a monster in a play. The nature of monsters, Dapple thought as she crouched in the ravine, was folly. That was the thing she had to concentrate on, not her own sense of fear and horror.

After a while the boy said, "They're gone. I didn't expect them to come this direction. But now that they've passed us, we'd better put as much distance as possible between us and them."

They rose and went on. Shortly thereafter, they found the robbers' camp: a forest clearing with the remains of a fire and Dapple's last companion, Manif's lover. He must have endured as much as he could, then fought back. There were various wounds, which Dapple did not look at closely, and a lot of blood, which had attracted bugs.

"Dead," said the boy. "They should have buried him, but we can't take the time."

Dapple went to the edge of the clearing and threw up, then covered her vomit with forest debris. Maybe the robbers wouldn't find it, if they came back this way. Though the moist ground should tell the bandits who'd been here.

The boy must have thought the same thing. After that, they traveled through streams and over rocks. It was a hard journey.

Late in the afternoon, they descended into a valley. At the bottom was a larger-than-usual stream. The forest canopy was less thick than before. Sunlight speckled the ground. "We are close to the border of our country," the boy said. "From this point on, it will be best to follow trails."

One ran along the stream—narrow and used more by animals than people, Dapple thought. The travelers took it. After a while, a second stream joined the first. Together, they formed a river where small rapids alternated with pools. At sunset, turning a corner, they discovered a group of men swimming. Clothes and weapons lay on the river bank.

The boy stopped suddenly. "Ettin."

"What?" asked Dapple.

"Our enemies," he answered, sounding fearful, then added, "The people I am bringing you to. Go forward. I cannot." He turned to go back the way they had come. Behind him the sky was sunset red; the boy's face was in shadow. Nonetheless Dapple saw his mouth open and eyes widen.

A harsh voice said, "Neither can you go back, thief."

She turned as well. A man stood in the trail, short and broad with a flat ugly face. A metal hat covered the top of his head and was fastened under his chin with a leather strap. His torso was covered with metal and leather armor. A skirt made of leather strips hung to his knees. One hand held a sword, the blade bare and shining. She had never seen anyone who looked so unattractive.

"Who are you?" she asked.

"A guard. You can't believe that men of Ettin would bathe without posting guards."

"I'm from the north," said Dapple. "I know nothing about Ettin, which I imagine is your lineage."

He made a noise that indicated doubt. "The north? And this one as well?" The sword tip pointed at her companion.

"I was traveling with actors," Dapple said. "Robbers killed my comrades and took me prisoner. This lad rescued me and was guiding me to safety."

The guard made another noise that indicated doubt. Other men gathered. Some were guards out of the forest. The rest were bathers, their fur slick with water and their genitalia exposed. She knew what male babies and boys looked like, of course; but this was the first time she'd seen men. They weren't as big as she'd imagined after Cholkwa's plays. None the less, the situation was embarrassing. She glanced back at the first guard, meeting his eyes.

"Are you threatening me?" he asked.

"Of course not."

"Then look down! What kind of customs do you have in the north?"

She looked at the ground. The air smelled of wet fur. "What's this about?" the men asked. "What have you captured?"

"Some kind of foreigner, and a fellow of unknown lineage, though local, I think. They say they've escaped from the robbers."

"If done, it's well done," said a swimmer. "But they may be lying. Take them to our outpost, and let the captain question them. If they're spies, he'll uncover them."

Who is talking about uncovering? Dapple thought. A man with water dripping off him and his penis evident to anyone who cared to look. Not that she glanced in his direction. It was like being in an animal play, though less funny.

Other men made noises of agreement. The swimmers went off to dry and dress. The men in armor tied Dapple's hands behind her back, then did the same for the boy. After that, they ran a second rope from Dapple's neck to the boy's neck. "You won't run far like this," one said when the second rope was fastened.

"Is this any way to treat guests?" asked Dapple.

"You may be spies. If you are not, we'll treat you well. The Ettin have always been hospitable and careful."

Tied like animals going to market, they marched along the trail, which had grown wider and looked better used. Half the men went with them. The rest stayed behind to guard the border.

Twilight came. They continued through darkness, though under an open sky. By this time Dapple was dazed by lack of sleep. One of the guards took her arm, holding her upright and guiding her. "You're a pretty lad. If you are what you say, maybe we can keep company."

Another guard said, "Don't listen, stranger. You can do better than Hattin. If you are what you say."

Her male disguise was certainly causing problems, though she needed it, if she was going to learn acting. What was she learning now? Danger and fear. If she survived and made it home, she would think about specializing in hero plays.

Ahead of them gleamed firelight, shining out of windows. A sword hilt knocked on a door. Voices called. Dapple could not understand what they were saying, but the door opened.

Entering, she found herself in a courtyard made of stone. On one side was a stable, on the other side a square stone tower.

She and the boy were led into the tower. The ground floor was a single room with a fireplace on one side. A man sat next to the fire in a high-backed wooden chair. His grey fur was silvered by age, and he was even uglier than his relatives.

"This is Ettin Taiin," said the guard named Hattin. "The man who watches this border with our help."

The man rose and limped forward. He'd lost an eye, though not recently, and did not bother to hide the empty socket. "Poor help you are," he said in a voice like stone grating against stone. "Nonetheless, I manage." He looked directly at Dapple. The one eye that remained was bright blue, the pupil expanded in the dim light, so it lay across his iris like a black iron bar across sky. "Who are you, and what are you doing in the land I watch?"

She told her story a second time.

"That explains you," said Ettin Taiin. "And I'm inclined toward belief. Your accent is not local, nor is your physical type, though you are certainly lovely in a foreign way. But this lad—" He glared at the boy. "Looks like a robber."

The boy whimpered, dropping to the floor and curling like a frightened *tli*. Because they were tied together, Dapple was pulled to her knees. She looked at the border captain. "There is more to the story. I am not male."

"What do you mean?" asked Ettin Taiin, his voice harsher than before.

"I wanted to be an actor, and women are not allowed to act."

"Quite rightly," said the captain.

"I disguised myself as a young man and joined a company here in the south, where no one knows me; and where I'm not likely to meet actors I know, such as Perig and Cholkwa."

"Cholkwa is here right now," said the captain, "visiting my mother and her sisters. What a splendid performer he is! I nearly ruptured myself laughing the last time I saw him. If he knows you, then he can speak for you; I am certainly not going to find out whether or not you're female. My mother raised me properly."

"An excellent woman," murmured the guards standing around.

"When the robbers captured me, I told them I was female; and they told this lad to impregnate me."

"With no contract? Without the permission of your female relatives?" The stony voice was full of horror.

"Obviously," said Dapple. "My relatives are on Helwar Island, far to the north."

"You see what happens when women run off to foreign places, without the protection of the men in their family," said the captain. "Not that this excuses the robbers in any way. We've been lax in letting them survive. Did he do it?"

The boy, still curled on the floor, his hands over his head, made a keening noise. The guards around her exhaled, and Dapple thought she heard the sound of swords moving in their scabbards.

"No," Dapple said. "He got me out of prison and brought me here. That's the end of the story."

"Nasty and shocking," said the captain. "We will obviously have to kill the rest of the robber men, though it won't be easy to hunt them down. The children can be adopted, starting with this lad. He looks young enough to keep. The women are a problem. I'll let my female relatives deal with it, once we have captured the women. I only hope I'm not forced into acts that will require me to commit suicide after. I'm younger than I look and enjoy life."

"We'd all prefer to stay alive," said Hattin.

"Untie them," said the captain, "and put them in separate rooms. In the morning, we'll take them to my mother."

The guards pulled the two of them upright and cut their ropes. The captain limped back to his chair. "And feed them," he added as he settled and picked up a cup. "Give the woman my best *halin*."

Leading them up a flight of stairs, Hattin said, "If you're a woman, then I apologize for the suggestion I made. Though I wasn't the only one who thought you'd make a good bedmate. Ettin Taiin is going to be hearing jokes about that for years."

"You tease a man like him?" asked Dapple.

"I don't, but the senior men in the family do. The only way someone like that is tolerable is if you can embarrass him now and then."

Her room had a lantern, but no fire. It wasn't needed on a mild spring night. Was the man downstairs cold from age or injuries? The window was barred, and the only furniture was a bed. Dapple sat down. The guards brought food and drink and a pissing pot, then left, locking the door. She ate, drank, pissed, and went to sleep.

In the morning she woke to the sound of nails scratching on her door. A man's voice said, "Make yourself ready." Dapple rose and dressed. The night before she'd unbound her breasts in order to sleep comfortably. She didn't rebind them now. The tunic was thick enough to keep her decent, her breasts weren't large enough to need support, and the men of Ettin were treating her like a woman. Better to leave the disguise behind, like a shell outgrown by one of the animals her male relatives pulled from the sea.

Guards escorted her and the boy downstairs. There were windows on the ground floor, which she hadn't noticed the night before. Open shutters let sunlight in. The Ettin captain stood at a table covered with maps. "Good morning," he said. "I'm trying to decide how to trap the robbers. Do you have any suggestions, lad? And what is your name?"

"Rehv," the boy said. "I never learned to read maps, and I will not help you destroy my family."

Ettin Taiin rolled the maps—they were paper, rather than the oiled leather her people used—and put them in a metal tube. "Loyalty is a virtue. So is directness. You'll make a fine addition to the Ettin lineage; and I'll decide how to destroy your lineage later. Today, as I told you before, we'll ride to my mother."

They went out and mounted *tsina*; the captain easily in spite of his lame leg, Dapple and the boy with more difficulty.

"You aren't riders," said Ettin Taiin. "And that tells me your families don't have many *tsina*. Good to know, for when I hunt the robbers down."

They spent the day riding, following a narrow road through forested hills. A small group of soldiers accompanied them, riding as easily as the captain and joking among themselves. Now and then they saw a cabin. "Hunters and trappers," said Ettin Taiin. "There are logging camps as well. But no women. The robbers are too close. Time and time again we've tried to clean them out; but they persist, growing ever more inbred and nasty."

Riding next to her, the boy shivered, hair rising on his arms and shoulders. Now that she was apparently safe, Dapple felt pity and respect for him. He'd been confronted by the kind of decision a hero faces in a play. Should he side with his kin or with right behavior? A man without kin was like a tree without roots. The slightest wind would push him over. A man without morality was like—what? A tree without sunlight and rain.

In most cases, hero plays ended in death. It was the easiest resolution. Unable to make a definite choice, the hero blundered through a series of half-actions and mistakes, until he was killed by enemies or friends and the audience exhaled in relief. May the Goddess keep them from this kind of situation!

Most likely, the boy would live to see his relatives die, while he was adopted by the Ettin. It was the right ending for the story of a child. Their duty was to live and grow and learn. Honor belonged to older people. Nonetheless, the story disturbed Dapple, as did the boy's evident unhappiness and fear.

Late in the afternoon, they entered a wide flat valley. The land was cultivated. The buildings scattered among fields and orchards were made of planks rather than logs. Many were painted: blue-grey, green, or white.

"Barns," said the Ettin captain. "Stables. Houses for herdsmen."

She was back in the ordinary world of people who understood rules, though she wasn't certain the Ettin followed the rules she had learned on Helwar Island. Still, the pastures were fenced, the fields plowed in straight lines, and the orchard trees—covered with pale orange blossoms—were orderly.

They reached the captain's home as the sun went down. It was a cluster of buildings made of wood and stone, next to a river crossed by a stone bridge. The lower stories had no windows, and the doors were iron bound. Built for defense, but no enemies were expected today. The largest door was open. Riding through it, they entered a courtyard surrounded by balconies. Children played in the early evening shadows, though Dapple couldn't make out the game. It stopped the moment they appeared.

"Uncle Taiin!" cried several voices.

The captain swung down stiffly and was surrounded by small bodies.

"An excellent man," said one of the guards to Dapple. "Affectionate with children, respectful toward women and violent toward other men."

"Even men of your family?" Dapple asked.

"We win, and most of us come home; we don't expect kindness from a leader on campaign."

A woman came into the courtyard, tall and broad, wearing a sleeveless robe. Age had whitened her face and upper arms. She carried a staff and leaned on it; but her head was erect, her blue eyes as bright as a polished blade.

The children fell silent and moved away from their uncle. He lifted his head, looked straight at the old woman and gave her a broad, boyish grin. Beyond question, this was his mother. Could actors replicate this moment? No. Children were not used in plays; and everything here was small and quiet: the man's grin, the woman's brief returning smile.

"Taiin," she said in greeting. Nothing more, but the voice rang—it seemed to Dapple—with joy. Her steel blue eyes flashed toward Dapple and the boy. "Tell me the names of our guests."

He did, adding, "The girl, if this is a girl, says that Cholkwa the actor will speak for her. The boy is almost old enough to be killed; but if he saved her, then he's worth saving."

"I will form my own judgement," said the Matriarch. "But she's clearly a girl."

"Are you certain?"

"Use your eye, Taiin!"

He obeyed with a slow sideways look. "She does seem more feminine than she did yesterday. But I'd be happier if she had on female clothing. Then, maybe, I could see her as a woman entirely. Right now, she seems to shift back and forth. It's very disturbing!"

"I'll give her a bath and new clothes," said the matriarch with decision. "You take care of the boy."

Dapple dismounted. The old woman led her through shadowy halls to a courtyard with two pools built of stone. Steps led down into each. One seemed ordinary enough, the water in it colorless and still; but the other was full of bright green water. Steam rose from its surface; the air around it had an unfamiliar, slightly unpleasant odor.

"It comes from the ground like this," said the matriarch. "We bring it here through pipes. The heat is good for old bones, stiff muscles and the kind of injuries my son Taiin has endured. Undress! Climb in!"

Dapple obeyed, pulling off her tunic. The matriarch exhaled. "A fine looking young woman, indeed! A pity that you won't be bred!"

Because she had bad traits. Well, she didn't mind. She had never wanted to be a mother, only an actor. Dapple entered the steaming water, sinking until she was covered. Hah! It was pleasant, in spite of the aroma! She stretched out and looked up. Though shadows filled the courtyard, the sky above was full of light. A cloud like a feather floated there. Last night she slept in a guard house. The night before she'd scrambled through a dark forest; and before that she'd been in a cave full of robbers. Now she was back in a proper house, not entirely like her home, but close enough.

Women appeared, bringing a chair for the matriarch and a clothing rack, on which they hung new clothes for Dapple. Then they left. The matriarch sat down, laying her staff on the court's stone floor. "Why did you disguise yourself as a man?"

Dapple told her story, floating in the steaming pool. The old woman listened with obvious attention. When the story was done, she said, "We've been negligent. We should have cleared those people out years ago. But I—and my sisters and our female cousins—didn't want to adopt the robber women. They'll be nothing but trouble."

This was true, thought Dapple, remembering the women in the cave, especially the robber matriarch. This was not a person who'd fit herself quietly into a new household. Hah! She would struggle and plot!

"But something will have to be done. We can't let these folk rob and murder and force men to breed. No child should come into existence without the agreement of two families. No man should become a father without a proper contract. We are not animals! I'm surprised at Cholkwa. Surely it would be better to die, than to reproduce in this fashion."

She might have agreed before her recent experiences; but now life seemed precious, as did Cholkwa and every person she knew and liked. If he had refused to cooperate with the robbers, she would have lost him when she barely knew him; and the boy who saved her would never have come into existence. The thought of her fate without the boy was frightening.

Maybe none of this would have happened if Cholkwa had died before she saw him act. Without him, she might have been content to stay in Helwar. Hardly likely! She would have seen Perig; and he was the one she wanted to imitate. Comedy was fine, and Cholkwa did it beautifully. But she didn't want to spend her life making rude jokes.

Nor did she want to do exactly what Perig did. His heroes were splendid. When they died, she felt grief combined with joy. They were so honorable! Perig had so much skill! But her recent experiences suggested that real death was nothing like a play. Manif and his comrades would not rise to shouts of praise. Their endings had been horrible and final and solved nothing. Death was the problem here, rather than the problem's solution. Why had they died? Why was she alive? Were tragedy and comedy the only alternatives? Did one either die with honor or survive in an embarrassing costume?

These were difficult questions, and Dapple was too young to have answers; maybe too young to ask the questions clearly. But something like these ideas, though possibly more fragmentary, floated in her mind as she floated in the steaming pool.

"That's enough heat," the matriarch said finally. "It will make you dizzy, if you stay too long. Go to the second pool and cool down!"

Dapple obeyed, pausing on the way to pick up a ball of soap. This water was pleasant too. Not cold, but cool, as the matriarch had suggested, and so very fresh. It must come from a mountain stream. The soap lathered well and smelled of herbs. She washed herself entirely, then rinsed. The robbers would stay in her mind, but the stink of their cave would be out of her fur. In time, her memories would grow less intense; though she didn't want to forget the boy; and, was it right to forget Manif and the other actors?

She climbed out of the second pool. A towel hung on the clothing rack, also a comb with a long handle. She used both, then dressed. The young women in this country wore kilts and vests. Her kilt was dark blue, the fabric soft and fine. Her vest was made of thicker material, bright red with silver fasteners down the front. The Ettin had provided sandals as well, made of dark blue leather.

"Beyond question you are a handsome young woman," the matriarch said. "Brave and almost certainly intelligent, but far too reckless. What are we going to do with you?"

Dapple said nothing, having no answer. The matriarch picked up her staff and rose.

They went through more shadowy halls, coming finally to an open door. Beyond was a terrace made of stone. A low wall ran along the far side. Beyond the wall was the river that ran next to the house, then pastures rising toward wooded hills. Everything was in shadow now, except the sky and the very highest hill tops. Two men sat on the terrace wall, conversing: Ettin Taiin and Cholkwa. The robber boy stood nearby, looking far neater and cleaner than before. Like Dapple, he wore new clothes: a kilt as brown as weathered bronze and sandals with brass studs. Looking from him to Cholkwa, she could see a resemblance. Hah! The boy would be loved by many, when he was a little older!

"I have introduced Cholkwa to his son," Ettin Taiin said to his mother.

Cholkwa stood and made a gesture of greeting. His gaze met Dapple's briefly, then passed on as if she were a stranger. "What a surprise, Hattali! When I left the cave, running as quickly as possible, I did not know the woman was likely to produce a child."

"You should have come to us, as soon as you escaped," the matriarch said. "If we'd known what the robbers were doing, we would have dealt with them years ago. Do you know this young woman?"

"She is Helwar Ahl, the daughter of a family that's dear to me. A good young person, though Taiin tells me she has some crazy idea of becoming an actor."

"I told you that!" cried Dapple.

"I told you it was impossible. My life is dangerous and disreputable, Ahl. No woman should lead it." He glanced toward the matriarch. "My stay with the robbers occurred during my first trip south. I didn't know your family or much of anyone. After I escaped, I fled to the coast and took the first ship I could find going north. Hah! I was frightened and full of self-disgust! It was several years before I came south again. By then I had convinced myself that the woman could not have been pregnant. I half-believed the story was a dream, caused by a southern fever. How could I think that such people were possible and real?"

"I am," said the boy. "We are."

"Think of the men who have died because you did not tell your story," the matriarch said to Cholkwa. "Think of the children who have been raised by criminals. How can they possibly turn out well? What kind of person would turn away from children in such a situation?"

Cholkwa was silent for a moment, then said, "I have no excuse for my behavior. I did what I did."

"Remember that he makes his living as a comic actor," said the Ettin captain. "How can we judge a man who spends his time portraying small animals with large sexual organs? Let's put these lost-past happenings off to the side. We have enough problems in the present."

"This is true," said the matriarch. "For one thing, I need a chair."

"I'll tend to that," said Cholkwa, and hurried off.

The captain, still lounging comfortably on the wall, glanced at his mother. "Have you decided how to deal with the robbers?"

The old woman groaned, leaning on her staff and looking morose. "You will have to kill the men and we will have to adopt the women and children, though I do not look forward to having females like these in our houses."

"This is a relief! I thought, knowing your opinion of the robber women, that you might ask me to kill them."

"Would you do it?"

"If you told me to, yes."

"And then what?"

"Why ask, Mother? The answer is obvious. I have always wanted to be famous, not infamous. If I had to do something so dishonorable, there would be no alternative left except suicide."

"This is what I expected," the matriarch said. "Listening to Helwar Ahl's story, I asked myself, 'What is worse? Taiin's death or a house full of unruly women?' No one should have to make such a decision! But I have made it, and I will endure the consequences."

"Be more cheerful! If you spread the women out among many houses, they may not be much of an aggravation."

"We'll see. But I'm glad to know that you are an honorable man, Taiin, though it means your old mother will suffer."

"Think of the pleasure you'll be able to take in my continued survival," the captain said. "Not every mother of your age has a living son, especially one with my excellent moral qualities."

What a fine pair they were, thought Dapple. She could see them in a play: the fierce soldier and his indomitable parent, full of love and admiration for each other. In a hero play, of course, the captain would die and the matriarch mourn.

—What a sight she would be, alone on a stage, standing over the captain's body!

Women came onto the terrace with chairs and lanterns. The matriarch settled herself. "Bring food!"

"Now?" asked a middle-aged woman. "When you are with company?"

"Bring food for them as well," said the matriarch.

"Mother!" said the captain.

"I'm too old and hungry to care about that kind of propriety. Manners and morality are not the same."

The rest of them sat down, all looking uneasy. The women brought food. Dapple discovered she was ravenous, as was the boy, she noticed. The two men poured themselves cups of *halin*, but touched no food. The matriarch ate sparingly. It wasn't as bad as Dapple had expected, since no one spoke. This wasn't like a pack of carnivores snarling over their downed prey, or the monsters in old stories who chattered through mouths full of people. This meal was like travelers in a tavern, eating together because they had to, but quickly and in decent silence.

Soon enough they were done. The matriarch took a cup of *halin* from her son. "One problem has been solved. We will adopt the robber women. Cholkwa's behavior will be forgotten. My son is right! We have no ability to judge such a man, and Taiin—I know—wants to keep Cholkwa as a friend."

"This is true," said the captain.

"Only one problem remains: the girl, Helwar Ahl."

"No," said the robber boy. "I also am a problem." He glanced at Cholkwa. "I don't want to stay here and watch these people kill my male relatives. Take me with you! I want to see foreign harbors and ships as large as caves!"

Cholkwa frowned. For a moment there was silence.

Ettin Taiin refilled his cup. "This might be a good idea for two reasons. The boy is likely to suffer from divided loyalties. That's always a problem when one adopts a child as old as he is. And I find him attractive. If he stays here and becomes Ettin, I will be troubled with incestuous thoughts. As much as possible, I try to keep my mind free of disturbing ideas. They cause sleepless nights on campaign and slow reflexes in battle."

"What about Helwar Ahl?" asked Cholkwa, obviously trying to go from one topic to another.

"She can't go with you," the matriarch said. "A woman with an unrelated man! And we are not ocean sailors, nor are the other families in this region, the ones we trust. Take the boy, if he's going to give Taiin perverted ideas; and tell the girl's family, when you get north, that she's here with us. They can send a ship for her."

"I want to be an actor," said Dapple.

"You can't," said Cholkwa.

The matriarch frowned. "There are two things that men cannot do. One is have babies, because it's impossible. The other is harm women and children, because it's wrong. And there are two things that women cannot do: father children and fight in a war. These are absolute prohibitions. All other kinds of behavior may be difficult or disturbing, but they can be done. Granted, I would not want a daughter of mine to become an actor; though it might help make plays more interesting. There are too many penises in comedy, and too many honorable deaths in tragedy. These are male interests. Maybe the world would benefit from a play about real life."

"Surely you don't mean that, mother," the Ettin captain said.

"You're a fine lad and my favorite child, but there is much you don't know. The world does not consist entirely of sex and violence. It isn't only men who take action, and there are kinds of action that do not involve violence or sex."

Dapple said, "I will run away again, I promise."

"From here?" asked the matriarch. "Surely you have learned how dangerous the south can be."

"From anywhere," said Dapple.

Ettin Hattali sipped *halin*. The others watched her. By this time the sky was dark and full of stars, which shed enough light so Dapple could see the old woman's pale face. "Life is made of compromises," Hattali said finally. "I will offer you one. Stay here until your family sends for you, and I will argue for you with them. You are useless for breeding already. A girl who runs off in all directions! This is not a trait any family will want to continue. I'll say as much and argue that the world needs women who speak for women, not just in our houses and the meetings between families, but everywhere, even in plays. Who knows where the current interest in drama will lead? Maybe in time plays will be written down, though this seems unlikely to me. But if they remain at all, in any form, as spoken words or memory, women should have a share in them. Do we want men to speak for us to future generations?

"Cholkwa, who has broken many rules before, can certainly break another one and teach you. If he wants the story of his behavior with the robbers kept quiet, if he wants to keep my son Taiin as a lover, he will cooperate."

Taiin and Cholkwa—lovers? For a moment, Dapple was distracted. This certainly explained why Taiin found the boy attractive.

How could Cholkwa betray his long-time lover, Perig, for a lame man with one eye?

Her family's old friend sighed. "Very well, I'll take the boy. No question I behaved badly when I mated with his mother. To create life without a contract! It was shameful! And you are right that I should have told my story. Then he would have gotten a proper home as a baby. Now he is old enough to love and mourn those criminals. I will not leave him here to watch his family die.

"And I will take your message to the Helwar. But I don't like the idea of teaching the girl to act."

"If you don't do it, I will ask Perig or run off in disguise again."

"Have the young always been this much trouble?" Cholkwa asked.

"Always," said the matriarch in a firm tone.

The captain stood up. "My leg aches, and I want either sleep or sex. Take the boy north, so he doesn't bother me. Take the message, so my mother can be happy. Worry about teaching the girl next year."

The two men left, the boy following. He would be put in a room by himself, the captain said as they walked into the house. "It's been a hard few days for you, Rehv my lad, and I don't think you need to deal with Ettin boys."

Dapple was alone with the matriarch, under a sky patterned with darkness and light.

"He made me angry when he used the word 'can't' for a woman," Ettin Hattali said. "No man has the right to say what women can and cannot do. Hah! I am old, to lose my temper and talk about women acting! But I will keep our agreement, young Ahl. What I said about plays is true. They are fine in their way, but they do not tell my story. So many years, struggling to keep my family going toward the front! The purpose of life is not to have honor and die, it's to have honor and survive and raise the next generation to be honorable. Who says that in any play?"

"I will," said Dapple and felt surprise. Was she actually going to become an actor and write plays? For the first time, her plan seemed possible rather than crazy. Maybe she wouldn't be dragged back to safety. Maybe, with the matriarch on her side, she could have the life she wanted.

The moment an idea becomes solid is the moment when another person reaches out and takes it in her grasp. How frightening this is! The fur on Dapple's shoulders rose. "Do you think Cholkwa will agree to teach me?"

" Most likely, when he gets used to the idea. He's a good man, though foreign, and we have been his hosts many times over. That is a bond—not equal to kinship, perhaps, but strong; and there is also a bond between Cholkwa and Taiin. You may not believe this of my son, but he can persuade."

They sat a while longer under the stars. A meteor fell, then another. Dapple's fur was no longer bristling. Instead, her spirit began to expand.

Two Knots that Tie Off the Story

Cholkwa took the boy, as promised, and Rehv traveled with his father's acting company for several years. But he had no gift for drama and no real liking for travel. Finally, in one harbor town or another, he fell in love. The object of his desire was a glassblower who made floats for fishing nets: good plain work that brought in an adequate income. The two men settled down together. Rehv learned to make glass floats and went on to finer work: *halin* cups, pitchers for beer, bowls for holding sand or flowers.

Sometimes he made figures, cast rather than blown: actors, soldiers, matriarchs, robbers, decorated with gold and silver leaf. The actors' robes were splendid; the weapons held by the soldiers and robbers gleamed; only the matriarchs lacked decoration. They stood on the shelves of his lover's shop—as green as the ocean, as red as blood, as black as obsidian.

Most people knew he had been an actor and had settled down because of love. Only his lover knew the entire story. He had grown up amid desperation and craziness; through luck and his own actions he had managed to achieve an ordinary life.

Dapple's relatives agreed to let her learn acting; and Perig agreed to teach her. She traveled with him for several years, accompanied by one of her male cousins, who ended by becoming an actor himself. In time, she established her own company, composed of women. She was always welcome in Ettin; and Ettin Hattali, who lived to be 110, attended Dapple's performances whenever possible, though toward the end she could no longer see the actors. She could still hear the voices, Hattali told her relatives, and they were the voices of women.

Fantastic and Religious Romances

The official *hwarhath* religion is monotheism. Worship, if that is the right word, is directed toward a female deity who created the universe and sometimes intervenes, though not in any consistent way, in *hwarhath* affairs. Though they are certain the Goddess is female, the *hwarhath* admit that she has many aspects; and these can manifest separately. When the Goddess deals with monsters and violent forces, she is almost always male. At times she becomes a pair of identical twins: one female, the other male. At other times she is a group of five or ten godlings: the Ten Unexpected Women of Atu or the Five Just Warriors. Often she is a shabby old woman who wanders around, asking difficult questions or giving advice that does not always make sense.

All these visions of the Goddess are, most *hwarhath* believe, equally close to (or far from) the truth. "The Great Mother is bigger than our minds." They have no official theology and no sacred texts, though some writings about religion are more valued than others—not for truth, but for good writing and thinking. When religious stories are condemned, it's because they offend against public morality, not because they say something untrue about the Great One.

Like the historical romances in the previous section, these stories—to one extent or another—question traditional ideas. The two origin stories are modern tales that pretend to be old myths, yet give us a new view of the Goddess and people. "The

Small Black Box of Morality" is, frankly, a joke; "Origin Story" is a horrific vision of how the world came into existence, involving heterosexuality, incest, patricide, and cannibalism.

"The Gauze Banner" is a distinctly quirky look at the Goddess. Like much humor, it is designed to upset the way people (*hwarhath* and human) think.

The two remaining stories are faux folk tales centered on two women who refuse to live by the rules of *hwarhath* life. Both are solitary, a clear danger sign. *Hwarhath* women almost always live in the middle of large families. A woman alone is a deeply disturbing idea. In the case of the women here, solitude leads them into unwomanly, unacceptable, and frightening behavior. What can one say about a woman who breeds on her own, without the supervision of older women? And what can we say about a woman who does not care for her child?

The Small Black Box of Morality

After the Goddess created the world, she went off to do other things. In time, it occurred to her that she would like to see how the world was doing. So she hiked up her robe and fastened it, and crossed the universe with long, quick strides, coming at last to the right place.

The world was there, exactly where she had left it. Everything on it flourished, and all the plants and animals behaved as she had intended.

This gave her pleasure, and she decided to spend some time admiring her handiwork. She let down her robe and refastened her belt, and stepped out of the sky.

Back and forth she went, over mountains and valleys, across wide prairies and into the ocean. She examined everything and muttered words of praise and self-congratulation. But finally it occurred to her that something was missing.

"None of my plants and animals have any judgement. They can't discriminate. They don't know right from wrong. My world needs morality," the Goddess said.

She took a handful of darkness and shaped it into a box. Into the box she put the ability to tell right from wrong.

Where did she get this ability? Out of herself.

In some versions of the story, this wisdom came from her mouth. It was a small animal that rested on her tongue, and she spat the animal into the box. In other versions, she put blood into the box or milk from her upper left breast. Still other versions claim that she took out her right eye and pulled morality out of her brain through the empty socket. She put the eye back in, but it never saw as sharply after that.

When people behave in a wrong and unjust fashion and get away with it, they are said to live "on the right side of the Goddess."

Wherever it came from, moral judgement was in the box, and the Goddess set out to find someone who wanted her gift.

She went to the trees first. Of all her creatures, they were the least violent and had the most dignity. But they were happy with their slow lives. "Why should we worry about right and wrong? These ideas sound like the chattering animals who live in our branches. They bother us as much as we are willing to be bothered. Leave us, Great Mother, to what you have already given us: sunlight and starlight and rain."

Next she offered her gift to the little plants that covered the ground. But they were happy with their quick lives. "We grow. We flower. We make seeds and die. Surely that's enough, Great Mother. Don't ask us to think as well."

The Goddess turned to her animals. They were all satisfied with what they had already.

The predators praised the teeth and claws she had given them. The herd animals praised their horns and quick feet. The sneaky animals were happy with being sneaky. The animals who were good at hiding thanked her for this skill. No one wanted judgement. They all said, "You have provided for us splendidly. We aren't greedy. We don't need anything else."

Finally the Goddess came to the first people. There were only two of them, a woman and a man. The woman was named First Woman. The man was named First Man. At that time, they had no tools and no knowledge of fire. They were not yet hunters. Instead, they wandered through the world looking for things to eat that were small and slow: roots in the ground, bugs and worms. It was a miserable life.

All the fine and handsome animals had turned her down, so the Goddess made her offer to First Woman and First Man.

They listened to her. First Man frowned and looked unhappy. As bad as his life was, he was used to it. Morality was an innovation. That bothered him.

But First Woman said, "It's worth a try. As animals go, we aren't much to speak of. We are small and slow and lack the abilities that other animals have. We aren't even attractive. Look at the fur that covers us! It's a very ordinary shade of grey, and it isn't especially thick or soft or glossy. Many animals have coats that are much handsomer.

"The same is true of every part of us. Our teeth can't tear like the teeth of a predator, and they can't grind like the teeth of an animal that grazes. Our nails are blunt. We can't see half as well as that hunting bird in the sky."

"Where? Where?" asked First Man and peered upward.

First Woman ignored him. "Our hearing is not especially keen. Our sense of smell is worse than our sense of hearing.

"If we take this gift that the Great Mother has offered us at least we'll be different. And maybe the Goddess will take an interest in us. Maybe she will help us now and then."

First Man scratched his crotch and picked his nose and tried to think of an argument. But nothing came to him, since he lacked judgement and discrimination.

So the woman held out her hand, and the Great Mother put the small black box of morality on her palm.

The woman opened the box, though it wasn't easy, since she lacked judgement and had never seen a box before. Inside was the ability to think about ideas. She took it out and divided it.

Since she was bigger than the man, she took the piece that was larger and ate it greedily.

First Man turned his piece over and over and sniffed it and touched it with the tip of his tongue.

By this time, the woman had judgement, and she knew that it hadn't been a good idea to take the bigger piece, since it meant that First Man would always have a less good sense of morality. But what's done is done.

"Eat it up," she said and praised the wonderful flavor of the thing and how full she was now and how satisfied she felt. This was not all entirely true, but she knew that people had no future unless both sexes could tell right from wrong.

Finally, the man ate his piece of morality.

"What happens after this ought to be interesting," said the Goddess.

Origin Story

Translator's Introduction:

Like humanity, the *hwarhath* have many origin stories. Most involve a mother goddess. The dominant cultures on the *hwarhath* home planet are monotheistic, and almost all believe their deity is female. After all, they argue, there are animal species that are entirely female and reproduce by parthenogenesis. But no known animal species is entirely male, nor can any male animal reproduce alone. If the universe reflects its creator, as most creations do, then a male originator of life seems unlikely.

Is it possible to believe in an asexual creator? Yes, and the members of a few small sects do. But most *hwarhath* find the idea as disturbing as the idea of a male creator. A god like a microbe that buds or splits apart? Surely this concept lacks dignity!

In spite of these firmly held and well-reasoned ideas about creation, there are anomalous myths. The one that follows is from the *hwarhath* Fifth Continent, the most isolated and peculiar region on the home planet. In it the world does not begin with the considered actions of a wise Mother. Instead, it begins with forbidden love and violence. The story's actors are several in number, their actions are ambiguous, and it would be difficult to call any of them—even the Goddess—wise.

∞ ∞ ∞

In the beginning two things existed. One was a wide, thick sheet of ice. The other was the sun, which shone on the ice daily. At first it was above the horizon for a brief time only, and the ice did not melt. Then, day by day, it rose higher and remained longer, till it never set. Warmed by continuous sunlight, the ice began to melt. Two forms emerged from it. One was a woman, the other a man. Both had fur the blue-white hue of ice, and their eyes—when these opened—were the color of sunlit sky.

The first thing each saw was the other; both were immediately filled with lust. When their bodies were completely free of ice, they fell into each other's arms, groping and kissing, like two male or two female lovers. Then they mated, with no bed except ice.

After that they wandered over the ice sheet, looking for something besides themselves. But there was nothing. Ice was their food and drink. They mated often, and the woman began to swell.

All this time, while they wandered and mated and the woman swelled to an ever-greater size, the land around them was changing, shaped by thaws and freezes, splitting ice and falling snow. In some places, the land rose into ice-mountains. In other places, it sank into valleys and lakes. When the woman was ready to give birth, she stopped in a valley under a cliff of blue-green ice. Ice rubble lay at the cliff's bottom. Ice boulders were scattered through the valley. On the sides of the boulders opposite the wind, drifts of snow formed. The man shaped one of these drifts into a shelter. He crouched beside the woman, not knowing what else to do. Soon she began to groan with pain.

This was the first birth in the world and among the worst. The woman had no female kin to help her. The man had no idea what was happening. When blood gushed from between her legs, he stood up, crying with horror. As ignorant as he was, he knew the red flood was dangerous. But he did not flee.

Soon a baby followed the blood into sunlight. The man picked her up, marveling at her tiny size and loud voice. She began crying at once.

As he looked at his daughter, a second child—a monster—was born. The moment it arrived in light, it attacked the man. In order to free his hands, and maybe to save his daughter, he tossed the child away. She landed on snow and slid into a deep crevasse. There she lay, lodged between two blue walls, while the monster killed her parents and ate them voraciously. Blood ran into the crevasse. The baby drank it silently.

Opinions vary as to why the second child was a monster. Maybe because the parents mated improperly. In a sense, they were sister and brother, both born of ice and heat. In addition, their mating had not been arranged—or approved—by senior relatives. They should have asked the ice for permission. If she did not answer, they should have asked the sun. Instead they gave in to an unnatural lust, and lust consumed them during their long journey across the melting ice.

Their purity—for they were surely pure, having been created from ice and sunlight at the beginning of the world—gave them one perfect child. Their lust and lack of consideration made their second child a monster.

This is only one opinion. There are others. Maybe it's the nature of existence to contain both good and bad, beauty and ugliness. Each calls forth the other. Therefore, the perfect child—who became our Goddess—had as her twin a monster.

There are even more opinions, but two are enough for a story as short as this one.

The monster ate every part of its parents, except for the marrow in their bones, the woman's ovaries and the testicles on the man. It left the bones scattered, not knowing how to break them open or that they contained food. But it buried the ovaries and testicles in snow. Maybe it intended to keep them as a treat later. Then it wandered off and was not seen again for a long time.

The baby grew strong, nourished by her parents' blood. Finally she was able to crawl out of the crevasse. She found her parents' bones scattered across the valley where they'd died. Being magical, she was able to crack the bones and suck out the marrow. This gave her more strength, and she grew to full size.

Imagine her a thick, tall woman, her fur streaked various shades of brown by the blood that had fallen on her in the crevasse. Her eyes are deep orange, the color of the sun when it rises and sets. Her teeth are ice-white.

By taking her parents' blood and flesh into her body, she learned their story. She knew they had been murdered by her twin, and she knew where their sexual organs were hidden. She dug the organs up. They were hard as stone, a material that did not yet exist. Holding the organs in her hands, the Goddess had an idea. She found some pieces of sinew that her twin had not eaten; these she made into a sling. Then she gathered her parents' split bones. The long ones became spears. The short ones became knives. The pieces that were too small to be knives, she formed into a basket, held together by sinew. She used this to carry her parents' organs, which were too cold to carry in her hands. Finally, she set out to find the monster.

In time she saw it in the distance: a great, hulking, spiny, ugly beast. She came on it from behind, seeing first its twitching tail, then its bony hindquarters, then its forequarters and neck and narrow head. Its long snout was snuffling over the ice, trying to find something—anything—as delicious as its parents.

"Greetings, Twin," the Goddess said and drove a bone spear into the monster's side. With a roar, it turned and attacked her. They fought for ten days, till the Goddess was steaming blood from many wounds, and numerous spears and knives stuck out of the monster. Finally, as the tenth day ended, the Goddess used her last weapon: the sinew sling. Her father's first testicle hit the monster in the rump, and it staggered. The second testicle hit the monster's side, and her twin stumbled to its knees. Her mother's first ovary hit the monster's shoulder. It fell over. The second ovary hit the monster's skull. It died.

The Goddess gave a yell of triumph. Then she gathered snow to staunch her many wounds. When the bleeding stopped, she returned to the monster and used its body to build the world we know.

The bony back became mountains. The wide, soft belly became the world's plains and valleys. The monster's hair became vegetation. Its scales became rocks and boulders.

She kept the sun to light her world, but turned most of the ice into water. It became the ocean, rivers, and lakes, though some of it remains in its original state.

When the world was complete, she put her parents' sexual organs between her thighs and held them there, till they were soft and warm. Then, when they were completely malleable, she used them to form all the world's creatures, including people.

How was she able to imagine a world like this one, when all she had experienced was ice and sunlight and blood? There is no good answer to this question. Maybe the world was somehow implicit in the monster's body and her parents' organs. Maybe the Goddess could see into the future. Her abilities are many and not well understood. If so, she was able to use the world-that-came-into-existence as a model for the world-not-yet-made; and we, living and acting now, may be shaping the world at its moment of origin.

In any case, when she was done, everything was used up, except for the sinew sling. She made it into a bracelet, which she wore on her dominant arm. This is how our oldest statues show her: a broad woman garbed only in her own fur, with no ornament except a narrow bracelet on her left arm or wrist.

THE GAUZE BANNER

Translator's Note:

The following purports to be a modern-day version of an ancient myth. There is no question that this version of the story is modern. (Notice the references to galaxies, singularities, holograms and the people of Dirt.) However, no earlier version can be found. The story belongs to the category of lying or invented myths.

The *hwarhath* do not consider such myths to be blasphemous or heretical. In their opinion, the mind of the Goddess is unknowable and her behavior often impossible to explain. Therefore, any story or explanation may (or may not) be true.

Though the *hwarhath* do not ban stories for religious reasons, they believe art should be decent and lead people in the direction of good behavior. Their various governments are perfectly willing to ban stories that seem destructive of public morality.

Beyond question, "The Gauze Banner" is a candidate for censorship. It contains at least three elements an ordinary *hwarhath* reader would find offensive or disturbing: (1) the ambiguous gender of the Goddess; (2) the explicit description of her as a hermaphrodite, which can only be described as shocking, at least to a *hwarhath*; and (3) the argument that the Goddess is not responsible for *hwarhath* sexual mores and therefore, implicitly, that *hwarhath* sexual mores are arbitrary.

The story has not been banned so far, probably because it came out in a small edition done in ink on paper and distributed via a not-entirely-hidden network of avant gardists, free thinkers, and people with odd sexual interests. In recent years *hwarhath* official society has ignored this kind of underground, so long as the people involved keep quiet and out of sight. No electronic version of the story has appeared, nor is one likely to. In all likelihood, this translation will reach more readers than the original, and "The Gauze Banner" will be better known on Earth than on its native planet.

∞ ∞ ∞

This story takes place early in the era called the Unravelling, before the formation of the system of alliances that led, centuries later, to a world government.

As yet there were no groups of families tied firmly together, no great armies, no leaders such as Eh Manhata, known forever as the Bloody Sword of Eh. There were only separate lineages, none large, all more or less equal, quarreling and skirmishing on a wide, flat, dusty plain.

Into this age of petty violence the Goddess came one morning in early summer, stepping out of a clear blue sky. The moment she landed on the plain, she turned into an old woman dressed in rags, carrying a heavy bundle. She didn't come in response to the Unravelling, which she probably had not noticed, but out of curiosity, to see what was happening in this particular world. As to why she chose to become a beggar woman, who can say?

Those who have true power need not worry about the appearance of power. She who wears the stars as ornaments need not put on jewels less bright.

In any case, she trudged along a road. On every side of her was the wide treeless plain. A light wind blew up dust, which covered her, turning her grey fur white. Her mouth was soon dry. Her old bones soon ached. Hah! How interesting, the Goddess thought, and looked at the bugs, which buzzed and hopped in the vegetation beside the road. At last she came to a bottle tree, standing alone. Its fat trunk and short branches cast barely enough shade for the man who rested there, along with his worn old riding *tsin*.

The man's name was Hai Tsa. He came from a small lineage in the south. His older brothers were quarrelsome bullies who envied Tsa because he was their mother's favorite, and for good reason. He was handsome, mannerly, decent, and generous, the kind of son every mother dreams of.

Once he was grown up, Tsa—like all other boys—moved from the world of women into the world of men, and his brothers did everything they could to make him miserable. He endured their behavior as long as he could, thinking of his mother. Finally the situation became impossible to endure. Hai Tsa left home and went looking for work on the plain. There was less in those days than later, in Eh Manhata's time, but a few of the quarreling lineages were willing to hire loose soldiers. Hai Tsa became a mercenary. When he met the Goddess, he was traveling to a new job.

The moment he saw the Goddess, emerging out of a haze of heat and dust, Hai Tsa stood. He tugged at his sword, making sure it would move freely if he needed it, and shaded his eyes against the white noon glare.

Soon it was evident who was coming: a bone-thin, ragged old woman. Hah! That such a one was wandering, instead of being safe at home! He walked out to meet her. The Goddess, bent under her bundle, gazed up at him with bleary eyes.

"Good day, great-aunt," the man said courteously. "Can I help you with your bundle?"

"How do I know you won't steal it?"

"I'm poor, but not that poor; and if I wanted to steal from you, I could do it."

This was, of course, not true, but the man didn't realize he was speaking to the Maker of the Universe.

The Goddess refused to let go of her bundle. Who knows what may have been in it? Hai Tsa, acquiescing, escorted her into the shadow of the tree. "Settle yourself," he told the old woman. "Be comfortable." He pulled a water bag off his *tsin* and held it out to her. The Goddess drank messily, water dripping off her chin.

The plain is dry, especially in summer, and water has always been precious there, but Hai Tsa did not complain. His manners were excellent!

When she finished drinking, he asked if she wanted to eat. Not at the moment, she replied. He moved the *tsin*, so she would have room, and settled himself at the edge of the bottle tree's shadow. Now the Goddess noticed how lovely this man was, his fur as grey as steel, his eyes the pale yellow of petrified resin. Her withered old body responded to his beauty and kindness. Hah! She could feel lust between her bony legs and in each of her four thin, hanging breasts. But she could tell that he was a self-respecting man, who would never have sex with a woman, unless his female relatives told him to fulfill a mating contract; and she, in her present form, was past the age for breeding. Still, he was beautiful to look at, his fur dappled with sunlight; and she, being the Goddess, did not need to pay attention to decency or right behavior.

They remained under the bottle tree until midday was past, then he lifted the old woman and her bundle onto his *tsin* and led the animal along the road. In this manner they traveled through the long afternoon. The Goddess fell more and more in love.

When evening came the two of them made camp. The sky darkened. Stars appeared and then the pale shining band of light that is called the Banner of the Goddess. They ate food from the man's supplies. Tired from his long walk, he went to sleep. Gathering her bundle, she stepped into the sky.

There she changed her appearance, becoming a man of extraordinary beauty. Her rags became armor. Her bundle became a well-fed, glossy *tsin*. That done, she grabbed a spiral galaxy. In her hand it became a mirror rimmed with light. She admired her new face, which was broad and dark with eyes the color of a summer sky and large, handsome ears. Excellent! the Goddess thought. No man could resist her now. She returned the galaxy to the place she'd found it and led her new animal onto the plain.

Being the Goddess, she was not bothered by such things as coincidence; but she knew that some of her creatures were. Hai Tsa might be suspicious if he woke in the morning and found his ancient female traveling companion had been replaced with a beautiful young man. Therefore, she went ahead of him to the war camp that was his destination. The war leader hired her. When Hai Tsa arrived, there she was among his new comrades, like a diamond among pebbles. Of course, he fell in love.

Because she was not interested in quarrels at the moment, she made sure the other men did not notice her beauty. Hai Tsa had no rivals. In almost no time, they were sharing the same tent.

Now Tsa discovered something unusual about his new lover. Though the man had ordinary looking genitalia, he did not have erections. An old injury, the Goddess explained. It no longer bothered her; and she had learned other ways to give and gain pleasure. Hai Tsa looked dubious. She placed her hand on his erection. "This is a fine thing you have; and I'm sure you are proud of it, as no doubt you ought to be. A penis is one of the more entertaining objects the Goddess has devised. But her universe is rich. She did not stint. Nor does she lack imagination. Most of the time, she has provided us with more than one way to do a job or reach a destination."

If you are thinking the Goddess is vain, maybe so. Though this speech might be a joke. The Goddess is famous for her sense of humor.

In any case, the two of them made love. Her hands were skillful and her tongue was in no way short of miraculous. Hai Tsa had never enjoyed a partner more. They fell asleep tangled together, the air around them reeking of satisfied desire.

Why had the Goddess, who can do anything, failed to give herself a working penis? Maybe as a joke or to make this romance more interesting. Or maybe because she had fallen in love with Hai Tsa while in the shape of a woman. In order to win him, she had to become male, but it's possible that she was not entirely happy with this transformation.

Whatever her reason, her decision caused no trouble. As she had discerned, Hai Tsa was proud of his male member, which was large and capable. It didn't bother him that he was the partner entering rather than the partner being entered, once he was sure the Goddess was equally comfortable. Initially, he'd been afraid that his lover would turn out to be touchy and difficult about her—or rather his—incapacity. In addition, a natural feeling of sympathy made him unhappy and even queasy, when he thought of what the other man could not do.

The Goddess turned her attention to another problem now. She was a warrior, and the band she had joined was preparing for war. But she had no interest in killing any of the beings she had created. Maybe her lack of interest in violence was due to the incomplete nature of her male guise, or maybe it was simply that she was in the mood for making love rather than war. In any case, she had to come up with an excuse for not killing men.

She thought for several days as the camp packed. Nothing occurred to her. Finally, on the last evening before they were due to leave, their leader complained that he had no proper flag. The Goddess was leaning against her lover, gazing up at the starry sky. Hah! she thought.

The next morning she rose before the others. As soon as the last star faded from sight, she reached up and grasped her banner, pulling it from the sky. In her hands, it became a flag of fine white gauze that had even now—in the bright light of sunrise—a glow of its own. How lovely, the Goddess thought as she folded the material. What excellent work!

She took the banner to the leader of their band and offered to become his standard bearer.

"Isn't that an unlucky color?" he asked. "Bones are white."

"And snow," the Goddess said in agreement. "Also clouds, waterfalls, the foam on the ocean, sunlight at certain times of day and many stars. Are these things unlucky or ominous? In any case, this isn't pure white." She unfolded the banner. The leader could see the material was full of dim gleams and sparkles: blue, red, orange, and yellow.

"I assure you, it will bring good luck," the Goddess said.

Something about her made the leader wonder if this was an ordinary warrior. He agreed to use the flag.

You may wonder why the Goddess decided to pull her banner from the sky. After all, there is no limit to her power: she could have turned anything into a flag or made a flag out of nothing. But if you look at her universe, you will see that most of her work is slap-dash. As a rule, she makes do with whatever is close at hand, and changes things as little as possible. Does this mean she's lazy or lacks imagination? Who can say? She is the Goddess.

For the rest of the summer she rode with the war band. When they fought, she was the standard bearer. She never had to defend the flag she carried. Something about it kept enemies at a distance, or maybe it was her. In battle, her extraordinary beauty became visible to everyone. No one wanted to strike a man whose dark fur seemed as lovely as night, whose armor glittered in an uncanny fashion, whose banner—held aloft and flying in the wind—was like a river of stars flowing.

When the fighting ended, her appearance became ordinary again. The various warriors remembered what they'd seen only dimly. The man must be touched by battle-frenzy, they decided. Rage and fear transformed some people in such a way.

After a while the Goddess became tired of pulling her banner out of the sky every morning and putting it back every evening before dark. There had to be a better method. She made a box: flat, square, and covered with a black lacquer that seemed as deep as space. In modern times, we would call the box a teleportation machine or a singularity or some other thing that twists the ordinary rules of physics and fiction. In those days it was merely magic.

Every morning at sunrise, the Goddess opened the box and found the banner neatly folded. Every evening she made sure the banner was in the box. When the sky turned dark, there the banner was, shining overhead. A neat trick, the Goddess thought.

Summer became autumn, though the autumn rains held off; and the plain was still dry enough for war. The Goddess continued to enjoy making love with Hai Tsa, but she was beginning to wonder how the rest of her universe was doing. She was especially curious about a world named Dirt, inhabited by almost hairless people with perverse habits, though they were (she had to admit) ingenious, especially when it came to getting into trouble.

She decided to visit Dirt, leaving her present body behind. As lovely as it was, it would be conspicuous among the hairless people of Dirt.

She told Hai Tsa she was going to sleep. "I don't know for how long. Don't worry about me. I'll be fine. Leave me alone. Don't try to wake me, unless a serious emergency comes forward; and don't touch my banner or the box that contains it, no matter what dangers come into view."

Hai Tsa agreed to all this. The Goddess went off, leaving her body apparently asleep. What happened on the world of Dirt is not part of this story, which is going to stay with Hai Tsa and his comrades.

After the Goddess had been asleep for several days, they began to discuss her, or rather him. Surely this man was a magician or diviner. The white banner was unusual; so was the sleep into which their companion had withdrawn. Hai Tsa listened and thought. According to rumor, magicians and diviners had unusual sexual habits. Some were insatiable and had huge organs, often oddly shaped. These were usually magicians rather than diviners. More often the behavior of holy people went in the opposite direction. They were moderate in their sexual behavior or entirely abstinent. Rather than exaggerated sexual characteristics, they had characteristics that seemed between the sexes: flat chests for the women, small genitals for the men. So this story tells us, though not all stories agree.

Hai Tsa's lover was not abstinent. Nor could he be called moderate. But surely impotence was a sign of something. Hai Tsa felt doubtful and uneasy. To have a magician for a partner! This had to be dangerous! His mother would not approve.

Nothing more happened for a while. The Goddess continued to sleep. Her comrades continued to gossip. Then a scout came in with disturbing news.

Another band, much larger and belonging to a hostile lineage, was coming toward them. They would have to fight.

"We need the banner," the war leader said to Hai Tsa. "Wake your lover."

He tried. Maybe he was timid, or maybe the Goddess was preoccupied. In any case, he could not rouse her.

"Open the box," the war leader said.

Hai Tsa tried to argue, but the leader would not listen. Their situation was perilous. The banner was clearly magical. If they did not have it, they would be destroyed.

Finally Hai Tsa capitulated and opened the box. The banner lay inside, shining like a starry night.

"You will be my standard bearer," the war leader said.

Reluctantly, Tsa lifted the banner. The wind took it at once, extending the gauzy fabric, undoing every fold. The morning sunlight made it glitter, or maybe it glittered by itself.

The band rode out, Hai Tsa beside the leader.

The battle was at the ford of a river, wide and summer-shallow. The enemy war bands met in water, between low banks overgrown with rust-brown vegetation. Swords flashed in the sunlight. Men shouted. *Tsina* screamed. The white banner shone as usual, but this time the opposing soldiers were not afraid of the warrior who carried the banner. Hai Tsa had to defend himself, drawing his weapon.

Blood spurted. Soldiers fell. *Tsina* reared, lunged, and turned. At last the banner made of gauze went down, its pole hacked through. Hai Tsa leaped into the bloody river water and pulled the fabric—drenched, torn and discolored—out from under a *tsin.* The leader of his band protected Tsa as he regained his saddle.

Something of his partner's frenzy came into Hai Tsa then. The sodden banner over his knees, he rode against the enemy, yelling like a demon or a ghost. His comrades followed. Their opponents were driven back, out of the bloody river, onto the dusty plain. So the battle was won, while Hai Tsa's lover slept.

Tsa and his comrades returned to their camp late in the afternoon, leaving guards at the river to make sure their opponents did not return. As night came on, Hai Tsa examined the banner, trying to think of a way to repair it. But the delicate material was in tatters, and blood had dimmed its glow. How was he going to explain this to the sleeping magician?

Close by him a fire burned. Around it his weary comrades cleaned their armor. At last, when Hai Tsa had given up hope of repairing the banner, one of the other soldiers glanced up. The man cried out, his voice sharp with fear: the sky was cloudless, but no stars shone there.

The world of Dirt has a companion that lights its sky at night, but the world of the *hwarhath* is moonless. Without their home galaxy, the night sky was black. Of course the man shouted in fear, and so did his comrades, when they realized what had happened.

Hai Tsa looked at the banner in his hands. Dirty as it was, he could see that the fabric gleamed dimly; and there were sparkles in it, dull and almost colorless, which reminded him of stars seen through haze.

What a magician! This person, his lover, had taken the Banner of the Goddess out of the sky and made it into a battle flag. Now they, through their folly, had ruined the banner and turned the night sky black.

He told his comrades his suspicions. They examined the torn banner, observing the dim glow and the dull sparkles. Yes, indeed. This looked like the band of light which made night tolerable.

"We have to do something," the war leader said.

"Kill the magician," suggested one of the soldiers. "Otherwise, he's likely to kill us when he wakes."

"No," said Hai Tsa.

But his comrades hurried to the tent where his lover slept. They pulled back the flap and looked in: the Goddess was still fast asleep, a lamp hanging from the pole above her, lighting her dark body, naked except for a blanket, which she'd mostly thrown off. Something made them reluctant to go any farther, though she looked like an ordinary man at the moment. The leader dropped the tent flap and led his comrades back to the fire.

"You are the standard bearer," he said to Hai Tsa. "And the magician is your lover. This is your responsibility. Put that thing back in the sky."

"How can I?" Tsa asked.

"Throw it," suggested a soldier.

The leader nodded in agreement. Hai Tsa balled up the fabric, trying to make it into something that could be thrown, and tossed it up, knowing that this was impossible. He wasn't magical. The banner wasn't going to make it into the sky.

As soon as the ball of fabric left his hands, a gust of wind caught it. The ball unfolded, becoming a banner once again, and floated on the mild early-autumn wind, just out of Hai Tsa's reach.

"Jump! Grab!" the leader cried.

Everyone obeyed, but no one could reach the banner. Carried by the wind, it drifted over the soldiers' fire. A draft of hot air took hold of it. The gossamer fabric twisted and fluttered, dipping toward the fire. The soldiers cried out in horror. The banner burst into flame. For a moment the fire was too brilliant to look at. Then the banner was gone.

Hah! The despair the soldiers felt! Nothing remained of their home galaxy except tiny ashes floating in the wind, though their world was somehow spared, as was their sun.

How did this happen? Our world and sun are part of the galaxy, as everyone now knows. They should have been consumed along with everything else. But the Goddess can do anything, and this is only a story.

"You have certainly made a mess," the leader said to Hai Tsa.

"I did what you asked."

"I didn't ask you to burn the Banner of the Goddess."

"Shouldn't we make another effort to kill the magician?" asked a soldier.

Everyone went back to the tent, but no one could manage to go in.

"We could burn the tent," said the soldier who was most intent on killing the Goddess.

"This person has clearly surrounded himself with magical protections," the leader said. "We aren't likely to be able to get through them. The best thing to do is leave. But someone has to stay behind and explain what happened. You, Hai Tsa. The magician is your lover. Maybe he'll forgive you."

"Hai Tsa will run as soon as we're gone," another soldier said.

"We'll chain him," said the leader.

The *hwarhath* have never kept prisoners for long. But sometimes in the old days it was necessary to keep enemy soldiers safe until they could be questioned. In addition, there have always been men who find it amusing to cause other men humiliation and pain, and such entertainment requires prisoners who are— for the moment—alive. Because of this, most war bands used to carry chains.

They had a smith, a fine craftsman, who fastened a circle of iron around one of Hai Tsa's ankles, then attached a chain that ended in a long spike. This the smith drove deep into a tree at the edge of camp. The chain was long enough so Tsa could move around and relieve himself on the far side of the tree. He would not have to sit next to his own excrement. His comrades meant no cruelty.

Dawn came. The soldiers struck camp. Hai Tsa watched, sitting under the tree, which was a *halawa*. He recognized the scent.

They worked quickly and were done a little after sunrise. The leader came over to Hai Tsa's tree, bringing a bag of water and a loaf of bread. He laid them down.

"We can't leave any tool or weapon," he said. "You might be able to use them to get free."

"What if a wild animal comes?"

"You'll have to deal with that situation as best you can. I have nothing against you, Tsa. But maybe if the magician has you, he won't come after the rest of us; and maybe he'll forgive you, since you have been lovers."

"Forgive me for destroying his banner and turning the night sky black? Does that seem likely?"

"No," said the leader.

The war band mounted and rode off in silence. Nothing remained of the camp except the magician's tent and Hai Tsa under his tree.

As the day brightened, he glanced up and saw the tree had fruit, dark red in color, which meant it was almost ripe. Tsa stood and grabbed, but the fruit was out of reach. Fortunately for him the tree was diseased. Great lumps of some malign growth dotted the trunk. Even wearing a chain, he was able to use the lumps as a ladder. Climbing up to the lowest branches, he gathered several pieces of fruit.

Back on the ground, he tried one. It was in exactly the condition he liked: the flesh hard, but also juicy, the flavor an intermingling of sweet and sour. He ate the fruit with enjoyment, drank water and examined his chain. It was well made; Hai Tsa could not think of any way to escape from it.

What should he hope for? His lover to awake? Or other soldiers to come, who might free him, but were more likely to kill him?

He tore off a piece of bread and chewed it, noticing how hard and tough it was. What had he done to deserve this fate? Chained to a tree in the middle of nowhere, waiting for something—a soldier or animal or magician—to end his life.

Maybe he had picked the wrong lover, or obeyed an order he should have refused to obey. Maybe it had been a bad decision to leave home. A man is always best off when he has senior relatives to tell him what to do. Though his senior relatives, his brothers, were malicious bullies.

None of this seemed sufficient. Maybe he hadn't taken a single bad step, but rather a series, which led finally to this tree. Or maybe there was no reason or explanation for what had happened.

Night came, the sky as black as tar. In the absence of a campfire, he could see a few blurry lights, which were other galaxies, though he didn't know this. He was afraid to stay on the ground and climbed the tree trunk, settling into a crotch.

After a while, something came to the bottom of his tree. Hai Tsa heard it snuffling and scratching, then felt a tug on his chain. The animal was chewing on the iron links. Tsa braced himself.

The chewing kept up for some time, and there were several more tugs. One almost pulled him out of the tree. Finally the creature, whatever it was, went off toward his lover's tent. He could tell this by the sound. All at once, Hai Tsa became worried. His comrades hadn't made a serious attempt to test the magician's spells of protection. Would they be enough? Should he care? He remembered how the magician looked, lying asleep, as lovely as always.

Would it make his situation any worse if he warned the man? Or managed to distract the animal? Hai Tsa shouted and swung his leg, making his chain rattle. The animal ignored him. He shouted again and rattled his chain more fiercely. Maybe he moved too vigorously in doing this: he felt himself begin to slip and grabbed for a branch, slipped farther and found himself hanging under the branch. For a moment or two he swung back and forth in darkness. Then he fell, landing on his feet. His water bag came after him and brushed his shoulder before it hit the plain with a squelching, leathery sound.

The animal, only a short distance away, paused and produced an interrogatory whine. Hai Tsa grabbed up the water bag. With his other hand, he gathered a length of chain, thanking the Goddess that his comrades had been so generous in the matter of extra links. He peered into the darkness, trying to see the beast; but it was sound that told him that the animal had turned and was coming toward him, snuffling and breathing heavily. Was it old? Or did it have a bad infection of the nose and throat? He waited till the heavy breathing had almost reached him, then swung the chain out and down with all his strength. It hit. The animal roared with pain, and Hai Tsa thrust his water bag toward the roar. Thinking it had found its enemy, the animal seized the bag in its jaws. At the same moment Hai Tsa gave a shove, pushing the bag as far as he could into the creature's mouth. There was a stifled choking noise. He had a sense that the animal had stopped, uncertain.

Before it had time to recover from its surprise, he wrapped his length of chain around the creature's neck, then shifted position, so the animal was between him and the tree. As soon as this was done, he pulled the chain taut. The beast struggled fiercely, but the chain was held on one side by Hai Tsa, pulling with all his weight, and on the other side by the long spike, which Tsa's comrade the smith had driven into the tree. Neither end gave. The beast, in the middle, could not free itself. Nor could it reach Tsa.

The struggling grew weaker. The animal went limp. Hai Tsa continued to pull, though by this time he was shaking and breathing as heavily as the animal had been before. Finally he let go of the chain and fell to his knees, too weak to stand. After he had rested for a while, he crawled to the animal, listening before he risked a touch.

The body was motionless. No breath moved the chest. The mouth was still stuffed full of his water bag, and it didn't seem likely any air could go in or out. He touched the creature's nose and felt no exhalation. He pressed the throat. There was no pulse.

Hah! The monster was dead! He was still alive!

He tugged at his water bag, managing finally to pull it from the animal's mouth. Sharp teeth had gone through the leather.

Most of the water had leaked away. He drank what remained, then took his chain from around the animal's neck and crawled back to his tree. There he sat till dawn, drifting in and out of sleep.

When the sun came up, he looked at the animal. It was a rangy quadruped covered with rough, yellow fur: a wild *sul*. The four legs ended in long claws. The large head had a mouth well provided with teeth. Hai Tsa felt a certain satisfaction, though the corpse would soon begin to stink, drawing bugs and carrion birds. Too bad no one would know about this battle.

As mentioned before, the Goddess has no problem with coincidences. At just that moment, she walked out of her tent.

It wasn't his peril that brought her or a desire to learn about his battle with the *sul*. Instead, she came to find out what had happened to her banner. Like the home world of the *hwarhath*, Dirt had survived the holocaust, along with its primary. But like the home world of the *hwarhath*, it had lost its stars. The Goddess, looking up at a suddenly dark night sky, remembered that she'd left her banner in the care of certain soldiers far away. She returned to her *hwarhath* body, rose, pulled on a robe and went outside.

As is well known, the Goddess combines both male and female traits, but she seems to prefer the female, and when she appears to diviners, she is usually a woman. Maybe she had forgotten this particular body was supposed to be male, or maybe she was preoccupied, wondering what had happened to her banner. In any case, she had reverted to the form she preferred. Although her body remained dark and powerful and lovely, it was now clearly female.

"You are a woman," Hai Tsa said.

"Yes."

The last couple of days had been difficult for Hai Tsa. Much of what happened was impossible to understand. But now he found a problem that made sense. Destroying a galaxy was beyond his comprehension. How could he feel shame about something so vast? Having sex with a woman, on the other hand, was a crime of reasonable size. It fit in his mind, and he was able to feel all the proper shame, grief, and self-hatred. Hai Tsa curled up, his arms around his knees, and groaned.

"If I were you, I'd worry more about what you've done with my banner," the Goddess said.

He ignored her, busy with self-loathing.

At this point, she became angry. "Look up," she told him and pulled her robe open.

There was no way to ignore that tone of voice. Tsa lifted his head and saw four breasts, covered with fur and tipped with dark nipples. The two upper nipples oozed milk, which gleamed in the light of the rising sun. Horrified, the man glanced down and saw the Goddess's penis, which was erect and as thick (it seemed to him) as a war club. A second kind of liquid shone at the tip. Beneath the penis hung the Goddess's scrotum, like a bag well-packed for a long journey. Hai Tsa covered his eyes.

"If you want to have rules about who you can and can't have sex with, I don't mind. The rules are not something I would have thought up, but they're interesting and seem to work. At least you get into less trouble than those people on Dirt. But understand, your rules are not my rules, and they do not apply to me.

"Now, take your silly hand from in front of your silly eyes and tell me what you've done with all my stars."

"Could you close the robe?" he asked timidly.

She laughed and changed her body, her full breasts sinking until they were flat. Her genitals shrank. Her penis became flaccid. She was Hai Tsa's lover once again, entirely male.

Tsa straightened up and shivered.

"Now," the Goddess said. "Tell me what's happened. I left you in good condition, and I return to find you chained to a tree with a dead *sul* in front of you, and my banner missing. You seem to have accomplished a lot. But first—" She touched the *sul*. It groaned and got up on four feet. "Be off," the Goddess told the animal. "I'm not in the mood to look at your ugly body." The *sul* made a whining noise, that was either a thank you or an apology, and loped onto the plain. The Goddess spread her robe on the ground under the tree and settled there, next to Hai Tsa. Ripe fruit fell around her. Reaching out a hand, she touched his chain. The links fell apart. She gathered two pieces of fruit and offered one to him.

It was sweeter and softer than he liked, but one can't complain to the Maker of the Universe. He ate the fruit, while telling her about the fate of the banner.

"What a stupid group of men," she said. "I told you to stay away from the box. I told you to keep your hands off the banner."

"We needed it, and we couldn't wake you."

"You should have come up with some other way out of your problem."

"That's obvious now," Hai Tsa said. "But you never told us you were the Goddess; and you never told us that the banner contained all the stars in the sky."

"I can't go around explaining everything to everyone. People usually don't understand me, anyway. I could tell you stories about those people on Dirt!" She stood up and stretched. "I suppose I'd better recreate the banner."

"You can?"

The Goddess gave him a look. "Of course."

After that she examined the remains of the war band's fire. Hai Tsa watched as she crouched and poked, picking up handfuls of ash and sorting through them. Finally, she rose, holding something between two fingers. "This might do." She held the thing up and blew on it, so it floated into air.

The plain vanished, and they were in a forest of huge trees.

The Goddess looked vexed. "I thought it was ash from the banner, but it's ash from a piece of wood."

The forest vanished. They were back on the plain. Hai Tsa felt dizzy.

The Goddess crouched and continued searching through the remains of the fire. Once again she found something, held it up, and blew on it. Once again ash floated into air. This time it glowed brightly, and the glow spread into a network of shining filaments. The Goddess looked up, her expression pleased. The filaments multiplied and interwove; the network lengthened and widened. A mild wind was blowing, and the edges of the network fluttered, but it stayed in place above its maker. By now the glow had almost vanished, except for an occasional gleam or sparkle; the network seemed made of thread rather than of light; and it was thick enough to cast a shadow over the Goddess.

She continued to watch with pleasure. Hai Tsa realized she was like his old comrade the smith. Both loved making.

The weaving ended. The network had become a banner, pale and sparkling. The Goddess held out her hands. The banner floated down. She gathered it into a ball and tossed it into the sky. It did not return.

"Did you have to remake it that way?" Hai Tsa asked.

"No," the Goddess said. "But if I'd made it out of nothing, it would not have been exactly the same, and people—here and on Dirt and in other places—would have noticed. The ash contained a memory of the banner, recorded in the manner of a hologram. By examining it, I was able to remake the galaxy as it was before."

Hai Tsa didn't know what a hologram was, of course. But he listened gravely, his head tilted.

The making of the banner must have taken longer than he'd thought. It was sunset now: the wide plain shone with ruddy light. The Goddess took food from her tent. They settled under the *halawa* tree and ate. When she was done, the Goddess said, "We'll wait till dark and make sure the banner looks all right. After that, it seems to me it would be pleasant to make love out here, under my stars."

"You and I?" asked Hai Tsa.

"Who else is present?"

"It can't possibly be decent to have sex with the Maker the Universe."

"You aren't telling me you have a rule about sex with the Goddess? Whatever for? It's a problem that very few people encounter. And I'm beyond rules. I can do whatever I want."

"You may be beyond rules, but I'm not."

The Goddess made an impatient noise.

"Also, you frighten me," Hai Tsa added.

"I have not done a good job with this universe," the Goddess said. "It's full of small-minded people."

They sat without speaking for a while. The sky darkened. The stars came out, and the Banner of the Goddess was visible.

"It looks fine," said Hai Tsa after a moment.

"So it does." The Goddess touched him lightly on the shoulder, and he discovered that he was less frightened than before, also less concerned about religious and moral questions.

He reached over and ran his hand down her front, which remained—thank the Goddess!—flat and male. Her crotch was male as well.

"Can't you do better than this?" Hai Tsa asked, his hand on the Goddess's penis. "If you can fill the sky with stars, why not come up with one little erection?"

She laughed and came up with an erection; and they made love. Afterward, they lay on her robe beneath the *halawa* tree. Stars shone around them.

"I need to go back to this other world," the Goddess said. "The one named Dirt. Do you want to accompany me? I'll have to change your appearance. The people there are almost entirely without fur."

"It sounds ugly," Hai Tsa said.

"You'll get used to it. What else do you have to do? You've lost your job, and if you stay here, you'll lose me as well."

"How long will this last?" Hai Tsa asked.

Being the Goddess, she knew he was asking more than one question. How long will this journey last? How long will we be comrades? How long will we be lovers?

"I make no promises," she told Hai Tsa.

He thought for a while. Lying next to her, he felt safe in a way he hadn't since he was a child with his mother. The feeling was illusory, he knew. The Goddess had no reputation for reliability. Still, it would probably be interesting to go with her; and she was right about his job. It was gone.

"Very well," he said.

She stood, holding out her hand. He took it, and she pulled him into the sky.

THE SEMEN THIEF

There was a woman who is nameless now. She belonged to a small lineage in a remote part of the third continent. The area was troubled by strange behavior and supernatural events, and this may explain what happened to the woman.

Her lineage was defeated in a war. As is customary, the men who belonged to the defeated lineage were killed, and the women and children adopted by their victorious neighbors. But this particular woman refused to join her new family. The ghosts of her dead male relatives haunted her, whispering angry ideas.

She went off by herself into the mountains and lived like an animal. But this wasn't enough to satisfy her. In the dark forest, the ghosts drew closer and became more real. This is how it is with ghosts. We are not haunted by what is good and happy in our dead relatives. After the time for grieving is over, these beneficent aspects or qualities move away from us into whatever country the dead inhabit. At most, they visit us briefly in dreams. But the parts of our relatives that were bad and unhappy—their anger, hunger, malice, pain, the quarrels that were never settled, the longings that were never fulfilled—these are reluctant to leave. If we let them, they will stay in our houses and villages and assume the forms of the people who died, though they are not the dead, but only shadows or vestiges.

The nameless woman sat alone by her fire night after night, and night after night her dead kin came and stood at the edge of the firelight in bloody armor. Their hoarse voices gave her bad advice.

The lineage, which had been destroyed, should be recreated. It was her duty to breed a new family.

How? The woman asked. There were men living in the mountains, outlaws and perverts, who might be willing to mate with someone like her. But these would be bad fathers. She didn't want their traits in her new lineage. No ordinary decent man would father a child unless the women in his lineage had arranged a breeding contract. For this is the way that breeding has always occurred. The decision lies with women, and the agreement is between families rather than individuals.

The ghosts said, "There is a woman living in this area who knows magic and is untroubled by ideas of right behavior. Go to her and ask for help."

"Very well," said the nameless woman, and she went and found the sorceress in question.

This person lived in a cave or deep hole, which the nameless woman entered. At the back was a low fire, and the sorceress crouched there. She was huge, more than twice the size of an ordinary woman, and the cave, though deep, was not large. Her head brushed the ceiling. An unpleasant odor came off her, like meat that is starting to go bad. She wore no clothing, and her skin was entirely bare. She had no fur. Not a hair.

A disgusting spectacle. The nameless woman wanted to turn and flee. But she was held in place by anger and a desire for revenge.

The sorceress lifted her horrible bald head and asked, "What do you want, little one?" Her voice was deep and harsh.

The woman explained her problem: she wanted to recreate her lineage, but she needed fathers who came from good lineages and had good traits, so her children would be strong and intelligent.

The sorceress thought for a while, wrinkling her hairless forehead. Then she said, "I have come up with a plan. First of all, you must disguise yourself as a man. Do you think you can do this?"

The woman said, "Yes."

"Then you must set up an inn on a road that has some travelers, but not many. Can you do this?"

"Yes."

"Finally, I will teach you to make five potions. The first will put men to sleep. The second will daze them, so they don't understand what is going on. The third will make them feel lust. The fourth potion you must take. It will ensure fertility. The fifth potion is a never-failing poison.

"Now, do exactly as I tell you. After you have built your inn, set up as the innkeeper and wait till a man arrives who is traveling alone. Talk with him. Find out his lineage and what kind of journey he is on. The best kind of man will be far from home and far from the end of his journey. If he vanishes, no one will know where it happened. You won't fall under suspicion.

"Once you have picked your man, give him the sleeping potion and then drag him to a room remote from all the others. Chain him there. When he wakes, give him the second potion. When it is obvious that he has become confused, give him the third potion and take the fourth yourself. Soon it will be possible to mate with him. No matter how careful and decent he is, he will respond to my magic.

"After you have gotten what you want from the man, you must kill him."

The nameless woman made a noise of protest.

"This must be done. You can't keep him prisoner in the inn. What if the other guests found him chained in a back room? It would certainly make them wonder what you've been up to. If you let him go, he will return home and report what's happened, as well as he can remember, and his lineage will send people to investigate.

"Most likely, the man will go to sleep after you have mated. You can strangle him or cut his throat. But if he remains lively, coax him to take a drink of my never-failing poison. Even a drop will finish him.

"Now," said the sorceress. "There is one final thing you must do. By this time, you will have gotten everything you need from the man, but a lot of him remains, and this is my portion.

"After the man is dead, go outside—making sure that no one else is around, of course—and call me in the following manner:

'Old Bald Pate, hairless one,
    come and gather another man.'

"If you follow my instructions exactly, you will live to see yourself surrounded by children."

The nameless woman agreed to all this. She learned to make the magic potions and then went to build an inn next to a rarely traveled road. When the inn was built, by her own effort entirely, except that the rear part was a natural cave, she assumed the guise of a man. This wasn't difficult for her. She was shorter than usual for a woman and lacked the sturdy build that is characteristic of most females, and her breasts were small and flat. All she had to do to be mistaken for a man was to wear a thick vest over her upper body.

She took Hrul Atig as her name and said that she was one of those men who enjoy solitude and don't have a lot of interest in fighting. She had left her lineage, with their permission of course, and wandered into the mountains. And because she wanted to do something useful, so long as it didn't involve warfare or too many people, she had established this inn.

She waited patiently for the right kind of man to arrive. He came finally, young and handsome and from a good family, traveling alone on a long journey.

Hrul Atig did as she'd been told, and everything happened as the sorceress had predicted.

After they had mated in the back room under the mountain, she strangled him. He was the only guest at the time. She walked fearlessly out into the daylight and called:

"Old Bald Pate, hairless one,
    come and gather another man."

An instant later, the sorceress appeared. Before, when Hrul Atig had seen the woman, she had been crouched in a badly lit cave. Now she was upright under the sun. Her four limbs were bony and knobby. Her four breasts hung down like empty bags. Her belly drooped. Below it, her female opening was clearly visible. Unprotected by fur and surrounded by wrinkled skin, it was entirely unattractive. Worst of all was the color of the monster's skin. In the few places where bare skin shows in ordinary people—the palms of the hands, the soles of the feet, the insides of the ears, the four large nipples—it is always dark. But the monster was pale and blotchy like a bank of old snow.

The sorceress grinned and gathered up the dead man. Then she said, "If you ever need me for any kind of help, go outside and call:

> 'Naked Breast, old hairless one,
> Help your helper at a run.'"

Then the monster loped away over the mountain, carrying the dead man in her arms.

The nameless woman felt horror at what she'd done, but also satisfaction. That evening she cleaned the inn, then burnt the murdered man's belongings in a fire, along with all other evidence of the murder. The ghosts of her dead relatives gathered at the edge of the firelight. Glancing up, she saw their torn clothing and broken armor and the dark blood that shone in their fur. "Our new family has begun," they told her, and they praised her courage and determination.

After a while, it became evident to the woman that she was pregnant. But she was one of those women who don't show early, and she continued to run the inn for many days longer. Finally one of the travelers, someone who had been at the inn before, remarked in a joking way that Atig was getting portly and this was no good thing in a man so young.

Hrul Atig waited till the traveler was gone, then called the sorceress, using the new verse. At once, the monster appeared, looking as horrible as before, though better fed.

"What am I going to do?" asked the nameless woman. "I'm not going to be able to pretend to be a man much longer. And who will help me bear the child?"

"You really aren't very bright," said the sorceress. "And this doesn't bode well for the children you bear. But maybe intelligence will come from the father. Shut up the inn and put a notice on the door, saying that you have gone to visit your lineage. You will be able to keep living here, if you keep an eye out for travelers and hide when they come by. As for help in childbirth, call me." Then the monster leaped up the cliff in back of the inn, and that was the last of her for a while.

The nameless woman did as she was advised. At the end of fifty days, she felt the pains that accompany birth, and cried out:

> "Naked Breast, old hairless one,
> help your helper at a run!"

The monster arrived and helped with surprising skill. The child, when it finally appeared, was female and covered with lovely soft pale grey fur. No mother could wish for a better looking child. Hrul Atig's mind filled with happiness.

The monster stayed until Hrul Atig was up and about. Then she said, "My advice to you is to reopen the inn as quickly as possible. If you bind your breasts and pad the nipples, people won't notice that you have milk. The child can stay in the back of the inn. I have brought her something to play with." She opened a bag and spilled out bones, as white as fresh snow. The child, young as she was, seemed able to focus her eyes. She looked at the bones and made a cooing noise.

"What are these?" asked Hrul Atig with a feeling of horror.

"Her father's bones, which I have cleaned and polished. I can tell you don't like them. But if you want my help to continue, you will let the child have these toys. I promise you, they will keep her quiet."

Reluctantly, the woman agreed. The inn was reopened. The woman returned to her male disguise, and her child played in the back room with the bones.

For many years after this, the nameless woman kept her inn. She was always careful and patient in what she did, and no one realized that she was the cause of men vanishing in that range of mountains. The young man I have told about was only the first. Others fell victim to her potions and died and were carried off by the sorceress. Other children were born. Some were male, and these the woman killed, following the advice of the sorceress.

"It's better to have girls if you want to recreate your family. These male children will take your time and your milk and not increase the size of the lineage-to-be. Kill them, and try again."

There were a number of female children, all of them healthy and good-looking. When there were no guests around, they played throughout the inn and in the surrounding forest. When travelers came, and the children could smell them at a long distance, the girls would withdraw to a special room deep in the mountain that their mother had built for them. There they played with the polished bones of their fathers.

Now the story turns in another direction, to the lineage named Hrul, which actually existed, though its home country was nowhere close to the forest where Hrul Atig kept her inn.

The Hrul were a very small family, whose land consisted of a single valley. A rare kind of tree grew there. The Hrul gathered bark from this tree and cooked it, making a dark blue dye that was highly valued throughout the entire region. They survived as a lineage because of their skill in making dye, and also because they had always had excellent relations with the neighboring lineages. This was so in spite of the odd problem the family had: the women of Hrul bore almost no male children. It made no difference who the father was. He might come from a lineage that produced mostly boys. Such exist, and they are very much pitied. But if such a man mated with a woman of Hrul, the result was almost certain to be a daughter. So Hrul had no warriors to protect them. Instead, they relied on intelligence, friendliness, and their craft.

Because there were so few men in the lineage, the women took on activities that are usually considered male. They hunted and patrolled the edges of their country and did the kinds of work that most families considered too dangerous for women: topping large trees, taming violent animals, and so on. The only male activity they did not take up was war. It wasn't necessary for them, since they got along with their neighbors, and they considered it unwomanly. Their few men were sent to the neighboring lineages when they reached adolescence and learned soldiering there. When their neighbors formed armies, the men of Hrul joined them, out of gratitude for their training and as repayment for the protection the neighbors gave to Hrul.

So this was the lineage whose name had been stolen by the nameless woman. It was many years before they heard about the inn in the wilderness, but finally a merchant came to purchase their fine blue dye and mentioned that he had met a relative of theirs in a distant part of the mountains.

Because they had so few males in their family, they kept track of all of them. They knew at once that this person was no true member of Hrul. They said nothing to the merchant, who was male and a stranger. But after he had loaded his animals with bags of powdered dye and ridden off, the Hrul gathered in council. There were only two men present: an old, lame great-uncle, and a lad just returned from military training. The rest were women of all ages. As a group, the women of Hrul were large, with grey fur that was usually solid but sometimes had barely visible stripes. Their hands were dyed blue from their craft, and the color extended up their arms to the elbow.

They gathered in the main room of their one great house. A fire burned in the firepit. Smoke curled around the rafters. Their eyes, blue like their hands, shone with reflected light. The lad, slender and as grey as smoke, leaned against a wall in back of his mother. The great-uncle sat stiffly in a chair.

This was a bad situation, the senior women declared. A large lineage was like a tall mountain: visible from a distance and known to everyone. Its true nature could not be hidden. Its reputation could not be destroyed by accident or rumor or the actions of a handful of people. If some of its members were immoral or unlucky, this would not change the world's opinion of the lineage.

But their lineage was small and almost unknown. A single person could ruin their name, and it was obvious that this innkeeper was up to something. Why else would he lie about his family?

They talked back and forth, wondering out loud what the man was doing and why he had picked their name to hide behind and make dirty. The two men remained silent, until the conversation became repetitious. Then the boy looked restless, and the great-uncle spoke in his light, quiet male voice. "You are settling nothing, and nothing can be settled, until we have more information. A person must be sent to investigate."

The boy offered to go, of course. The women looked at each other with consternation. He was so young! It was hard enough to send him off with their neighbors, who were good soldiers and could be relied on to take care of him. But to go alone into the wilderness—

The boy's elder sister leaned forward. According to the story, she was one of the daughters of Hrul who behaved in a male fashion, hunting and logging in the high forest above Hrul Valley. "If we knew for certain that the man needed killing, then we could send my brother. But we don't know this as yet. I suggest that I go. Everyone knows that I am comfortable in wild country. My dreams are often useful, and things appear to me that are invisible to other people. These are the kind of abilities our envoy ought to have. Let me find out what's going on. Then we can decide what to do about the man."

It was true that she had the kind of abilities that are most often found in diviners. But her gift was erratic and could not be relied on. For this reason, she had not become a diviner. Nonetheless, she was strong and clever and resourceful. She had been bred once and produced twin daughters, who were healthy but not remarkable. If she did not return, her genetic material would not be lost to the lineage, but there was no obvious reason to breed her again. By this time, the daughters had been weaned. Her female relatives were raising them, since she was not especially maternal. A good person to send, the women decided after more talk.

"There is a problem that must be dealt with," the great-uncle said. They all looked at him. "If the innkeeper knows anything about us, it is that we make dye. If our kinswoman appears with blue hands and arms, he will be suspicious."

"What shall we do?" the women asked.

"Dye her. Not blue, but black. It will cover the blue. Our kinswoman can say that she comes from the southwest coast of our continent. The people there have dark fur. Some are almost black.

"And I suggest, as well, that she take men's clothing and a traveling sword." He looked at the sister. "Put these on before you reach the inn. The innkeeper will be more comfortable with another man and more likely to tell his story. But don't change clothes until you are almost at the inn. It's too dangerous to travel as a man."

All this was agreed to, though it was some time before the woman was able to leave. First her relatives had to dye her, then she had to learn how to wear male clothing. She was slender enough to pass for a tall man, and (as mentioned before) she had spent much of her life doing things that were violent and dangerous. She knew how to use an axe and a long hunting knife. Blood did not bother her. She could move quickly and climb like the *olb* that live on cliffs. A very good choice for this journey, her great-uncle said. If any woman could carry forward this deception, she was the one.

She left finally, riding a hardy *tsin* and with a second animal following her. Her male clothing was in its pack, along with a sword.

At this point, she needs a name. After her story became known, people—though not her relatives—began to call her Blue Hands, and this name will be used here.

Why Blue Hands, if she had been dyed? Because the dye had taken hold everywhere except on her few areas of bare skin. Her nipples and the soles of her feet were still grey, as were the insides of her ears. The palms of her hands were blue-grey, and there was a definite blue tinge to her narrow, curving, claw-like fingernails. This would not show in firelight, her great-uncle said. "Be careful in daylight, and take gloves."

Her journey was a long one, and she had adventures, which will not be told here. In the end, she arrived in the area where the innkeeper lived. This was her last day as a woman, at least for a while. She made camp in a little hollow off the trail, and ate the food she had brought: hard bread and dried fruit. Night came. She built a fire and sat by it, watching the flames.

After a while, she got the impression she was being looked at. She glanced up. Men stood at the edge of the firelight. There were maybe ten, though she had trouble counting them.

"Who are you?" Blue Hands asked.

One of the men took a step forward. He was young and handsome, dressed for travel in shorts, a jacket and high soft boots. A sword hung from his belt. He met her gaze directly. "Greetings, woman of Hrul."

She knew then he was a ghost. No ordinary man would have known her family name, and no ordinary man would have looked directly into the eyes of an unrelated woman. "What do you want from me?" she asked.

"We have been watching along this road, some of us for years, looking for someone to deal with the innkeeper. We think you are the person and that you ought to know what lies ahead of you."

She opened her mouth to speak, though she wasn't certain what words would come out.

A second man stepped forward, almost as dark as she was in her disguise. His clothes were richly embroidered in an unfamiliar way. His voice had an accent. "We know the reputation of ghosts is not good, and for the most part, that reputation is merited. The innkeeper is haunted by ghosts who are as bad as can be imagined. We are not going to haunt you or give you advice. Our days for advising and being advised are over. But listen to our story."

Another voice, speaking out of the shadows, said, "All of us ask this, woman of Hrul."

She agreed. "Will it bother you, if I put more wood on the fire?"

"A little more will not be a problem," said the first man, who was silver-grey with faint markings on his arms and shoulders: large, cloudy-looking spots that were shaped like broken rings. "We are most comfortable in shadow. Don't fill this hollow with light."

She added two branches. They caught. The fire brightened, and it became less easy to see the ghosts. But they remained, most of them, anyway, and they told Blue Hands how they had been trapped and killed.

The story was painful to hear and must have been painful to tell, even for ghosts. But their voices were quiet and even. They remained at the edge of the firelight, most standing, but one squatting as people do on the high plateau, rocked back on his heels, looking comfortable. No one moved much. What excellent manners they had! What a pity they had died in such a way!

Each man had been traveling alone, they said. Usually the inn was empty when he arrived, though several times there had been other travelers at the inn, who left without noticing what was going on. The innkeeper made each man welcome.

"Though he didn't seem to be the kind of man who finds it easy to be friendly," said the man with spots. "I wondered about that, but maybe he felt that an innkeeper ought to be friendly. Or maybe he was lonely. The Goddess knows it is a lonely place!"

They sat together, drinking and talking. If there were other people in the inn, the innkeeper paid only as much attention to them as he had to. It was clear that he was interested in the solitary traveler.

"Maybe that should have warned us," said the man who was squatting, his arms resting easily on his thighs. "But all of us were young and good looking. We were used to attention from other men."

In the end, the traveler fell asleep, sometimes in the common room of the inn and sometimes upstairs. When he awoke, he was in a new place entirely.

By this time the fire had burned down a little, and it was easier to see the ghosts. A new man spoke. His fur was grey with faint stripes. A fine sword with a golden hilt hung at his side. A necklace of gold links shone at his throat. "This is where the story becomes difficult to tell," he said. "Most of us spent the rest of our lives, which were not long, crazy in one way or another. We don't remember those last few days with any clarity. But I was one of the first to be murdered. I saw what happened to the men who came after me. Let me tell this part of the story."

When the traveler woke, the striped man said, he was in a new place: a cave in the mountain behind the inn. The walls and floor and ceiling were solid rock. The man was naked, without anything that could be used as a tool or weapon, and held by a chain made of thick iron links. At one end was an iron ring, fastened around his ankle. At the other end was an iron bolt, sunk deep into the wall.

"You have to remember," said the striped man in his quiet voice. "The room was entirely dark. Everything I tell you was happening in darkness and in silence, except for the noise that each man made. Some of us were quiet, so there was only the

225

sound of breathing and the clinking of the chain as we moved. Some of us called for help or cried out in anger or groaned in fear."

Another man spoke out of the shadows. "It was not a comfortable situation. There is nothing shameful about being afraid, so long as it does not affect one's actions."

The striped man glanced toward the speaker in the shadows and smiled briefly. "As you might be able to tell, he was one of the quiet ones. Even his breathing remained even and slow."

"I lacked imagination," the speaker in the shadows said. "Everyone in my family told me this. When I was put into an unusual situation, I became slow and quiet because I had no idea what else to do."

Usually, the man was fed a second potion before he woke properly. He went directly from sleep into craziness. Sometimes, the innkeeper was delayed, and the man woke fully to realize his situation. If the man explored, feeling his way around the unlit room, he found nothing except a basin cut in the rock floor and full of a liquid that had a faint, sweet odor. If he drank the liquid, he went crazy.

Two men refused to drink. So they had clear memories of the innkeeper when she returned, carrying a lantern. She entered through a heavy door made of wood and iron, which none of her prisoners had been able to reach. The chain was not long enough. She stood at a safe distance, holding up the lantern and looking, then asking questions to determine whether or not the prisoner was crazy. If he was still rational, she said, "I am a murderer and a thief, as you may suspect by now. There is no way out of this situation, except death, and you might as well take dying into your own hands. The water in the pool is poisoned. Scoop it up and drink it. Otherwise, you will die slowly of thirst and starvation and without the satisfaction of determining your own moment of death."

The man who was squatting said, "Maybe I shouldn't have listened to her. But I could not imagine what was in her mind; and given the choice, every man prefers to keep hold of his death."

Another man came forward, shorter than the others, his fur solid grey. "I did not drink even then. She waited till thirst made me weak, then came and fed me her potion, and I went crazy like all the others."

It was not a useful kind of craziness. The man became confused and suggestible, unable to think for himself. It was easy for the innkeeper to persuade him to drink yet another potion. This one caused lust.

The second potion did not wear off. The man remained crazy, unable to distinguish good from evil or dreams from the waking world. While he was in this condition, the innkeeper mated with him, though there was no contract between their families, and the man was not able to understand what was happening or to agree to it.

The dark man said, "I remember strange animals and landscapes such as I have never seen, and then I thought I was with my lover at home. But when I began to make love with him, he turned into a monster, and it seemed that the monster was sucking everything inside me out, though not through its mouth but rather through another opening in another part of its body." He paused and glanced down, then back up, meeting her gaze with pale yellow eyes. "Everything came out of me. I was like a bag made of skin. Empty."

The striped man said, "When she was finished with us, she killed us, and she called the witch who was her teacher: a horrible, big, hairless creature. The witch came and carried our bodies away. She flayed us and tanned our skins. Our flesh went into her cooking pot. Our bones she cleaned and made into toys for our children to play with."

That was the end of the story. The woman of Hrul put more wood on the fire. The ghosts became indistinct, drawing back into the forest shadow.

"This may be untrue," she said finally. "You may be trying to trick me into evil. On the other hand, my family believes this innkeeper is up to something. But I think I will have to take a look myself."

"As we told you before," the dark ghost said. "We haven't come to advise you. But I will say this: be careful and observant. Remember our story! And remember that we can do nothing in the world of the living. You will be on your own in dealing with the innkeeper, though we will try to keep the ghosts who haunt her at a distance. They hang around the inn and watch what is happening there, and they give the innkeeper advice and help. If they are unable to get close to her, she will be less dangerous, we hope.

"If everything turns out well, and you manage to deal with the innkeeper, please take our bones away from our daughters."

"You needn't worry about trying to separate the bones," said the spotted man. "We have gotten used to having them mixed together. But burn them and bury the ashes."

The short man said, "I wish we could tell you our names, so our families would learn what happened to us and perform the right ceremonies of farewell. But that doesn't seem to be possible. When I try to speak my name, it vanishes from my mind. At times, I think I can remember where my family lives and who is in it. But at the moment, all of that is unclear, as if they are creatures in a dream or I am a creature in a dream."

She glanced down, tired and distressed. When she lifted her head, the ghosts had vanished. Grey dawn was showing between the trees. Her fire was out, and she was sprawled next to it.

Blue Hands sat up and rubbed her body. She felt as if she'd been lying all night on the cold ground. Maybe the ghosts had been a dream, though a dream that was so vivid and full of detail had to be taken seriously.

It was obvious what she had to do: dress as a man and go to the inn. The innkeeper's behavior ought to tell her whether or not this story was true.

She reached the inn late that afternoon. It was a small building, solid-looking, set against a cliff wall next to the road, which at this point went through a narrow valley. A small swift river rushed through the valley bottom, around boulders and over drops.

Blue Hands rode into the courtyard and dismounted. The innkeeper came out, dressed in a kilt and a vest that was fastened across the front with chains. He was tall enough to be a woman, but not as broad as was (and is) typical of women of the People. He greeted Blue Hands with apparent pleasure, though when he wasn't speaking or smiling, his expression became grim. This was his natural expression, she thought, which he hid with glances and grimaces and twists of his lips.

She unsaddled her two animals and put them in the stable. There were other *tsina* there already, and a family party was gathered in the common room: two matrons and three young men. Was this lucky or not? wondered Blue Hands. The innkeeper might not reveal his true nature with so much company present.

Blue Hands sat down at a table. She carried a bag with her. Inside it was a cloak and a jug full of *halin*. She had given thought to the story the ghosts had told, and she had devised a plan, though she wasn't certain that it would work.

The innkeeper brought food over: a meat stew and a tall goblet full of a liquid that smelled like *halin*. "Those others can entertain themselves," he said. "Families always like to speak to one another. I'll sit with you, if you don't object."

"No," said Blue Hands, wondering about the meat in the stew. Was it possible that she was about to eat another person? There was no way of telling, and the innkeeper would become suspicious if she left the food alone. She dug in.

The young men with the family called for more to drink. The innkeeper sighed and got up. While he was gone, Blue Hands spilled some of the liquid in her goblet on the table, then emptied the rest into her bag. The heavy fabric of the cloak soaked it up. Moving quickly, she wiped the goblet out and refilled it with *halin* from her jar. If she was lucky, the scent of the *halin* she had spilled would keep the innkeeper from noticing that her *halin* was not quite the same as his. She smeared the spilled liquid across the table, rubbing it into the wood.

The innkeeper came back, complaining about the demands of the family. Blue Hands drank her *halin*. He sat down and asked about her travels. She told the story she had made up, after speaking with the ghosts.

She came from a small, far-distant lineage. (This much was true.) They'd had bad luck in recent years, and the local diviners had not been able to find a cause. Blue Hands was the son of the most important woman in the lineage and had been sent to consult with a famous diviner in the north. She—or, rather, he—had gotten an answer from the diviner and was going home by the most direct route, though it was more dangerous. "But my family needs to act quickly to end the cause of our bad luck. The diviner has assured me that if we do as she advises, our bad luck will vanish, and we will become known for good fortune." She drank more *halin*. "My family will be surprised when I return! They expected me to take the long route both ways."

The innkeeper looked satisfied and asked her if she wanted more *halin*.

"Yes," said Blue Hands.

He refilled her cup, then went to serve the family. Once again, Blue Hands emptied her goblet, refilling it with the *halin* she had brought.

The innkeeper returned, and the two apparent men continued their conversation. After a while, the matrons in the family went up to bed, as did one of the young men. But the other two stayed in the common room.

"They'll be drunk tonight and sick tomorrow," the innkeeper said, his voice angry. "Men should behave with more decorum when they are traveling with women."

It was excellent good luck that the family was in the inn, Blue Hands decided. Without them, she would have had a difficult time.

The next time the young men called for *halin*, she emptied the innkeeper's goblet and refilled it with the *halin* he had given her. Then she filled her goblet with her own *halin*.

The innkeeper returned. They continued their conversation. The two young men finally had too much to drink, and the innkeeper had to help them upstairs. Once again, Blue Hands emptied her goblet into the innkeeper's.

She had been drinking slowly, but nonetheless she had taken in more *halin* than was usual for her, and maybe there had been some residue in the goblet. Her thinking was unclear, and she was beginning to have some trouble focusing her eyes. It didn't feel like drunkenness, but rather like taking a medicine. A residue then. The potion must be very powerful. She closed her eyes, trying to think more clearly.

All at once, she could see the entire inn: the lit common room and the darkness outside it. In the darkness, beyond the outer walls, a battle was taking place. The warriors shone faintly, so she was able to make them out. Her ghosts, the murdered young men, were fighting other ghosts who were dressed in bloody armor. Sword met sword, producing no sound. The men who had been murdered were holding off the other ghosts, keeping them out of the inn, and the situation was clearly making the bloody ghosts angry. Their mouths opened and closed, as if they were screaming or cursing. Blue Hands heard nothing, except the crackle of the fire in the common room. Her ghosts, the murdered young men, fought with calm determination.

They should not have been able to win against the angry ghosts, since they wore no armor and carried only the short swords that men take with them on journeys. But she could see that they were doing well. Maybe the difference was in the kinds of ghosts they were. Her young men had kept the qualities that relatives like to remember: intelligence, skill, calmness, discipline, comradeliness. The other ghosts were made of everything that should be forgotten about a person once he is dead: anger, malevolence, stupidity, selfishness, lack of skill.

She knew then—looking at the battle that ringed the inn, shining dimly before her inner vision—that the story told by the ghosts was true. The innkeeper was a murderer and a thief.

The innkeeper returned, swaying now. "I can't understand it," he said. "I am usually able to drink much more than this."

Blue Hands slouched over the table, keeping her head down so the false man would not be able to see that her pupils were a normal size. Her voice stumbling, she said, "The same for me. I am not certain I will be able to stand."

"In your case, it must be the journey," the innkeeper said, his voice full of satisfaction. "You are tired. Don't worry. I'll help you to bed."

They settled down to drink some more. Every time Blue Hands closed her eyes, she saw the ghostly battle, still continuing in the darkness around the inn.

Finally, the innkeeper fell forward, unconscious. When this happened, the angry ghosts all screamed, though their voices were inaudible, and turned and fled into the night. The ghosts of the murdered men remained where they were, swords in their hands, guarding.

Blue Hands made sure the innkeeper was not likely to wake. Then she searched the inn and found the room described by the ghosts: empty except for an iron chain. She carried the innkeeper there and chained her. The basin cut in the floor was empty. Blue Hands filled this with water, so the innkeeper would have something to drink, and then she went upstairs and found an empty room and went to sleep. She did this out of necessity. Even the small amount of potion left in her goblet had been almost enough to render her unconscious. And she did it out of trust. Surely the ghosts would keep her safe from anything supernatural, and she was not worried about ordinary people.

She woke in the morning before the family did and cleaned the common room. Then she made breakfast and served it to her fellow travelers, saying that the innkeeper—a cousin of hers—was ill.

They ate and went on their way, the two young men moving stiffly and wincing from time to time. The matrons glared their disapproval. The third young man, who had gone to bed early, looked smug.

While this was happening, the innkeeper woke and found herself in her own prison, chained in the same way as the men she had raped and murdered.

Hah! This was troubling! She shouted for help. After a while, several of her daughters came out of the room where they played with their fathers' bones. One of them carried a lantern. They opened the door of the prison and peered in.

"Help me," the innkeeper cried.

The daughters consulted together in whispers. One of them spoke finally, "No."

"But I'm your mother," the innkeeper said.

"Our fathers are our fathers, but we play with their bones. Why should we care for you any more than we care for them?"

The innkeeper pleaded, but the little girls would not listen. They left, taking the lantern, and she was in darkness. Now she remembered the monster and chanted the verse that summoned her:

> "Naked breast, old Hairless One,
> Help your helper at a run."

A moment later, the sorceress was in the room with her. She carried no light, but a faint pale illumination shone out of her. As usual, she was huge and hideous, but this time she wore a garment over her nakedness: a robe made of pieces of fur, grey and dark grey, spotted and striped, the pelts of the men who had been murdered. It covered her from neck to ankle, and the long full sleeves came down over her wrists.

The innkeeper explained her problem.

"Too bad," said the monster. "But I think your usefulness to me is over, so I am not going to move a finger to help you."

"What do you mean?" asked the innkeeper.

"Have you never wondered what I got out of our agreement? I am not able to have children directly. In order to create more monsters, I have to use an ordinary woman. One of the potions I taught you to make changes the child inside you, so it is mine instead of yours. Now I have ten fine young daughters, who will prey on people and cause harm in the world, and I have finished this excellent coat, which will keep me warm and covered, even though I have no fur.

"You are reaching the age when women become less fertile and more likely to produce children who are unhealthy. It's time that I abandoned you."

"But we have an agreement!" cried the innkeeper.

"Surely you don't expect an agreement made with a monster to hold," said the sorceress. She grinned, showing a mouth full of teeth as white as fresh new bone. "Farewell," she said, and vanished.

Once again the nameless woman was left in darkness. She screamed and struggled with the chain. Finally, exhausted, she cried out to her male relatives. But the bloody ghosts could not come near her. The ghosts of the men she had murdered held them off.

She ended by sitting hunched on the stone floor and groaning, as the People do, when they have reached a condition of complete despair. This was how Blue Hands found her.

"You have choices," Blue Hands said. "I can leave you here to starve or I can give you a knife, if you agree to use it."

"My life has been meaningless," the nameless woman said. "My kin have abandoned me. Nothing is left. Give me the knife."

Blue Hands threw it to her, and she used it to cut her throat.

When this happened, the ghosts who guarded the inn sheathed their swords and left, striding off into the morning forest. Blue Hands saw them briefly, when she closed her eyes against the sight of the innkeeper spurting blood. The young men faded among the trees like mist in sunlight. After a moment or two, they were entirely gone.

Blue Hands opened her eyes and saw the false man lying in a pool of blood.

She took her lantern and left. After a while, she found the room where the innkeeper's children played. They were there: ten daughters ranging in age from a baby to a tall, thin girl at the edge of puberty. Around them were the bones of their fathers and of other men who had not produced living children. White and polished, the bones filled most of the room. Two of the girls squatted on an empty area of floor and threw knucklebones like dice. Another pair of children had gathered up the small narrow bones that are found in hands and feet and were using them to play a pick-up game. In one corner a tower rose, made of leg bones and arm bones. In another corner was a cave made largely of ribs, with a child of three or so huddled inside. The littlest girl lay nestled in a pelvic girdle as if in a cradle.

Blue Hands stood at the door of the room, holding a second knife, feeling horror at the sight, but also disconcerted. The children looked like quite ordinary little girls. They lifted their heads and gazed at Blue Hands, obviously frightened.

"Don't kill us," the oldest daughter said. "We had nothing to do with the crimes of our mother."

Her vision failed her then. She did not see the children as monsters, and she could not harm them.

"What will happen to you?" she asked.

"I'm almost grown," said the oldest daughter. "I can care for my sisters, and we have a relative who lives nearby. She's a recluse, but she won't refuse to help her own kin."

Blue Hands gathered the bones of the murdered men and burned them outside the inn. She burned the innkeeper as well and then went on her way, leaving the children. She ought to have cared for them, but she knew there was something wrong with them, and, though she could not kill them, she wanted nothing to do with them.

The children fled into the mountains and lived in the high forest like animals. If their true mother, the sorceress, helped them, it isn't known. When they reached maturity, their fur dropped off and they looked exactly like the sorceress, though they did not have her great size and power. They became petty monsters called *tlugha*, who prey on children who are disobedient, destructive, uncooperative, or lazy. Little boys are especially likely to draw the attention of a *tlugh*. Mothers warn their male children: if they don't act properly, a *tlugh* will come down out of the mountains and carry them off to its lair and eat them, starting at the toes.

The inn fell to ruins, and there were rumors that it was haunted. Travelers tried to get past it during daylight hours. Only a fool would camp near it.

As for Blue Hands, she returned to her family and became an impressive matriarch, respected by everyone in the region.

This story has five morals:

(1) Don't let your life be run by ghosts.

(2) Never come to an agreement with a monster.

(3) Never breed without a contract.

(4) Don't try to take and use what belongs to other people: their fur, their flesh, their bones, or their procreative powers.

(5) Be careful with compassion. There are some things that should not live.

The Woman Who Fooled Death Five Times

A *Hwarhath* Folk Tale

For the most part, the *hwarhath* do not think of death as a person. But there are remote regions on the home planet where education levels are low and superstition levels are high. In these places, people tell stories about Death.

This is one.

When the Goddess built the world, she worked like a good cook making a meal, tasting as she went along. She tasted the fruit to make sure it was sweet and the bitter herbs to make sure they were bitter. She tried other things as well: rocks, clay, water, bugs, fish, birds, and animals with fur. Cooked or raw, everything went onto her tongue.

In the end, the world was done and seemed more than adequate. As for the Goddess, she felt bloated and over-full. She made herself a medicinal tea and drank it. Then she had an enormous bowel movement.

After she had finished, she looked at the heap of dung. "Well, that looks nasty and smells nasty, too."

The heap moved, and a voice came from it. "Don't be too critical. I am a creation of yours, just as the world is." The heap heaved itself up, assuming the shape of a man, though it was a badly formed man, lumpy and drippy. Its eyes were like two black

237

fruit pits; its leathery tongue looked like a piece of skin pulled from a roasted bird; and its fingernails were like fish scales.

"I didn't plan on you," the Goddess said. "What *are* you?"

"I am the end of everything," the man-shaped heap replied. "I am Death."

The Goddess considered for a while and decided to let Death exist. Maybe he would prove useful. As he had said, he was her creation, and she rarely did anything that lacked point or meaning.

The dung-man dried, until he was smooth and dark brown. He became better shaped in the process, though he never grew fur, and he was always rather lumpy. Once he was completely dry, he took on his job, which was escorting life forms off the planet when their time was done.

Now the story turns to a woman named Ala. She lived in a cabin with her young son, a pet bird and a loyal *sul*.

One night Death came to her door and scratched on it.

"Who is there?" Ala asked.

"I am Death, and I have come for Ala."

"I'm her sister," Ala replied.

"Then I won't bother you, but tell Ala to come out and meet me."

The woman hastily rolled up a quilt and tied it, then opened the door and handed it to Death. "Here she is."

Death had poor eyesight, especially in the dark, but he could feel. The quilt felt round and comfortable, like a woman of Ala's age. He thanked Ala, put the quilt in his sack, and headed home.

You may think Death was stupid to mistake a rolled-up quilt for a woman. You are right. Remember that his brain, like the rest of him, was made of dung; and his job was comparatively simple. He didn't need the intelligence and skill of a space pilot or a research doctor or even an ordinary person.

When Death got home, he pulled out the quilt. A fire burned on the hearth, and there were several lanterns, which he lit as soon as he got in the door. He could see that he held a quilt.

"I have been tricked," he said. "But now I have a fine, thick quilt to put on my bed, which only had a worn sheet before. This is all to the good. Tomorrow I will go back for the woman."

He spread the quilt on his bed and slept in comfort. The next night he went back to Ala's cabin. "You tricked me, but you won't do it a second time. I will feel to make sure the thing you give me is warm and living. "

Ala took her pet bird, which was sleeping on its perch, and handed it out to Death. Even his clumsy hands could tell it was warm and living. He thanked Ala and put the bird in his sack and headed home.

After a while, the bird began to sing: a wonderful, liquid music.

"That doesn't sound like a person on her way out of existence," Death said.

He stopped by a wayside tavern. Light shone from its windows. Standing in the light, Death opened his sack and took out the bird. "You aren't Ala, and your time is not over. Go on your way."

The bird spread its wings and flew to the top of a nearby mountain. There it sang and sang, until it attracted a mate. Together, they built a nest and raised nestlings, above clouds and mist and the troubles of the world.

The next night Death went back to Ala's cabin. "You have fooled me twice, but you won't do it again. I can tell if something is warm and alive and covered with fur rather than feathers. Give me your sister."

Ala gathered up her loyal *sul*, which was lying by the fire, and handed it through the door. *Sulin* have scales as well as fur, as everyone knows. But Death felt only the fur with his clumsy hands, and he put the *sul* in his sack.

"Thank you," he told Ala, and headed home.

On the way, the *sul* began to growl and snarl.

"That doesn't sound like a person on her way to the end," Death said.

He stopped in a high pass and waited for dawn. Then, when the sun's first rays lit the pass, he opened his bag and took out the *sul*, which snapped at him, but was afraid to bite.

"You aren't Ala, and your time is not yet. Go on your way."

The *sul* loped down from the pass into a thick forest. There it encountered a brave and honorable hunter. The two of them liked each other at once. In this way, the *sul* found a new master, who would never betray it. They lived together and hunted together in perfect harmony for many years.

The next night, Death, who may have been stupid but was certainly persistent, returned to Ala's cabin. "You have tricked me three times, but you won't do it again. I can tell if what you give me is warm and alive, covered with fur and shaped like a person. Give me your sister."

Ala looked around her cabin. The only thing that met Death's specifications was her son, a boy of four or five, well mannered, obedient, and quiet.

She picked him up. "I am sending you with this man. No matter what happens, remain quiet."

The boy inclined his head in agreement, and she handed him through the doorway to Death.

"Thank you," said Death, and popped the boy into his sack. Then he went on his way.

The bag was very dark, except for the dead people it contained, who glowed faintly. The boy did not see entire persons, but rather parts: a hand, a pair of eyes, a leg or foot, all glowing dimly. The ghosts took up no room, but floated through one another and through the boy, complaining in barely audible voices. For the most part, he did not understand what they said, though sometimes he made out a word or two or three: "Grief." "Pain." "Not now." "Not like this."

He was a stoic boy, but gradually he became frightened by the wisps of light and the sad, complaining voices. Nonetheless, he pressed his lips together and kept quiet, as his mother had told him.

Finally Death reached his house. He opened the bag and pulled the boy out. "Tricked again! You're not Ala, and your time has not come. Go on your way."

"Is your house near a town?" the boy asked.

'No. It's far into the wilderness."

"Then, I will die if you send me out alone; and you said this is not my time to die."

Death frowned deeply as he thought. "You are right."

"Why don't I stay here?" the boy asked, glancing around at the warm fire and shining lamps. A fine quilt lay on the bed. The rug on the floor was badly worn, but still looked friendly and comfortable. "I could help you keep the fire burning, and I know how to sweep and wash."

Death frowned some more, then tilted his head in assent. "You seem like a mannerly child, and one determined to be useful. I could use some company and help around the house. You are welcome to stay."

So the boy remained in Death's house, helping with the housework. At night, if Death was home, they played simple games together or the boy told stories as best he could. They were simple and childlike, but Death enjoyed them. Both were happy.

In the meantime, Death went back to Ala's house a fifth time.

"You have fooled me four times, but this is the end. Send your sister out."

Ala looked around her cabin. There was nothing more to give Death. She opened the door and said, "Your visits frightened my sister so much that she has fled south. Come in and look. You won't find her."

Death accepted her invitation, came in and looked around. The cabin seemed bare without quilt, bird, *sul,* and boy. He could find no second woman. "Very well," he said. "I will look for Ala in the south. Don't expect to see me again, until your time has come."

He left, and Ala exulted. She had fooled Death five times and was free of him. Granted: she had lost her fine quilt, her pet bird, her loyal *sul*, and her son. Her cabin seemed cold and empty now, and she wondered if she could have found other ways to fool Death.

Wondering this, grief and sadness crept into her mind. But it was mixed with the joy that came from being free of Death.

At dawn she went down to the river to get a bucket of water. Mist obscured her way, and the wooden steps that led to the river were glazed with ice, which she could not see in the dim light. When she had almost reached the river, she slipped, fell into the water, and drowned.

Her bucket floated free, bobbing in the rapid current. She followed, her body turning slowly. At length, a long way down river, she climbed out.

Because Death had not found her, she was not entirely dead. Rather, she existed in a strange place between life and death. Her fur was drenched with water. Her teeth chattered, and she shivered all over.

She tried to gather dry vegetation to huddle under, but her hands went through the branches and leaves.

Next, she looked for people and their fires. She found a group of hunters around a roaring bonfire. Her old *sul* was among the *sulin* and growled, but no one else noticed her. She moved closer and closer to the fire, till she should have been roasting or burning. But the heat did not reach her. She remained wet and cold. Crying out in despair, she fled into darkness.

So began years of wandering. She never dried off or grew warm, though she tried over and over to heat herself at every fire she found. Even on the hottest days of summer, when everyone else was panting, she remained wet and cold.

People could not see her, though they sometimes felt her as an icy draft. Her only company were angry ghosts, who gathered around her, complaining—not gently, like the newly dead, but in harsh, loud voices. Their deaths were unjust. Their families were

242

ungrateful. The neighbors had been out to get them. Malice and bad luck had followed them all their lives. Their voices pierced her like knives of ice, making her even colder.

Finally, after years of wandering, she came to Death's house. Her son was outside, sweeping the front step. By this time, he was nine or ten, a tall and promising boy. He looked at her and frowned.

"You look like my mother, though she was not soaking wet the last time I saw her."

"What house is this?" the woman asked.

"Death lives here."

"Then you must be my son. I gave him to Death years ago."

The boy paused, considering. "It hasn't been a bad life here, and Death has always told me to be courteous. So I will welcome you, though I never liked the way you handed me over. Come in!"

She entered the house and sat by the fire. Her son pulled the fine, thick quilt off the bed and folded it around her shoulders. At last, she stopped shivering and her teeth stopped chattering. The boy heated soup and gave it to her. At last, she was able to eat, though she hadn't eaten or drunk for years.

Hah! The warm soup felt good going down! The quilt felt good on her shoulders! The fire's heat felt good on her face and hands!

"Who is this?" asked Death, coming through the door.

"My mother," said the boy.

"I am Ala," the woman said. "I tricked you five times. Nonetheless, I died."

"You haven't died entirely, but you are mostly gone, as I can see," Death replied. "This is why a stupid person can do my job. No one can escape the rules of physics and biology."

"I died by accident, not physics," Ala replied angrily.

"All living beings die one way or another," Death replied comfortably. He helped himself to a bowl of soup and sat down to eat.

"What happens now?" Ala asked. "I can tell you I don't like my current existence. I have been cold and hungry and tired for years, unable to warm myself or eat or sleep."

Death gave her a considering look. "Usually, people die the moment I pop them in my bag. They may make a little noise, but they are gone. When I get them home, I take them out of the bag and divide them in two. The good parts go off to another place. I have no idea what happens there. The bad parts remain here as angry ghosts, complaining about their lives and deaths. Gradually, their anger wears them out. They grow thin and vanish entirely.

"But you are something new, neither alive nor dead. If I popped you into my bag, you might well become entirely dead. Then I'd have to divide you into good and bad. I'm worried about what would happen. You gave up a pet bird, a loyal *sul*, and a son to remain alive. This is bad; and it leads me to believe that most of you would become an angry ghost. Maybe I could drive you away; but since you tricked me five times, I'm not sure. I don't want an angry ghost screaming and crying around my house at night. It would be unpleasant and likely to bother the boy. What do you say, lad? Do you want the ghost of your mother screaming outside our door?"

"No," the boy said. "You have taught me to appreciate quiet. I don't want to hear my mother screaming in the night."

"I think I can see a few glimmers of good in you," Death said to Ala. "The good is small and dim, and it's tightly tangled with badness. It would be hard to pull free. Maybe this could change in time. Do you think you have learned any remorse?"

"I have learned there are worse things than death," Ala replied.

"That's a start," Death said. "Why don't you stay here? I would enjoy some grown-up company, and your son would enjoy his mother; and neither of us would have to deal with an angry ghost."

"Yes," said the boy slowly. "I think I would like to have my mother here, in spite of everything."

Ala frowned. "It's wrong for men and women to live together, unless they are members of the same lineage."

Death laughed, showing his dung-brown teeth. "You are thinking of mating and reproducing. I represent undoing rather than doing. That being so, I can neither mate nor reproduce. Think of me as an old uncle or great-uncle, an eccentric member of your family, tolerated and possibly loved.

"In any case, you are in no position to talk about right and wrong. There is a lot about morality you need to learn, though I do admire your cleverness. It might prove helpful the next time someone tries to trick me."

Ala looked at Death. He wore nothing except a cape, pushed back over his shoulders, and seemed to be a smooth, hairless man, though lacking any genitalia. She knew he was frightening, but at the moment he looked harmless. "I will stay," she said.

Death laughed again.

Ala kept her word and stayed with Death. For the most part, she was happy. So long as she stayed close to Death's house, she felt alive, able to eat and sleep and defecate. If she moved any distance, she began to feel herself grow thin and unreal. So she returned to the house.

She cooked meals and sewed clothing, told stories and helped raise her son. When Death came in with his bag, she tried to ignore the sorting process. Gradually, however, she began to watch. The boy had seen the ghosts in Death's sack as glowing body parts. But when Death took them out, they looked like badly snarled tangles of thread or yarn. They came in all colors, but most were black, white, gray, or red. Using his clumsy hands, which were surprisingly deft at this task, Death pulled the filaments apart. When he was done, the gray and black threads rose into the air and wove themselves into the image of a person.

"Thank you," the person said, rose to the ceiling, and vanished. That was the good part, going to an unknown place.

As for the white and red filaments, they wove themselves into the image of an ugly, angry person with burning eyes and a mouth full of tusks. Saying nothing, it stormed out through the door.

What about the threads of other colors? They lay on the floor a while, then faded, and were gone.

"Most people have fur that is either black or gray," Death told Ala, "and these are the colors of ordinary virtues, such as thoughtfulness and cooperation. Red is the color of rage and greed. White is the color of selfishness and indifference. These are the traits that destroy families and societies."

"What a moralist you are," Ala said angrily.

"I am the being the Goddess made," Death replied. "Maybe she shat her morality out, after she finished making the world. It isn't always clear to me that the universe is moral now, but I am. I have to be, in order to divide the dead."

"What are the other colors?" Ala asked.

"Yellow and green and so on? The ones that fade? They are the parts that have nothing to do with morality. A liking for flowers. An ability to sing. Good reflexes. They go back into a general pool of traits, from which they are taken by future generations. Nothing is wasted here."

When the boy was twenty, he left to find his own life. It is never easy to be a man alone, with no kin. But he found a job as a soldier, working for a large and contentious family that quarreled with all its neighbors. He was good at what he did, being strong and quick to learn, with an even temper and the good manners Death had taught him. In addition, he was not afraid of Death, though he certainly respected him. His calmness and lack of fear made him a very good soldier.

He and Death met from time to time on battlefields and in field hospitals. The man could always see his foster uncle, though no one else could, except those who were actually dead. They chatted before Death put the man's comrades and enemies into his bag and carried them away. Both Death and the boy, now a man, took comfort from their conversations.

As for Ala, one day Death said to her, "I think I could divide you now. You seem to have learned something about morality over the years. There is more good in you, and it's less mixed with the bad."

Ala considered. It seemed to her she was as selfish as ever, though she liked and respected Death, who had a hard job and did it carefully. "I'd rather stay here. I have no desire to leave the world, and I am terrified of becoming an angry ghost. Even though I am not entirely—or even mostly—alive, I can still take pleasure in flowers and food and in telling a story."

"Very well," Death said after a long silence, during which he frowned mightily.

They remained together like two old relatives.

Ala's son became the leader of a war band, respected by all. When he was sixty-five, a stray arrow killed him; and Death came for him. The man's spirit rose from his body, looking no more than twenty. "It's good to see you," he said to Death, and embraced the old monster. "Do I have to get into the bag? I didn't like it the first time."

"No," said Death. "Though I will put the other soldiers there."

They traveled home slowly, talking. In the meantime, many people on the edge of dying remained alive. Let that be as it was, Death thought. He treasured this journey with his foster nephew.

Hah! The forests they saw! The rushing rivers and tall mountains!

At last they reached Death's house. "Your mother is inside," Death said.

"Let her remain there," the man said. "She is afraid of dying, and that is what I'm here to do."

They sat down on the bare ground in front of the house. The man looked his age now, still solid, but no longer young. The long guard hairs over his shoulders were silver-white, as was the soft, thick fur around his mouth and along the line of his jaw. "Go ahead," he said.

Death reached in and pulled out the threads that were the man's spirit. Only a few were red and white, the colors of anger and selfishness. Many were gray and black, the colors of responsible behavior. Most were other colors: yellow, orange, green, blue, purple.

The red and white threads were too few to become anything. They faded at once. The black and grey threads wove themselves into the image of a person, who nodded politely to Death, then rose into the sky and vanished.

The rest of the threads wove themselves into another person, this one blue-green, dotted with yellow, orange and purple. The person floated on the wind like a banner. "What am I?" it asked Death.

"I don't know. I have never made anything like you."

"Then I must find out, but not here. I will come back for a visit, if I am able." It flew off on the wind, soaring and rippling.

Death rose and went inside, where Ala waited by the fire. Here the story ends.

Translator's note # 1: The *hwarhath* live in large families. A few are solitary, mostly because of their jobs: a forest fire-spotter or herder, the operator of a lift bridge in a remote location. But women with children are always surrounded by relatives. A *hwarhath* reader would know at once that something was disturbingly wrong about Ala, though we never find out why she is living on her own, except for her son.

Translator's note # 2: Human readers of the translation have complained that the story does not close the way a human story ought to. Ala has learned nothing from her experiences and does not suffer any consequences for her really awful behavior. The *hwarhath* (and the translator) would reply (a) some people do not learn from experience and (b) Ala does suffer consequences. At the story's end, she is trapped in Death's house, unable to go any distance from it; and she is stuck between life and death, not entirely dead, but not really living. In spite of all her cleverness, has she escaped the thing she fears? Do any of us escape the things we fear?

Scientific Romances

Hwarhath science fiction developed prior to human contact. As *hwarhath* civilization became more scientific, there began to be romances about science, real or imagined.[1]

As they moved into space, fiction about space travel and alien planets became inevitable. The male romances are about love and violence in far-distant places. The female romances describe the establishing of new families in space stations, on moons, and in other star systems. This has not happened in reality, where women rarely go beyond their home system and children are never raised anywhere except the home planet. Maybe *hwarhath* women and children will travel later, when the galaxy is better known and the human menace has been dealt with. In the meantime, women, especially young women, can and do dream.

Neither of the two stories here are planetary romances, though these are becoming common. Instead, we have a story about a discovery made too early and a man who does not want to go into space.

---

1   The *hwarhath* are not entirely comfortable with imaginary science, except for physics, which has become so strange (they say) that anything is possible. Once FTL becomes real, who knows what else might be real?

THE POTTER OF BONES

The northeast coast of the Great Southern Continent is hilly and full of inlets. These make good harbors, their waters deep and protected from the wind by steep slopes and grey stone cliffs. Dark forests top the hills. Pebble beaches edge the harbors. There are many little towns.

The climate would be tropical, except for a polar current that runs along the coast, bringing fish and rain. The local families prosper thanks to fishing and the rich, semi-tropical forests that grow inland. Blackwood grows there, and iridescent greywood, as well as lovely ornamentals: night-blooming starflower, day-blooming skyflower, and the matriarch of trees: crown-of-fire. The first two species are cut for lumber. The last three are gathered as saplings, potted, and shipped to distant ports, where affluent families buy them for their courtyards.

Nowadays, of course, it's possible to raise the saplings in glass houses anywhere on the planet. But most folk still prefer trees gathered in their native forests. A plant grows better if it's been pollinated naturally by the fabulous flying bugs of the south, watered by the misty coastal rains, and dug up by a forester who's the heir to generations of diggers and potters. The most successful brands have names like "Coastal Rain" and emblems suggesting their authenticity: a forester holding a trowel, a night bug with broad, furry wings floating over blossoms.

This story is about a girl born in one of these coastal towns. Her mother was a well-regarded fisherwoman, her father a sailor who'd washed up after a bad storm. Normally, a man such as this—a stranger, far from his kin—would not have been asked to impregnate any woman. But the man was clever, mannerly, and had the most wonderful fur: not grey, as was usual in that part of the world, but tawny red-gold. His eyes were pale clear yellow; his ears, large and set well out from his head, gave him an entrancing appearance of alertness and intelligence. Hard to pass up looks like these! The matrons of Tulwar coveted them for their children and grandchildren.

He—a long hard journey ahead of him, with no certainty that he'd ever reach home—agreed to their proposal. A man should be obedient to the senior women in his family. If they aren't available, he should obey the matrons and matriarchs near-by. In his own country, where his looks were ordinary, he had never expected to breed. It might happen, if he'd managed some notable achievement. Knowing himself, he didn't plan on it. Did he want children? Some men do. Or did he want to leave some-thing behind him on this foreign shore, some evidence that he'd existed, before venturing back on the ocean? We can't know. He mated with our heroine's mother. Before the child was born, he took a coastal trader north, leaving nothing behind except a bone necklace and Tulwar Haik.

Usually, when red and grey interbreed, the result is a child with dun fur. Maybe Haik's father wasn't the first red sailor to wash up on the Tulwar coast. It's possible that her mother had a gene for redness, which finally expressed itself, after genera-tions of hiding. In any case, the child was red with large ears and bright green eyes. What a beauty! Her kin nicknamed her Crown-of-Fire.

When she was five, her mother died. It happened this way: the ocean current that ran along the coast shifted east, taking the Tulwar fish far out in the ocean; and the Tulwar followed. Somewhere, days beyond sight of land, a storm drowned their fleet. Mothers, aunts, uncles, cousins disappeared. Nothing came home except a few pieces of wood: broken spars and oars. The people left in Tulwar Town were either young or old.

Were there no kin in the forest? A few, but the Tulwar had relied on the ocean.

Neighboring families offered to adopt the survivors. "No, thank you," said the Tulwar matriarchs. "The name of this bay is Tulwar Harbor. Our houses will remain here, and we will remain in our houses."

"As you wish," the neighbors said.

Haik grew up in a half-empty town. The foresters, who provided the family's income, were mostly away. The adults present were mostly white-furred and bent: great-aunts and -uncles, who had not thought to spend their last years mending houses and caring for children. Is it any wonder that Haik grew up wild?

Not that she was bad; but she liked being alone, wandering the pebble beaches and climbing the cliffs. The cliffs were not particularly difficult to climb, being made of sedimentary stone that had eroded and collapsed. Haik walked over slopes of fallen rock or picked her way up steep ravines full of scrubby trees. It was not adventure she sought, but solitude and what might be called `nature' nowadays, if you're one of those people in love with newfangled words and ideas. Then, it was called The Five Aspects or Water, Wind, Cloud, Leaf, and Stone. Though she was the daughter of sailors, supported by the forest, neither Leaf nor Water drew her. Instead, it was rock she studied—and the things in rock. Since the rock was sedimentary, she found fossils rather than crystals.

Obviously, she was not the first person to see shells embedded in cliffs; but the intensity of her curiosity was unusual. How had the shells gotten into the cliffs? How had they turned to stone? And why were so many of them unfamiliar?

She asked her relatives.

"They've always been there," said one great-aunt.

"A high tide, made higher by a storm," said another.

"The Goddess," a very senior male cousin told her, "whose behavior we don't question. She acts as she does for her own reasons, which are not unfolded to us."

The young Tulwar, her playmates, found the topic boring. Who could possibly care about shells made of stone? "They don't shimmer like living shells, and there's nothing edible in them. Think about living shellfish, Haik! Or fish! Or trees like the ones that support our family!"

If her kin could not answer her questions, she'd find answers herself. Haik continued her study. She was helped by the fact that the strata along the northeast coast had not buckled or been folded over. Top was new. Bottom was old. She could trace the history of the region's life by climbing up.

At first, she didn't realize this. Instead, she got a hammer and began to break out fossils, taking them to one of the town's many empty houses. There, through trial and error, she learned to clean the fossils and to open them. "Unfolding with a hammer," she called the process.

Nowadays we discourage this kind of ignorant experimentation, especially at important sites. Remember this story takes place in the distant past. There was no one on the planet able to teach Haik; and the fossils she destroyed would have been destroyed by erosion long before the science of paleontology came into existence.

She began by collecting shells, laying them out on the tables left behind when the house was abandoned. Imagine her in a shadowy room, light slanting through the shutters. The floor is thick with dust. The paintings on the walls, fish and flowering trees, are peeling. Haik—a thin red adolescent in a tunic—bends over her shells, arranging them. She has discovered one of the great pleasures of intelligent life: organization or, as we call it now, taxonomy.

This was not her invention. All people organize information. But most people organize information for which they can see an obvious use: varieties of fish and their habits, for example. Haik had discovered the pleasure of knowledge that has no evident use. Maybe, in the shadows, you should imagine an old woman with white fur, dressed in a roughly woven tunic. Her feet are bare and caked with dirt. She watches Haik with amusement.

In time, Haik noticed there was a pattern to where she found her shells. The ones on the cliff tops were familiar. She could find similar or identical shells washed up on the Tulwar beaches. But as she descended, the creatures in the stone became increasingly strange. Also, and this puzzled her, certain strata were full of bones that obviously belonged to land animals. Had the ocean advanced, then retreated, then advanced again? How old were these objects? How much time had passed since they were alive, if they had ever been alive? Some of her senior kin believed they were mineral formations that bore an odd resemblance to the remains of animals. "The world is full of repetition and similarity," they told Haik, "evidence the Goddess has little interest in originality."

Haik reserved judgment. She'd found the skeleton of a bird so perfect that she had no trouble imagining flesh and feathers over the delicate bones. The animal's wings, if wings they were, ended in clawed hands. What mineral process would create the cliff-top shells, identical to living shells, and this lovely, familiar-yet-unfamiliar skeleton? If the Goddess had no love for originality, how to explain the animals toward the cliff bottom, spiny and knobby, with an extraordinary number of legs? They didn't resemble anything Haik had ever seen. What did they repeat?

When she was fifteen, her relatives came to her. "Enough of this folly! We are a small lineage, barely surviving; and we all have to work. Pick a useful occupation, and we'll apprentice you."

Most of her cousins became foresters. A few became sailors, shipping out with their neighbors, since the Tulwar no longer had anything except dories. But Haik's passion in life was stone. The town had no masons, but it did have a potter.

"Our foresters need pots," said Haik. "And Rakai is getting old. Give me to her."

"A wise choice," said the great-aunts with approval. "For the first time in years, you have thought about your family's situation."

Haik went to live in the house occupied by ancient Rakai. Most of the rooms were empty, except for pots. Clay dust drifted in the air. Lumps of dropped clay spotted the floors. The old potter was never free of the material. "When I was young, I washed more," she said. "But time is running out, and I have much to do. Wash if you want. It does no harm, when a person is your age. Though you ought to remember that I may not be around to teach you in a year or two or three."

Haik did wash. She was a neat child. But she remembered Rakai's warning and studied hard. As it turned out, she enjoyed making pots. Nowadays, potters can buy their materials from a craft cooperative; and many do. But in the past every potter mined his or her own clay, and a potter like Rakai, working in a poor town, did not use rare minerals in her glazes. "These are not fine cups for rich matrons to drink from," she told Haik. "These are pots for plants. Ordinary glazes will do, and minerals we can find in our own country." Once again Haik found herself out with hammer and shovel. She liked the ordinary work of preparation, digging the clay and hammering pieces of mineral from their matrices. Grinding the minerals was fine, also, though not easy; and she loved the slick texture of wet clay as she felt through it for grit. Somehow, though it wasn't clear to her yet, the clay—almost liquid in her fingers—was connected to the questions she had asked about stone.

The potter's wheel was frustrating. When Rakai's old fingers touched a lump of clay, it rose into a pot like a plant rising from the ground in spring, entire and perfect, with no effort that Haik could see. When Haik tried to do the same, nothing was achieved except a mess.

"I'm like a baby playing with mud!"

"Patience and practice," said old Rakai.

Haik listened, being no fool. Gradually, she learned how to shape clay and fire it in the kiln Rakai had built behind the house. Her first efforts were bad, but she kept several to store her favorite pieces of rock. One piece was red iron ore, which could be ground down to make a shiny black glaze. The rest were fossils: shells and strange marine animals and the claw-handed bird.

At this point in the story, it's important to know the meaning of the word "potter" in Haik's language. As in our language, it meant a maker of pots. In addition, it meant someone who puts things into pots. Haik was still learning to make pots. But she was already a person who put stones or bones into pots, and this is not a trivial occupation, but rather a science. Never undervalue taxonomy. The foundation of all knowledge is fact, and facts that are not organized are useless.

Several years passed. Haik learned her teacher's skill, though her work lacked Rakai's elegance.

"It's the cliffs," said the old potter. "And the stones you bring back from them. They have entered your spirit, and you are trying to reproduce them in clay. I learned from plants, which have grace and symmetry. But you—"

One of Haik's pots was on the wheel: a squat, rough-surfaced object. The handles were uneven. At first, such things had happened due to lack of skill, but she found she liked work that was a little askew. She planned a colorless, transparent glaze that would streak the jar—like water seeping down a rock face, Haik suddenly realized.

"There's no harm in this," said Rakai. "We all learn from the world around us. If you want to be a potter of stones, fine. Stones and bones, if you are right and the things you find *are* bones. Stones and bones and shells."

The old potter hobbled off. Should she break the pot, Haik wondered. Was it wrong to love the cliffs and the objects they contained? Rakai had told her no. She had the old potter's permission to be herself. On a whim Haik scratched an animal into the clay. Its head was like a hammer, with large eyes at either end—on the hammer's striking surfaces, as Haik explained it to herself. The eyes were faceted; the long body was segmented. Each segment had a pair of legs, except for the final segment, which had two whip-like tails longer than the rest of the animal. No one she had met, not travelers to the most distant places nor the most outrageous liars, had ever described such an animal. Yet she had found its remains often, always in the cliffs' lower regions, in a kind of rock she had named "far-down dark-grey."

Was this one of the Goddess's jokes? Most of the remains were damaged. Only by looking carefully had she found intact examples; and no one else she knew was interested in such things. Had the Goddess built these cliffs and filled them with remains in order to fool Tulwar Haik?

Hardly likely! She looked at the drawing she had made. The animal's body was slightly twisted, and its tails flared out on either side. It seemed alive, as if it might crawl off her pot and into Tulwar Harbor. The girl exhaled, her heart beating quickly. There was truth here. The creature she had drawn must have lived. Maybe it still lived in some distant part of the ocean. (She had found it among shells. Its home must be aquatic.) She refused to believe such a shape could come into existence through accident. She had been mixing and kneading and spinning and dropping clay for years. Nothing like this had ever appeared, except through intent. Surely it was impious to argue that the Goddess acted without thought. This marvelous world could not be the result of the Great One dropping the stuff-of-existence or squishing it aimlessly between her holy fingers. Haik refused to believe the animal was a joke. The Goddess had better things to do, and the animal was beautiful in its own strange way. Why would the Goddess, who was humorous but not usually malicious, make such an intricate and lovely lie?

Haik drew the animal on the other side of the pot, giving it a slightly different pose, then fired the pot and glazed it. The glaze, as planned, was clear and uneven, like a film of water running down the pot's dark grey fabric.

As you know, there are regions of the world where families permit sex among their members, if the relationship is distant enough. The giant families of the third continent, with fifty or a hundred thousand members, say there's nothing wrong with third or fourth or fifth cousins becoming lovers; though inbreeding is always wrong. But Haik's family did not live in such a region, and their lineage was so small, and lived so closely together, that no one was a distant relative.

For this reason, Haik did not experience love until she was twenty and went down the coast on a trading ship to sell pots in Tsugul.

This was an island off the coast, a famous market in those days. The harbor was on the landward side, protected from ocean storms. A town of wood and plaster buildings went down slopes to the wooden warehouses and docks. Most of the plaster had been painted yellow or pale blue. The wood, where it showed, was dark blue or red. A colorful town, thought Haik when she arrived, made even more colorful by the many plants in pots. They stood on terraces and rooftops, by doorways, on the stairway streets. A good place to sell Rakai's work and her own.

In fact, she did well, helped by a senior forester who had been sent to sell the Tulwar's other product.

"I'd never say a word against your teacher, lass," he told her. "But your pots really set off my trees. They, my trees, are so delicate and brilliant; and your pots are so rough and plain. Look!" He pointed at a young crown-of-fire, blossoming in a squat black pot. "Beauty out of ugliness! Light out of darkness! You will make a fortune for our family!"

She didn't think of the pot as ugly. On it, in relief, were shells, blurred just a bit by the iron glaze. The shells were a series, obviously related, but from different parts of the Tulwar cliffs. Midway up the cliffs, the first place she found them, the shells were a single plain coil. Rising from there, the shells became ever more spiny and intricate. This progression went in a line around the pot, till a spiked monstrosity stood next to its straightforward ancestor.

Could Haik think this? Did she already understand about evolution? Maybe not. In any case, she said nothing to her kinsman.

That evening, in a tavern, she met a sailor from Sorg, a tall, thin, arrogant woman, whose body had been shaved into a pattern of white fur and black skin. They talked over cups of *halin*. The woman began brushing Haik's arm, marveling at the red fur. "It goes so well with your green eyes. You're a young one. Have you ever made love with a foreigner?"

"I've never made love," said Haik.

The woman looked interested, but said, "You can't be that young."

Haik explained she'd never traveled before, not even to neighboring towns. "I've been busy learning my trade."

The Sorg woman drank more *halin*. "I like being first. Would you be interested in making love?"

Haik considered the woman, who was certainly exotic looking. "Why do you shave your fur?"

"It's hot in my home country; and we like to be distinctive. Other folk may follow each other like city-building bugs. We do not!"

Haik glanced around the room and noticed other Sorg women, all clipped and shaved in the same fashion, but she did not point out the obvious, being young and polite.

They went to the Sorg woman's ship, tied at a dock. There were other couples on the deck, all women. "We have a few men in the crew this trip," her sexual partner said. "But they're all on shore, looking for male lovers; and they won't be back till we're ready to lift anchor."

The experience was interesting, Haik thought later, though she had not imagined making love for the first time on a foreign ship, surrounded by other couples, who were not entirely quiet. She was reminded of fish, spawning in shallow water.

"Well, you seemed to enjoy that," said the Sorg woman. "Though you are a silent one."

"My kin say I'm thoughtful."

"You shouldn't be, with red fur like fire. Someone like you ought to burn."

Why? wondered Haik, then fell asleep and dreamed that she was talking with an old woman dressed in a plain, rough tunic. The woman's feet were muddy. The nails on her hands were untrimmed and long, curling over the tips of her fingers like claws. There was dirt under the nails. The old woman said, "If you were an animal, instead of a person, you would have mated with a male; and there might have been children, created not as the result of a breeding contact, but out of sexual passion. Imagine a world filled with that kind of reproduction! It is the world you live in! Only people use reason in dealing with sex. Only people breed deliberately."

She woke at dawn, remembering the dream, though it made little sense. The woman had seemed like a messenger, but her message was obvious. Haik kissed the Sorg woman goodbye, pulled on her tunic and stumbled down the gangway. Around her the air was cold and damp. Her feet left prints on dew-covered wood.

She had sex with the Sorg woman several more times. Then the foreign ship lifted anchor, and Haik's lover was gone, leaving only a shell necklace.

"Some other woman will have to make you burn," the lover said. "But I was the first, and I want to be remembered."

Haik thanked her for the necklace and spent a day or two walking in the island's hills. The stone here was dark red and grainy and did not appear to contain fossils. Then she and her kinsman sailed north.

After that, she made sure to go on several trips a year. If the ship was crewed by women, she began looking for lovers as soon as she was on board. Otherwise, she waited till they reached a harbor town. Sometimes she remained with a single lover. At other times, she went from one to another or joined a group. Her childhood nickname, long forgotten, came back to her, though now she was known as Fire, rather than Crown-of-Fire. She was a flame that burned without being burned.

"You never feel real affection," one lover told her. "This is nothing but sex for you."

Was this true? She felt affection for Rakai and her family at home and something approaching passion for her work with clay and stone. But these women?

As we know, men are more fervent and loyal lovers than women. They will organize their lives around affection. But most women are fond of their lovers and regret leaving them, as they usually must, though less often in modern times; and the departures matter less now, since travel has become so rapid. Lovers can meet fifty times a year, if they're willing to pay the airfare.

Haik enjoyed sex and her sexual partners, but left with no regrets, her spirit untouched.

"All your fire is in your sexual parts," another partner said. "Nothing burns in your mind."

When she was twenty-five, her family decided to breed her. There was no way she could refuse. If the Tulwar were going to survive, every healthy female had to bear children. After discussion, the senior women approached the Tsugul, who agreed to a mating contract. What happened next Haik did not like to remember. A young man arrived from Tsugul and stayed with her family. They mated till she became pregnant, then he was sent home with gifts: fine pots mostly, made by her and Rakai.

"I won't have children in my pottery," the old woman said.

"I will give the child to one of my cousins to raise," said Haik.

She bore female twins, dun colored with bright green eyes. For a while, looking at them, she thought of raising them. But this idea came from exhaustion and relief. She was not maternal. More than children, she wanted fossils and her pots. A female cousin took them, a comfortable woman with three children of her own. "Five is always lucky," she told Haik.

It seemed to be. All five children flourished like starflower trees.

Rakai lasted till Haik was almost thirty. In her last years, the old potter became confused and wandered out of her house, looking for long-drowned relatives or clay, though she had turned clay digging over to Haik a decade before. One of these journeys took place in an early winter rain. By the time the old woman was found, she was thoroughly drenched and shaking with cold. A coughing sickness developed and carried her away. Haik inherited the pottery.

By this time, she had developed a distinctive style: solid, squat pots with strange creatures drawn on them. Sometimes, the handles were strange creatures made in molds: clawed birds or animals like flowers with thick, segmented stalks. Haik had found fossils of the animals still grasping prey. In most cases, the prey were small fish, so the creatures had been marine predators. But her customers thought they were flowers—granted, strange ones, with petals like worms. "What an imagination you have!"

The pots with molded handles were fine work, intended for small expensive plants. Most of her work was large and sturdy, without handles that could break off. Her glazes remained plain: colorless or black.

Though she was a master potter, her work known up and down the coast, she continued hunting fossils. Her old teacher's house became filled with shelves, and the shelves became filled with pieces of stone. Taking a pen, Haik wrote her name for each creature on the shelf's edge, along with the place where she'd found this particular example. Prowling through the rooms by lantern light, she saw eons of evolution and recognized what she saw. How could she fail to, once the stones were organized?

The first shelves held shells and faint impressions of things that might be seaweed. Then came animals with many limbs, then fish that looked nothing like any fish she'd ever seen. Finally came animals with four limbs, also strange. Most likely, they had lived on land.

She had a theory now. She knew that sand and clay could become solid in the right circumstances. The animals had been caught in muck at the ocean's bottom or in a sand dune on land. Through a process she did not understand, though it must be like the firing of clay in a kiln, the trapping material turned to stone. The animal vanished, most likely burnt up, though it might also have decayed. If nothing else happened, the result was an impression. If the hollow space in the stone became filled, by some liquid seeping in and leaving a deposit, the result was a solid object. Her clawed bird was an impression. Most of her shells were solid.

Was she too clever? Could no one in her age imagine such a theory?

Well, she knew about clay, about molds, about minerals suspended in water. What else is a glaze? There were people in her village who worked with mortar, which is sand that hardens. There were people in nearby villages who used the lost wax process to cast.

All the necessary information was present. But no one except Haik used it to explain the objects in the Tulwar cliffs. Why? Because her kin had barely noticed the fossils and were not curious about them, did not collect them and label them and prowl around at night looking at the pieces of stone and thinking.

Life had changed through time. It went from the very odd to the less odd to the almost familiar. In a few places on the cliff tops were animals that still lived. So, the process that led to the creation of fossils was still happening or had stopped happening recently.

How much time had this taken? Well, the old people in her town said that species did not change; and, as far as she knew, there were no traditions that said animals used to be different. Oh, there were a few stories about monsters that no one had seen recently. But nothing about strange shells or fish. So the time required for change was longer than the memories of people.

Think of what she had learned and imagined! A world of vast periods of time, of animals that changed, of extinction. Hah! It frightened her! Was there any reason why her people might not vanish, along with the fish and plants they knew? Their lineage was small, its existence precarious. Maybe all life was precarious.

One night she had a dream. She was standing atop the cliffs above Tulwar Town. The houses below her looked very distant, unreachable. There was nothing around her except space, stretching up and down and east over the ocean. (The forest was behind her, and she did not turn around.) Next to her stood an old woman with white fur and dirty feet. "You've come a long way," she said. "Maybe you ought to consider turning back."

"Why?" asked Haik.

"There is no point in your journey. No one is going to believe you."

"About what?"

"My creatures."

"Are you the Goddess?" asked Haik.

The woman inclined her head slightly.

"Shouldn't you look more splendid?"

"Did Rakai look splendid? She worked in clay. I work in the stuff-of-existence. I wouldn't call it clean work, and who do I need to impress?"

"Have things really died out? Or do they exist somewhere in the world?"

"I'm not going to answer your questions," the old woman said. "Figure existence out for yourself."

"Do you advise me to turn back?"

"I never give advice," the Goddess said. "I'm simply telling you that no one will believe you about time and change. Oh, one or two people. You can get some people to believe anything, but sensible people will laugh."

"Should I care?" Haik asked.

"That's the question, isn't it?" the Goddess said. "But as I've said already, I don't give advice."

Then she was gone, and Haik was falling. She woke in bed in Rakai's house. Outside her window, stars blazed and gave her no comfort.

She thought about her dream for some time, then decided to go on a voyage. Maybe her problem was lack of sex. Her best pots went into wicker baskets, wrapped in straw, along with large plates, some plain, but most with strange creatures painted on them: her lovely bird with claws, the many-legged bugs, fish that wore plate armor instead of scales, and quadrupeds with peculiar horny heads.

When a ship arrived, going north, she took passage. It was crewed by Batanin women, so she had plenty of sex before she reached their destination. But the feeling of loneliness and fear remained. It seemed as if she stood on the edge of an abyss, with nothing around her or below her.

She got off in a harbor town inhabited by the Meskh, a good-sized family. Although they had a port, they were mostly farmers, producing grain and dried fruit for export, along with excellent *halin*.

Her pottery brought good prices in Meskh Market. By this time she was famous as the Strange Animal Potter or The Potter of Shells and Bones.

"You are here in person," her customers said. "This is wonderful! Two famous women in town at once!"

"Who is the other?" Haik asked.

"The actor Dapple. Her troop has just given a series of plays. Now, they're resting, before continuing their tour. You must meet her."

They met that night in a tavern. Haik arrived escorted by several customers, middle-aged women with dark fur. At a table in the middle of the room, surrounded by dark Meskh women, was someone tall and slender, broad shouldered, her fur pale silver. Introductions were made. The actor stood. In lantern light, Haik could see the silver fur was dappled with small, dim spots. It was rare for people to keep their baby markings, but a few did.

"Hah! You're a lovely one," the actor said. "Red fur is unusual in this part of the world."

Haik sat down and told the story of her father, then how her mother died and how she had grown up in Tulwar Town. When she finally stopped, she saw the Meskh women were gone. She and Dapple sat alone at the table under the flaring lamp.

"What happened?" Haik asked.

"To the others? Most had the good sense to leave. Those who did not were removed by members of my company."

"And I didn't notice?"

"I don't believe," said Dapple, stretching, "that you are a person who notices much outside your interests. The Meskh have loaned us a house. Why don't you come there with me? We can drink more *halin* and talk more, if you wish. Though I have spent the past half an *ikun* imagining what you look like without clothing."

They went to the house, walking side by side through the dark streets. Inside, in a courtyard full of potted trees and lit by stars, they made love. Dapple pulled some blankets and pillows out of a room, so they weren't uncomfortable. "I have spent too much of my life sleeping on hard ground," the actor said. "If I can avoid discomfort, I will." Then she set to work with extraordinary skillful hands and a mouth that did not seem to belong to an ordinary woman made of flesh, but rather to some spirit out of ancient stories. The Fulfilling Every Wish Spirit, thought Haik. The Spirit of Almost Unendurable Pleasure.

The potter tried to reciprocate, though she knew it was impossible. No one, certainly not her, could equal Dapple's skill in love. But the actor made noises that indicated some satisfaction. Finally, they stopped. The actor clasped her hands in back of her head and looked at the stars. "Can you give me a pot?"

"What?" asked Haik.

"I've seen your work before this, and I would like a keepsake, something to remember you."

At last the flame felt burning. Haik sat up and looked at the long, pale figure next to her. "Is this over? Do we have only this night?"

"I have engagements," Dapple said. "We've arranged our passage on a ship that leaves tomorrow. Actors don't have settled lives, Haik. Nor do we usually have permanent lovers."

As in her dream, Haik felt she was falling. But this time she didn't wake in her bed, but remained in the Meskh courtyard.

The Goddess was right. She should give up her obsession. No one cared about the objects she found in cliffs. They did care about her pottery, but she could take leave of pots for a while.

"Let me go with you," she said to Dapple.

The actor looked at her. "Are you serious?"

"I have done nothing since I was fifteen, except make pots and collect certain stones I have a fondness for. More than fifteen years! And what do I have to show? Pots and more pots! Stones and more stones! I would like to have an adventure, Dapple."

The actor laughed and said, "I've done many foolish things in my life. Now, I'll do one more. By all means, come on our journey!" Then she pulled Haik down and kissed her. What a golden tongue!

The next morning, Haik went to her ship and gathered her belongings. They fit in one basket. She never traveled with much, except her pots, and they were sold, the money in a heavy belt around her waist.

Next she went to the harbor mistress. Sitting in the woman's small house, she wrote a letter to her relatives, explaining what had happened and why she wasn't coming home.

"Are you sure this is a good idea?" the mistress said as Haik rolled the letter and put it in a message tube, then sealed the tube with wax.

"Yes." The letter was to go south on the next ship, Haik told the mistress. She gave the woman half her money to hold, till the Tulwar came to claim it.

"This is a foolish plan," the harbor mistress said.

"Have you never been in love?" Haik asked.

"Not this much in love, I'm glad to say."

Haik had started for the door. Now she stopped. The shutters on the room's windows were open. Haik was in a beam of light. Her red fur shone like fire. Her eyes were as clear and green as a cresting ocean wave. Hah! thought the harbor mistress.

"I'm thirty-two and have never been in love, until last night," Haik said. "It has come to me recently that the world is a lonely place." She slung her basket on her back and walked toward Dapple's borrowed house.

A strange woman, thought the harbor mistress.

The actors' ship left on the afternoon tide, Haik with them, standing on the deck, next to her new love.

At this point, the story needs to describe Dapple. She was forty when Haik met her, the first woman to train as an actor and the first person to assemble an acting company made of women. Her early years had been difficult; but, by this time, she was successful and self-confident, a fine actor and even better playwright. Some of her writing has come forward to us, though only in a fragmentary condition. Still, the words shine like diamonds, unscratched by fate.

Dapple was her acting name. Her real name was Helwar Ahl, and her home—which she rarely visited—was Helwar Island, off the northeast corner of the Great Southern Continent. For the most part, she and her company traveled up and down the continent's eastern coast, going as far south as Ettin, where she had many friends.

They were going south now and could have taken Haik's letter, though Haik hadn't known this. In any case, their ship was a fast trader, bound for Hu and not planning to stop on the way. East they went, till the coast was a thin dark line, visible only when the ship crested a wave. The rest of the time, they were alone, except for the *peshadi* that swam in front of them and the ocean birds that followed.

The birds were familiar to Haik, but she had never seen a live *pesha* before. As the animals' sleek backs broke the water's surface, they exhaled loudly enough so Haik had no trouble hearing the sound. *Wah! Wah!* Then they dove, their long tails cutting through the water like knives. They had a second name: blue fish, which came from their hide's deep ocean color. Neither death nor tanning dimmed the hue, and *pesha* leather was a famous luxury.

"I had a pair of *pesha* boots once," said Dapple. "A wealthy matron gave them to me because they were cracked beyond repair. I used them in plays till they fell into pieces. You should have seen me as a warrior, strutting around in those boots!"

Years before, a dead *pesha* had washed up on a beach in Tulwar. They'd all gone to see it: this deep-sea animal their kin had hunted before the Drowning. It had been the size of a large woman, with four flippers and a tail that looked like seaweed, lying limp on the pebbles. The old men of Tulwar cut it up. Most of the women went back to work, but Haik stayed and watched. The flesh had been reddish-purple, like that of land animals; the bones of the skeleton had been large and heavy. As for the famous skin, she'd felt it. Not slimy, like a fish, and with no scales, though there were scaleless fish. She knew that much, though her kin no longer went to sea.

Most interesting of all were the flippers. She begged a hind one from the old men. It was small, the hide not usable, with almost no flesh on the bones. "Take it," her senior male relatives told her. "Though nothing good is likely to come from your curiosity."

Haik carried it to her teacher's house, into a back room that Rakai never entered. Her fossils were there, along with other objects: a bird skeleton, almost complete; the skulls of various small animals; and shells from Tulwar's beaches. Laying the flipper on a table, she used a sharp knife to cut it open. Inside, hidden by blue skin and reddish-purple flesh, were five rows of long, narrow, white bones.

She had cleaned them and arranged them on the table as she'd found them in the flipper. The two outer rows were short, the thumb—could she call it that?—barely present, while the three middle rows were long and curved. Clearly, they provided a framework for the flipper. What purpose did the outer rows serve, and why had the Goddess hidden a hand inside a sea animal's flipper?

"Well," said Dapple after Haik told this story. "What's the answer to your question?"

"I don't know," said Haik, afraid to talk about her theories. What did she know for certain? A group of puzzling facts. From these she had derived a terrifying sense of time and change. Did she have the right to frighten other people, as she had been frightened?

Beside them, a *pesha* surfaced and exhaled, rolling sideways to eye them and grin with sharp, white teeth.

"Rakai told me the world is full of similarities and correspondences. The Goddess is a repeater. That's what they always told me."

"And a jokester," said Dapple. "Maybe she thought it would be funny to make something that was a fish in some ways and a land animal in others."

"Maybe," Haik said in a doubtful tone. "I tanned the flipper hide and made a bag from it, but couldn't use the bag. It seemed dishonorable and wrong, as if I was using the skin from a woman's hand to keep things in. So I put the *pesha* bones in the bag and kept them on one of my shelves; and I made a pot decorated with *peshadi*. It was a failure. I didn't know how living *peshadi* moved. Now, I will be able to make the pot again."

Dapple ruffled the red fur on her shoulder. "Like fire," the actor said gently. "You burn with curiosity and a desire to get things right."

"My relatives say it will get me in trouble."

"The Goddess gave us the ability to imagine and question and judge," the actor said. "Why would she have done this, if she did not intend us to use these abilities? I question the behavior of people; you question rocks and bones. Both activities seem *chulmar* to me."

Then as now, *chulmar* meant to be pious and to be funny. Dapple's voice sounded amused to Haik; this made her uneasy. In Tulwar, after the Drowning, piety took the form of glumness, though the people there certainly knew the meaning of *chulmar*.

They did not mean to turn their children away from enjoyment of the world, but so much had been lost; they had become afraid; and fear is the end of piety.

The ship continued south, till it was far past the Tulwar coast. During this period, Haik was preoccupied with love. Hah! It had struck her like a strong blow in battle! She could think of little except Dapple's body: the four breasts, surprisingly large for a woman who'd never borne children; the rangy limbs; the prominent nipples, the same color as the "far-down dark grey" strata at home; and the place between the actor's legs, which was a cave of pleasure. Haik could model a breast in clay, make a covered pot of it, with a nipple for the handle. But how could she replicate the hidden place? Or Dapple's mouth with its golden tongue? It could not be done, especially now, with her kiln far behind her. Better not to think of pottery.

They made love often, usually on deck, under blazing tropic stars. She was drunk with love! Love had made her crazy, and she did not care!

Five days south of Tsugul Island, the ship turned west. They came to the wide harbor at Hu, guarded by white shoals. The *peshadi* were gone by then; the birds had become more numerous. A low green coast emerged from misty rain.

Haik and Dapple were on deck. Peering forward, Haik made out the buildings of Hu Town: white and blue, with red or green roofs. Fishing boats lined the harbor docks. Their furled sails were red, white, green, and yellow. "A colorful country."

"That's the south," said Dapple in agreement. As lovely as always, the actor was leaning on the ship's rail, looking happy.

"People in the north call these folk barbarians, who lack refinement and a sense of nuance. But drama is not made of nuance." She raised an arm and brought it down. "It's the sword blade descending, the cry of understanding and anger and pain. I could not write the plays I write, if I didn't visit the south."

They tied up among the fishing boats, empty in mid-afternoon. The acting company went on shore, Tulwar Haik among them. She had never been this far south. The people in the streets, dressed in bright tunics and kilts, were an unfamiliar physical type: broad chested, with short thick limbs. The women were taller than women in the north, towering a full head above their male relatives. Everyone had grey fur, and Haik got many sideways glances.

"I could lose you," said Dapple with amusement.

"They're ugly," said Haik.

"They are different, dear one. When you get used to them, they will begin to look handsome."

"Have you had lovers here?"

Dapple laughed. "Many."

Their destination was an inn built around a courtyard. There were potted trees in the courtyard: skyflower and starflower and a kind Haik did not recognize, which had silver-blue leaves and frilly, bright yellow flowers. Several of the pots had been made by Rakai; one had been made by her, an early work, not bad in its way. She pointed it out to Dapple.

The innkeeper appeared, a huge woman with arms like tree limbs and four enormous breasts, barely concealed by a vest. "My favorite customer!" she cried. "Are you going to perform?"

"Most likely, yes. Haik, this is Hu Aptsi." Dapple laid a hand on Haik's red shoulder. "And this beauty is my new lover, Tulwar Haik the potter. She has given up her pots to travel with me, until we tire of each other."

"Never!" said Haik.

"Excellent work you do in Tulwar," the innkeeper said. "I have neighbors who say nothing good comes from the north. Dapple and pots and flowering trees, I say."

They went into the common room and settled around tables. A round clay hearth bulged out of one wall. Logs burned in it. The innkeeper brought a large metal bowl, filling it with fruit juices and *halin*. Then she heated an iron rod in the fire and put the glowing tip in the full bowl. The liquid hissed and steamed. The innkeeper served. Haik wrapped her hands around a hot cup, sniffing the aromatic steam, thinking, *I am far from home, among strangers, about to drink something for which I have no name.* She tasted the liquid. Delicious!

"It will make you drunk quickly," said Dapple in a warning tone.

Beyond the room's windows, rain fell in the courtyard, and the potted trees quivered. *I am happy*, Haik thought.

That night, as she lay in Dapple's arms, she had a dream. The old woman came to her again, this time with clean hands and feet. "Existence is made to be enjoyed. Always remember that."

"Why did you kill my mother and my other relatives?" Haik asked.

"A storm killed them. Do you think every gust of wind is my breath? Do you think it's my hand that crushes every bug and pulls every bird from the sky?"

"Why did you make things that die?"

"Why do you work in clay? Sooner or later, all your pots will break."

"I like the material."

"I like life," the Goddess said. "And change."

The next day, Haik helped the actors set up their stage in a warehouse near the docks. Rain still fell. They would not be able to perform outside. The acting company was large: ten women, all from northern towns. Five were full members of the company. Three were apprentices. One was a carpenter; one made the costumes; though both of these last could fill small parts when needed. They all worked together easily. It was Haik who was awkward and needed to be told what to do. "You will learn," said Dapple.

Midway through the morning, she disappeared. "Off to write," said the carpenter. "I could see her thinking. These southerners like rude plays, and that isn't the kind of thing we usually do, except when we're down here. You'd think they'd like hero plays; they have plenty of real heroes among them. But no, they want comedy with lots of penises."

Haik could think of nothing to say.

They ate their evening meal in the inn. A light one, since acting should never be done on a full stomach. Then they went back to the warehouse, through still-falling rain. There were lamps on the walls around the stage. The wide, dark space beyond the lamplight was full of people. The air stank of oil, damp fur, and excitement.

"We know our business," said Dapple. "You keep off to the side and watch."

Haik did as told, leaning against a side wall, below a lamp that cast a yellow, flickering glow. Because she rarely thought about her appearance, she did not realize how she looked, her red fur and green eyes shining. Half the women in the audience wanted to have sex with her; half the men wished she were male. How could a woman of her age be so naive? By thinking too much and living too long in the glum family Tulwar became after the Drowning.

The play was about a *sul* with an enormous penis. Dapple played him in an animal mask. The penis, of which he was so proud, was longer than she was and limp, so it dragged on the ground. The *sul* tripped over it often, while he bragged about his masculine power and the lovers he'd had, all men of extraordinary beauty and talent. Once he was established as an irritating braggart, a *tli* appeared, played by the company's second actor. The two animals got into a betting contest, and the *tli* won the *sul's* penis, which struck the audience as funny. Getting it off was a problem, which struck the audience as even funnier. Finally, the *sul* stormed off, bereft of his male member and vowing revenge.

Now the *tli* delivered a soliloquy, while holding the huge limp object. Fine to win, the *tli* said, but he had no use for a penis this large. His own was adequate for his purposes; and the *sul* would come back with friends and weapons to reclaim the penis. This was the problem with giving into irritation. What was he to do? How could he escape the vengeance of the *sul*?

At this point, Dapple reappeared, wearing a sleek blue mask, the open mouth full of sharp white teeth. She was a *pesha*, she announced, an early version of this species. She lived in shallow water, paddling and catching fish. She wanted to move into the ocean, but her tail was too small; she needed a new one, able to drive her deep into the water or far out over the waves.

"I have just the thing," said the *tli* and showed her the *sul*'s penis. "We'll sew this on your backside, and you'll swim like a fish. But in return for this gift, you must carry me to safety; and once you are able to dive deeply, I wouldn't mind having some of the treasure that's sunk in the ocean."

The *pesha* agreed, and the two animals attached the penis to the back of Dapple's costume. Than she did a dance of happiness, singing praise of the ocean and her new life.

The other actors joined them with blue and white banners, which mimicked the motion of water, through which Dapple and the *tli* escaped, dancing and singing.

When everyone was gone, and the stage was bare, Dapple returned as the *sul*, along with two more *sulin*. "Foiled!" they cried. "We can't follow. Your penis is assuredly gone, dear relative. You are not going to be socially popular in the future."

That was the end of the play, except for a final dance, done by the *tli*, surrounded by the rest of the cast, waving golden banners. These represented the treasure he had gained. As for the grateful *pesha*, she was happy in her new home, and with luck the penis would not retain any of its old qualities.

The audience stamped their feet and made hooting noises. Clearly, the play had gone over well.

Haik thought, yes, she was certain that things could turn into other things. But not, in all likelihood, a penis into a tail. And change was not a result of trickery, but time.

People came to talk with the main actors. Haik helped the carpenter and costume maker clean up.

"Ettin Taiin," said the carpenter. "I didn't know he was in town."

"Who?" asked Haik, putting the *tli* mask in a box.

"The lame man."

She looked around and saw a short fellow limping toward the stage. His fur was grey, turning silver over the shoulders and on the face. One eye was missing; he didn't bother to wear a patch over the empty socket.

"He is the foremost war captain among the Ettin," the carpenter said. "And they are the most dangerous lineage in this part of the world. Dapple calls his mother 'great-aunt.' If you find him scary, as I do, then you ought to meet the old lady."

There was no way for him to reach Dapple, surrounded by admirers. He greeted the carpenter and the costume maker by name, without glancing at them directly. Good manners, thought Haik.

"Is Cholkwa with you?" asked the costume maker.

"South, among the savages of the Cold Ocean Coast. I sent men with him for protection, in case the savages didn't like his comedies. May I ask about your companion, or is that rude?"

"We can hardly object to rudeness, after the play we've done," said the carpenter.

"I laughed so hard I thought I would lose control of my bladder," said the one-eyed man.

The costume maker said, "This is Tulwar Haik the potter. She's Dapple's new lover."

The man lifted his head, apparently in surprise. Haik got a glimpse of his sunken eye socket and the remaining eye, which blazed blue as a noon sky. His pupil had expanded in the dim light and lay across the eye like an iron bar. "The Potter of Strange Animals," he said.

"Yes," said Haik, surprised to be known in this distant place.

"The world is full of coincidences!" the soldier told her. "And this one is pleasant! I bought one of your pots for my mother last year. She can barely see these days, but she likes the texture of it. She especially likes to feel the animals you have used for handles. Birds with clawed hands! What an idea! How can they possibly fly?"

"I don't think they did—or do," said Haik.

"These birds exist?" asked the soldier.

Haik paused, considering. "I have found their remains."

"You don't say. The world is full of two things, then: coincidence and strangeness. Considering the Goddess, this can't be called surprising." He glanced toward Dapple. Most of the admirers had gone. "Excuse me. I want to give her news of Cholkwa. They just missed each other. His ship left two days ago; and I was planning to ride home, having stayed with him till the last *ikun*. But then I heard that Dapple had arrived."

He limped away.

"He and Cholkwa are lovers," said the carpenter. "Though the true love of Cholkwa's life is the actor Perig. Perig's old now and in poor health. He lives on Helwar Island with Dapple's kin, who are my kin also, while Cholkwa still travels. Male actors are as promiscuous as women."

Haik finished putting away the masks. The *pesha* mask was new, she realized. The blue paint was still tacky, and the shape of the head had been changed, using cloth and glue.

"We keep blank masks," said the carpenter. "Then, when Dapple has a sudden idea, we can add new animals."

"This is something I can do," Haik said. "Shape the masks and paint them." She glanced up at the carpenter and the costume maker. "Unless the work belongs to you."

"We all do many things," said the costume maker. "If you stay with us you'll find yourself on stage."

278

When everything was packed up, they went back to the inn, sat in the common room and drank *halin*. The Ettin captain, who came with them, had an immense capacity. He left from time to time to urinate, but never got noticeably drunk. The idea of coincidence was stuck in his mind, and he talked about how it worked in war, sometimes to his benefit, sometimes against him.

There was the time he went to attack the Gwa and met their warband on the way, coming to attack Ettin. "We both picked the same exact route. So there we were in a mountain pass, staring at each other with mouths open. Then we fought." He spilled *halin* on the table and drew the disposition of troops. "A bad situation for both of us! Neither had an advantage, and neither had a good way to retreat. I knew I had to win and did, though I lost an eye and a brother; and enough Gwa soldiers escaped, so we could not surprise them at home. A nasty experience, caused by coincidence. Doubtless the Goddess does this to us so we won't take our plans too seriously. A good captain must always be ready to throw his ideas away."

When he finally left, walking steadily except for his limp, Dapple said, "I have sworn to myself, I will put him in a play some day. That is what a hero is really like. I'll have to make up a new story, of course. His life has not been tragic. He's never had to make difficult choices, and everything he's wanted—fame, the affection of his relatives, the love of Cholkwa—has come into his hands."

Well, thought Haik, she was certainly learning new things. The man had not seemed like a hero to her.

The next evening, they did the play a second time. The warehouse was packed, and Ettin Taiin was in the audience again.

Haik watched him as he watched the play, his expression intent. Now and then, he laughed, showing white teeth. One was missing, an upper stabber. Doubtless it had been lost in battle, like his eye and his leg's agility. Haik's male relatives fought nothing except the forest predators, which were not especially dangerous. When men died in the forest, it was usually from small creatures that had a poisonous bite or sting; or they died from accidents. Old people told stories about pirates, but none had attacked the northeast coast in more than a generation. The Tulwar feared water and storms.

Now, Haik thought, she was in the south. War was continuous here, and lineages vanished from existence; the men killed, the women and children adopted. A family that lacked soldiers like Ettin Taiin would not survive.

This idea led nowhere, except to the thought that the world was full of violence, and this was hardly a new thought. In front of her, Dapple tripped over the *sul*'s long dragging penis and tumbled into a somersault, which ended with her upright once again, the penis wound around her neck. The audience hooted its approval. The world was full of violence and sex, Haik thought.

Once again the captain joined them at the inn. This time he drank less and asked questions, first of the actors, then of Haik. Where exactly was her family? What did they produce besides pots?

"Are you planning to invade us?" she asked.

He looked shocked. "I am a soldier, not a bandit, young lady! I only fight with people I know. The purpose of war is to expand the size of one's family and increase the amount of land held by one's kin. That should always be done along existing borders. You push out and push out, gathering the land and the women and children immediately beyond your borders, making sure the land is always contiguous and protected—if possible—by natural barriers. Any other strategy leaves you with a territory that is not defensible."

"He's not planning to invade you," Dapple said in summary. "Your land is too far away."

"Exactly," the captain said. "Bandits and pirates use different tactics, since they want valuable objects rather than land and people. We've had both in the south and dealt with them."

"How?" asked Haik.

"The obvious way is to find where they came from, go there and kill all the men. The problem is, you have to do something with the bandit women and children. They can't be left to starve. But obviously no family wants members with bad traits."

"What do you do?"

"Adopt them. but spread them among many houses, and never let any of them breed. Often, the children turn out well; and after a generation, the traits—bad or good—are gone. This, as you can imagine, is a lot of work, which is a reason to kill enough men so the bandits will think twice about returning to Ettin, but leave enough alive so the women and children are provided for."

The carpenter was right. This was a frightening man.

Dapple said, "The Tulwar are foresters. For the most part, they export lumber and flowering trees. Haik makes pots for the trees."

"Do you have children?" the captain asked Haik.

"Two daughters."

"A woman with your abilities should have more. What about brothers?"

"None."

"Male cousins?"

"Many," said Haik.

The captain glanced at Dapple. "Would it be worthwhile asking a Tulwar man to come here and impregnate one of our women? Your lover's pots are really excellent; and my mother has always liked flowers. So do I, for that matter."

"It's a small family," said Dapple. "And lives far away. A breeding contract with them would not help you politically."

"There is more to life than politics," said the captain.

"The Tulwar men aren't much for fighting," said Haik, unsure that she wanted any connection with Ettin.

"You don't mean they're cowards?"

"Of course not. They work in our wild backcountry as foresters and loggers. They used to sail the ocean, before most of my family drowned. These kinds of work require courage, but we have always gotten along with our neighbors."

"No harm in that, if you aren't ambitious." He grinned, showing his missing tooth. "We don't need to breed for ambition or violence. We have those talents in abundance. But art and beauty—" His blue eye glanced at her briefly. "These are not our gifts, though we are certainly able to appreciate both."

"Witness your appreciation of Cholkwa," said Dapple, her tone amused.

"A great comedian. And the best looking man for his age I've ever seen. But my mother and her sisters decided years ago that he should not be asked to father Ettin children. For one thing, he has never mentioned having a family. Who could the Ettin speak to, if they wanted a breeding contract? A man shouldn't make decisions like these. We do things the right way in Ettin! In any case, acting is not an entirely respectable art; who can say what qualities would appear among the Ettin, if our children were fathered by actors?"

"You see why I have no children," Dapple said, then tilted her head toward the carpenter. "Though my kinswoman here has two sets of twins because her gift is making props. We don't tell our relatives that she also acts."

"Not much," said the carpenter.

"And not well," muttered the apprentice sitting next to Haik.

The captain stayed a while longer, chatting with Dapple about his family and her most recent plays. Finally he rose. "I'm too old for these long evenings. In addition, I plan to leave for Ettin at dawn. I assume you're sending love and respect to my mother."

"Of course," said Dapple.

"And you, young lady." The one eye roved toward her. "If you come this way again, bring pots for Ettin. I'll speak to my mother about a breeding contract with Tulwar. Believe me, we are allies worth having!"

He left, and Dapple said, "I think he's imaging a male relative who looks like you, who can spend his nights with an Ettin woman and his days with Ettin Taiin."

"What a lot of hard work!" the carpenter said.

"There are no Tulwar men who look like me."

"What a sadness for Ettin Taiin!" said Dapple.

From Hu Town they went west and south, traveling with a caravan. The actors and merchants rode *tsina*, which were familiar to Haik, though she had done little riding before this. The carrying beasts were *bitalin*: great, rough quadrupeds with three sets of horns. One pair spread far to the side; one pair curled forward; and the last pair curled back. The merchants valued the animals as much as *tsina*, giving them pet names and adorning their horns with brass or iron rings. They seemed marvelous to Haik, moving not quickly, but very steadily, their shaggy bodies swaying with each step. When one was bothered by something—bugs, a scent on the wind, another *bital*—it would swing its six-horned head and groan. What a sound!

"Have you put *bitalin* in a play?" she asked Dapple.

"Not yet. What quality would they represent?"

"Reliability," said the merchant riding next to them. "Strength. Endurance. Obstinacy. Good milk."

"I will certainly consider the idea," Dapple replied.

At first the plain was green, the climate rainy. As they traveled south and west, the weather became dry, and the plain turned dun. This was not a brief journey. Haik had time to get used to riding, though the country never became ordinary to her. It was so wide! So empty!

The merchants in the caravan belonged to a single family. Both women and men were along on the journey. Of course the actors camped with the women, while the men—farther out—stood guard. In spite of this protection, Haik was uneasy. The stars overhead were no longer entirely familiar, the darkness around her seemed to go on forever, and caravan campfires seemed tiny. Far out on the plain, wild *sulin* cried. They were more savage than the domestic breeds used for hunting and guarding, Dapple told her. "And uglier, with scales covering half their bodies. Our *sulin* in the north have only a few small scaly patches left."

The *sulin* in Haik's country were entirely furry, except in the spring. Then the males lost their chest fur, revealing an area of scaly skin, dark green and glittering. If allowed to, they'd attack one another, each trying to destroy the other's chest adornment. "Biting the jewels" was the name of this behavior.

Sitting under the vast foreign sky, Haik thought about *sulin*. They were all varieties of a single animal. Everyone knew this, though it was hard to believe that Tulwar's mild-tempered, furry creatures were the same as the wild animals Dapple described. Could change go farther? Could an animal with hands become a *pesha*? And what caused change? Not trickery, as in the play. Dapple, reaching over, distracted her. Instead of evolution, she thought about love.

They reached a town next to a wide, sandy river. Low, bushy trees grew along the banks. The merchants made camp next to the trees, circling their wagons. Men took the animals to graze, while the women—merchants and actors—went to town.

The streets were packed dirt, the houses adobe with wood doors and beams. (Haik could see these last protruding through the walls.) The people were the same physical type as in Hu, but with grey-brown fur. A few had faint markings—not spots like Dapple, but narrow broken stripes. They dressed as all people did, in tunics or shorts and vests.

Why, thought Haik suddenly, did people come in different hues? Most wild species were a single color, with occasional freaks, usually black or white. Domestic animals came in different colors; it was obvious why; people had bred according to different ideas of usefulness and beauty. Had people bred themselves to be grey, grey-brown, red, dun, and so on? This was possible, though it seemed to Haik that most people were attracted to difference. Witness Ettin Taiin. Witness the response of the Tulwar matrons to her father.

Now to the problems of time and change, she added the problem of difference. Maybe the problem of similarity as well. If animals tended to be the same, why did difference occur? If there was a tendency toward difference, why did it become evident only sometimes? She was as red as her father. Her daughters were dun. At this point, her head began to ache; and she understood the wisdom of her senior relatives. If one began to question anything—shells in rock, the hand in a *pesha*'s flipper— the questions would proliferate, till they stretched to the horizon in every direction and *why, why, why* filled the sky, like the calls of migrating birds.

"Are you all right?" asked Dapple.

"Thinking," said Haik.

At the center of the town was a square made of packed dirt. The merchants set up a tent and laid out sample goods: dried fish from Hu, fabric made by northern weavers, boxes carved from rare kinds of wood, jewelry of silver and dark-red shell. Last of all, they unfolded an especially fine piece of cloth, put it on the ground and poured out their most precious treasure: a high, white, glittering heap of salt.

Townsfolk gathered: bent matriarchs, robust matrons, slim girls and boys, even a few adult men. All were grey-brown, except the very old, who had turned white.

In general, people looked like their relatives; and everyone knew that family traits existed. Why else select breeding partners with so much care? There must be two tendencies within people, one toward similarity, the other toward difference. The same must also be true of animals. Domestic *sulin* came in different colors; by breeding, people had brought out variations that must have been in the wild animals, though never visible, except in freaks. She crouched in the shadows at the back of the merchants' tent, barely noticing the commerce in front of her, thinking difficult thoughts.

Nowadays, geneticists tell us that the variation among people was caused by drift in isolated populations, combined with the tendency of all people to modify and improve anything they can get their hands on. We have bred ourselves like *sulin* to fit in different environments and to meet different ideas of beauty.

285

But how could Haik know this much about the history of life? How could she know that wild animals were more varied than she had observed? There are wild *sulin* in the far northern islands as thick furred and white as the local people. There is a rare, almost extinct kind of wild *sulin* on the third continent, which is black and entirely scaly, except for a ridge of rust-brown fur along its back. She, having traveled on only one continent, was hypothesizing in the absence of adequate data. In spite of this, she caught a glimpse of how inheritance works.

How likely is this? Could a person like Haik, living in a far-back era, come so near the idea of genes?

Our ancestors were not fools! They were farmers and hunters who observed animals closely; and they achieved technological advances—the creation through breeding of the plants that feed us and the animals we still use, though no longer exclusively, for work and travel—which we have not yet equaled, except possibly by going into space.

In addition to the usual knowledge about inheritance, Haik had the ideas she'd gained from fossils. Other folk knew that certain plants and animals could be changed by breeding; and that families had traits that could be transmitted, either for good or bad. But most life seemed immutable. Wild animals were the same from generation to generation. So were the plants of forest and plain. The Goddess liked the world to stay put, as far as most people could see. Haik knew otherwise.

Dapple came after her, saying, "We need help in setting up our stage."

That evening, in the long summer twilight, the actors performed the *pesha* comedy. Dapple had to make a speech beforehand, explaining what a *pesha* was, since they were far inland now. But the town folk knew about *sulin*, *tli* and penises; and the play went well, as had the trading of the merchants. The next day they continued west.

Haik traveled with Dapple all summer. She learned to make masks by soaking paper in glue, then applying it in layers to a wooden mask frame.

"Nothing we carry is more valuable," said the costume maker, holding a thick, white sheet of paper. "Use this with respect! No other material is as light and easy to shape. But the cost, Haik, the cost!"

The *bitalin* continued to fascinate her: living animals as unfamiliar as the fossils in her cliffs. Her first mask was a *bital*. When it was dry, she painted the face tan, the six horns shiny black. The skin inside the flaring nostrils was red, as was the tongue protruding from the open mouth.

Dapple wrote a play about a solid and reliable *bital* cow, who lost her milk to a conniving *tli*. The *tli* was outwitted by other animals, friends of the *bital*. The play ended with Dapple as the cow, dancing among pots of her recovered milk, turned through the ingenuity of the *tli* into a new substance: long-lasting, delicious cheese. The play did well in towns of the western plains. By now they were in a region where the ocean was a rumor, only half-believed, but *bitalin* were known and loved.

Watching Dapple's performance, Haik asked herself another question. If there was a hand inside the *pesha*'s flipper, could there be another hand in the *bital*'s calloused, two-toed foot? Did every living thing contain another living thing within it, like Dapple in the *bital* costume?

What an idea!

The caravan turned east when a plant called fire-in-autumn turned color. Unknown in Tulwar, it was common on the plain, though Haik had not noticed it till now. At first, there were only a few bright dots like drops of blood fallen on a pale brown carpet. These were enough to make the merchants change direction. Day by day, the color became more evident, spreading in lines. (The plant grew through sending out runners.) Finally, the plain was crisscrossed with scarlet. At times, the caravan traveled through long, broad patches of the plant, *tsina* and *bitalin* belly-deep in redness, as if they were fording rivers of blood or fire.

When they reached the moist coastal plain, the plant became less common. The vegetation here was mostly a faded silver-brown. Rain fell, sometimes freezing; they arrived in the merchants' hometown at the start of the first winter storm. Haik saw the rolling ocean through lashes caked with snow. The pleasure of salt water! Of smelling seaweed and fish!

The merchants settled down for winter. The actors took the last ship north to Hu Town, where the innkeeper had bedrooms for them, a fire in the common room, and *halin* ready for mulling.

At midwinter, Dapple went to Ettin. Haik stayed by the ocean, tired of foreigners. It had been more than half a year since she'd had clay in her hands or climbed the Tulwar cliffs in search of fossils. Now she learned that love was not enough. She walked the Hu beaches, caked with ice, and looked for shells. Most were similar to ones in Tulwar; but she found a few new kinds, including one she knew as a fossil. Did this mean other creatures— her claw-handed bird, the hammer-headed bug—were still alive somewhere? Maybe. Little was certain.

Dapple returned through a snow storm and settled down to write. The Ettin always gave her ideas. "When I'm in the south, I do comedy because the people here prefer it. But their lives teach me how to write tragedy; and tragedy is my gift."

Haik's gift lay in the direction of clay and stone, not language. Her journey south had been interesting and passionate, but now it was time to do something. What? Hu Town had no pottery, and the rocks in the area contained no fossils. In the end, she took some of the precious paper and used it, along with metal wire, to model strange animals. The colors were a problem. She had to imagine them, using what she knew about the birds and bugs and animals of Tulwar. She made the hammer-headed bug red and black. The flower-predator was yellow and held a bright blue fish. The claw-handed bird was green.

"Well, these are certainly different," said Dapple. "Is this what you find in your cliffs?"

"The bones and shells, yes. Sometimes there is a kind of shadow of the animal in the rock. But never any colors."

Dapple picked up a tightly coiled white shell. Purple tentacles spilled out of it; and Haik had given the creature two large, round eyes of yellow glass. The eyes were a guess, derived from a living ocean creature. But Haik had seen the shadow of tentacles in stone. Dapple tilted the shell, till one of the eyes caught sunlight and blazed. Hah! It seemed alive! "Maybe I could write a play about these creatures; and you could make the masks."

Haik hesitated, then said, "I'm going home to Tulwar—"

"You are?" Dapple set down the glass-eyed animal.

She needed her pottery, Haik explained, and the cliffs full of fossils, as well as time to think about this journey. "You wouldn't give up acting for love!"

"No," said Dapple. "I plan to spend next summer in the north, doing tragedies. When I'm done, I'll come to Tulwar for a visit. I want one of your pots and maybe one of these little creatures." She touched the flower-predator. "You see the world like no one else I've ever met. It is full of wonders and strangeness, when looked at by you!"

That night, lying in Dapple's arms, Haik had a dream. The old woman came to her, dirty-footed, in a ragged tunic. "What have you learned?"

"I don't know," said Haik.

"Excellent!" said the old woman. "This is the beginning of comprehension. But I'll warn you again. You may gain nothing, except comprehension and my approval, which is worth little in the towns where people dwell."

"I thought you ruled the world."

"Rule is a large, heavy word," said the old woman. "I made the world and enjoy it, but rule? Does a tree rule the shoots that rise at its base? Matriarchs may rule their families. I don't claim so much for myself."

When spring came, the company went north. Their ship stopped at Tulwar to let off Haik and take on potted trees. There were so many plants that some had to be stored on deck, lashed down against bad weather. As the ship left, it seemed like a floating grove. Dapple stood among the trees, crown-of-fire mostly, none in bloom. Haik, on the shore, watched till she could no longer see her lover or the ship. Then she walked home to Rakai's pottery. Everything was as Haik had left it, though covered with dust. She unpacked her strange animals and set them on a table. Then she got a broom and began to sweep.

After a while, her senior relatives arrived. "Did you enjoy your adventures?"

"Yes."

"Are you back to stay?"

"Maybe."

Great-aunts and uncles glanced at one another. Haik kept sweeping.

"It's good to have you back," said a senior male cousin.

"We need more pots," said an aunt.

Once the house was clean, Haik began potting: simple forms at first, with no decoration except a monochrome glaze. Then she added texture: a cord pattern at the rim, crisscross scratches on the body. The handles were twists of clay, put on carelessly. Sometimes she left her hand print like a shadow. Her glazes, applied in splashes, hid most of what she'd drawn or printed. When her shelves were full of new pots, she went to the cliffs, climbing up steep ravines and walking narrow ledges, a hammer in hand. Erosion had uncovered new fossils: bugs and fish, mostly, though she found one skull that was either a bird or a small land animal. When cleaned, it turned out to be intact and wonderfully delicate. The small teeth, still in the jaw or close to it, were like nothing she seen. She made a copy in grey-green clay, larger than the original, with all the teeth in place. This became the handle for a large covered pot. The body of the pot was decorated with drawings of birds and animals, all strange. The glaze was thin and colorless and cracked in firing, so it seemed as if a film of ice covered the pot.

"Who will buy that?" asked her relatives. "You can't put a tree in it, not with that cover."

"My lover Dapple," said Haik in reply. "Or the famous war captain of Ettin."

At midsummer, there was a hot period. The wind off the ocean stopped. People moved when they had to, mouths open, panting. During this time, Haik was troubled with dreams. Most made no sense. A number involved the Goddess. In one, the old woman ate an *agala*. This was a southern fruit, unknown in Tulwar, which consisted of layers wrapped around a central pit. The outermost layer was red and sweet; each layer going in was paler and more bitter, till one reached the innermost layer, bone-white and tongue-curling. Some people would unfold the fruit as if it were a present in a wrapping and eat only certain layers. Others, like Haik, bit through to the pit, enjoying the combination of sweetness and bitterness. The Goddess did as she did, Haik discovered with interest. Juice squirted out of the old woman's mouth and ran down her lower face, matting the sparse white hair. There was no more to the dream, just the Goddess eating messily.

In another dream, the old woman was with a female *bital*. The shaggy beast had two young, both covered with downy yellow fur. "They are twins," the Goddess said. "But not identical. One is larger and stronger, as you can see. That twin will live. The other will die."

"Is this surprising?" asked Haik.

The Goddess looked peeved. "I'm trying to explain how I breed!"

"Through death?" asked Haik.

"Yes." The Goddess caressed the mother animal's shaggy flank. "And beauty. That's why your father had a child in Tulwar. He was alive in spite of adversity. He was beautiful. The matrons of Tulwar looked at him and said, 'We want these qualities for our family.'

"That's why tame *sulin* are furry. People have selected for that trait, which wild *sulin* consider less important than size, sharp teeth, a crest of stiff hair along the spine, glittering patches of scales on the sides and belly, and a disposition inclined toward violence. Therefore, among wild *sulin*, these qualities grow more evident and extreme, while tame *sulin* acquire traits that enable them to live with people. The *pesha* once lived on land; the *bital* climbed among branches. In time, all life changes, shaped by beauty and death.

"Of all my creatures, only people have the ability to shape themselves and other kinds of life, using comprehension and judgment. This is the gift I have given you: to know what you are doing and what I do." The old woman touched the smaller *bital* calf. It collapsed. Haik woke.

A disturbing dream, she thought, lying in darkness. The house, as always, smelled of clay, both wet and dry. Small animals, her fellow residents, made quiet noises. She rose and dressed, going to the nearest beach. A slight breeze came off the ocean, barely moving the hot air. Combers rolled gently in, lit by the stars. Haik walked along the beach, water touching her feet now and then. The things she knew came together, interlocking; she achieved what we could call the Theory of Evolution. Hah! The Goddess thought in large ways! What a method to use in shaping life! One could not call it quick or economical, but the Goddess was—it seemed by looking at the world—inclined toward abundance; and there was little evidence that she was in a hurry.

Death made sense; without it change was impossible. Beauty made sense; without it, there couldn't be improvement or, at least, variety. Everything was explained, it seemed to Haik: the *pesha*'s flipper, the claw-handed bird, all the animals she'd found in the Tulwar cliffs. They were not mineral formations. They had lived. Most likely, they lived no longer, except in her mind and art.

She looked at the cloudless sky. So many stars, past all counting! So much time, receding into distance! So much death! And so much beauty!

She noticed at last that she was tired, went home and went to bed. In the morning, after a bad night's sleep, the Theory of Evolution still seemed good. But there was no one to discuss it with. Her relatives had turned their backs on most of existence after the Drowning. Don't think badly of them for this. They provided potted beauty to many places; many lineages in many towns praised the Tulwar trees and pots. But their family was small, its future uncertain. They didn't have the resources to take long journeys or think about large ideas. So Haik made more pots and collected more fossils, saying nothing about her theory, till Dapple arrived late in fall. They made love passionately for several days. Then Dapple looked around at the largely empty town, guarded by dark grey cliffs. "This doesn't seem like a good place to winter, dear one. Come south with me! Bring pots, and the Ettin will make you very welcome."

"Let me think," said Haik.

"You have ten days at most," Dapple said. "A captain I know is heading south; I asked her to stop in Tulwar, in case your native town was as depressing as I expected."

Haik hit her lover lightly on the shoulder and went off to think.

She went with Dapple, taking pots, a potter's wheel and bags of clay. On the trip south—through rolling ocean, rain and snow beating against the ship—Haik told Dapple about evolution.

"Does this mean we started out as bugs?" the actor asked.

"The Goddess told me the process extended to people, though I've never found the bones of people in my cliffs."

"I've spent much of my life pretending to be one kind of animal or another. Interesting to think that animals may be inside me and in my past!"

On the same trip, Haik said, "My family wants to breed me again. There are too few of us; I'm strong and intelligent and have already had two healthy children."

"They are certainly right in doing this," said Dapple. "Have you picked a father?"

"Not yet. But they've told me this must be my last trip for a while."

"Then we'd better make the most of it," Dapple said.

There had been a family argument about the trip; and Haik had gotten permission to go only by saying she would not agree to a mating otherwise. But she didn't tell Dapple any of this. Family quarrels should be kept in the family.

They spent the winter in Hu. It was mild with little snow. Dapple wrote, and Haik made pots. Toward spring they went to Ettin, taking pots.

Ettin Taiin's mother was still alive, over a hundred and almost entirely blind, with snow-white fur. But still upright, as Taiin pointed out. "I think she will go to the crematorium upright and remain upright amid the flames."

He said this in the presence of the old lady, who smiled grimly, revealing that she'd kept almost all her teeth.

The Ettin bought all the pots Haik had, Taiin picking out one with special care. It was small and plain, with flower-predators for handles, a cover and a pure white glaze. "For my mother's ashes," the captain said quietly. "The day will come, though I dread it and make jokes about it."

Through late winter, Haik sat with the matriarch, who was obviously interested in her. They talked about pottery, their two families and the Theory of Evolution.

"I find it hard to believe we are descended from bugs and fish," Ettin Hattali said. "But your dreams have the sound of truth; and I certainly know that many of my distant ancestors were disgusting people. The Ettin have been improving, due to the wise decisions of my more recent ancestors, especially the women. Maybe if we followed this process far enough back, we'd get to bugs. Though you ought to consider the possibility that the Goddess is playing a joke on you. She does not always speak directly, and she dearly loves a joke."

"I have considered this," said Haik. "I may be a fool or crazy, but the idea seems good. It explains so much that has puzzled me."

Spring came finally. The hills of Ettin turned pale blue and orange. In the valley-fields, *bitalin* and *tsina* produced calves and foals.

"I have come to a decision," the blind old woman told Haik.

"Yes?"

"I want Ettin to interbreed with your family. To that end, I will send two junior members of my family to Tulwar with you. The lad is more like my son Taiin than any other male in the younger generation. The girl is a fine, intelligent, healthy young woman. If your senior female relatives agree, I want the boy—his name is Galhin—to impregnate you, while a Tulwar male impregnates Sai."

"It may be a wasted journey," said Haik in warning.

"Of course," said the matriarch. "They're young. They have time to spare. Dapple's family decided not to breed her, since they have plenty of children; and she is definitely odd. It's too late now. Her traits have been lost. But yours will not be; and I want the Ettin to have a share in what your line becomes."

"I will let my senior female relatives decide," said Haik.

"Of course you will," said Ettin Hattali.

The lad, as Hattali called him, turned out to be a man of 35, shoulder high to Haik and steel grey. He had two eyes and no limp. None the less, his resemblance to Taiin was remarkable: a fierce, direct man, full of good humor. Haik liked him at once.

His half-sister Sai was 30, a solid woman with grey-brown fur and an excellent, even temperament. No reasonable person could dislike her.

Dapple, laughing, said, "This is Ettin in action! They live to defeat their enemies and interbreed with any family that seems likely to prove useful."

Death and beauty, Haik thought.

The four of them went east together. Haik put her potter's tools in storage at the Hu Town inn, Dapple took leave of many old friends, and the four found passage on a ship going north.

After much discussion, Haik's senior relatives agreed to the two matings, impressed by Galhin's vigor and his sister's calm solidity, by the rich gifts the Ettin kin had bought and Haik's description of the southern family.

Nowadays, with artificial insemination, we don't have to endure what happened next. But it was made tolerable to Haik by Ettin Galhin's excellent manners and the good humor with which he handled every embarrassment. He lacked, as he admitted, Tai-in's extreme energy and violence. "But this is not a situation that requires my uncle's abilities; and he's really too old for mating; and it would be unkind to take him from Hattali. Who can say how long she will survive? Their love for each other has been a light for the Ettin for years. We can hardly separate them now."

The two foreigners were in Tulwar till fall. Then, both women pregnant, the Ettin departed. Haik returned to her pottery. In late spring, she bore twins, a boy and a girl. The boy died soon after birth, but the girl was large and healthy.

"She took strength from her brother in the womb," said the Tulwar matriarchs. "This happens; and the important child, the female, has survived."

Haik named the girl Ahl. She was dun like her older sisters, but her fur had more of a ruddy tint. In sunlight, her pelt shone red-gold; and her nickname became Gold.

It was two years before Dapple came back, her silver-grey fur beginning to show frost on the broad shoulders and lean upper arms. She admired the baby and the new pots, then gave information. Ettin Sai had produced a daughter, a strong child, obviously intelligent. The Ettin had named the child Haik, in hope that some of Tulwar Haik's ability would appear in their family. "They are greedy folk," said Dapple. "They want all their own strength, energy, solidity, and violence. In addition, they want the beauty you make and are.

"Can you leave your daughter for a while? Come south and sell pots, while I perform my plays. Believe me, people in Hu and Ettin ask about you."

"I can," said Haik.

Gold went to a female cousin. In addition to being lovely, she had a fine disposition; and many were willing to care for her. Haik and Dapple took passage. This time, the voyage was easy, the winds mild and steady, the sky clear except for high, thin clouds called "tangled banners" and "schools of fish."

"What happened to your Theory of Evolution?" Dapple asked.

"Nothing."

"Why?"

"What could be done? Who would have believed me, if I said the world is old beyond comprehension; and many kinds of life have come into existence; and most, as far as I can determine, no longer exist?"

"It does sound unlikely," Dapple admitted.

"And impious."

"Maybe not that. The Goddess has an odd sense of humor, as almost everyone knows."

"I put strange animals on my pots and make them into toys for Gold and other children. But I will not begin an ugly family argument over religion."

You may think Haik lacked courage, but remember that she lived in an era before modern science. Yes, there were places where scholars gathered, but none in her part of the world. She'd have to travel long distances and learn a new language, then talk to strangers about concepts of time and change unfamiliar to everyone. Her proof was in the cliffs of Tulwar, which she could not take with her. Do you really think those scholars—people devoted to the study of history, mathematics, literature, chemistry, and medicine—would have believed her? Hardly likely! She had children, a dear lover, a craft, and friends. Why should she cast away all of this? For what? A truth no one was likely to see? Better to stay home or travel along the coast. Better to make pots on her own and love with Dapple.

They reached Hu Town in early summer. The inn's potted trees bloomed scarlet and sky-blue.

"The Potter of Strange Animals!" cried the innkeeper. "I have bought five of your pots for my trees."

Indeed the woman had. Haik wandered around the courtyard, admiring her own work. Four were the kind she'd made when she first returned from the south, decorated with scratches and glazed white or black. The fifth had an underwater scene, done in low relief. Beaked fish swam around the top. Below them, rising from the bottom of the pot, were long sinuous plants. Haik had named them "ocean whips." It was possible that they were animals; once or twice she had found shadows that might be mouths with teeth. Between the plants (or animals) were segmented bugs. The glaze was dark blue with touches of white.

"This is more recent," Haik said.

"I bought it because you are the Potter of Strange Animals. But I prefer the other pots. They set off my trees."

Who can argue with opinions about art, especially with someone who has bought five large pots?

Dapple's company was at the inn, having arrived several days before. Haik knew all of them, except the apprentices. For a while, they traveled through the little coastal towns of Hu, Tesh and Ta-tesh, performing comedies and now and then a tragedy. These last were a surprise to Haik, especially the tragedies about women. They were so subdued! Instead of tumbling and rude jokes, there were small gestures, turned heads, a few words spoken quietly. The actors wore plain robes in sober colors; their faces were unmasked. Most of the time, the music became a single flute. Its sound reminded Haik of a thread floating on moving water, coiling and uncoiling in the current.

"It's my observation that women suffer as much as men," said Dapple in explanation. "But we are expected to be solid and enduring. As a result, our suffering is quiet. I'm trying to show it in the way it happens. Hah! I am tired of loud, rude comedies! And loud, sad plays about the suffering of men!"

At last, in far southern Tesh, they turned inland, traveling without merchants. The borders between Ettin and its eastern neighbors were all quiet. The various families had been allies and breeding partners for generations; and none tolerated criminal behavior. By now, it was late summer. The plain baked under a sun like polished brass. The Ettin hills were hot and dusty. When they reached Hattali's house, it was with relief. Household women greeted them. Men took their *tsina* and the packs of props and costumes. Their rooms opened on a courtyard with two bathing pools. The water in one was colorless and cold. The other bubbled, bright green. The entire acting company stripped and climbed in. What a pleasure! Though both pools were crowded. Well, thought Haik, she'd take a slow bath later, soaking the travel aches from her muscles and bones.

When they were done and in fresh clothes, a woman came for Dapple and Haik. "Ettin Taiin wants you to join his mother."

"Of course," said Dapple.

They went through shadowy halls, silent except for birds calling in the house's eaves. They sounded like water running over stones. The woman said, "Thirty days ago, Hattali fell. She seemed unharmed, except for damage to one foot. It drags a little now. But since the fall she's been preoccupied and unwilling to do much, except sit and talk with Taiin. We fear her great strength is coming to an end."

"It can't be!" said Dapple.

"You know about old age and death. We've seen them in your plays." Saying this, the woman opened a door.

Outside was a terrace, lit by the afternoon sun. Hattali sat in a high-backed chair, leaning against the back, her eyes closed. How old she looked! How thin and frail! Her warrior son sat next to her on a stool, holding one of his mother's hands. He looked at them, laid Hattali's hand gently in her lap and rose. "Cholkwa is in the north. I'm glad to see you, Dapple."

They sat down. Hattali opened her eyes, obviously seeing nothing. "Who has come, Tai?"

"Dapple and her lover, the potter."

The old lady smiled. "One last play."

299

"A play, yes," said Dapple. "But not the last, I hope."

A look of irritation crossed Hattali's face. "Did the potter bring pots?"

Haik excused herself and went to find her pack. Now she understood the house's quiet. Most likely, the children had been sent out to play; and the adults—she passed a few in the halls—moved softly and gravely. A matriarch like Hattali, a woman with so much dignity, should not be bothered with noise while deciding whether to live or die.

When Haik returned to the terrace, Hattali seemed asleep. But the old woman took the pot Haik put in her hands, feeling it with bony fingers. "What is it?"

"There's a skull on top, a replica of one I found in stone."

"It's shaped like a *tli* skull," Hattali said.

"A bit, but the teeth are different. I imagine from the teeth that the animal had scales, not hair."

Hattali exhaled and felt more. "On the sides of the pot?"

"The animal as I imagine it must have been, when alive. I found the skull first and made a pot that Dapple bought. But now I have found the entire animal, and it wasn't the way I showed it on the first pot. So I made this."

"The animals are in relief?"

"Yes."

"What do they look like, if not *tli*?"

Haik thought. "An animal about as long as my arm, four legged with a tail. Spines protrude along the back, as if the animal had a fin there like a fish. That was the thing I did not imagine: the spines. And the tail is different also, flat from side to side, like the tail of a fish."

"What color is the glaze?"

"Black, except the skull, which is white."

"Tai," said the old woman.

"Mother?"

"Is it beautiful?"

"She is the Potter of Strange Animals. The pot is strange, but well made."

"I want it for my ashes."

"You will have it," he said.

She gave her son the pot. He turned it in his blunt, strong-looking hands. Hattali turned her blind face toward Haik. "You must still believe your crazy idea, that we are descended from bugs."

"That the world is old and full of change, yes," said Haik.

"Sit down and tell me about it again."

Haik obeyed. The old woman listened as she explained about beauty, death, and change.

"Well, we have certainly improved our lineage through careful breeding," said Hattali finally. "The child your kinsman fathered on Sai is a fine little girl. We hope she'll be as clever as you are, though I'm still not certain about your idea of time and change. Why didn't the Goddess simply make people? Why start with bugs?"

"She clearly likes bugs," said Haik. "The world is full of them. They are far more common than people and more varied. Maybe her plan was to create a multitude of bugs through beauty and death, and we are an accidental result of her breeding of bugs."

"Do you believe that?"

"No. She told me we have a gift no other living creature had: we know what we do. I believe this gift is not an accident. She wanted comprehension."

Haik was wrong in saying this, according to modern scientists. They believe life is entirely an accident, though evidently an accident that happens often, since life has appeared on many planets. Intelligent life is far less common, but has clearly appeared on at least two planets and may be present elsewhere in a form we do not recognize. It also is an accident, modern thinkers say. This is hard for many of us to believe; and Haik, living in the distant past, could hardly be expected to bring forward an idea so disturbing.

"Well, you certainly ought to listen to the Goddess, if she talks to you," said Hattali. "When will I hear your play, Dapple?"

"It will take a few days to prepare."

The matriarch tilted her head in acquiescence.

They left Hattali then, going back to their room. "I want you to make masks for a new play," Dapple said. "Five of your strange animals. They interest Hattali. Sit with her while you work, and tell her about your ideas. Taiin is an excellent man. None better! But her illness has got him frightened, and his fear is not helping her mood. Maybe she knows what she's doing, maybe it is time for her to die. But I wonder if the fall has frightened her as well as her relatives. A woman like Hattali should not die from fear."

"Has she no daughters?"

"Two. Good women, but not half what she is; and she's never gotten along with either. The love of her life has always been Taiin."

He left the next morning, called to the western border. Gwa scouts had been seen. Their old enemies might have heard that Hattali was dying. What better time to attack?

"They expect that grief will break me," Taiin said, standing in the house's front court, dressed in metal and leather armor. A sword hung at his side, and a battle axe hung from a loop on his saddle. "It may, but not while there's work to be done." He swung himself onto his *tsin* easily, in spite of age and his bad leg. Once settled on the animal, he looked down at Haik and Dapple.

"She is the last of her generation. What people they were, especially the women! As solid as stone walls and towers! I have lived my entire life in their protection. Now, the walls are broken. Only one tower remains. What will I do, when Hattali is gone?"

"Defend Ettin," said Dapple.

He gathered the *tsin*'s reins, grinning. "You're right, of course. Maybe, if I'm lucky, we'll capture a Gwa spy."

A moment later he was through the house's gate, moving steadily along the dusty road, his men following, armed and armored.

"You may be wondering about his last remark," Dapple said.

Haik opened her mouth to say no.

"There are men who take pleasure in raping prisoners before they kill them. Or in harming them in other ways. I have suspected Taiin is one such. Now I'm certain."

This was how he'd deal with his grief at Hattali's illness: by making someone else's end unpleasant.

"Beauty and death," Dapple said. "This is the way the Goddess has organized her world, according to you and your bones."

They spent the next several days on Ettin Hattali's terrace. The weather remained dry and sunny. Haik worked on the masks, while Dapple sat with paper and brush, sometimes writing, more often listening.

There was a folding table next to Hattali's chair. The matriarch's relatives brought out food and drink. In any ordinary circumstance, it would have been rude to eat while conversing with other people, especially guests, but the old lady had not been eating. Good health always goes in front of good manners.

At first Hattali ignored everything except water, brought in a glass goblet. This she held, turning the precious object between her bent fingers.

The first mask was the animal on Hattali's funeral pot: a long, narrow head, the jaw hinged and moved with a string, the mouth full of pointed teeth. Snap! Snap!

The skin would be mottled green, Haik decided; the eyes large, round and red. There were existing animals—small hunters with scaly hides—that had triangular pupils. She would give this creature the same. The spines on the back would be a banner, supported by a harness over Dapple's shoulders. Hah! It would flutter when her lover danced! As she worked, she described the mask to Hattali.

"Have you ever found large animals?" the old woman asked.

"Not complete. But large bones, yes, and teeth that are longer than my hands. The layer they are in is high on my native cliffs and was laid down when the country was above water. They were land-dwellers, those animals, larger than anything living now, at least in the regions I've visited, and with teeth that remind me of birds' teeth, though more irregular and much larger."

"What eyesight you have!" Hattali exclaimed. "To see into the distant past! Do you really believe these creatures existed?"

"They did," said Haik firmly.

Gradually, as their conversation continued, the old lady began to eat: hard biscuits first, then pieces of fruit, then *halin* in a small, square, ceramic cup. Hattali was sitting upright now, her bony shoulders straight under an embroidered robe. Hah! She was licking her fingers! "Can you write, Haik?"

"Yes."

"I want you to write down your ideas and draw the animals you've found in stone. I'll have one of my female relatives make a copy."

"You believe me," said Haik in surprise.

"Most of what you've told me I knew already," Hattali answered. "How could any woman not know about inheritance, who has lived long enough to see traits appear and reappear in families of people, *sulin,* and *tsina?* But I lacked a framework on which to string my information. This is what you've given me. The frame! The loom! Think of the patterns the Ettin will be able to weave, now that we understand what the Goddess has been doing with sex and death and time!" The old woman shifted in her chair. There was a cup of *halin* next to her on the folding table. She felt for it, grasped it and drank, then reached for a piece of fruit. "I have been wondering whether it's time for me to die. Did you notice?"

"Yes," murmured Dapple.

"The blindness is hard to endure, but life remains interesting; and my kin tell me that they still need my judgment. I can hardly refuse their pleas. But when I fell, I thought—I know this illness. It strikes women down like a blow from a war club. When they rise, if they rise, who can say what the damage will be? Paralysis, stupor, the loss of speech or thought.

"This time the only damage was to one leg. But I may fall again. I have seen relatives, grave, senior female cousins, turn into something less than animals—witless and grieving, though they do not remember the cause of their grief. Maybe, I thought, it would be better to stop eating now and die while I am still able to choose death.

"But I want your book first. Will you write it for me?"

Haik glanced at Dapple, who spoke the word "yes" in silence.

"Yes," said the potter.

The matriarch sighed and leaned back. "Good! What a marvel you are, Dapple! What a fine guest you have brought to Ettin!"

The next day Haik began her book, drawing fossils from memory. Fortunately, her memory was excellent. Her masks went to the costume maker, who finished them with the help of the apprentices. It was good work, though not equal to Haik's. One apprentice showed real promise.

The old lady was eating with zest now. The house resumed the ordinary noise of a house full of relations. Children shouted in the courtyards. Adults joked and called. Looking up once from her work, Haik saw adolescents swimming in the river below the terrace: slim, naked girls, their fur sleeked by water, clearly happy.

By the time the Ettin war party returned, Taiin looking contented as he dismounted in the front courtyard, the book on evolution was done. Taiin greeted them and limped hurriedly to his mother's terrace. The old woman rose, looking far stronger than she had twenty days before.

The war captain glanced at Dapple. "Your doing?"

"Haik's."

"Ettin will buy every pot you make!" the captain said in a fierce whisper, then went to embrace his mother.

Later, he looked at Haik's book. "This renewed Hattali's interest in life? Pictures of shells and bones?"

"Ideas," said Dapple.

"Well," said Taiin, "I've never been one for thinking. Ideas belong to women, unless they're strategic or tactical. All I can be is thankful and surprised." He turned the folded pages. "Mother says we will be able to breed more carefully, thinking of distant consequences rather than immediate advantage. All this from bones!"

The actors did their play soon after this, setting their stage in the house's largest courtyard. It began with a fish that was curious about the land and crawled out of the ocean. In spite of discomfort, the fish stayed, changing into an animal with four legs and feet. Hah! The way it danced, once it had feet to dance with!

The fish's descendants, all four footed animals, were not satisfied with their condition. They fell to arguing about what to do next. Some decided their ancestral mother had made a mistake and returned to water, becoming animals like *peshadi* and *luatin*. Others changed into birds, through a process that was not described; Haik knew too little about the evolution of birds. Other animals chose fur, with or without a mixture of scales. One animal chose judgement as well as fur.

"How ridiculous!" cried her comrades. "What use are ideas or the ability to discriminate? You can't eat a discrimination. Ideas won't keep you warm at night. Folly!" They danced away, singing praise for their fur, their teeth, their claws.

The person with fur and intelligence stood alone on the stage. "One day I will be like you," Dapple said to the audience. "No spines on my back, no long claws, no feathers, though I had these things, some of them at least, in the past. What have I gained from my choice, which my relatives have just mocked? The ability to think forward and back. I can learn about the past. Using this knowledge, I can look into the future and see the consequences of my present actions. Is this a useful gift? Decide for yourselves."

This was the play's end. The audience was silent, except for Hattali, who cried, "Excellent! Excellent!" Taking their cue from the old lady, the rest of the Ettin began to stamp and shout.

A day later, the actors were on the road. They left behind Haik's book and the new masks. Dapple said, "My play doesn't work yet, and maybe it never will. Art is about the known, rather than the unknown. How can people see themselves in unfamiliar animals?"

Haik said, "My ideas are in my head. I don't need a copy of the book."

"I will accept your gifts," said Hattali. "And send one copy of the book to another Ettin house. If anything ever happens here, we'll still have your ideas. And I will not stop eating, till I'm sure that a few of my relatives comprehend the book."

"It may take time," said Haik.

"This is more interesting than dying," Hattali said.

The story ends here. Haik went home to Tulwar and made more pots. In spite of Taiin's promise, the Ettin did not buy all her work. Instead, merchants carried it up and down the coast. Potters in other towns began to imitate her; though they, having never studied fossils, did not get the animals right. Still, it became a known style of pottery. Nowadays, in museums, it's possible to find examples of the Southern Fantastic Animal Tradition. There may even be a few of Haik's pots in museum cabinets, though no one has yet noticed their accuracy. Hardly surprising: students of art are not usually students of paleontology.

As for Dapple, she continued to write and perform, doing animal plays in the south and heroic tragedies in the north. Her work is still famous, though only fragments remain.

The two lovers met once or twice a year, never in Tulwar. Dapple kept her original dislike of the place. Often, Haik traveled with the actor's company, taking pots if they were going to Ettin.

Finally, at age fifty, Haik said to her senior relatives, "I am leaving Tulwar."

The relatives protested.

"I have given you three children and trained five apprentices. Let them make pots for you! Enough is enough."

What could the relatives say? Plenty, as it turned out, but to no avail. Haik moved to a harbor town midway between Tulwar and Hu. The climate was mild and sunny; the low surrounding hills had interesting fossils embedded in a lovely, fine-grained, cream-yellow stone. Haik set up a new pottery. Dapple, tired of her rainy home island, joined the potter. Their house was small, with only one courtyard. A crown-of-fire tree grew there, full-sized and rooted in the ground. Every spring, it filled their rooms with a sweet aroma, then filled the courtyard with a carpet of fallen blossoms. "Beauty and death," Dapple sang as she swept the flowers up.

Imagine the two women growing old together, Dapple writing the plays that have been mostly lost, Haik making pots and collecting fossils. The creatures in those hills! If anything, they were stranger than the animals in the cliffs of Tulwar!

As far as is known, Haik never wrote her ideas down a second time. If she did, the book was lost, along with her fossils, in the centuries between her life and the rediscovery of evolution. Should she have tried harder? Would history have been changed, if she had been able to convince people other than Ettin Hattali? Let others argue this question. The purpose of this story is to be a story.

The Ettin became famous for the extreme care with which they arranged breeding contracts and for their success in all kinds of far-into-the-future planning. All through the south people said, "This is a lineage that understands cause and effect!" In modern times, they have become one of the most powerful families on the planet. Is this because of Haik's ideas? Who can say? Though they are old-fashioned in many ways, they've had little trouble dealing with new ideas. "Times change," the Ettin say. "Ideas change. We are not the same as our ancestors, nor should we be. The Goddess shows no fondness for staying put, nor for getting stuck like a cart in spring rain.

"Those willing to learn from her are likely to go forward. If they don't, at least they have shown the Great Mother respect; and she, in return, has given them a universe full of things that interest and amaze."

THE GARDEN

There was a boy who belonged to the Atkwa lineage. Like most of his family, he had steel grey fur. In the case of his relatives the color was solid, but the boy's fur was faintly striped and spotted. In dim light this wasn't visible. In sunlight his pelt looked like one of the old pattern-welded swords that hung in his grandmother's greathouse. They were rarely taken outside, usually to be polished, though sometimes for teaching purposes, when adult male relatives were home. Not that anyone used swords in this period, except actors in plays. But children ought to learn the history of their family.

The boy's pelt was due to a recessive gene emerging after generations, since the Atkwa had not gone to a spotted family for semen in more than two hundred years. This was not due to prejudice. Unlike humans, the *hwarhath* find differences in color more interesting than disturbing. Their prejudices lie in other directions.

It was circumstance and accident that kept the Atkwa solid grey. They lived in a part of the world where this was the dominant coloration, and—being a small and not especially powerful family—they did not look to distant places when arranging breeding contracts.

As a toddler, the boy was forward and active, but not to an extraordinary degree. At the age of eight or so, he lengthened into a coltish child, full of energy, but also prone to sudden moods of thoughtfulness. These worried his mother, who consulted with

309

her mother, the family matriarch: a gaunt woman with fur frosted by age, her big hands twisted by joint disease.

"Well," the matriarch said after listening. "Some men are thoughtful. They have to be, if they're going to survive in space, with no women around to do their thinking."

"But so young?" the mother asked. "He spends hours watching fish in a stream or bugs in a patch of weeds."

"Maybe he'll become a scientist." The matriarch gave her daughter a stern look. "He's your only boy. He's been strange and lovely looking from birth. This has led you to pay too much attention and to worry without reason. Straighten up! Be solid! The boy will probably turn out well. If he doesn't, he'll be a problem for our male relatives to handle."

At ten, the boy discovered gardening—by accident, while following a *tli* that had come out of the nearby woods to steal vegetables. The sun was barely up. Dew gleamed on the vegetation around his grandmother's house. The air he drew into his mouth was cool and fragrant.

The *tli*, a large specimen with strongly marked stripes, trundled over his grandmother's lawn, its fat, furry belly gathering dew like a rag wiping moisture off something bright. A metal blade maybe, the boy thought. A dark trail appeared behind the animal, and it was this the boy followed at a safe distance. Not that a *tli* is ever dangerous, unless cornered, but he didn't want to frighten it.

The animal skirted the house, entering the garden in the back. There the *tli* began to pillage, a messy process with much (it seemed to the boy) unnecessary destruction. He ought to chase it away. But he was hit, suddenly and with great force, by the beauty of the scene in front of him. The perception was like a blade going into his chest. Don't think of this as a figure of speech, exaggerated and difficult to believe. There are emotions so intense that they cause pain, either a dull ache or a sudden sharp twinge. Under the influence of such an emotion, one's heart may seem to stop. One may feel wounded and changed, as one is changed by a serious injury.

This happened to the boy when he didn't, as yet, understand much of what he felt. If he'd been older, he might have realized that most emotions go away, if one ignores them. Instead, he was pierced through by beauty. For the rest of his life he remembered how the garden looked: a large rectangular plot, edged with ornamental plants, their leaves—red, purple, yellow, and blue—like the banners of a guard in a military ceremony.

Inside this gaudy border were the vegetables, arranged in rows. Some grew on poles or trellises. Others were bushes. Still others rose directly from the soil as shoots, fronds, clusters of leaves. The variety seemed endless. While the garden's border was brightly colored, most of these plants were shades of green or blue. Yet they seemed, if anything, more lovely and succulent, beaded with dew and shining in the low slanting rays of the sun.

So it was, on a cool summer morning, the air barely stirring, that Atkwa Akuin fell in love—not with another boy, as might have been expected, if not this year, then soon—but with his grandmother's garden.

He spent the rest of that summer in the plot, helping the two senior female cousins who did most of the house's gardening. In the fall, he turned soil, covered beds with hay, trimmed what needed trimming, and planted chopped-up bits of root. Black and twisted, they looked dead to him. But they'd send up shoots in the spring, his cousins promised.

Akuin's mother watched doubtfully. The boy was settling down to a single activity. That had to be better than his former dreaminess, but she would have been happier if he'd taken up a more boyish hobby: riding *tsina*, fishing in the nearby river, practicing archery, playing at war.

"Give him more time," said Akuin's grandmother. "Boys are difficult, as I know."

She'd raised three. One had died young in an accident. Another had died in space, killed in the war that had recently begun. The enemy—humans, though their name was not yet known—had come out of nowhere in well-armed ships. Almost everything about them remained hidden in darkness as complete as the darkness from which they'd emerged. But no one could doubt their intentions. The first meeting with them had ended in violence; so had every encounter since.

The matriarch's third son was still alive and had reached the rank of advancer one-in-front. This should have given her satisfaction, but the two of them had never gotten along. Akuin's uncle rarely came home for a visit. The matriarch lavished her attention on her one daughter, her nieces and their children.

Now she said, folding her twisted hands, "Maybe Akuin will become a gardener in a space station. Such people are useful. An army needs more than one kind of soldier."

When he was fifteen, Akuin went to boarding school, as do all boys of that age. In these places they learn to live without women and among males who belong to other lineages. This becomes important later. A boy who can't detach himself from family and country is little use in space. In addition, the boys complete their education in the ordinary *hwarhath* arts and sciences—the ones learned by both females and males—and begin their education in the specifically male art and science of war.

Akuin's school was on the east coast of his continent, in an area of sandy dunes and scrub forest: poor land for gardening. Nonetheless, the school had a garden. Botany is a science, and horticulture is an art.

It was on the landward side of the school complex, sheltered by buildings from the prevailing wind. Akuin found it the day after he arrived. To the west was a row of dunes, with the afternoon sun standing just above them. Long shadows stretched toward the garden. The gardener—a man with a metal leg—moved slowly between the rows of plants, bending, examining, picking off bugs, which he pressed between the fingers of his good hand. His other arm hung at his side, clearly damaged and not recently. It had shrunk till little remained except black fur over bone.

Akuin thought he was unnoticed. But the gardener turned suddenly, straightened and glared at him with yellow eyes. Akuin waited motionless and silent. He might be a little odd, but there was nothing wrong with his manners.

"You're new," said the man finally. "Where from?"

Akuin told him.

"Inland. Why aren't you on the beach? Or exploring the school? We have a fine museum, full of things that former students have sent back."

"I like gardens," Akuin said.

The man glared at him a second time, then beckoned, using his good hand. The boy came forward into the garden.

The man's name, it turned out, was Tol Chaib. He'd gone to this school years before, gone into space, then come back to teach. He said nothing more about himself in that first encounter. Instead he talked about the difficulty of growing healthy plants in sand. Partly, he said, he worked to change the soil. The school provided him with compost and manure, more than was needed. "If there's anything certain about boys and *tsina*, it's that they will produce plenty of fertilizer." Some of the excess went into lawns and ornamental borders. The rest was sold to local farmers.

Mostly, he found plants that fit the local soil and weather. "No other strategy works well. This is why it's so difficult to grow our plants on other planets. The light is different; so is the invisible radiation. The soil has the wrong minerals or minerals in the wrong proportions. A plant always grows best on its home planet, unless—as sometimes happens—it proliferates unnaturally in a strange place."

Akuin had been feeling lonely and afraid. How could he survive five years in school? At the end of his school years stood a fate even worse. Few *hwarhath* men remain on the home planet. From 20 to 80, their lives are spent in space, exploring and preparing to meet the enemies who will inevitably appear. The universe is a dangerous place, and the *hwarhath* are a careful species. So the men go into space, looking for trouble, while

313

their female relatives stay home, raising children and practicing the arts of peace.

Sixty years in metal corridors, with only brief visits home. Hah! The prospect was terrible.

Now, listening to Tol Chaib, he felt a little comfort. Maybe he'd be able to survive school. He could certainly learn much from the crippled man.

The school had a curriculum, of course. There were classes, labs, field trips, military exercises. Most of what Akuin did was required. But when he could decide for himself, he went to Tol Chaib's garden or to the greenhouses where Chaib kept flowers growing all winter.

This was a comfort on days when snow lay over the campus and a knife-wind blew off the ocean. The glass walls were covered by condensed moisture, making the world outside invisible. Inside was damp, warm air; the smell of dirt and growing things; flowers that blossomed as brightly as a campfire; the gardener's dry, harsh voice.

At first he told Akuin about the plants around them, then about the gardening he'd done in space. Gardens up there—Tol Chaib waved at the ceiling—are necessary for five reasons. Men are healthier if they eat fresh fruit and vegetables. The plants help keep air breathable by removing carbon dioxide and providing oxygen. "This can be done by inorganic chemical reactions or by microbes, but a garden is more pleasant and produces air with a better aroma."

In addition, Tol Chaib said, every station and ship is supposed to be self-sufficient. "Ships become lost. A station might be cut off, if the war goes badly. If this happens, the men on board will need ways to provide themselves with air, food, and medicine."

"You've given me three reasons for gardens in space," Akuin said. "Health, clean air, and self-sufficiency. What are the other two?"

"Joy," the gardener said. "Which is not usually produced by vats of microbes or inorganic chemical reactions. And hope that we will finally come home."

Toward the end of winter Akuin learned how Tol Chaib had been injured.

He'd been the foremost gardener in a small station designed for research rather than war. A supply ship arrived, and the pilot made a mistake while docking—several mistakes, since he panicked when he realized the coupling of ship and station was going badly. The station's outer skin had been punctured. There was a sudden loss of pressure." Tol Chaib grinned. "The air lock system in my section of the station was new and had improvements, which did not work as planned."

When the rescue workers reached the garden, they found most of the plants gone, sucked out into space. The garden's equipment was mostly in pieces. Tol Chaib lay under a heap of debris, next to a lock that had finally closed.

"They think—I don't remember—that I was pulled from one end of the garden to the other, through several rooms. Most likely I hit things on the way. I certainly hit the airlock after it closed; and the debris hit me."

What a story! Akuin shivered.

"The pilot of the ship killed himself. The engineer in front of the air lock design team asked to die. But his senior officers decided the problem with the system had not been caused by anything he did, and could not have been foreseen."

"What was the problem?" Akuin asked. "Why did the system malfunction?"

"I never learned. At first, I was in no condition to pay attention. Later, I didn't care."

"Did the pilot have permission to kill himself?"

"That's another thing I don't know." Tol Chaib said.

The pilot had panicked in an emergency. That was the one thing Akuin knew about him. Maybe, after he saw the damage he'd done, the pilot had panicked a second time and made the decision to die on his own. A terrible idea! "If he asked for permission and got it, then what he did was right," Akuin said finally. "And it was right for the engineer to live, after permission had been refused to him, though—hah! He must have wanted to die."

"Maybe," said Tol Chaib.

There was another thought in Akuin's mind, which he did not express.

"You're wondering why I'm still alive," Tol Chaib said. "I gave serious thought to taking the option." He paused, his good hand gently touching the frilly edge of a tropical bloom. "I was a handsome man. Many approached me or watched from a distance, hoping for encouragement. Hah! It was fine to know that I could make another man happy by saying "yes."

"Then I woke and discovered my leg was gone. What a surprise! Where was the rest of me?"

Akuin felt uncomfortable. No child wants to know that adults can be unhappy. Heroes in hero plays—yes. They can suffer, and a boy Akuin's age will be inspired. But a man like Tol Chaib, a teacher and crippled, should never reveal pain.

"I had no desire to limp and crawl through life," the teacher said, his dry voice inexorable. "I wanted to be quick and lovely and loved.

"One of my senior male relatives came to visit me while I was in sick bay. I asked him for permission to die. He said, 'wait.' So I did. My male relatives consulted with each other and with the officers in front of me. This is how such things are done," the dry voice said. "Except in hero plays."

"I know," Akuin said. In a sense he hadn't known. Before this moment, the rules for killing oneself had been unreal, something learned as one learns formulae one is never going to use. How fine that I can use sticks and triangles to determine the height of that tall tree! Do I want to know the tree's height? No.

"In that kind of situation," Tol Chaib added. "The kind that occurs in hero plays, when a man is entirely alone or the people around him are confused and wrong, it makes sense for the man to take his fate into his own hands. What choice does he have? But it's a good idea to be sure that one *is* a hero, and in a heroic situation, before acting in such a way.

"It was decided I ought to live—for various reasons. My skill as a gardener was remarkable; and I'm good at teaching. Also, I'm an only child; and my mother is well-loved in our family. It was thought she might grieve too much, if I killed myself."

Akuin left the greenhouse soon after, trudging back to his dormitory through a new fall of snow. Overhead the sky was full of stars. For once the air was almost still, though stabbingly cold. The boy walked in a cloud of his own breath.

He reached the middle of a playing field and looked around, first at the snow, unmarked except by the trail he was in the process of making, then at the sky. How brilliant! How many-colored! How difficult to measure!

All at once he lost his sense of position and direction. Up and down seemed no longer different. The ground beneath his feet was gone; so was his body's weight; he was falling into the innumerable stars.

It was a terrible sensation. Akuin closed his eyes. For a moment, the sense of falling continued. Then it was gone, as quickly as it had come. When he opened his eyes, everything was ordinary again.

Later, he wondered if this had been a vision. Most likely not. He'd never shown any signs of having a diviner's ability, nor did he want it. Seeing what other people can't see is unsettling. Diviners tend to be odd, ungraceful folk, who go through life out-of-step and off-balance, never fitting into any group. No rational boy wants a fate like this.

More likely, Akuin thought, he was tired and disturbed by his mentor's story. In any case, the experience was over and did not recur.

He completed school in the usual period of time. Education is not a race for the *hwarhath*. No one finishes before the others. How can they? Every *hwarhath* male goes into the army as soon as he graduates; and no one can enter the army until he has reached the age of adulthood.

At twenty, Akuin left school, going home for a long visit. As usual, on visits home, he worked in the family garden. His mother watched with her usual concern. He had turned into a lovely young man, slim and graceful; his pale, stippled pelt reminded her of sunlight moving over metal or water moving over stones. But he was too quiet for a youth his age: too thoughtful and too in love with the plants he tended.

With luck, she told herself, he'd be assigned to work as a gardener. The teachers at his school had recommended this. According to her male relatives, the officers in charge of making assignments often paid attention to such recommendations. Though not always, of course.

A little before harvest, Akuin's assignment came. As expected, it was in space, though where in space the message did not say. He packed the one bag permitted him and said goodbye to his family. It wasn't easy to bid his mother farewell. Unlike humans, the *hwarhath* do not express grief by excreting water from the corners of their eyes. Nor do they have the human love of making noise. Given any reason—grief, anger, happiness, a flash of irritation, a momentary surprise—humans will be noisy. An uncomfortable kind of behavior. Maybe it comes from their ancestors, who spent their time (we are told) screaming at the tops of trees. The *hwarhath* must be descended from animals who spent more time on the ground, where they could see one another, and where noise might attract unwelcome attention. In most situations, they are quiet, at least in comparison to humans.

But what man wants to see a look of grim endurance on his mother's face?

It was a relief to get outside. The plants that bordered the garden were waist-high now. Their long sharp leaves seemed to Akuin like a fence of swords, inlaid with precious metals and encrusted with jewels, so they shone red, blue, yellow, green. The green especially was a shade so intense and pure that it seemed to pierce him. Hah! He could feel it in his throat and chest!

Bugs with the same rich late-summer colors floated in the hot air. Bending down and peering, Akuin could see ripe fruits and vegetables nestled among the leaves of the plants raised for food. He found a few last pests, pressed them to death between his fingers, then turned toward the waiting car.

One of his female cousins drove him to the nearest rail line. They parted quietly. He went by train to the regional airport, then by plane to one of the rocket islands. From the island he went to a keeping-pace-with-the-place-below station. At each stage of this journey, his environment became more closed-in and artificial, till at last in the station it was a maze of grey metal corridors. No windows opened out on space. If they had, what would he have seen?

His unreachable home planet.

Akuin felt his spirit shrink like a plant shriveling in a drought. How was he going to survive? His grandmother's voice, speaking in his mind, gave the answer: through loyalty and discipline. In his imagination he made the gesture of acknowledgment.

An FTL transport carried him along with other men to a station in the most remote region of *hwarhath*-explored space. This was not a place where the *hwarhath* would usually have built a station; it was too far out, and the route that led to it was not easy to follow.

But when the *hwarhath* came to this region, they found many stars in close proximity. By itself this would have been interesting. The stars in *hwarhath* space are, for the most part, scattered as thinly as trees on Great Central Plain; and in general they are solitary rather than communal. It's rare to find more than two or three together.

If ordinary stars are like a bottle tree, standing alone on the dusty plain, with at most a couple of offshoots or companions, then this group was like a grove or thicket, gathered around some hidden reason for their gathering: a spring or sunken pool.

Of course the *hwarhath* scientists wanted to study the grove, and they had enough influence to get the station built. But they did not get the resources they wanted. Remember that a war was on. This region was far distant from the *hwarhath* home planet and from the region where humans were a recurring problem. The work done here did not seem important to the men who made decisions. Akuin's new home was inadequately funded.

Imagine a metal cylinder orbiting a dim and dusty, unimpressive star. The cylinder is small and plain, with none of the additions characteristic of the great stations, which unfold over time like flowering plants, producing metal stalks, blossoms, and pods. Around them move attendant bodies: maintenance craft, shuttles, satellites devoted to research or specialized manufacture, so the great station seems enveloped in a cloud of glittering bugs.

Akuin's destination was nothing like this. There was only the cylinder, a simple geometric shape, orbiting its primary, which had no planets. In the distance were other stars, packed closely together, all of them dim and red.

"Like an army camped on a plain," said one of the new arrivals. "How long the night has been! The army's fires have burnt down. Now they are almost out."

"It may look like an army to you," another soldier commented. "To me it looks like a group of stars."

Scattered through the star-grove (or, if you like the image, the army-camp of stars) were other bodies, which the new arrivals could not see. These came in several varieties. Most were burning-into-darkness stars, which had exhausted their fuel, turning into the stellar equivalent of cinders. Others, less numerous, were breaking-into-pieces stars, which had become so dense that gravity had crushed their matter, so it became a kind of *puree* or thick soup. The last group, least numerous of all, were called falling-into-strangeness; and these were the stars that interested the *hwarhath* scientists.[1]

Akuin paid little attention to the grove (or camp) of stars. Instead he noticed the interior of the station: a cramped maze of corridors and rooms. There were no windows, of course, and most of the holograms (there were some, though not as large and splendid as the ones in a great station) showed more impressive parts of the galaxy.

At the end of one corridor a huge planet turned, surrounded by moons and braided rings. At the end of another corridor was a human ship, which exploded over and over, hit by *hwarhath* missiles. Hah! It was a thing to see! Dramatic and encouraging!

He was assigned to a room with four other young men, also new arrivals. Each got a bed, a storage locker, and a niche in the wall, where a hologram could be installed. Three of his companions put scenes of home, as did Akuin: his grandmother's garden at midsummer. The last man, a thin lad with the most amazingly ugly markings on his pale grey fur, put nothing in his niche.

The ugly lad was named Gehazi Thev. He seemed remarkably calm and friendly, for a man who looked as if he'd been used to blot up ink. How could any family have kept a child like this one?

"Easy enough to explain," Thev said on the second or third day that Akuin knew him. "My mother is a mathematician, the best in our lineage; and the semen used to produce me came from a family—the Thevar—who are famous scientists. They also have a tendency toward splotchiness, which shows up rarely. It's a defect they have tried to eliminate.

"In any case—" No question that Thev was a talker. "My mother had a terrible pregnancy. Not only did she feel sick, but her ability to think about math vanished almost entirely, either due to her queasiness or to some change in her hormones.

---

1   Black dwarves, EDSOs, and clothed singularities. There is no reason to believe the hwarhath have discovered a stellar cluster as odd as this one turns out to be.

"When I was born, they thought of killing me. Just look!" He ran one hand over an arm disfigured by a great, dark blotch. "How could I possibly have a normal life? But my mother had already announced that she would never allow her family to breed her again. These were her good years, when she could do original work. She wasn't going to waste them on motherhood." The calm, friendly voice sounded amused. "My relatives could kill me and lose my mother's genetic material, or they could keep me. There was no reason to believe that I would be stupid."

"It doesn't bother you?" asked Akuin.

"My lack of stupidity? No. The Goddess has made sure that the universe is well provided with stupid people. As far as I can tell from their behavior, humans are as dim as most *hwarhath*. What is this war about, for example? How can we fight people when we can't even talk with them? What has war been about, through our entire history? The taking of land! The acquisition of women and children! But what good are human females to us? If they do have females, as we understand that term. For all we know, humans may have five different sexes, none of them producing children in a way we understand. As for their land, how can we use it? It isn't likely that our plants will grow on their planet. So, what are we fighting for? Women who cannot mother *hwarhath* children, and land that is—for us—infertile. The humans are just as stupid. Unless, of course, they have another reason for killing people." Thev tilted his head, considering the idea of a new reason for war.

"I was talking about your looks," said Akuin. He touched a patch of fur that wasn't blotchy. Instead, it shone like silver. "If you had been like this all over—"

"Hah! I would have been something! There would have been men lined up at our door, and very inconvenient it would have been for the rest of you." Thev paused. He was sprawled on his bed, resting on his elbows, regarding Akuin with resin-yellow eyes. "Yes, it has bothered me at times," he said at last. "When I first realized how very ugly I was, and again when I was in school and the age when boys begin to fall in love. No one would ever love me, I thought. I would have to be content with my hands and the programs the Public Health Corps makes about how to have sex that's both pleasant and healthy."[2]

"Has that happened?" Akuin said.

Thev smiled. "I have seen a lot of public health programs. But I have discovered that some men like intelligence. Believe me, I am intelligent!"

They became friends, though the other roommates couldn't understand why. Akuin was lovely and also sad, the kind of youth that older men—some older men—liked to comfort. No one would ever try to comfort Thev. He was too confident and happy. In addition, they were slightly different ages. Thev had stayed on the home world for two extra years, studying at the famous Helig Institute. Instead of being 20 or 21, he was 23, though he didn't seem especially old. His time had been devoted to ideas rather than experience. It was stars he knew, not manners.

They stayed together through the period when new arrivals were oriented to life in space. "Like two burrs," said the other roommates, who began to suspect it was Akuin's beauty that drew the other man. But what drew Akuin to a man whose conversation was so often impossible to understand? All these kinds of stars that fell into themselves, changing (as they did so) the nature given them by the Goddess, and even in some cases (according to Thev) falling out of the universe the Goddess had created. This was unexpected! Who could make sense of it? Who could find it interesting or erotic?

When the orientation period was over, Thev began to spend his time with other physicists. Akuin started his new job, in the station's garden.

---

2   Hwarhath Public Health Corps programs about sex are deliberately erotic and often made with the assistance of the Arts Corp, the theory being that the audience will pay more attention to something that is beautiful and sexy than to something that is ugly and dull.

A garden, you may think. The lad had been saved. He'd found his natural environment.

The garden occupied a series of rooms, grey metal like everything else in the station. The plants, all useful rather than ornamental, grew in raised beds like metal boxes. Light came from panels in the ceiling. Moisture was provided by a network of tubes, which dripped water directly on the roots. Nothing was wasted. Nothing was present unless it was needed.

Akuin discovered that gardening, for him, comprised many things besides the garden itself. He missed sunlight, clouds, rain, bugs, raiding *tli*, the sight of hills rising in the distance, the smell of a nearby forest or ocean. It was home he missed: the home world in its entirety. Most especially he missed his home country: the valleys full of stones and stony rivers, the indomitable granite mountains.

But he could not go home, except for an occasional brief visit, until he was eighty. To think of sixty years in stations like this one! The idea was horrible!

"Don't be morose," Thev said. "You have a gift for gardening. The senior gardener has said that often. In time you'll be transferred to one of the big stations, where there are ornamental plants and bugs, maybe even a hologram of the home world sky. Think of that above you, while you pick suckers off stems! I, by then, will be a distinguished physicist. They'll bring me in to lecture, and we'll make jokes about the way our lives used to be."

Akuin felt doubtful and said as much.

"And then, finally, when you are a success, I'll confess to you that I've always loved you. And only the Goddess can know why, because you have an awful disposition."

Akuin looked at his friend. "Do you mean that?"

"About your disposition? Absolutely!"

"About loving me?"

"From the first moment I laid eyes on your shining pelt. From the first time I heard you complain."

"Why?"

"I have no idea. Remember that my area of competence is stars, not people."

Akuin kept looking at Thev, who was (as usual) sprawled on his bed, under the empty wall niche. He'd just come from the communal shower. Naked, it was possible to see all the blotches on his front. One covered half his forehead. Another, even larger and just as badly shaped, covered half a thigh.

"Did you ever think of coloring your fur?" Akuin asked.

"My aunts tried dying me when I was young. I hated it, a horrible messy process that stank and had to be done over and over. When it was time, when I smelled the dye cooking, I'd run away and hide, and they would come hunting. They made my cousins join in, until they began to refuse. 'If Thev wants to be ugly, let him be. We don't want to hunt him down like an animal.' My aunts gave up finally."

"You never rethought that decision?"

"What are you telling me, Akuin? You are willing to become my lover if I turn myself black? But not otherwise? Can't you be content to be the lovely one? I am certainly content to be the smart one."

No question the spots were ugly. But the thin body was good enough, and so was the voice, even and friendly and amused. The mind was in front of any mind he'd ever encountered. What would it be like to make love with someone who could peer into the center of stars and see what lies beyond ordinary experience? Akuin kissed his friend. Thev responded with passion. Ugly he might be, and intellectual, but he was also passionate.

They became lovers. This is always a difficult situation when the couple is young, without much privacy. Either they waited till their roommates were gone, or they used the rooms-for-sex-and-other-intimate-behavior, which are associated with gymnasia.

It would be better to do these things, Akuin thought, in the woods of Atkwa or in a secluded part of his grandmother's garden. Even the dunes next to his boarding school would have been better. Love did not belong in the station. Though Thev didn't seem to mind the grey rooms and the air that smelled of machinery.

Would life have been different, Akuin wondered later, if he'd chosen a more appropriate lover? One of the older men, who showed an interest in him? The senior gardener, for example?

The problem now, aside from the uncomfortable places they made love, was Thev's other passion. He was onto something interesting about the star grove.

Maybe, if Akuin had loved his work as much, he would have been able to endure Thev's periods of abstraction or his long discussions of the behavior of aging stars. He tried to be as boring, telling Thev about the garden's problems. It is always difficult to keep an incomplete ecology in balance. This particular garden had recurrent infestations of a parasitic organism that was neither a plant nor an animal, but rather alive in its own way. It was native to the *hwarhath* home world, but had changed after the *hwarhath* had inadvertently carried it into space, a region it liked; or rather, it liked the conditions of gardens in space. It thrived under lights that did not have the exact spectrum of the *hwarhath* home star; and soil that wasn't full of the home world's microorganisms seemed like a gift from the Goddess.

Thev listened patiently, but what he heard—more than anything else—was complaining. Obviously, a garden in space was going to be different from a garden on the home planet. Obviously, there were going to be difficulties and problems. But to a man of his temperament, optimistic and determined, problems were something one overcame or suffered cheerfully, the way he suffered his spots.

If Akuin's plants were covered with mold, well then, Akuin would have to find a cure. If a cure could not be found, the garden would have to grow other kinds of plants.

"Does nothing discourage you?" asked Akuin.

"You do, sometimes. Why not enjoy life? Is anything improved by moping? Think of how handsome you are! Think of my devotion! Do you think mold is any worse than my equations, which are *not* going where I want them to?"

In spite of his excellent heritage, Thev said, he was not a first rate mathematician. Rather, he had an instinct for how things are. "Where that came from, I don't know. The same place as my spots, maybe. In any case, I don't reason out what the Goddess has done with the universe. It comes to me almost as a vision; and if you think it's easy to see things in more than the usual five dimensions, you are wrong.[3] That's what the grove is like: a place that requires far more than five dimensions, if I'm going to understand it. There are so many stars here, and they are packed so closely!"

Maybe the problem was a difference in magnitude. Mold seemed like a trivial problem, compared to Thev's struggles with his equations. More likely it was a difference in temperament. Thev's energy made everything he did important. When he struggled, it was a real struggle. Akuin's sadness, which was chronic now, diminished his concerns. Nothing he did seemed really worth doing to himself or to those around him.

His first year in space ended. The second began. According to messages from relatives, everyone at home was doing well, though his grandmother's garden didn't thrive as it had when he tended it. Beyond doubt, he had a gift. "How lucky that you can use it where you are," his mother said.

The mold was under control now. He had convinced the senior gardener to introduce a few ornamental plants.

"Just in the corners, lad," the senior gardener said. "The places we aren't using. This isn't a great station. If the officers here want flowers for their lovers, too bad. And no matter how you beg, I'm not going to send for bugs. They aren't in the budget."

---

3   Pre-modern *hwarhath* math and physics recognized five aspects of objects in space. These were: location, extension, expansion-to-the-side, expansion-up-and-down, and relation or change. The human equivalents to these are: point, line, plane, volume and time.

At first he put in plants with colored leaves. They shone like jewels at the corners of beds full of green and blue-green vegetation.

"Like fire in the night," said one of the station's senior officers. "Are flowers possible?"

"Talk to the man in front of me. He says we don't have the money."

The officer, a physicist and a good one, according to Thev, ran his hand along a bright red leaf. "Maybe something can be worked out, though he's right that research and beauty never get the funding they deserve." The man glanced at Akuin. "You are Gehazi Thev's friend."

"Yes."

"You've made a good choice. He's going to have a future, in spite of being as ugly as a wall made of mud. Beauty isn't everything." The man touched the leaf a second time. "But it's something."

Money was found for flowers, though not for bugs. The senior officer picked the first bloom that opened. "To give to someone dear."

"I know who that is," Thev said. "A man who gets ahead on charm. He'll go into administration. He hasn't got the mind for research. But he isn't a bad fellow, and he'll make sure the men who can think get the chance to think. Do you think charm can take a person all the way to the front, Akuin?"

"I never got the impression that the Frontmen-in-a-Bundle were charming."

"Research scientists don't make it to the Bundle," Thev said. "Accountants, yes, and administrators, though I'm not sure they are especially charming administrators. Also experts on warfare. But not experts on how the universe really works."

"Are you ambitious?" Akuin asked.

"Yes, but not in that way. What I want, aside from you—" He rolled over and took hold of Akuin, pulling him close. "Is fame that goes on forever and a good teaching position."

At the end of his second year in space Akuin got leave and went home, like any other young man, to his native country and the house where he'd been raised. He was there for the usual length of time, working in his grandmother's garden and taking hikes in the stony hills. For the most part, he spent his time alone.

Hah! He had grown, his female relatives told him. He was handsomer than ever! They didn't mention his aloofness, which troubled them, or the expression of sadness that appeared too often on his face.

"It may be nothing," his grandmother said in private. "There are men who have trouble adjusting to space, but almost everyone manages in the end. This other young man sounds encouraging. I've done research on the family. They are a small lineage, not rich, but they have made excellent alliances; and their traits seem fine. If this romance works out, and Akuin stays involved with the Gehazi boy, we ought to think of approaching them for semen."

"It's the other side of the planet!" Akuin's mother exclaimed. "And the young man has spots!"

"He'd be a poor choice to father children," the grandmother admitted. "Though he is apparently a genius. But I agree with you. It would be better to go to his male relatives. He has plenty who look normal, and most are bright. As for Gehazi's location, these are modern times. We can't be provincial. Who can say which alliances will prove useful?"

At the end of his leave, Akuin visited his former school. It was almost empty, the students on vacation, but Tol Chaib was there, getting his garden ready for winter. The air was cold already and smelled, when the wind came off the land, of drying vegetation.

He spent a day working with his mentor, digging into the sandy soil, cutting stalks and branches, gathering fallen leaves. In the evening they drank *halin* and talked, alone together in Tol Chaib's quarters. The rest of the building was unoccupied.

After they were both drunk, Tol Chaib said, "I always wanted to have sex with you. It wasn't possible, until you became a man. But the longing was there. It frightened me. I'm not usually attracted to boys."

What was it, Akuin wondered, about him and ugly men? Maybe they could see the wrongness in him, though it was different from their ugliness. There was nothing wrong with Thev except his spots. In every other way, he was a model young man: loyal, determined, direct, pious. Though not violent. Thev lacked the fifth male virtue. Well, no one was perfect, and Thev's other traits—his intelligence and cheerfulness—ought to count for something.

Tol Chaib was more disturbing. Looking at him, Akuin saw loneliness and grief for things lost: his old beauty, his life in space. The old man was like a mirror, reflecting Akuin's future. He could end like this. Though he didn't think he would ever be attracted to boys. That was a perversion, after all, and his wrongness—whatever it was exactly—seemed unconnected with perversity. He was a gardener who wanted to garden at home. A shameful ambition! But not the same as wanting to molest children.

In the end, after another cup of *halin*, he went to bed with Tol Chaib, though he was never certain exactly why. The old man wanted this to happen, and he felt he owed his mentor something. That was as good an explanation as any. In the morning they parted, Tol Chaib giving him a tropical flower from the school greenhouse. It was huge and intricate and as blue as the sky, though almost scentless. Akuin carried it until it wilted, then threw it in the ocean. This was on one of the rocket islands. An *ikun* later he boarded a rocket that carried him into space.

Gehazi Thev greeted him with affection when he got back to their station. "Though it was a good idea to have time away from you. I thought about stellar evolution instead of sex. There is much to be said for both, of course, but my job is stars."

During his absence, Thev had moved into a new dormitory, this one occupied by four young physicists.

"There didn't seem to be any reason to stay in my old room. I have nothing in common with the other men. It was only habit that kept me there. Habit and you, and you were gone."

Their romance continued, though it might have ended. Who can say what ties men or women together? They returned to their old habits, exercising in the station's gymnasia, going to its one theater to see recordings of plays put on in the great stations, places such as Tailin. Both enjoyed soaking in the pools-for-soaking. Both enjoyed sex in the rooms-for-privacy.

These last were small, like everything in the station. There was a low bed, fastened to the floor, and two stools that moved in grooves. The ceiling had a mirror, which could be turned off, though the lovers usually kept it on. The wall opposite the bed could be replaced with a hologram. Thev liked scenes of space: galaxies, nebulae, stars and planets. Akuin (of course) preferred scenes of home.

During one of their stays in a private room, Thev spoke about the work he was doing. They'd had sex and were lying together on the bed's thin mattress. A trio of stars—orange, red and yellow—blazed at the room's end. The mirror above them showed their bodies, quiet now, Thev resting on his belly, Akuin on his back.

Later, Akuin remembered the scene, as he remembered the day he first fell in love with his grandmother's garden.

Thev had been working with geometry. "Making models, so I can visualize what is happening in this region of space. Mind you, it isn't easy. We evolved to see five dimensions, and that's the number we insist on seeing, no matter how many there may be.

"But it is possible, especially if one uses a computer. How did our ancestors get anything done, before the existence of computers? Imagine trying to understand the universe by counting on fingers! Or making lines in the dirt! No wonder the universe was small in those days! No wonder it was simple!

"What one does—"Thev rolled over and began to go through his uniform's pockets.[4] A moment later he was kneeling by the hologram projector. The triple star vanished. In its place was an

---

4   The *hwarhath* male uniform is a pair of shorts: knee-length, loose, and abundantly provided with pockets. This, plus sandals, is adequate for life in a space station or ship.

irregular object made of glowing white lines. It floated in midair, turning slowly and changing shape as it turned.

"—Is eliminate one of the ordinary visible dimensions and replace it with a dimension that can't be seen. Obvious, you may say to me; and certainly it has been done many times before; and certainly it isn't adequate to show what's happening in this region of space.

"But if one makes a large number of these partial models, each one showing an aspect of reality—"

Now the room was full of floating objects, all made of glowing lines, but not all the same color. Some were red, orange, or yellow, like the vanished stars. Others were green, blue-green, blue. Hah! It was like a garden, except these flowers were all deformed and deforming. Some expanded like leaves opening in spring. Others folded in and seemed to be swallowing themselves. As one diminished, the one beside it grew, either in size or complexity. Akuin began to feel queasy.

"The problem, of course, is fitting all these partial models together. This is where a computer is essential."

"What is this about?" Akuin asked. "Does this array of ugly objects serve any purpose?"

"Ugly!" said Thev. "Dear one, they are the achievement of my life!" He was back on the bed now, sitting with his arms around his knees, admiring the things. "Of course, I'm young and likely to do better. But this isn't bad, I assure you."

"You have told me," Akuin said, "that you are trying to see what can't be seen, and comprehend what isn't comprehensible. Maybe you can do this. Everyone agrees that you are brilliant. But I'm not going to understand these things swallowing themselves."

"You want another kind of model. Something that has to do with plants and bugs."

"That's what I know," Akuin said.

Thev was silent for a while, watching his things, which continued to grow, change shape, divide, diminish, and vanish. A garden out of a bad dream. A sorcerer's garden.

Thev spoke finally. "Think of this region, this grove of stars, as a grove of trees growing in a dry place, so the trees are forced to seek water. We think the ground is dirt and stone, we think it's solid. In reality, a multitude of roots go down and out, forcing their way through dirt and stone, twisting around each other. It's possible the roots are connected."

Akuin had grown up in a part of the home world where many species of trees were communal, their various trunks rising from a single root system. But he had trouble imagining stars connected in the same way. This suggests that he hadn't paid attention to his physics class in school, which is true.

"We know that strange stars can be connected with other strange stars. Usually, the partners are not in close proximity. Here, I think they are. Imagine what this must do to reality. Strangeness loops back on itself. The fabric of space is pierced again and again by strangeness.

"What I've said so far is ordinary. Few scientists would disagree, except about the strangeness looping. That's not a generally accepted idea, though I'm not the only person who's come forward with it. But from this point on—" Thev glanced and smiled. "The ideas are mine.

"According to the usual theory, the ground under our grove of trees is stable. Yes, the roots have pushed through it, causing stress—most evidently at the surface, where the ground may buckle, forced up from below. In areas settled by people, this pressure-from-below is easily perceived. Sidewalks are lifted. The walls of buildings crack and fall. All done by roots." Thev wiggled his fingers, showing the action of roots.

"But let's imagine that the ground is not stable. Maybe the land is limestone and full of caves. The roots, burrowing down, are cracking stone that forms the roof of one of these caves. In time the roof will break. The grove will fall into a sinkhole."

This was understandable. There are places in the Great Central Plain where the ground is limestone, and water is usually found in pools at the bottom of sinkholes. Nowadays, windmills bring the water up. In the old days, people cut steps in the stone walls and carried buckets. Akuin knew all this, and knew that sinkholes could appear suddenly. But how could a sinkhole appear in space? After all, a sinkhole was an absence of stone. But space wasn't there in the first place. How could one have an absence of something already absent?

"Let me give you another model," Thev said. "Think of this region of space as a cheese."

"What?" said Akuin.

"A large, round one." Thev spread his arms to show the cheese's size. "Bugs have infested it. It looks solid, but inside is a maze of tunnels. If one bends the cheese a little, or twists it, if any extra strain is put on it—hah! It breaks apart! There's nothing left but crumbs. The bugs have destroyed their home."

"These are disturbing images," Akuin said. "What are you saying with them? That this region of space could break into crumbs? I find it hard to imagine such an occurrence. What is a space crumb like?"

"Maybe the grove is a better model than the cheese, though you wanted plants and bugs, and I have given you both. I think it's possible this region will collapse. More than possible. In time, collapse is certain."

"But what will it become? Not a sinkhole?"

"My guess would be a large area of strangeness. Spherical, of course. Such things always are."

"What would happen to the station?" By this time Akuin was sitting up and looking at Thev with horror. This wasn't a pleasant situation that Thev was describing. But Thev's voice was full of interest and pleasure. What Thev was enjoying, of course, was his own cleverness. In addition, it's possible that he saw the situation as one of the many fine jokes with which the Goddess has filled her universe. A pious man will always enjoy the Great Mother's tricks.

"It depends on the size of the collapse," Thev said. "If it takes the entire region out, the station will be destroyed. But if it's the right size, and happens at the right distance, we'll be able to observe the process."

Akuin was getting a headache, either from the conversation or from his lover's ugly things, which still filled the room and continued to change in disturbing ways. He mentioned the headache. Thev stopped the recording. The garden remained, but everything in it was motionless.

Much better! Akuin lay back. The mirror above him reflected his own dark body. On one side of him was a funnel made of bright red lines. It appeared to be dissolving and pouring itself down itself, though nothing moved now; and the center of the funnel was empty.

On the other side of him was a blue sphere, which had apparently stopped in the middle of turning itself into something full of many sharp angles. Both the angles and the sphere's smooth surface were visible. Akuin closed his eyes.

Thev kept talking. More research was needed. He'd written a proposal. "But you know the funding situation. If an idea can't be turned into a weapon at once, the frontmen aren't interested; and I can't see any obvious way to do harm with my ideas. Maybe some day we'll be able to use strangeness as a weapon, but not soon."

Thev must be getting tired. His conversation was beginning to wander. So much was uncertain. So many things might happen. If the station wasn't swallowed, it might still be destroyed by the event. "I don't think this process of collapse will be entirely quiet and peaceful." Or, if the station survived, and the men inside were alive, they might find that they'd lost their Heligian gate.[5]

"We'd be trapped," Akuin said. No one had ever warned him to beware of sex with physicists. Maybe they should have. It would be easier to have a lover who thought about more trivial problems.

"We could send information home," Thev answered in an encouraging tone. "Though only at the speed of light. But that

5   The *hwarhath* name for an FTL transfer point.

would be sufficient. It would take less than five years for a message to reach the nearest working gate. Surely the frontmen would post a ship there, after our gate vanished."

"What is most likely to happen?" Akuin asked.

"The station will be destroyed."

"Soon?"

"I don't know," Thev said. "Some of the work done here suggests the space in this region is badly strained already; and it's possible that our presence is making things worse."

"How?" Akuin asked.

"Through the coming and going of star ships. They do have an effect on the fabric of space, though not one that matters in ordinary situations. And there is at least one experiment being done here at the station that may be acting like roots pushing through a crack in limestone, or maybe like a slight twist of the cheese." Thev smiled briefly. "The experiment is continuing, though I've mentioned that it may cause trouble. The men running it don't believe the risk is significant."

"Aren't you worried?" Akuin asked.

"What can I do, except put my ideas out in front? Maybe I'm wrong. I have sent my theory, and recordings of my models, to the Helig Institute. If I die here, I will become famous. If I don't die here, if this region does not collapse, then I'll become famous later for something else. One cannot live in fear of thoughts, Akuin."

That was the end of the conversation. Akuin found he couldn't get Thev's ideas out of his mind. They haunted him: the collapsing grove, the cheese eaten out by bugs, the garden of ugly things.

Bad enough to think of living for years in the station. But to think of dying here! How could he feel the same affection for Thev? A man who came up with such ideas and models!

Gradually the two lovers drew apart. Thev accepted this with his usual calm good sense. Nothing pushed him back for long. He always recovered and went forward. Soon he found a lover among the physicists: not a thinker, but a hands-on builder, who said that Thev's models were likely to prove useful, though he didn't believe the station was in danger.

"You theoreticians love terrifying ideas! The Goddess may be sloppy in her details. We know she is, from looking around. But the basic structure of her universe is solid. Space doesn't fall to pieces like a bridge with bad mortar. It lasts! And will outlast everything!"

As for Akuin, he took a series of sexual partners. All were casual. This didn't especially bother him. Some men must have a true love, a companion for life. He wasn't such a man. Sex was fine. So was friendship. But his real love, the center of his life, was plants.

Another year passed. Once again he traveled home. His grandmother had died suddenly, shortly after his previous trip. Now it was time to put her ashes in the ground and carve her name on the monument for Atkwa women.

When he reached his home country, it was spring. In his grandmother's garden flowers bloomed, attracting early bugs. The house was full of female relatives, busy with details of the coming ceremony.

There was nothing for Akuin to do, so he went hiking. South and west of the house were hills, not high, but made impressive by huge outcroppings of igneous rock. No limestone here, eroding easily. His country had bones of granite! An *ikun* from home, he came to his favorite spot for looking into the distance. Up he climbed, until he was atop the great bald knob. Now he could see the folded hills, covered with pale green foliage. They stretched in every direction. Here and there were patches of color: yellow, pale orange, and lavender, flowering shrubs and trees.

All at once, he realized he had reached the limit of his endurance. He could not bear to leave this place again. He would not return to space.

Why did this happen? How can any man turn away from duty? His grandmother, the most formidable member of his family, was dead. He'd lost his lover. His mentor had turned out to be a pervert, attracted to children. The garden in the station was not an adequate substitute for the country here, extending around him in every direction under a cloudless sky.

Always, in the station, he was aware of the space outside: dark, cold, airless, hostile to life. If Thev was right, the emptiness outside the station was not even reliable. It might collapse at any moment, becoming something worse.

Here he stood on granite.

By the time he returned to his grandmother's house, he was already making plans. His female relatives continued to be busy, his mother especially. She would be the new matriarch. Akuin gathered supplies, sneaking them out of storerooms and hiding them in a forest. Tools. Clothing. A rifle and ammunition. A hunting bow and arrows. Medical supplies. Plenty of seeds. A computer full of information.

By the time his grandmother was underground, he was ready. There was a final ceremony: cutting his grandmother's name in the stone that memorialized the family's dead women. When that was over, his mother bid him farewell. A cousin took him to the train station. He climbed on board, then climbed out the far side and ducked behind a bush. The train pulled away. His cousin returned to her car. Akuin took off for the forest and his hidden supplies.

He reached them without trouble. With luck, it would be several days before his family realized that he had vanished: time enough to get into the high mountains, the wilderness. He was strong, determined and not afraid of anything in his homeland. Pack on back, he set off.

There's no reason to tell his life in detail from this point on. The important thing had happened. Akuin had decided to turn away from loyalty and obligation. Now, he lived for himself rather than his family or his species. This is something humans do, if the stories we hear are true. This is why their home planet is full of violence and has far too many inhabitants, produced not by careful breeding contracts, but random acts of heterosexuality.

He found a valley high in the mountains, away from all trails with a hard-to-find entrance. There he built a hut and established his garden. The first year was difficult. So was the second. But he persisted. At times he was lonely, but not often. He'd always been comfortable with solitude. The things around him—sunlight, rain, wind, his garden, the mountains—were a constant source of joy.

In the third year he built a solid cabin. Having done this, he began to wonder what was happening in the house where he'd grown up. He waited till harvest was over, and his cabin full of food. Then he went home.

He couldn't arrive openly, of course. He was a criminal now, and the women of his family had always been law-abiding and respectful of tradition. Instead, he lurked in the forest shadow and crept close after dark, peering in windows. There his family was, the same as always. Only he had changed. For a while he felt regret. Then he remembered the station, and Gehazi Thev's terrifying ideas. He had made the right choice.

The next fall he came down again. This time he did a little stealing. There were tools he needed, and he could always use more seeds.

The fifth year of his exile, he decided to visit the library in his grandmother's house, which was held by his mother now. He crept in after midnight, when the house was entirely dark, and made his way without trouble to the room. Some of the houses in Atkwa were old. Their libraries were full of actual books, ancient cherished objects. This house had been built a century before. There were a few books, brought from other places, but most of the glass-fronted cabinets held modern recordings. When his electric torch played over them, they glittered like so many jewels: garnet-red novels, poetry like peridots, topaz-yellow plays. The music was shades of blue. What a fool he'd been to take only nonfiction before! Quickly, he picked the recordings he wanted and copied them into his computer, then replaced the shining bits of silicon and metal in their proper resting places.

When he was almost done, he heard a noise. Akuin turned and saw his mother, standing in the doorway.

She reached out a hand. The ceiling light went on. Akuin stood ashamed, his hands full of music, like a jewel thief holding sapphires.

His mother stepped into the room, closing the door behind her. "It was you who stole from us last fall."

He tilted his head in agreement.

"I thought so, and I thought, 'he's alive.' That idea brought me joy, Akuin, though it shouldn't have. What's wrong with you? Why was it so difficult for you to live like other men? When you came home the first time, your grandmother and I made plans. If your romance worked out, she wanted to asked the Gehazi for semen. A young man of so much promise! A family worth forming an alliance with! We thought—we hoped—you had overcome your oddness at last."

No words of explanation came to him. Instead, he said, "what?" and stopped. His voice sounded harsh. The tone was wrong. He was no longer used to speaking.

"What am I going to do? Nothing. By now the neighboring families have forgotten about you. If I give you to the male police, it will bring our shame into daylight. People will know for certain that you ran from duty. Before, there was a possibility that something happened—an accident, a murder."

"You could tell me to die," Akuin said in his new strange voice.

"Would you kill yourself, if I asked you to?"

He didn't answer.

"No," his mother said. "I think not. Go back to your mountains. Every family has embarrassing secrets. You will be ours."

He set the music on a table. How it glittered!

"Don't come into the house again," his mother added. "I'll see that things are left in the far barn for you."

He opened his mouth to thank her.

"Go."

Akuin left, carrying his computer.

The next year he came home twice, though not to the great-house. Instead he found his mother's gifts in the far barn: tools, small boxes containing seeds, recordings of music, favorite pieces from when he was young, a letter full of family news.

After this, there were no changes in his life for many years. Bit by bit, he expanded his garden and made his cabin more comfortable. Slowly he read his way through most of the great male plays, which are—as everyone knows—about honor and the making of difficult choices. The heroes, the men who must chose, usually die, as he should have. Or they sacrifice their happiness to obligation. Another thing he had failed to do.

In addition, he read many of the plays written about women and their lives. These deal with endurance and compromise, which are not male virtues.

Maybe he would have made a better woman, though it didn't seem likely. Nothing about him seemed especially feminine. He certainly didn't have his grandmother's solidity. His mother was the same. Women like the mountains of Atkwa! Nothing ordinary could wear them down!

Akuin's mother died prematurely, when he was only forty. Coming down from the mountains through an early snow, he found the usual kind of supplies in the far barn, also a letter. It was from one of his female cousins, telling him the news: a sudden illness that should not have killed a woman so healthy, not yet old. But it did! "Life is full of these kinds of surprises," his cousin wrote in an elegant, flowing script, though Akuin was not thinking about calligraphy at the moment.

He fell to his knees, chest heaving. The groans inside him would not come out. Beyond the barn's open door, snow fell in thick soft flakes.

The gifts would continue, his cousin wrote. She had promised his mother while the woman lay dying. "This is not the kind of promise one breaks. Though I have to say, Akuin, that I do not approve of your behavior."

"So, so," Akuin said. He got up finally, walking into the snow. No chance the people in the house would see him through this whiteness. He lifted his head and hands, as if to catch something, though he didn't know what. The life he should have had? The snow flakes melted when they touched his palms.

More time passed. This is what the real world is like. Instead of the sudden important decisions that heroes must make in plays, everything solved in less than an *ikun*, real life is gradual.

His cousin kept her promise. He continued to find gifts in the barn. For many years he saw no people, except at a distance. He always managed to avoid them.

One summer morning, when he was almost fifty, Akuin stepped out his cabin door and saw a monster in his garden. That was his first impression. The thing stood in brilliant sunlight. Akuin, coming out of his cabin's dimness, could make out nothing except the creature's shape: upright on two legs like a person, but far too thin and tall. A stick-person. A person made of bones. Like bones, the monster was pale.

He stepped back into his cabin, picked up his rifle and waited, hoping the monster had not seen him. Maybe it would go away. He'd never had a problem with monsters before.

The thing remained in the middle of Akuin's vegetables. He saw it more clearly now. It had on clothing, pants and a red checked shirt. A head rose above the shirt. The face was hairless, the features like no *hwarhath* features he had ever seen: everything narrow and pushed together, as if someone had put hands on either side of the creature's head and pressed, forcing the cheeks in, the nose out, the forehead up, the chin into a jutting bulge.

"It's a magnificent garden," the creature said in Akuin's own language.

He'd been spotted. Akuin raised his rifle.

A second voice said, "You are looking at a human. This one is friendly. Put the gun down."

Akuin glanced around, until he made out the second person, standing at the forest edge. He was short with steel grey fur, dressed in hiking shorts and boots. A *hwarhath* male, beyond any question. But not a relative. Like the monster, he spoke with an accent that wasn't local. In the case of this man, the accent was southern.

"Believe me," added the *hwarhath* in a quiet voice. "Neither one of us will do you any harm. We are here with the permission of the Atkwa, for recreational purposes."

"Hiking in the mountains," said the monster in agreement.

"Enemy," Akuin said in the voice he almost never used. Hah! The word came out like a branch creaking in the wind.

"The war has ended," the *hwarhath* said. "We have peace with the humans."

This didn't seem possible, but the news Akuin got from his cousin was all family news.

"Put the gun down," the *hwarhath* male repeated. "You really must not kill this human. He works for us. His rank is advancer one-in-back."[6]

Akuin had been a carrier. The monster far outranked him. It was definitely wrong to point a gun at a senior officer. He lowered the rifle.

The *hwarhath* man said, "Good. Now, come out."

Slowly, Akuin moved into the sunlight. The monster remained motionless. So did the man at the edge of the forest.

What next? Akuin stood with his rifle pointing down. He was making out more details now. There was a patch of hair, or possibly feathers, on top of the monster's head. The patch was bone-white, like the hairless face. Even the monster's eyes were white, though a dark spot floated in the middle of each eye. Was this a sign of disease? Could the monster be blind? No. Akuin

6   The equivalent human rank is major. There is no easy (or politically neutral) way to discuss the two characters just introduced. Therefore they will not be discussed, except to note that any ordinary *hwarhath* reader would recognize the pair at once. Much of the humor in the rest of the story lies with Akuin's attempts to figure out things all other *hwarhath* know.

had a clear sense that the thing was watching. The dark spots moved, flicking from him to the *hwarhath* male, then back again.

"I think it would be easier to talk if you put the gun down entirely," the *hwarhath* said.

A calm voice, low and even, but Akuin recognized the tone. This was authority speaking. He laid the rifle on the ground and straightened up, trying to remember the way he used to hold himself, back when he was a soldier.

"Much better," said the *hwarhath*. He walked forward and picked up the rifle, handing it to the monster.

For a moment, Akuin was afraid. But the monster held the rifle properly, barrel pointed down. The oddly shaped hands did not reach for the trigger. The backs of the hands were pale and hairless. Was the creature the same all over? White and as hairless as a fish?

The *hwarhath* man looked at Akuin, who glanced down at once. This was a very senior officer. It showed in his tone of voice, the way he moved, the way he treated the monster, expecting obedience, which the monster gave him. Not a man you looked at directly.

If the man had questions, he did not ask them. Instead, he explained their arrival. It had been an accident. They'd gotten off their trail and lost. "Though not by much, I suspect. If your relatives become worried, they will be able to find us."

The night before had been spent at the entrance to Akuin's valley. This morning, curious, they had hiked in. "I don't think we could find this place again. In fact, we'll need your help to get back to our trail."

"I'll give it in return for news," Akuin said, then felt surprise at what he'd said.

The *hwarhath* man tilted his head in agreement. "That can be done."

Akuin remembered he was the host and got busy making tea. The two visitors wandered through his garden. The human still carried Akuin's rifle. There was another rifle in the cabin. If necessary, Akuin could kill both of them.

But if they vanished, Akuin's relatives would look for them and keep looking till the men were found. Hospitality required as much. So did respect for rank and the connections far-in-front officers always had. The *hwarhath* picked a flower—a yellow midsummer bloom—and handed it to his companion, who took it with a flash of teeth. A smile. Then the two of them strolled back toward the cabin, the *hwarhath* first, the monster following, rifle in one hand, flower in the other.

This was a peculiar situation! And likely to turn out badly. If the men became curious about him, they'd discover that he was AWOL. His family would be shamed in public. He would have to kill himself.

His mother should have turned him in twenty-five years before. The result would have been the same for him: death by suicide or execution. But the Atkwa would have escaped embarrassment. At least his mother wasn't alive to see the result of her affection.

Maybe it would be better to ask no questions, send the men off as quickly as possible, and hope they did not become curious. But his longing for information was intense. In any case, they must suspect that he was a runaway. How could they not? He was alone in the mountains and so ignorant that he didn't know the war with the humans was over.

There was a flat rock near his cabin door. He used it as a table, setting out the teapot and cups. His two guests settled down, the monster leaning Akuin's rifle against the cabin where Akuin could not reach it, though the monster could. He kept the flower, twirling its stem between oddly proportioned fingers. "It really is a very fine garden."

"What kind of news do you want to hear?" asked the *hwarhath*.

"The war," Akuin said.

"It turned out to be a mistake. Humans can be reasoned with, though I can't say the process is easy; and we live at such great distances from one another that there isn't much to fight over."

"Some fool, apparently a human fool, fired at the first strange ship he encountered," the monster added. "That's how the war began." He showed his teeth to Akuin, another smile. It wasn't quick and friendly like a *hwarhath* smile, but wide and slow, disturbing. "It continued because the two sides lacked a way to communicate, unless one calls the firing of weapons a form of communication. In the end, we learned each other's languages."

"That helped," the *hwarhath* said. "Though once a war has gotten going, it's hard to stop. This proved no exception."

Akuin asked about the station where he'd been assigned. The *hwarhath* man was silent.

"It's not an important place," Akuin said. "Maybe you haven't heard of it."

"Why do you want to know about it?" the man asked.

"I had a friend who was assigned there, a man named Gehazi Thev."

"The physicist."

"You know about him," said Akuin. "Is he still alive?"

"He wasn't at the station when it disappeared."

Hah! Akuin thought, and refilled the cups. The monster had barely touched his tea, but the *hwarhath* male was obviously a drinker. "Did the region collapse, as he said it would? Was the station swallowed by strangeness?"

"We couldn't get back in the usual way," the *hwarhath* said. "The local gate had vanished, along with everything else. But we were able to survey the area from a distance; and we sent a robot probe. The stars that had been in the region were gone. No question about that. But, as far as we could tell from a distance, they hadn't been replaced by strangeness, and there wasn't the kind of release of energy we expected. When the probe reached the region, it found nothing special. There was nothing there except empty space."

"How is that possible?" Akuin asked.

"Gehazi Thev revised his theory." The *hwarhath* gave a proper smile, small and quick, which did not threaten at all. "If you know him, you know that nothing pushes him back. His first ideas did not explain what happened, so he brought new ideas to the fore. He now thinks the collapse served to separate the region from our universe."

"What do you mean?" Akuin asked. "What happened to the station? Does it still exist?"

"How can we know?" the man said in answer. "If it has survived, then it's in another universe, along with the stars that vanished. A very small universe, according to Gehazi Thev, who has described the place. There is no way to check his ideas, but it's a fine description.

"At first, according to Gehazi Thev, the new universe would be dark, except for the stars around the station. Imagine how that would look!" The man exhaled. Akuin couldn't tell if the exhalation meant horror or interest. Horror seemed more reasonable. "In time the light produced by the stars will be bent back. Then it will seem that new stars are appearing in the distance, all dim and red, like the stars around the station. If the men in the station had good enough instruments, they'd be able to see themselves. They will certainly be able to see and hear the messages they send."

"The men in the station must be dead," Akuin said.

"Most likely, though Gehazi Thev thinks—or did, the last time I heard him speak—there's a slight possibility they are alive. It depends on what happened to all the strangeness in the region when it collapsed, not to mention the energy that should have been generated by the collapse. If these went into this new universe, then the universe is almost certainly uninhabitable. But if the strangeness and energy were in some way dissipated or used up in the creation of the universe—"

It was, Akuin realized, another one of Thev's terrible ideas. "When did this happen?"

"Twenty-one years ago," the *hwarhath* said.

Akuin could have been there, when the station vanished. He almost certainly knew men who had died or gone into their own universe. Had Thev's lover, the hands-on physicist, been among them? He could no longer remember the fellow's name. Akuin looked toward his garden, but did not see its midsummer brightness. Instead, for a moment, he imagined darkness and isolation, relieved—finally—by dim red stars that were an illusion, light bent back toward its origin. What a fate!

"Most likely the station was destroyed," the *hwarhath* said in a comfortable tone, then excused himself and went off to eliminate tea.

The monster stayed where he was, his cup still full. "I have bad reactions to a number of *hwarhath* foods," he said. "It's better not to experiment."

"How did you end up working for us?" Akuin asked.

"I was offered a job. I took it."

"Was this after the war ended?"

The monster smiled his slow, disturbing smile. "No."

"Is this acceptable behavior among humans?" Akuin asked.

"To change sides in the middle of a war? No."

Obviously Akuin found the monster interesting. This was a person who'd done something worse than running away. "What would happen if your people got hold of you?"

"Nothing now. There is a treaty. I'm a *hwarhath* officer. That should protect me. But the usual penalty for disloyalty is death."

Akuin wanted to ask the monster why he'd changed sides, but there wasn't time.[7] The *hwarhath* male was returning, moving through Akuin's garden, pausing to pick another flower, this one red. He laid the flower down on Akuin's rock table, then resettled himself on the ground. "Is there anything else you want to know?"

7   Most *hwarhath* believe that Nicholas Sanders changed sides because of love.

"What are you going to do about me?" Akuin asked and was surprised by the question. Surely it would have been wiser to keep quiet.

The *hwarhath* tilted his head, considering. "We're both on leave at the moment. Our work, when we are at work, is not for the Corps that keeps track of *hwarhath* men; and we are guests in this country. I assume the Atkwa know about you. Let them deal with you. I don't see that your behavior is our business."

He was not going to die. His relatives were not going to suffer embarrassment. In his relief, he offered them vegetables from his garden.

"We can't carry much," the *hwarhath* said. "And my friend can't eat most of our edible plants. Either they don't nurture him, or they make him ill. So he lives on specially prepared rations. It's a hard fate for a human. Eating is an amusement for them. They expect their food to be as entertaining as a good play. Our human rations are—dull, I have been told."

"This is true," the monster said.

"But I'll accept your offer," his *hwarhath* companion concluded. "I don't know that I've ever seen handsomer looking vegetables. This is something worthy of respect, though I don't have the human interest in food."

That afternoon, Akuin led them back to their trail. After he left them, heading back toward home, he realized that he hadn't learned their names. Nor had they learned his, but he was obviously Atkwa. If they wanted to find his records, they'd be able to do it without difficulty. He reached his cabin late in the afternoon. Shadows covered the valley's floor and lower slopes, but light still filled the sky and touched the eastern hilltops. A copperleaf tree stood high on one of these, shining as if it were actually made of uncorroded copper. Lovely!

He gathered the teapot and cups, carrying them inside, then came out and picked up the yellow flower, which had been left. The red one had gone with his visitors, tucked under a flap on the *hwarhath* man's pack. He'd seen it go bobbing down the trail, as the *hwarhath* followed his long-legged companion. Easy to see who the athlete in the pair was.

Holding the withered flower, Akuin realized the two were lovers. It was as clear as something seen in a vision, though he was not a diviner and did not have visions. Nonetheless, he knew.

Impossible! was his first reaction. But how could he tell what was possible these days? He'd heard a monster speak his native language and been told it was a *hwarhath* officer. If this could happen, and a station vanish out of the universe, who could say what other unexpected events could occur?

He laid the flower down, unwilling to discard it yet, and watched as sunlight faded off the copperleaf tree. A disturbing day, though he was glad to hear that Thev was still alive and apparently famous. It was what Thev wanted. The news brought by the two men made him feel isolated and ignorant, for a moment doubtful about the choice he'd made.

Overhead the sky seemed limitless: not a roof, but an ocean into which he could fall and sink—if not forever, then far enough to drown.

Hah! That was an unpleasant idea, and also untrue. He stood with his feet in the dirt of Atkwa. Below the dirt was granite and the great round planet, which held him as a mother holds a child. There was no way for him to fall into the sky.

As for the choice he'd made, this was what he'd always wanted, as intensely as Thev had wanted fame: the garden in front of him, the copperleaf tree shining on its cliff, evening bugs beginning to call in the shadows. Only a fool mourns for the impossible or asks for everything, as if the Goddess had made the universe for his comfort.

If he had lost through his choice, he had also gained. Surely this valley—the bugs, the scent of his garden carried on a slight cool wind—was better than a lifetime spent in grey metal corridors. It was certainly better than vanishing into a very small universe of dim red stars. Thev and his ideas!

350

He stayed at the cabin doorway, watching day end. The sky was a roof again. The ground beneath his feet was solid. Gradually his uncertainty—his sense of loss—faded, like sunlight fading off the copperleaf tree. He regretted nothing. This was the right place for him to be.

That evening Ettin Gwarha and Sanders Nicholas made their camp next to the trail. A stream ran in a gully below them, producing a pleasant quiet noise. Ettin Gwarha ate fresh vegetables, while his companion made do with human rations. Then the son of Ettin turned on a map and studied it. "We'll take a different route out than the one we originally planned," he said.

"Why?" asked Sanders Nicholas.

"The original plan had us ending at one of the Atkwa greathouses. I'd just as soon avoid the family."

"Is there a reason?"

"If they realize how close we came to that man's territory, they'll worry, and that will force me to reassure them. As much as possible, I want nothing to do with this situation."

"But you told the man you wouldn't turn him in."

"Every family has its secrets, and we are guests in the country of the Atkwa. But never think that I approve of behavior such as his. There is no acceptable reason to run away from duty." The frontman turned off his map and closed it, then added, "I'm not going to comment on the behavior of the Atkwa women in letting their male relative go wild. Only women can judge women."

Sanders Nicholas considered this for a while. Maybe Ettin Gwarha could read the expression on his pale hairless face. No ordinary *hwarhath* can. "I have another question," he said finally.

The frontman looked at him.

"Why do you know so much about Gehazi Thev and the station that vanished? Physics has never been one of your areas of competence."

"Negotiation is my great skill, as you know. When the station disappeared, the Bundle had two questions it wanted answered; and they wanted one question at least to be asked diplomatically. It was a disturbing question, and they had to go—I had to go—to the Helig Institute for an answer."[8]

Sanders Nicholas waited.

"The first question was: had some kind of weapon caused our station to disappear? Was it possible that humans—or another alien species—had so much power? Remember that an entire grove of stars vanished with the station. This was a serious event! If intelligent beings caused it to happen, then we were in trouble.

"The next question was: could such an event be caused? Was there a way to make a weapon out of whatever had happened?"

Sanders Nicholas gave his lover the wide, slow, unfriendly-seeming smile of humans. "You were hoping you could force the human home system into another universe."

"It was a thought that occurred to several men," Ettin Gwarha admitted. "Surely you can imagine the appeal of the idea, Nicky! The human threat could be eliminated without doing harm to humanity. We wouldn't have to go to our female relatives and say, 'We have destroyed women and children.'"

Sanders Nicholas sat quietly, looking at the small fire they had made. It was dying to embers already. Overhead the sky was dark. The Banner of the Goddess stretched across it, a wide swathe of dimly shining light. "I have two objections," he said finally. "How could the Bundle be certain that people would not be harmed? It would be an untested procedure, after all; and I find it hard to believe that any universe, even a small one, comes into existence quietly."

Ettin Gwarha inclined his head, perhaps in agreement. "What is your other objection?"

8   The Helig Institute is on the home planet and thus under the control of the *hwarhath* female government, rather than the Bundle. As far as can be determined from a distance, the two halves of *hwarhath* society treat each other as genuine sovereign governments, whose interests are not always identical.

"Even if it could be done without immediate physical harm, think of the consequences. You would be depriving humanity of this—" He looked up, gesturing toward the starry sky. "Would you like to live in a very small universe, Ettin Gwarha?"

"No."

"I may be showing a bias, but I think this universe would be diminished if it lost humanity, though there's no question we are a difficult species."

"We could have found better neighbors," Ettin Gwarha said in agreement. "But it doesn't seem likely we'll be able to get rid of you. The scientists at the Helig Institute say there's no way to reproduce whatever happened at Kushaiin. Gehazi Thev does not agree. He believes we could cause such an event, but only in a region on the verge of collapse. Such a region would be full of old stars and strangeness. It's not the kind of place one would expect to find intelligent life. At most, in such a place, we might find a research station." Ettin Gwarha smiled briefly, his teeth flashing in the red light of the fire. "Hardly worth destroying in such an elaborate fashion. 'Avoid force in excess of the force needed,' as the old proverb says."

"Well, then," Sanders Nicholas said. "We are stuck with each other and with a very large universe."

"A disturbing situation," his lover said in agreement. "Though I think we can endure it.

"There is a final aspect that I pointed out to the Bundle. The situation at hand—the idea that worried us—was not likely. Destroying an entire system, or moving it out of our universe, is beyond any science we know, and I don't believe humanity will develop a weapon able to do this. Human technology, at least in the relevant areas, is not impressive, and their economic and political problems are so severe I don't think they can afford the necessary R & D. But if there are two star-faring species in the galaxy, there ought to be three and four and five. Suppose one of these other species is as hostile as humanity and better organized. Could they create a weapon able to destroy an entire area of space? How can we know?

"That's one thing to consider. The other is, it's comparatively easy to make a single planet uninhabitable. Even the humans could do it. Our home world was safe during the war because humanity didn't know where it was. At some point they are going to learn. It's possible the human government knows already."

"Maybe," said Sanders Nicholas. "I certainly think you ought to assume they know. But they'd have to fight their way here, and I think the *hwarhath* can stop them. In addition, as you ought to remember, there's a peace treaty."

"Some treaties last. Others don't. This one has no breeding clause.[9] How can we trust an agreement that hasn't been made solid—knotted—through the exchange of genetic material?"

Sanders Nicholas did not answer this question, though the answer is obvious. No treaty can be entirely trusted, if it lacks a breeding clause.

"Humans send their women to the stars. Destroying the Solar System would not destroy their species. But our women prefer to stay at home. If something happened to our home planet, we would not be able to reproduce."

"You could borrow human biotechnology," Sanders Nicholas said.

"And produce cloned children who are raised by men?" asked Ettin Gwarha. His voice combined disgust and horror, as it should, of course.

"They wouldn't have to be clones."

"Well, suppose we decided to combine genetic material from men belonging to different lineages. Who would arrange the breeding contract, if our women were all gone? And how could men possibly raise children?"

9   As every reader ought to know, humans and *hwarhath* can't interbreed.

354

"That leaves one obvious alternative," Sanders Nicholas said. "The *hwarhath* could do what humans have done: move women out of the home system. You must have thought of this."

"The Bundle has discussed the idea," Ettin Gwarha admitted. "And we have suggested it to the female government. Unfolding such a plan required far-in-front diplomatic ability. I was sent." He smiled briefly. "The idea was to establish colonies of young women in distant systems—in stations initially, since they are safer than the surface of any inhabitable planet.

"'To live without the advice of their mothers and senior female relatives?' the Weaving said. 'Absolutely not! It's the job of men to keep the home system safe. If you can't do it, then we need to talk about your failings and limitations. But we won't send our daughters to the stars.'"

"Did you suggest sending older women as well?"

"The Weaving didn't like the idea; nor was the Bundle entirely happy with it. There are frontmen whose mothers are still living, not to mention other female relatives. Space might become considerably less comfortable, if senior women began to travel."

"This is true," said Sanders Nicholas. "But comfort is not the only important aspect of life. I think the Weaving and the Bundle are making a mistake." He glanced at Ettin Gwarha. "There's a human proverb that warns against putting all one's ova in one container. If anything happens to the container—"

Ettin Gwarha tilted his head in agreement. "Nonetheless, the Bundle isn't going to argue with the Weaving over an issue that concerns women. Most likely, the home system is safe. Anyone seeking to destroy this world would have to get past many armed and armored ships. But I'd like to see women among the stars. Some of them would enjoy the experience."

Sanders Nicholas made no answer, possibly because he was tired.

Soon after, the two of them went to sleep. In the morning they continued their journey, going down out of the mountains to a railroad junction. There, at day's end, they caught a local train. All night they rattled through the Atkwa foothills, riding in a freight car, since there wasn't a passenger car for men. He'd had worse accommodations, Sanders Nicholas said. At least there were windows, though not much to see: the hills as areas of darkness against a starry sky, now and then the lights of a station, flashing by quickly, showing nothing except an empty platform. By sunrise they had reached the plain.[10]

10 There is no reason to believe that the Bundle, or any *hwarhath* senior officer, has advocated an idea as radical as putting women into space. It belongs to the author, who is almost certainly female, though the story (like most *hwarhath* fiction) was published anonymously. Apparently, there are hwarhath women who want to travel outside the home system; and the real point of the story, what the *hwarhath* would call its center or hearth, seems to be this final argument in favor of travel for women. Why didn't the author argue her point directly, by writing a story about women actually going to the stars? Maybe because she felt that would be fantasy, at least at present, and she wanted to write science fiction.

A Romance of Investigation

Hwarhath mysteries are a result of human contact. Prior to contact, there were stories about secrets and the discovery of truth, but they were not the kind of puzzles that classic human mysteries are. Why did hwarhath, so similar in humanity in many ways, not develop this classic human art form? We might as well ask why human mysteries appeared as a genre in the nineteenth century and not earlier.

"Holmes Sherlock" is an attempt to create a classic human mystery, written by an author who has obviously been exposed to human literature.

HOLMES SHERLOCK

A Hwarhath Mystery

There was a woman who fell in love with the stories about a human male named Holmes Sherlock. Her name was Amadi Kla, and she came from a town on the northeast coast of the Great Northern Continent. It became obvious, when she was a child, that she was gifted at learning. Her family sent her to a boarding school and then to college in the capital city. There she learned several languages, including English, and became a translator, working for a government department in the capital.

She did not translate military information, since that was done by *hwarhath* men in space. Nor did she translate technical information, lacking the requisite technical knowledge. Instead, she translated human fiction.

"There is much to be learned from the stories people tell," the foremost woman in her department said. "If we are going to understand humans, and we must understand them since they are our enemies, then we need to study their stories."

The fiction came out of computers in captured human warships. At first the Department of Translation picked stories out of the human computers randomly. Most were as bad as the novels read by *hwarhath* young men and women. But it turned out that the humans made lists of important stories, so their young people would know the stories they ought to read. Once these lists were found, the Department began to pick out famous and well-considered works for translating.

The foremost woman said, "It may be possible to learn about a culture by reading trivial fiction. There are people who will argue that. But humans are not a trivial species. They are clearly dangerous, and we should not underestimate them. If we study their least important work, we may decide they are silly. No one who can blow apart a *hwarhath* warship is silly."

After nine years in the capital, Kla began to long for the steep mountains, fjords, and fogs of her homeland. She requested permission to work from home.

"This is possible," the foremost woman said. "Though you will have to fly here several times a year for meetings."

Kla agreed, though she did not like to fly, and went home by coastal freighter.

Her hometown was named Amadi-Hewil. It stood at the end of a fjord, with mountains rising above it. Most of the people belonged to one of two lineages, Amadi or Hewil, though there were some members of neighboring lineages; and the government kept a weather station on a cliff above the fjord. The two men who cared for the station were soldiers from another continent. Of course, they were lovers, since there were no other men of their age in the town. Almost all young males went into space.

Most of the people in the town—women, girls, boys, old men, and old women—lived off fishing. The cold ocean outside their fjord was full of great schools of silver- and copper-colored fish, insulated with fat. There was a packing plant at the edge of the town that froze the fish or put it in cans, while smaller operations made specialty foods: dried seaweed and smoked or pickled marine animals.

The town had rental apartments and rooms for fishers whose family homes were farther in the mountains. Kla decided to take one of these, rather than move back into one of the Amadi houses. She had gotten used to living on her own.

Her room was furnished with a bed, a table, and two chairs. There was a bathroom down the hall. She had a window that looked out on a narrow street that went steeply down toward the harbor. There were plenty of electrical inlets, which was always good. She could dock her computer and her two new lamps on any wall. A shelf along one side of the room gave her a place for books and recordings. She settled in and began to translate.

It was in this period that she discovered Holmes Sherlock. There was little crime in her town, mostly petty theft and drunken arguments. But there was plenty of fog, rain, and freezing rain. The street lamps outside her window glowed through grayness, and she could hear the clink and rattle of carts pulled by *tsina* coming in from the country with loads of produce.

The human stories seemed to fit with her new life, which was also her childhood life. Much human fiction was disturbing, since it dealt with heterosexual love, a topic the *hwarhath* knew nothing about. Holmes Sherlock lived decently with a male friend, who might or might not be his lover. While the male friend, a doctor named Watson John, eventually took up with a woman, as humans were expected to, Holmes Sherlock remained indifferent to female humans.

The stories were puzzles, which Holmes Sherlock solved by reason. This appealed to Kla, who was not a romantic and who had to puzzle out the meaning of human stories, often so mysterious!

After a while, she went to a local craftsman and had a pipe made. It had a bent stem and a large bowl, like the pipe that Holmes Sherlock smoked in illustrations. She put a local herb into it, which produced an aromatic smoke that was calming when taken into the mouth.

Holmes Sherlock wore a famous hat. She did not have a copy of this made, since it looked silly, but she did take an illustration that showed his cape to a tailor. The tailor did not have the material called "tweed," but was able to make a fine cape for her out of a local wool that kept out rain and cold. Like Holmes Sherlock, Kla was tall and thin. Wearing her cape, she imagined she looked a bit like the famous human investigator.

For the rest, she continued to wear the local costume: pants, waterproof boots and a tunic with embroidery across the shoulders. This was worn by both women and men, though the embroidery patterns differed.

Twice a year she flew to the capital city and got new assignments. "You are translating too many of these stories about Holmes Sherlock," the foremost woman said. "Do it on your own time, if you must do it. I want stories that explain humanity. Therefore, I am giving you *Madame Bovary* and *The Journey to the West*."

Kla took these home, reading *Madame Bovary* on the long flight over winter plains and mountains. It was an unpleasant story about a woman trapped in a life she did not like. The woman—Bovary Emma—had a long-term mating contract with a male who was a dullard and incompetent doctor. This was something humans did. Rather than produce children decently through artificial insemination or, lacking that, through decent short-term mating contracts, they entered into heterosexual alliances that were supposed to last a lifetime. These were often unhappy, as might be expected. Men and women were not that much alike, and most alliances—even those of women with women and men with men—did not last a lifetime. The *hwarhath* knew this and expected love to last as long as it did.

Bored by her "husband," a word that meant the owner of a house, Bovary Emma tried to make herself happy through sexual liaisons with other human males and by spending money. This did not work. The men were unsatisfactory. The spending led to debt. In the end, Bovary Emma killed herself, using a nasty poison. Her "husband" lived a while longer and—being a fool with no ability to remake his life—was miserable.

A ridiculous novel! Everyone in it seemed to be a liar or a fool or both. How could humans enjoy something like this? Yes, there was suffering in life. Yes, there were people who behaved stupidly. But surely a story this long ought to remind the reader—somewhere, at least a bit—of good behavior, of people who met their obligations, were loyal to their kin, and knew how to be happy.

Maybe the book could be seen as an argument against heterosexual love.

When Kla was most of the way home, she changed onto a seaplane, which landed in her native fjord and taxied to dock. The fishing fleet was out. She pulled her bag out of the plane and looked around at the fjord, lined by steep mountains and lit by slanting rays of sunlight. The air was cold and smelled of salt water and the fish plant.

Hah! It was fine to be back!

She translated *Madame Bovary* and sent it to the foremost woman via the planet's information net. Then she went on to *Journey*, an adventure story about a badly behaved stone monkey. But the monkey's crimes were not sexual, and it was obvious that he was a trickster, more good than bad, especially after he finished his journey. She enjoyed this translation, though the book was very long.

While she was still working on the monkey's story, she met a woman who lived on another floor of her rooming house. The woman was short and stocky with pale gray fur and almost colorless gray eyes. She was a member of Hewil lineage, employed by the fishing fleet as a doctor. She didn't go out with the boats. Instead, sick and injured fishers came to her, and the fleet paid her fees. Like Kla, she preferred to live alone, rather than in one of her family's houses. She walked with a limp, due to a childhood injury, and she enjoyed reading.

They began to meet to discuss books. The doctor, whose name was Hewil Mel, had read some of Kla's translations.

"Though I don't much enjoy human stories. They are too strange, and I can't tell what the moral is."

"I'm not sure there is one," Kla said and described *Madame Bovary*.

"I will be certain to avoid that one," Doctor Mel said firmly. "Do you think your translation will be published?"

"No. It's too disturbing. Our scientists will read it and make up theories about human behavior. Let me tell you about the story I am translating now."

They were walking along the docks on a fine, clear afternoon. The fleet was in, creaking and jingling as the boats rocked amid small waves. Kla told the story of the monkey.

"What is a monkey?" asked Doctor Mel.

"An animal that is somehow related to humans, though it has fur—as humans do not—and lives in trees."

When she finished with the story, leaving out a lot because the book really was very long, Doctor Mel said, "I hope that one is published in our language."

"I think it will be, though it will have to be shortened, and there are some parts that will have to be removed. For the most part, it is decent. Still, it seems that humans can never be one hundred percent decent. They are a strange species."

"They are all we have," Doctor Mel said.

This was true. No other intelligent species had been found. Why had the Goddess given the *hwarhath* only one companion species in the vast darkness and cold of interstellar space? Especially since humans were more like the *hwarhath* than anyone had ever expected and also unpleasantly different. Surely if two similar species were possible, then many unlike species ought to be possible, but these had not been found; and why was a species so like the *hwarhath* so disturbing? Kla had no answer. The Goddess was famous for her sense of humor.

In the end, Kla and the doctor became lovers and moved to a larger apartment in a building with a view of the fjord. When she had free time, Kla continued to translate stories about Holmes Sherlock and handed them around to relatives, with the permission of the foremost woman. Some stories were too dangerous to spread around, but these were mostly safe.

"People need to get used to human behavior," the foremost woman said. "But not all at once. Eh Matsehar has done a fine job of turning the plays of Shakespeare William into work that we can understand. Now we will give them a little more truth about humans, though only in your northern town. Be sure you get your copies back, after people have read them, and be sure to ask the people what they think. Are they interested or horrified? Do they want to meet humans or avoid them forever?"

When Kla and the doctor had been together almost a year, something disturbing happened in the town; and it happened to one of Kla's remote cousins. The girl had taken a rowboat out into the fjord late one afternoon. She did not come back. In the morning, people went looking for her. They found the rowboat floating in the fjord water, which was still and green and so clear that it was possible to look down and see schools of fish turning and darting. The rowboat was empty, its oars gone. People kept searching on that day and days following. But the girl's body did not turn up, though the oars did, floating in the water only a short distance away.

The girl was a good swimmer, but the fjord was cold. She could have gotten hypothermia and drowned. But why had she gone out so late in the afternoon? And how had a child from a town full of skilled sailors managed to fall out of a boat and been unable to get back in? Where was her body? It was possible that the ebbing tide had pulled it out into the ocean, but this was not likely. She ought to be in the fjord, and she ought to float to the surface.

All of this together was a mystery.

After twenty days or thereabouts, Kla's grandmother sent for her. Of course she went, climbing the steep street that led to the largest of the Amadi houses, which was on a hill above the town. The house went down in layers from the hilltop, connected by covered stairways. Kla climbed these to the topmost building. Her grandmother was there, on a terrace overlooking the town and fjord. The day was mild. Nonetheless, the old lady was wrapped in a heavy jacket and had a blanket over her knees. A table with a pot of tea stood next to her.

"Sit down," the grandmother said. "Pour tea for both of us."

Kla did.

"You still wear that absurd cape," the grandmother said.

"Yes."

"I have read some of your stories about the human investigator."

"Yes?" Kla said. "Did you like them?"

"They seemed alien." The grandmother sipped her tea, then said, "We have a mystery in our house."

Kla waited.

"The girl who vanished," her grandmother said after a moment. "People are saying she must have weighted herself down and jumped into the water deliberately. Otherwise, her body would have appeared by now. This is possible, I think. But we don't know why. She had no obvious reason. Her mother is grieving, but refuses to believe the girl is gone. I would like you to investigate this mystery."

"I am a translator, not an investigator."

"You have translated many stories about investigation. Surely you have learned something. We have no one else, unless we send to the regional government or the capital. I would like to keep whatever has happened private, in case it turns out to be shameful."

Kla considered, looking down at the green fjord, edged with mountains. Rays of sunlight shone down through broken clouds, making the water shine in spots. "I will have to talk to people in this house and look at the girl's computer."

"The girl erased all her files and overwrote them. We have not been able to recover anything. That is a reason to think she killed herself."

"Then she must have had a secret," Kla said.

"But what?" the grandmother said. "It's hard to keep secrets in a family or a small town."

Kla could not refuse. Her grandmother was asking, and the woman was an important matriarch. In addition, she wanted to see if she could solve a mystery. She tilted her head in agreement and finished her tea. "Tell the people in the house I will be asking questions."

"I will do that," the grandmother said. "The girl was only eighteen, not yet full grown, but she was clever and might have become an imposing woman. I want to know what happened."

Two days later, Kla went back to the house and questioned the women who had known the girl, whose name was—or had been—Nam.

A quiet girl, they told her. She had no close friends in the family or elsewhere. When she wasn't busy at household tasks or studying, she liked to walk in the mountains around the town. She always carried a camera and did fine landscape photography.

One aunt said, "I expected her to go to an art school in the capital. She had enough talent."

"Can I see her work?" Kla asked.

"Most is gone. It was on her computer. You know she erased it?"

"Yes."

"But some of us have photographs she gave us. I'll show you."

Kla followed the woman around the Amadi house. The photographs hung on walls in public and private rooms. They were indeed fine: long vistas of mountain valleys and the town's fjord, close-ups of rocks and low vegetation. The girl had potential. It was a pity she was gone.

Kla went home to her apartment and filled her pipe with herb, then smoked, looking out at the docks and the water beyond. When Doctor Mel came home from looking at a fisher with a bad fracture, Kla described her day.

"What will you do next?" Mel asked.

"Find out where the girl went on her walks. Do you want to come with me?"

"With my leg? I'm not going to limp through the countryside."

"Let's rent *tsina* and ride," Kla said.

They went the next day, which was mild, though overcast. Now and then, they felt fine drops of rain. The *tsina* were docile animals, used to poor riders, which was good, since neither Kla nor the doctor was a practiced traveler-by-*tsina*.

They visited the town's outlying houses. Most were too far away to be reached by walking. Nonetheless, they contained relatives, Amadi or Hwil, though most of these were not fishers. Instead, they spent their days herding or tending gardens that lay in sheltered places, protected by stone walls. Some of these people remembered the girl. They had seen her walking along farm roads and climbing the hillsides. A shy lass, who barely spoke. She always carried a camera and took pictures of everything.

Some had photographs she had given them, fastened to the walls of herding huts: favorite livestock, the mountains, the huts themselves. The girl did have an eye. Everything she photographed looked true and honest, as sharp as a good knife and balanced like a good boat that could ride out any storm.

"This is a loss," Doctor Mel said.

"Yes," Kla replied.

After several days of exploring the nearby country, they returned their *tsina* to the town stable and went home to their apartment. A fog rolled in at evening, hiding the fjord and the neighboring houses. Streetlights shone dimly. Sounds were muffled. Kla smoked her pipe.

"What next?" the doctor asked.

"There are paths going up the mountains above the fjord. No one lives up there, except the two soldiers at the weather station. We'll ask them about the girl."

"It's too steep for me," Doctor Mel said.

Kla tilted her head in agreement. "I'll go by myself."

The next day she did. The fog had lifted, but low clouds hid the mountain peaks. The fjord's water was as gray as steel. Kla took a staff and leaned on it as she climbed the narrow path that led to the station. Hah! It seemed perilous! Drop offs went abruptly down toward the gray water; and cliffs hung overhead, seeming ready to fall. She was a townswoman, a bit afraid of heights, though she came of mountain ancestry. Her gift was language and a curious mind.

The station was a prefab metal building, set against the cliff wall. Beyond it was a promontory overlooking the fjord. Equipment stood there, far more complicated than an ordinary weather station. Well, it was maintained by the military. Who could say what they were watching, even here on the safe home planet? No doubt important women knew what was going on here.

A soldier came out of the prefab building, a slim male with dark grey fur. He wore shorts and sandals and an open jacket.

Casual, thought Kla.

"Can I help you?" he asked.

She explained that she was looking for people who had met Amadi Nam, a shy girl who loved photography.

"No such person has been here," the soldier replied.

"Hah!" said Kla and looked at the magnificent view of the fjord beyond the equipment.

Now the second soldier appeared. He was the same height as the first male, but much broader, with thick, white fur that was lightly spotted. He also wore shorts, but no jacket. His fur must be enough, even on this cool, damp day.

He agreed with the first man. The girl had never been to the station.

Kla thanked them and went back down the mountain. She arrived home at twilight. Lamps shone in the apartment windows. The electric heater in the main room was on. Doctor Mel had bought dinner, fish stew from a shop in town.

They ate, then Kla smoked, settled in a low chair close to the heater. Doctor Mel turned on her computer and watched a play on the world information net, her injured leg lifted up on a stool. Kla could hear music and cries of anger or joy. But the dialogue was a mumble, too soft to understand.

The play ended, and Doctor Mel turned the computer off. "Well?"

"I have a clue," answered Kla.

"You do?"

Kla knocked the dottle out of her pipe. "It is similar to the dog that made noise in the night time."

"What is a dog?"

"A domestic animal similar to a *sul*, though smaller and less ferocious. The humans use them to herd and guard, as we use *sulin*. In this case, in a story you have apparently not read, the dog did not make any noise."

"Kla, you are being irritating. What are you trying to say?"

"The dog did not do what was expected, and this was the clue that enabled Holmes Sherlock to solve the problem."

"You met a *sul* on the mountain?"

"I met two young men who said they never met my cousin, though she climbed every slope in the area and loved to photograph splendid vistas."

"They are lying?"

"Almost certainly."

"Why?"

"I have no idea."

Doctor Mel looked confused. "They belong to far-off lineages and have no relatives in town. Why would they become involved in something here? If Amadi Nam had been a boy, one might suspect a romance. But she was a girl, and the soldiers are lovers, as everyone knows."

"This is true," Kla replied. "But I am certain the soldiers are lying. I need to confront them."

Doctor Mel rose and went to pour two cups of *halin*. She gave one to Kla and settled back in her chair. "If they are telling the truth, they will think you are crazy and may tell people in town. You will have to endure joking. More important, if they are lying, then they are crazy and may be dangerous. I'd go with you, except for the climb."

"I'll go to my grandmother tomorrow and explain the situation. She will know what to do."

"Good," said Doctor Mel.

The next day was clear and cold. Ice rimmed puddles in the streets and made the street paving stones slippery. Kla could see her breath.

Her grandmother was inside, next to an old-fashioned brazier full of glowing coals.

"Help yourself to tea and pour a cup for me," the old lady said. "Then tell me what you have found."

Kla did as she was told. When she had finished her story, the matriarch said, "The soldiers must be confronted."

"My lover has suggested that they may be dangerous."

"Hardly likely. But this story is disturbing. Something unpleasant has happened." Her grandmother drank more tea. "I want to keep this in the family. I'll pick two of your cousins, large and solid fisher-women. They'll go with you up the mountain. Even if the soldiers are crazy, they will hardly do harm to three women, all larger than they are, though you are thin. The fishers will not be."

A day later, Kla went back up to the weather station. It was another clear, cold day. The fjord sparkled like silver.

The two fisher-women were named Serit and Doda. Both were second cousins to Kla, and both were tall and broad, with big knives in their tunic belts. Serit carried a harpoon gun, and Doda had a club.

"Is that necessary?" Kla asked.

"Always be provided," Serit replied in a deep, calm voice.

"The soldiers have been trained for war," Doda added. "But the war they were trained to fight is fought by ships in space. How can that help them here? We, by contrast, have struggled with many large and dangerous fish, while the fish thrashed on the decks of our boats. If the soldiers threaten us, though that does not seem likely, we will know what to do."

When they reached the station. Both men came out.

"How can we help?" the dark soldier asked.

"We are certain Amadi Nam came here," Kla said. "Since you lied about this, we are going to search your building."

What did she hope to find? Some evidence that Nam had been there—a picture that had been printed out or her camera, full of pictures. People did not easily throw away Amadi Nam's work.

The dark soldier frowned. "This is a military installation. You can't examine our equipment or building until you get permission from the officers in front of us."

Serit lifted the harpoon gun. "This is not space, where your senior officers make decisions. This is our town, our country, and our planet. Our senior women are in charge, and you are here on this mountain with their—and our—permission. If we want to know what you do in your building, we have the right."

"We will go in," Kla said.

"Women do not fight and kill," the dark soldier said, as if trying to reassure himself.

"What nonsense," Serit replied. "Doda and I fight large and dangerous fish and other sea animals."

"But not people," the dark soldier said.

"Of course not. We are fishers, and we are still young. But who decides which newborn children will live? Who gives death to those who have nothing left but suffering?"

"The old women," said the spotted soldier in a resigned tone.

"So," Serit continued in a tone of satisfaction. "Women can fight, and we are able to kill. We will go into this building."

Kla felt uneasy. As a rule, men and women did not interfere with each other's activities. If it had been up to her, she would have waited for the soldiers to consult their senior officers, though she suspected they were stalling. What did they have hidden that could be better hidden, if they had time?

But her grandmother had picked Serit and Doda. She must have known how aggressive they were.

The spotted soldier exhaled. "I will not fight women, Perin, even for you."

The dark soldier made the gesture that meant, be quiet!

So, thought Kla, there was a secret. "I will go in and search. The two of you watch the soldiers."

Doda made the gesture of assent, and Serit tilted her head in agreement.

Kla entered the building. It was messy, as was to be expected, with two young men living alone, no senior officers near them. Unwashed dishes stood on tables. The beds were unmade. Kla saw no sign of the girl, even in the closets and under the beds. But there were pieces of paper under one bed. She gathered them. Printouts of photographs. They showed the green fjord, the black and white surrounding mountains, and the dark soldier, Perin.

She took the printouts into sunlight. "What are these?"

"I took them," the spotted man said quickly.

This was almost certainly a lie. Kla knew Nam's work when she saw it. She gave the printouts to Doda and went back in the building, going through it a second time. An uncomfortable experience! She was a translator, not someone who poked around in other people's homes.

This time she found the girl, wedged into a low cabinet and folded over like the kind of scissors that bend back on themselves, the blade points touching the handles.

"Come out," said Kla.

"No," said the girl, her voice muffled.

"Don't be ridiculous," Kla replied. "I might not be able to get you out, but I have two large, strong fisher-women with me. They can easily pull you from that hole."

After a moment or two, the girl squeezed herself out, groaning as she did so. Once she was upright, Kla could see her clearly: a plump young woman with badly rumpled clothing and fur. She looked miserable and angry.

Kla gestured, and the girl followed her outside.

"Now," Kla said to the girl and the soldiers. "What is this about?"

The girl looked sullen. The soldiers looked more unhappy than before. No one spoke.

"Very well," Kla said. "We will all go to see my grandmother. If the girl has a jacket, get it."

The spotted soldier did.

"Put it on and pull the hood up," Kla said to the girl. "I don't want people to know you are alive until Grandmother has made a decision."

The girl obeyed, and they all went down the mountain, Serit last, holding the harpoon gun ready.

Once again her grandmother sat by an old-fashioned brazier, though it was difficult to see the glow of the coals this time. The room was full of sunlight, coming in through east-facing windows. The red floor tiles shone, and it was easy to see the paintings on the walls: flowers and flying bugs.

Doda pushed the girl in front of the old woman, then pulled back her hood.

"Well," the old lady said. "You've had all of us worried, Nam." Then she glanced around at everyone. "Pull up chairs. I will hurt my neck, if I look up at you."

The men brought chairs from the walls and arranged them in front of the old woman.

"Sit!" Kla's grandmother said. "You found Nam at the weather station. That much is evident. But why was she there? Why was the boat left floating empty? And why was her computer erased?"

"I think the soldier with spots might tell us," Kla answered. "He seems to be the most reasonable of the three."

The man clasped his hands tightly together. "I know I am dead. May I tell this the way it happened?"

"Yes," said the grandmother. "But try to be brief. And tell me your name."

"I am Sharim Wirn."

"Go on."

"My lover always took walks. I did more of the work than he did, but willingly, out of love. Recently, he has taken longer walks, and I began to notice food was disappearing. I do the accounting. I knew how much food we bought and how much we usually ate." The man paused, glancing briefly at his comrade. "I thought he might have a new lover. But where had he found the man? And why would he feed him? It made no sense. So I followed Perin. He went to a cave in the mountains. I went inside after him, expecting to find Perin with another man. Instead, I found him with the girl, sitting by a little fire and sharing food. Not eating with her, that would be indecent, but giving her food from our supplies.

"I asked what this was about. At first he refused to speak. At last, he told me the story. He had met the girl during his walks. They both liked the mountains, and they were both solitary. The girl had no one to love, apparently, and Perin had only me. I was not enough." The soldier's voice was bitter. "They began by talking and ended by having sex."

The two fishers drew breath in sharply. Kla's grandmother hissed. Kla was too shocked to make a noise. Men and women had mated in the past, before artificial insemination, but only after their families had agreed to a breeding contract, and only to make children.

Of course there had been perverts. But they were not common, and she had never expected to meet any. She certainly had not expected to have one in her family.

"Go on," the grandmother said, sounding angry.

"The girl became pregnant and came to Perin, insisting on his help," the spotted soldier went on. "He knew he would be told to kill himself, if this story became known. So he hid the girl, until I found them. I insisted on bringing her to our building. The cave was cold and damp. She would become sick. I was not willing to be responsible for the death of a woman, even one as foolish and selfish as this girl."

He lifted his head, glancing briefly at the old lady. "I know that I should have told my senior officers, but I love Perin. I knew he would die for what he did, and it would be my fault for telling. I could not bear the idea of him dying."

"How could you love him after he had sex with a woman?" Serit asked.

The man looked down at his clasped hands. "I don't know. But it became obvious to me, after spending time with her, that the girl has the stronger will. I believe she seduced him; and then she entangled him with her plan."

This did not seem likely. Nam was only eighteen, two years away from adulthood.

Kla looked at the girl and saw her grim, determined, angry face.

"What plan?" asked the grandmother.

"She emptied her computer, so no one would know where she had been and what she photographed; and then she left evidence of her death—the boat, floating in the fjord, empty. Then she went to Perin and insisted on his help. He had no choice. If she told her family—you—what had happened, he would die. Or, if not that—his family has influence—he would get a really bad assignment.

"She could not stay here in this town because her family would discover what she'd done. And she could not travel while pregnant. A woman alone in that condition would arouse too much interest and concern. People would stop her and offer help or ask about her family. Where were they? Why was she alone?"

"You say that you love this man Perin, but now you tell this terrible story," Kla's grandmother said.

"There is no good ending," the spotted soldier replied. "If the girl gave birth, she would do it alone, with no one to help except Perin and me. That was frightening! If the child lived, what would happen to it? Children don't appear out of nowhere. They are the result of breeding contracts. They have families. No mother with a child is ever alone."

"This is true," Kla's grandmother said.

"It became apparent to me that the child would die, even if it was healthy. How else could Perin and the girl hide what they had done?" He paused and took a deep breath. "The girl said she would travel to the capital after the child was born. There are people there who live in the shadows and make a living in irregular ways. She planned to become one of those. She never spoke of the child.

"All the time, while this was happening, my love for Perin was wearing away. How could he be so stupid? It was obvious to me that the girl had the stronger will. He was acting the way he did out of weakness and fear of discovery. I would have told your family or my senior officers, except by this time I had gotten myself entangled. I was at fault. I would be told to kill myself, once this was known."

"True," said Kla's grandmother. She looked at Nam. "Well, child, why did you do this?"

"I love him." Nam said stubbornly, though Kla was not sure the girl meant it. How could love endure this mess?

"How can you?" the old lady asked. "He is male."

"I cannot change what I feel."

"Certainly you can."

"No," the girl replied.

"Tell them all to kill themselves," Serit put in. "They are disgusting."

The old woman looked at Kla. "You have studied human crimes. What is your advice?"

"Two suicides close together would cause talk." Kla replied. "Though we might say it was some kind of lovers' quarrel. But why would both commit suicide? No one was stopping their love. It would be a mystery. There would be talk and wondering and possibly an investigation by military. We don't want that.

"As for the girl, everyone thinks she is dead. If she killed herself now, we would have to hide her body. Otherwise, people would wonder where she had been before her death. And she is pregnant. That is another problem. If Sharim Wirn is right, the girl planned to kill the child or let it die. We have no reason to believe the child is defective. I am not comfortable doing what the mother planned to do."

"Yes." The grandmother leaned back in her chair and closed her eyes. "Be quiet, all of you. I need to think."

They sat, as sunlight moved across the floor and out of the room. Kla needed to pee and would have liked a cup or tea or *halin*. But she kept still.

At last, the grandmother opened her eyes. "The important thing is to keep this story secret. One solution would be for all three of you to die. But as Kla says, that might cause talk and wondering; and there is the problem of the child. So—" She gestured at the two soldiers. "You will volunteer for service in space, far out in the war zone, where you will not meet women. My family has relatives who are important in the military. They will make sure you get the assignments you desire.

"As for you, Nam, you will stay in this house until your child is born. You have a cousin who is pregnant now. We will say that she had twins. I am not comfortable with this, since I will be deceiving the lineage that provided semen for your cousin. But we do what we have to do; and I hope you are ashamed at the lies you are forcing your relatives to tell."

Kla looked at the girl. She did not show any evidence of shame.

"After the child is born—" the grandmother said. "I will give you two choices. Either you can stay here and study art on the world information net, or you can leave and go into the shadows. If you stay here, we will watch you for further signs of misbehavior. We cannot trust you, Nam. You have initiative, a strong will, no self-control, and no sense of family obligation. This is a dangerous combination."

"I will go," Nam said.

The grandmother exhaled. "If you want to live in the shadows in the capital, fine! But do not tell anyone your family name."

"I won't," the girl said. "I despise all of you and this town."

"Why?" asked Kla, surprised.

"Look at you," the girl said. "In your silly cape, pretending to be a human."

"What harm does it do?" Kla asked.

"And you," the girl stared at Kla's grandmother. "Pretending that none of this happened because you are afraid of gossip."

"Gossip can cause great harm," the old lady said.

"The world is changing," Nam said. "There are aliens in the sky! But your lives remain the same, full of fear and pretense."

"There are no aliens in the sky," Kla's grandmother said firmly. "The humans remain a long distance from our home system." She paused for a moment. "I hope your child has your gift for art, without your difficult personality. This has been an unpleasant conversation. I'm tired now. I want to take a nap. Everyone go."

"You stay in the house," Serit said to Nam. "We don't want anyone outside the family to know you are alive."

The girl made the gesture of assent, though she looked sullen.

Kla left the house with the soldiers. "Thank you," the spotted soldier said before they parted. "You said that our suicides would cause talk. For this reason, Perin and I will remain alive."

"Behave better in the future," Kla said.

The man showed his teeth in a brief smile. "We will have no chance to behave badly in a war zone." He glanced around at the mountains. "I will miss this country. But space may be safer."

The two men took off, walking rapidly. They kept well apart, as people do who have quarreled.

Kla went back to her apartment. It was late afternoon by now, and the sun was behind the mountains, though the light still touched the high peaks, streaked with a little snow. The fjord was still and gray.

Doctor Mel was in the main room, drinking tea. Kla sat down and told the story. Even though Mel belonged to another lineage, she was a doctor and knew how to keep secrets.

At the end, Mel said, "You have solved your mystery."

"It's an ugly story," Kla said. "I wish I still believed the girl had drowned."

"That is wrong," Mel said firmly. "Her life may be hard, but she still has a future. The dead have nothing." She refilled her cup and poured tea for Kla. "Most likely, she will give up her un-natural interest in men. If she does not—well, there are people in the shadows who know about contraceptives."

"There are?" Kla asked.

Mel grinned briefly. "You know more about crime in the an-cient human city of London than you know about bad behavior here. Of course there are *hwarhath* who behave in ways we do not find acceptable; and of course these folk learn to deal with the consequences of their behavior. Doctors know this, though we rarely talk about it."

"In the stories I have translated, the solution to the puzzle is satisfying. The ending seems neat and finished, though—of course—I do not understand everything. Humans are alien, after all. I can translate their words, but not their minds. This ending does not satisfy," Kla said.

"How could it? Most likely the young men will be fine, once they are in a military unit with officers to watch them; and most likely the child will be fine, born in your grandmother's house and raised by members of your family. But the girl is an unsolved problem. Maybe she will decide to stay here and study photog-raphy. Her work is full of possibility."

"I don't believe she'll stay. She is angry, though I don't know why. Maybe it is shame. She said our lives are full of fear and pretense."

"We live with rules and obligations," Doctor Mel said. "Most of us fear what will happen if we break the rules; and we may—as in this case—pretend that a rule has not been broken, rather than deal with the idea of broken rules. Is this wrong? I don't think so. I would not like to live in chaos, without the net of kinship that holds us all, and without front-and-back relations. The girl may want more honesty. However, most of us want a comfort-able life."

Mel paused, obviously thinking. "The girl is right about one thing. Our universe is changing in ways that people could not have imagined a century ago. Look at your job, translating human literature. It did not exist in the past. Now, through your work, we learn about Holmes Sherlock and the shadows of London, and about that irritating woman who lived in her own shadow."

"Bovary Emma. That translation will never be released. It is too disturbing."

Mel smiled briefly. "See how we protect ourselves!"

"Rightly!"

Mel gave Kla a look of affectionate amusement, then continued her line of thought, like a *sul* following a scent. "There have always been people who feel constrained by our rules. Most stay in their families and are unhappy. Others leave, going into the shadows. Some are criminals. Others are outcasts or eccentrics. Doctors know about them because we must watch everyone—even people who are difficult—for signs of illness. Public health requires that we treat everyone, even those we don't approve of.

"Is it possible to be happy in shadows? I think so. Holmes Sherlock was happy, though he lived outside a family and made his own rules, and so was Watson John, who was odd enough to enjoy living with Holmes Sherlock. The irritating woman—remind me of her name."

"Bovary Emma."

Doctor Mel tiled her head in thanks. "Was unhappy, but she does not sound—from your description—like a person able to live a difficult life. Or even an ordinary life."

"These are humans, and they are imaginary!"

"We can still learn from them. We can always learn from other people."

"Are you saying the girl might be happy, even among outcasts?" Kla asked.

"Happier than in her—your—family. I will give you a name. Please give it to Nam before she leaves home. It's a doctor in the capital city, a good woman who treats people in the shadows and collects art. She can help Nam get settled. If she likes Nam's work, she can find a dealer-in-art. A good photographer should not be wasted."

Kla looked at Mel with speculation. This woman she loved, who lived in a small town and treated the injuries of fishers, knew more about people than she did, although she had lived in the capital city and had been translating human novels for years. People were more difficult to understand than she had believed, even the people she loved. But Mel was right. A good photographer should not be wasted. Maybe this situation would work out. Best of all, the disturbing girl would be gone from Kla's life.

Doctor Mel got up and limped to the room's window. After a moment, Kla joined her. The street lamps were on, and lights shone on the fishing boats anchored by the docks. High up on the mountain, a gleam showed that the soldiers were home.

Appendix A: On Pronunciation

Consonant sounds are about what you would expect from English, except that the "h" sound is always noticeable.

Vowel sounds are pronounced as follows:

a is approximately "ah," though modified by the following consonant;

ai as in hay;

ei as in pet or (sometimes) pear;

eh as in feh;

i as in tin;

long i (which should be spelled with an acute accent over the i) as in tea;

u as in hull;

long u (which should be spelled with an acute accent over the u) as in hue.

Tsin has a long i. So does *tli*.

Tulwar has a short u.

The language is accented, and the accent tends to fall on the first syllable of any given word.

The double t in certain names (Ettin, Hattin) reflects an orthographic peculiarity present in the written versions of several related languages on the Fourth (or Large Southern) Continent, and has no effect on pronunciation.

Appendix B: On Time

The home planet of the People has a rotation period of ten *ikun* or 23.1 hours.

One *ikun* = 100 *ha-ikun*.

One *ikun* = 2.31 hours.

One *ha-ikun* = 1.386 minutes.

One minute = .7215 *ha-ikun*.

15 minutes = approximately 10 *ha-ikun*.

One hwarhath year = 402.2 hwarhath days.

AUTHOR BIOGRAPHY

Eleanor Arnason was born in New York City in 1942. Her mother, Elizabeth Hickcox Yard, was a social worker who grew up in a missionary community in western China. Her father, Hjorvardur Harvard Arnason, was the son of Icelandic immigrants and an art historian. She grew up in New York, Chicago, London, Paris, Washington DC, Honolulu, St. Paul, and Minneapolis. She received a BA in art history from Swarthmore College and did graduate work at the University of Minnesota, before quitting to learn about life outside art museums and institutions of higher learning. She made her first professional sale in 1972 while living in the Detroit inner city. Since then she has published six novels and over fifty works of short fiction. Her fourth novel, *A Woman of the Iron People* (2001), won the James Tiptree, Jr. award for gender-bending science fiction and the Mythopoeic Society Award for adult fantasy. Her fifth novel, *Ring of Swords* (1995), won a Minnesota Book Award. Since 1994 she has devoted herself to short fiction. Her story "Dapple" won the Spectrum Award for GLBT science fiction and was a finalist for the Sturgeon Award. Other stories have been finalists for the World Fantasy, Hugo, and Nebula Awards, and for the Sturgeon and Sidewise Awards. Her collection *Big Mama Stories,* from Aqueduct Press in 2013, was on the Tiptree award honor list.

She lives in Minnesota and is currently a full time writer. Her interests include politics, economics, bird-watching, and hanging out in local coffee shops.